The Devil's Playg

Stav Sherez is the author of three other novels; a standalone thriller, *The Black Monastery* (2009), which was described as 'dynamite fiction' in the *Independent* and as 'truly exceptional' by Lee Child, and two novels in his acclaimed Carrigan and Miller series, *A Dark Redemption* and *Eleven Days*, the first of which was shortlisted for the Theakston's Old Peculier Crime Novel of the Year in 2013.

You can find him on Twitter @stavsherez and also at www.stavsherez.co.uk

Praise for Stav Sherez:

'Sherez is superb at evoking the unfamiliar world of immigrant communities . . . Although there is nothing more conventional than an unconventional cop, Sherez has beaten the odds and created an original detective in Carrigan.' Jake Kerridge, *Daily Telegraph*

'Powerful . . . Sherez is emerging as a very interesting crime novelist indeed, pursuing dark themes with impressive authority.' Andrew Taylor, *Spectator*

'Sherez belongs in the top league of British crime writers.' Eva Dolan

STAV SHEREZ

The Devil's Playground

FABER & FABER

First published in 2004
by Michael Joseph, an imprint of
Penguin Books, 80 Strand, London WC2R ORL

First published in 2014
by Faber and Faber Limited
Bloomsbury House
74–77 Great Russell Street, London WC1B 3DA

Printed and bound by CPI Group (UK) Ltd, Croydon CR0 4YY

A CIP record for this book
is available from the British Library

ISBN 978-0-571-31235-1

FSC
www.fsc.org
MIX
Paper from
responsible sources
FSC® C101712

To my Father and Mother with love

Acknowledgements

To my wonder-agent Lesley Thorne and super-editor Beverley Cousins – without the two of you this book would still exist in a small room.

Thanks: James Sallis, Steve Wynn, Matt Dornan, Leo Hollis, Lisane Radice, Jane Gregory and Bill Hamilton.

I am indebted to Mary Lowenthal Felstiner's biography *To Paint Her Life: Charlotte Salomon in the Nazi Era* (Harper Perennial).

Author Note

As anyone with knowledge of Amsterdam might guess, I have moved things around to suit my purposes and will put them back together one of these days.

All characters are fictional – even the real ones.

Prologue

Amsterdam is full of butch dogs. Lean, tough beasts who can weather out any frozen Baltic wind or spray that assails them as they slouch along the canals.

But not this one. This one is small and wiry and shivering in the pelting rain. All he wants to do is find some shelter.

He runs ahead. A compact, dripping bundle of fur and legs, pulling his master along, the leash outspinning, past the Old Church and into the park. His muzzle breaks through a tangle of bushes and he sees the old man lying there, barefoot and face-down. Yet it is not for him to make sense of this but for his master, who comes puffing along, out of breath and ready to be annoyed, ready to shout, to blame the dog for all this rain and discomfort, when he too sees it.

It doesn't take him long. It is a scene intimately familiar from movies he has watched, books and plays. All this stuff crammed into his head is finally of use. He calls the police from his mobile phone and, as he's waiting for someone to answer, he's thinking about whether they'll want to interview him for the evening news. The thought of this makes him smile.

The rain refuses to pause for the scene. It has been raining for weeks. The canals are high and turbulent and a strange fatalism has crept into the minds of the city's inhabitants. Unnoticed, the beagle wanders off, bored by the whole scene, trying to find some shelter from the awful rain. His master stands guard beside the body. He doesn't look down. It is the police's problem now, not his. The Oude Kerk keeps off the worst of the weather. It is the oldest building in the city but the man takes no account of this, he walks by it every day and it is no more to him than a shape, something to delineate the streets and canals. Instead he watches the window-girls standing in their booths, smiling and trying to entice through the rain. A line of tourists waits patiently at the gated entrance to the church, their second-day-in enthusiasm and protective mountain-wear more than enough to make up for the weather. But the man is more concerned with his dog. He feels the hard jerk against his wrist. He reels the leash in and smiles at the window-girls as he hears the approaching police sirens, straightening his hair and wishing he'd worn his new burgundy jacket. He doesn't like the idea of people seeing him in his jogging gear.

Van Hijn watched as Christ was airlifted out of Rome. The great open-armed statue wobbling precariously in the wind under the insect chop and buzz of the helicopter, leaving the city to bikinied sunbathers waving from rooftops and the snarl and flash of hungry journalists.

Then the beeper on his hip went off.

The other five people in the cinema turned towards him and, even in the dark, he could see their angry stares. The pulse echoing through the almost empty room, disturbing the immersion of the film, that wonderful longed-for loss of control. All gone now.

He let it ring a couple of times more, then pressed the small black button, got up, adjusted his trousers, sighed and said goodbye to *La Dolce Vita*.

He'd left his umbrella at the cinema and by the time he got to the scene he was soaked and in a bad mood. He'd intended to spend the afternoon locked away in the shelter of the screen; a Fellini double bill, a thermos of coffee and a slice of blackcurrant cheesecake. There was nothing else to do on such days. Days when the rain seemed like a dark cloud, permanently orbiting the city.

'Detective Van Hijn.'

Someone was calling him but he was still thinking about the face of Anouk Aimée, the way her eyes seemed to dance when she spoke, the small upcurl of her top lip.

'Detective!'

He saw the lieutenant approaching hesitantly and he made an effort to smile, to pretend he was glad to see him. Jan was one of the few officers who didn't laugh behind his back these days. Who had seen the incident at the canal as just a stupid accident, nothing more. The kind of thing that happened to all cops, even the best ones.

'What is it this time, Jan?' He looked towards the park, the hedges glistening with rain, the huddle of people staring at something on the ground.

'Take a look.' The lieutenant shrugged. Van Hijn could see he was tired. 'He was found, by a dog, half an hour ago,' Jan added.

'A dog? Did this dog also call us and report it?' Immediately he felt bad about this but it was too much to say sorry in the rain, too much just now, and he let it ride.

'No. His owner's over there. Seems eager to talk about it.'

'Aren't they all?' Van Hijn wiped the rain from his eyebrows. 'Get him off the scene. Take his statement and send him home.'

Van Hijn watched as the lieutenant turned away and disappeared into the rain. He saw the gradually forming pack of spectators, all whisper and expectancy, standing on the other side of the road. He didn't understand these people who congregated around murder scenes and accidents, straining for a glimpse, taking home-movies, popping flashbulbs, impersonating journalists. They were like the dark twins of those birth addicts who roam hospitals pretending to be expectant fathers, shivering and sweating in anticipation of glimpsing the shuddering bloody expulsion that brings us all into this life. It *was* like watching something being born, he had to admit to himself. But as he got older he was becoming less and less tolerant of these people and the way they interfered with his work. Their foolish belief that they could learn something in observing death. Their hunger for tragedy.

He lit a cigarette, postponing things for at least another few minutes. He managed to smoke it a third of the way down before the rain got to that too.

The man lay face-down between two sets of bushes in a small hedged-in space, a pinprick of green amid the purples and blues of Amsterdam's red-light district. Van Hijn took a deep breath that tasted of diesel and sweat and approached the body.

The dead man wore a dirty brown overcoat, once expensive perhaps but now rubbed and lined with street debris, mud and rain. Blue jeans that were no longer blue but a shade Van Hijn had never seen before, somewhere between stone white and the colour of sea mist in late Ruisdael. No shoes or socks.

Van Hijn knelt down and had a closer look. He felt the cheesecake coming up and had to turn away, take a deep breath of wet air, before he was able to continue. He cursed the fact that he'd put a new battery in his beeper that morning. Should have just let the damn thing run out.

There was something wrong about the man's feet. The dark and calloused skin. The white flash of scars running up and down, disappearing into the cuffs of his jeans. Van Hijn took a sharp swallow of air, felt it crease into his stomach – not just another dead tramp then, but something else.

He looked back down. Took note. Small black spots that he knew would prove, when measured, to be the exact diameter of a cigarette end. He took out his pen and used it to lift the trouser cuff. The marks continued up the man's hairless leg. Van Hijn remembered the body of the girl they'd recently found near the Heineken factory. A similar pattern of marks had decorated her body too. And there were others, as every newspaper reader in the city knew, a whole row of faces and mutilations stretching back nine months. His hand was shaking. The pen clattered to the ground. Another one then, he thought, and lit a cigarette to cover the smell that was coming off the corpse and still his shaking hands. The ninth so far. A man. The first time the killer had chosen a man.

Van Hijn noted the position of the body. Its relation to the shrubs that surrounded it. To the tiny park that it lay in and the shadows of the Old Church beyond. He sketched out the crime scene in a small notebook and then leaned down once again, braced himself, and turned the body over.

He'd expected someone older from the withered state of the feet, small husks wrinkled and torn, but the man lying on the ground was only in his early sixties. Maybe younger. Van Hijn drew back. A flutter of something echoed through his chest, rumbling palpitations whispering: this is it, the quirk, the crack and shift that would mark the break in this case. A man. An old man this time. Maybe now they would believe him.

He looked down. The white beard which had been smeared across the man's face by the rain held in it an assortment of leaves and twigs, the wind's things. The man's eyes were closed and his skin was blue.

7

He put his gloves on, stretching his fingers to loosen the latex and carefully undid the buttons on the dead man's coat. A warm, dark smell came from underneath the cloth, a smell of basements and stagnant water. He searched for a wallet, some identification, but there was nothing. The inside left pocket, the one covering the heart, had been cut out.

It was when he pulled the coat back together that he noticed the book. A tiny glint of white peeking from the outside pocket, almost totally submerged in that brown funk. He cautiously pulled it out, brushed some of the dirt and leaves away. He called over one of the policemen and asked him to hold up his umbrella while he studied the book.

It was an old Faber edition of Pound's *Selected Cantos*. Worn, ribbed by water damage, it seemed as dead as the man on the ground. Van Hijn carefully opened it. He felt a slight surge in his belly. On the inside front cover he saw a name and a phone number. He could just make them out although the rain had smudged the ink.

The number wasn't local. The name wasn't Dutch.

He flicked through the rest of the book, feeling the wet bend and droop of the pages under the rubber skin of his glove. On the third page, sunk halfway down, was a plain white bookmark, a string of numbers written on it by a shaky hand. They didn't seem to mean anything but they were too precise, too neatly spaced to have meant nothing, an idle doodle while waiting for the phone to ring or the train to pull in.

He forced himself not to think about these things. It was too early. Nothing had any context. There was no point in speculating. Evidence had to be gathered first, sifted and comprehended.

He jotted the two sets of numbers down in his notebook,

then called over for an evidence bag and sealed the book and bookmark away. It was time for others to take over. The ones who would study the dirt with magnifying glasses. Spray chemicals and fill test-tubes. Photograph the scene before clearing it away. He could already see them making their way towards the enclosure in their white boiler suits and plastic gloves, the forensics team, setting up borders, marking their territory like a ragged troop of Arctic explorers.

There was nothing else he could do at the scene. Some of the younger officers were whispering, their eyes flicking in Van Hijn's direction every now and then.

He knew what they were saying. He'd heard it ever since the canal incident; at the station, in a bar, passing on the street. The whole gamut of Dirty Harry jokes. At times, it seemed as though the whole of Amsterdam knew. Yet, it had never reached the papers. The man had been given a cheap burial. No one mentioned that he'd been killed by mistake. The fact of his crimes was enough to keep things quiet and discreet. The whole thing was buried. Elections were close and bad publicity was bad publicity. No one wanted that kind of thing to besmirch the department as a whole. They'd struck a deal: a quiet transfer, a pension hearing, a desk – the prospects of a belly, a bad back and endless cups of cheap coffee awaited him.

'Detective. I'm surprised to see you here.'

Van Hijn turned and saw Captain Beeuwers approaching, shaking off the rain like an annoyed dog, trailing young fresh-faced replacements in his stream.

'I got the call,' Van Hijn replied, wishing he hadn't, wondering how much of the film he'd missed.

'That's all fine, but you'll hand the case over to Zeeman now that he's here.' The captain's eyes seemed to shift over

Van Hijn's face, as if scanning for any weakness, ready to target.

Van Hijn smiled. Perhaps it was just as well he'd had to miss the film. Perhaps this little encounter would be worth it. 'I'm still the one in charge until the transfer comes through,' he said.

The captain's face seemed to freeze almost as if someone had pressed a button. 'A deal was made, and besides, we don't want you going off all half-cocked again. It doesn't look good for the department.'

'The man wasn't innocent,' Van Hijn drily replied. He knew he was falling for the captain's bait but every time it came up he felt the need to explain himself anew.

Beeuwers spat into the rain. 'He wasn't the guy we were looking for. You seem to have forgotten that. We can't just go out shooting people hoping that, after the fact, they'll turn out to be guilty of something. Everyone's guilty but not everyone deserves to be gunned down in the street. He was only a rapist. There's no death penalty for rape.'

'There should be,' Van Hijn replied, remembering that peculiar, yet vaguely familiar smell, unsettling somehow, when they entered the dead man's flat. And how the man with him, a uniform, started vomiting and collapsed on to the floor almost immediately. Not that you could really tell what constituted the floor. That was the thing. The man had wallpapered his whole flat with porn, torn from magazines, jagged edge of flesh overlapping flesh, creating monstrosities and freaks unbelievable and disturbing. A tableau like something from the tormented mind of Hieronymous Bosch. But it wasn't just the walls. That wouldn't have made the uniform so sick, nor given Van Hijn a dizzying nauseous headache like the constant spinning after stepping off a fairground ride. No, it was the fact that *everything* had been wallpapered.

All the surfaces had been meticulously covered with porn: the ceiling, totally covered, the chairs and the tables and the table legs, the phone, the whole border and back of the TV, everything but the screen. Within a couple of minutes Van Hijn had lost all sense of perspective and depth. The room seemed to pulsate, the floor to float. He reached out for objects that turned out to be much further away than he anticipated. Eyes followed him around the room. A woman with six legs and thirteen breasts seemed to smile. And he remembered the keepsakes that the rapist had mounted on a porn-splashed altar, the reason for that smell, all thirty of them, tagged and dated, with names and small photos attached to each. They had to carry him out of there.

Van Hijn snapped out of the dark tangle of his memories and stared at Beeuwers. The rain made him look like a piece of discarded furniture. Van Hijn stepped forward and leaned into the captain's sweating face. 'This is my case, always has been, since the first body and I'm not going to let your goon take over. I don't care what the fuck you think about it.'

'In that case you'll find your transfer coming sooner than even you anticipated, I assure you.' The captain tried to smile, to show him that yes, he was still in control, but he couldn't make it, his lips refusing to rise. He knew that the detective had got the better of him this time. He would have to do something about that.

Van Hijn winked at the captain. A faint smile, barely discernible in the rain. He turned away before the captain could answer. He didn't care. There was nothing left to lose.

He hit the streets hard, his feet splashing the puddled rain, his head hunched down, fists stuffed into his pockets. The dialogue with the captain had angered him more than he'd realized. Hadn't demoting him been enough? Yet, there was always this tendency to push home the further humiliation, to consolidate the gain and destroy the enemy. He shouldn't have been surprised, or only at his own naïveté perhaps.

He could go back to the cinema, catch the last hour of the film, pretend he'd been there all along. No, somehow he didn't think that was going to work today. He could still see the man's scarred feet and the way the passers-by had wrestled with each other to get a glimpse of the body before it was carried away. His mouth felt dry and bitter, his head heavy. He stopped at a café, ate two pieces of chocolate pecan cheesecake, too fast, and stared at a poster advertising a forthcoming fashion show. The redhead looked at him from its surface, smiling, saying, who cares about all that and what does it matter anyway? When the sugar hit, he felt his whole body relax, deflate and soften like an old sponge soaked in a bath. He smoked a cigarette and headed back to the station, back to life and to the phone call that he has to make.

I

I

This is how it begins. With Jon staring out of his window at the space where the tramp once stood. Wondering where the old man was. If he would come back again to this spot. If he would come back at all.

He turned to the empty room, bare except for the clutter and murmur of the accusing computer, the deadline looming, the work still undone. His mind was filled not with paragraphs and grammar but with thoughts of Jake, the short snap of time they'd spent together, the meagre two weeks that the old man had stayed in Jon's flat. The aching throb of the space where someone used to sit.

Jon stared at the flickering screen of the computer monitor, the impossibly complex rendering of a man's body overlaid by meridian lines snaking and spiralling like telephone cables connecting the parts, keeping the system in flow. He could feel a headache's claw creeping up the back of his neck, spreading wider, like a ratcheting of the skull, and he closed his eyes and saw Jake's face once again, the straggly beard and high forehead, the eyes wide and alive, and he forced himself not to think of these things, squeezed his eyelids down hard as if that would be enough to expunge this vision. And it almost was.

Jon rubbed his ankle. Dante could not have found words to describe this pain. Maybe the doctor had been mistaken. It seemed to be getting worse rather than better, a slow and dull throb that had become all insistent making him feel as if he was wearing an iron boot. He'd taken some painkillers and now, as he stared out at the people withdrawing money, huddling around the cashpoint like conspirators sharing a secret, he felt so angry, so ashamed for what had happened that morning.

He'd been on the bus, standing on the exposed edge of the Routemaster, when he'd seen Jake, the tramp, walking along Oxford Street, or at least thought he'd seen him. Looking back on it now he realized that the man had been shorter, moved in a different way. Jon had jumped off the bus, hit the ground and went flying, face-down in the street. The bus behind screeched to a stop. He could smell the black smoke spewing from its front and hear the driver cursing.

Everyone was staring at him. The constantly moving mass of pedestrians had stopped dead in their tracks and was watching with an unnerving intensity, a sort of group spirit that seizes people in the vicinity of an accident. He smiled, tried to get up and collapsed straight back on to the asphalt, unable to stifle unmanly screams of pain. His ankle felt broken. He was sure of it.

He tried again. Arrows of pain shot up his legs, his stomach lurched, the earth shifted and spun. This is what happens when you black out, he thought and slumped back down, surrendering to gravity. He lay on the road, paralysed by pain and embarrassment, hoping the police, or someone – anyone – would come and get him out of this.

The doctor had said the ankle was only sprained but it felt like it was broken. The doctor had suggested a pair of crutches, ease the weight off it for a couple of days, but Jon had refused, horrified at the thought of trying to navigate London on anything but two good legs.

Had he really thought it was Jake? Or only hoped so much, desired it to such an extent that it had become real? For the first time, he understood how much he wanted it to have

16

been the old man. The way he'd spent the past week searching the faces of the crumpled figures on the streets for him, wondering if he'd driven him out or if it was something else, one of the demons that haunted his past, hoping somehow, against everything, that he'd still come back, ring the buzzer, act as though nothing had . . .

The phone made him jump. He peeled himself away from the window, eyes squinting at the light. He fumbled for the receiver. He had put his phone number in a book he'd given Jake. Perhaps the old man was calling him.

'Jon Reed.' Breathless with an underlay of expectancy, a slight tremulous uplift of tone.

'It's me, Jon. Just calling to check on progress.'

Jon exhaled, his heart slowed, he reached for his cigarettes. He couldn't tell his editor that he hadn't started yet. Not with the deadline at noon tomorrow. He couldn't begin to explain.

'It's going fine,' he said, lighting a cigarette.

'That's good to hear. And how are you?' There was always this rigmarole of genial inquiry following the reminder.

'I'm fine,' he replied, disappointed, though he knew there was no chance that Jake would call, but disappointed none the less.

'You still have your guest staying?'

His boss had a way of turning even the most innocuous word, 'guest' for instance, into a pejorative oozing loathing, bile and suspicion.

'No.'

'Good. Crazy thing, Jon. Could have got yourself killed. Or worse. Think about it. Drugged, raped and video-taped. Before you know it you're big in Bangkok. A star in Singapore. Maybe it's already happened. Maybe you didn't even realize.'

'Thanks, Dave, but I don't need you to make me any more paranoid than I already am.' He wanted to get off the phone, check the window again.

'I still don't understand you, Jon. What did you think you were trying to achieve?'

'I thought that . . .'

'What? I can't hear you.'

He was mumbling. He coughed, spoke again. 'I was drunk. I thought it would be a good thing to do. Something that I found hard, that would challenge me. I didn't want to just give money every now and then. I wanted to see if I really was what I believed myself to be.'

'For someone so cynical, Jon, you really are endearingly naïve.' Dave chuckled to himself. 'Tomorrow noon. Don't blow this one.'

Jon put the receiver down. His fists were clenched and his jaw tight. Why did such an act as inviting an old man off the streets cause such astonishment in people? Shouldn't it have been the other way around?

He tried to breathe deeply but that didn't work. It only made his chest hurt. He smoked a cigarette down fast and that was better.

The job was a massive task of sub-editing, link-checking and laying out of a to-be-launched-tomorrow website for a derivation of Shiatsu called Seiki. He lit another cigarette and stared at the page in front of him. Japanese characters and dense little packets of text. Tiny annotated diagrams. The body mapped and reduced to a flow-chart. Many hyper-links. His head spun. Everything began to merge. Lines slipped over and under each other, entwined. Photos blurred, ran down the page like water.

He forced himself to concentrate. He had chosen this after all, he had to keep reminding himself, and it was better than writing. There was no responsibility involved here, he was a gardener pruning and tidying up someone else's creation. He was the invisible ghost that lived in the spaces between. And that was good, that was the way he liked it. There were only the hard, sure rules of grammar and apostrophe, the tight strictures of syntax, like the cloistered halls of a cathedral, there to keep everything in check.

Once he had written. Oh yeah. Published a small, hexagonal quarterly music journal that had been read by the industry and perhaps no one else. He'd prided himself on the integrity of content, the eschewing of fads, the reliance on treating each record on its own merits.

And then he'd written that review.

Nothing much, at the time. Three hundred words about a bad country album that was getting good press. The review mentioned medieval torture devices and Noriega. The review was funny. It was honest and straight, though he would now admit that there was a certain relish in the rhetoric of the piece. He received a one-line email from the artist thanking him for his knowledgeable and erudite review. He received a small and scrunched-up newspaper clipping, a fortnight later, from the man's wife, now widow, after the singer had hanged himself in an EconoLodge two blocks away from his own home.

Everyone told him it wasn't his fault. These things happen. They cited examples. They bought him drinks and said *fuck it*. But he couldn't and so, quietly and without much fuss, he folded the magazine and retired to the indoor life, the pull of a small room, the way it feels almost like an extra layer of clothing protecting you from the world.

He'd cut out the review and had pressed it under the glass of a cheap clip-frame, sometimes, he thought, to remind him of the smallness of this thing that had loomed so large, as if there, framed and sequestered, it had been made discrete, answerable only to itself. But at other times he looked at it and it winked back, a confirmation of his worst and darkest fears.

But that was four years ago, he thought, tapping his fingers on the desk, looking for a way into this grid of blinking pixels. Four years, and he somehow understood that those years, that era even, as he could now call it, had come to an end the day he had invited a homeless man called Jake into his flat.

Jake had always stood by the cashpoint. A tall, bearded man in a blue lumberjack shirt and a pair of faded jeans, barefoot, whispering almost inaudibly out of the side of his mouth, never seeming to ask for change from the blank-faced passers-by. Jon hadn't even noticed him at first, so used to avoiding unnecessary glances in the London streets that the tramp made no impression. When he did begin to notice him, he was amused at how the man so resembled Hemingway, as if he were a strayed contestant from one of those lookalike competitions held annually in Florida.

As the long days of sunlight dragged through the first part of September, he grew more and more intrigued with the tramp. He'd been giving him money whenever he went past, he couldn't help doing that, was always doing that, and they were now on nodding terms; a brief hello, a morning smile. Jake was so different from the other homeless men, almost Dickensian characters crouched in doorways, defeated and bent, or swaying drunkenly in front of shops full of gleaming objects. There was a certain dignity to Jake, in his rake-like posture and eyes that always met yours, that even the streets had not managed to scrape off.

Jon began to spend an inordinate amount of time thinking

about him. He would get up from the computer and sneak peeks through the net curtains. Watch as the man arrived every morning, always carrying a pile of books and a notepad, though he'd never seen him using them. He speculated, spun stories, and imagined a spectrum of possibilities as he strolled through his own dull daily life. It was a way of writing, invisible writing that harmed no one, a way of passing the time. He had him as an undercover police agent, a former man of good standing gone to pot after the death of a spouse, an escaped child molester, and sometimes, in his most fuzzy late-night haze, he convinced himself that it was indeed the ghost of old Hem come back to beg in the London streets.

Then the weather turned. Brooding black skies spread overhead and the rain began its endless onslaught. The gutters overflowed, clotted and sticky with dead leaves. The days got shorter and harsher.

Jon found himself becoming – well, sometimes he admitted it – a little obsessed, though he passed it off as just one of those things that happens when nothing else happens. His morning strolls were punctuated by the smile of the old man, by his bare feet and by the faces of the people who passed him by oblivious. When he walked up Notting Hill, he saw the face of the tramp in every homeless person, on every street corner, in their gap-toothed smiles and resigned pleas, their ragged clothes and sad-eyed dogs.

Jon even started to feel disappointed when he looked out in the morning and the tramp wasn't there; it was as if his day were incapable of starting without the old man. He had got as used to seeing him as he was to his morning cigarette, his first espresso. Like those things, the old man had some-how become esssential to Jon's life, an underlying recurrent, something to hold it all together by, and he felt strangely resentful of the tramp at times, as if his sole purpose was to ensnare him in this need.

But he found himself returning to the window time and again, unable to keep away, promising himself he would just check and then get back to the TV, invariably spending the night watching, wondering *Who are you? Why do you draw me like this? Are you a ghost?*

As the weather worsened it tested his resolve. The thought of inviting the old man to stay had, at first, seemed rash, idealistic, the kind of thing his twelve-year-old self would have done. He'd dismissed it instantly and given the old man a fiver the next time he'd passed. But he kept watching from the window. The rain constant and dark. The old man like a statue standing still in the wet soup. And slowly the idea took shape in his head. It had a certain clarity to it that he found seductive. It was something so unusual, a wild leap, and he knew that only such an act, such an un-Jon-like act, could break through the ice he'd been petrified in these past few years.

And he was scared. Absolutely terrified. He thought about the old man slaughtering him in his sleep. He remembered stories splashed across newspapers and TV discussions, heads nodding in patronizing they-should-have-known-better gestures. Or how about: the old man stealing his favourite CDs; the old man inviting a crew of juiceheads to wreck the place; the old man burning down the flat.

He chided himself for thinking like this, for the spew and sputter of images that seemed to come so readily. And this was another reason to do it. Disprove all this bullshit once and for all. Yes. He unconsciously inventoried his flat, appraising what there was of value.

After the seventh day of torrential rain, Jon's resolve and paranoia finally broke and all the reasons for not inviting the tramp in were washed away like the summer leaves. He'd been thinking about it so much, it had swallowed up his life and he knew that there was only one thing to do. He got drunk. Stared at the wet old man two floors below. Drank more. Went out into the rain, shouted over the noise of the thunder. Made his offer.

Now, staring at the empty space, rubbing his engorged ankle, Jon could understand a little better the reasons that had made him invite the old man to stay. At the time, he only vaguely pressed against the surface of his motivation, afraid that probing it too deeply might make it wilt. And he was glad that he had done it, even if Jake was back on the streets. His mother would have been proud. She'd always taught him to think about the men who lived on the fringes of life. She had taken him to parts of town that his father hadn't even known existed. She'd led him through small, crowded, smelly streets that for the twelve-year-old boy were like a window, a gateway into a world that bubbled under the surface of this one.

The first time he had cried so much that his mother apologized. He'd told her that it wasn't fair that they were going home to dinner while these men and women had to sleep in cardboard boxes. His mother just nodded sadly, and something in the world had shifted slightly.

At first the tramp had mumbled and demurred, but Jon insisted, the rain hissed and splattered, and they walked back into the building together, dripping and cold, exchanging names and wet handshakes as they waited for the lift.

They sat opposite each other in the living room and didn't say a thing.

Jon stared at his bookcases, crushed by a sudden feeling that he'd made a terrible mistake. He'd invited a stranger into his house. More than a stranger. A tramp. Who was to say he hadn't come from an institution? Or prison? Jon suddenly realized that he knew nothing about this man, that all his assumptions and speculations were just that. He tried to think of something to say, but nothing came.

There was a tired smell exuding from Jake, like the whiff of old books or attic-rescued toys. He just sat there, almost a part of the armchair, his head bowed, his hand running through the straggle of his beard.

Jon tried not to stare at Jake's feet. He was barefoot, as always, but it was only now in the small confined light of the room that he could see that the marks and patterns on the old man's feet were not just from sleeping rough. His feet were dark and sunburned, crisscrossed with tiny white lines, the flesh sometimes folded over itself, sometimes stretched tight to the bone, a latticework of streets and alleys carved into the skin or an ancient map of places still unseen. They looked hard and worn like an athlete's feet, as if the flesh was slowly turning to leather.

He glanced up and noticed that Jake was watching him.

He shivered, a real body snap and jerker, the kind that makes you feel as if 100 volts have just surged through your system. He coughed to make it seem like something else, hoping Jake hadn't caught it, thinking of exiled Chilean academics he'd seen in a documentary once and the torture scars they carried like a secret tattoo beneath their clothes.

'I wonder if I could have a bath.'

Jon jumped. Then laughed, or tried to, but it came out wrong and Jake didn't smile back or make things any easier. His face held still like the face of a man carved in stone.

'It's been a couple of weeks. I must smell awful.'

Yes he did, Jon thought, but he'd been way too polite, too

embarrassed, to say anything. 'There's towels in the racks and you can use whatever soaps, shampoos I've got,' he said, trying not to let the relief show in his voice.

'Thank you,' Jake replied and got up, leaving big wet, soggy footprints on the faded carpet.

When the door closed, Jon felt a sudden surge of relief, a welcome spasm of privacy. What had he done? But it was too late for that now, of course. He couldn't ask him to leave. Couldn't change his mind. That would be worse, and more difficult. He suddenly remembered his toothbrush, wondering whether Jake would use it, it was the only one he had, and he made a decision to buy a new one tomorrow, but one that was identical so that the old man wouldn't feel insulted.

Jon lit a cigarette and put the first side of Zappa's *Waka/Jawaka* on the stereo. As the horns began blasting the melody, reaching ever higher, counter-phrasing and spinning across the wild, propulsive beat, he went to the kitchen, buoyed by the screaming trumpets, and started to make an omelette, figuring the old man must be hungry, wanting to do something for him, even if it was just this.

He thought about his father's funeral while the eggs slowly turned opaque in the pan. The sound of the sizzling fat like the rain on the roofs of the cars that morning . . . another grey rain-lashed day . . . his inability to look anyone in the eye, hiding behind the cortège of hearses; a small child again, weeping for a father that he'd hated in life, filled with shame, regret and the massiveness of all that had been left unresolved.

He took out the milk and made some coffee, hearing the pipes squeak and whistle as Jake ran his bath. Thinking about his father again made Jon's body tense up and he spilled sugar all over the floor, cursing himself and the way his memory always lay in wait like a densely packed minefield, impossible to avoid, fracturing the present.

It made his ankle throb. Thinking about his father, about the past, Jake's disappearance, all the things that were still raw and painful. He didn't want to think about any of that.

He got up, poured another drink. Stared out at the cash-point, deserted now. He was glad that he'd invited Jake in. It was the one thing in his life he was unmitigatedly proud of. The one time when he overcame his fears and quibbles and actually did something without reservation. Not that it had made any difference. The old man was gone.

Jon thought about the tissues on the floor, the unexpected sight of the old man naked, but surely it was more than that. The thought that he'd somehow driven him off was not something he wanted to contend with. Not now. Not with all this work still to be done, this flickering mass of pixelated crap.

He pulled the curtains shut, drained the scotch, shut down the computer and turned on the dying minutes of a football game. Took a couple more painkillers. His headache had settled behind his eyes, fine white pins of pain piercing his retinas.

The phone rang.

It sounded like something snapping inside his head.

Each ring seemed to get louder. Dave checking he was working. Dave hassling him. He almost didn't pick it up. But what if it was Jake? He picked up, said, 'Hello', trying not to slur, to sound too drunk or drugged.

'Mr Jon Reed?'

'Yes?' he said, muting the TV.

'My name is Detective Ronald van Hijn, Amsterdam police.' There was a pause in which the detective seemed to be lost for words. Jon stared blankly at the mute players dancing across the brilliant green. The detective coughed. His voice sounded thin and far away. 'I'm afraid I have some bad news for you, Mr Reed.'

2

Wouter tied her to the four corners of the bed using pairs of tights he had taken out of her drawer. The arms came first; small wrists covered by smooth Lycra, pinioned to the brass ends of the headboard. When he was satisfied that her arms were safely pinned, he began tying her feet, wrapping the tights around her ankles, ankles he dearly loved, and pulling them across to either side of the bed.

Suze said nothing, didn't struggle, let him continue with his slow seduction as she stared at the black of the blindfold that covered her eyes and saw the desert appear in front of her.

It was a good image. An image drawn from the vast repository of her youth. Before things had turned bad. Before . . .

She focused on the lone mesa in the distance, black and mysterious in the corners of her memory, as she heard him taking off clothes, coughing, getting on top of the bed and mumbling something in Dutch.

She told him to hit play on the deck. The sound of the Geraldine Fibbers' second album, *Butch*, alternatingly soft and savage, saturated the room. She felt his tongue, warm and sticky, slide up her thigh, and though it was almost like being tickled, she tried not to move or squirm, instead letting the creeping sensitivity drown her as it raced across her body making nipples stand cold and rosy, skin prick up as if expecting an unexpected guest. He noticed this and began to play with her breast, grabbing the nipple slightly between his teeth, tightening the grip and gently releasing as he heard her moan.

He lit a cigarette, reached over to the bedside table and picked the two clothes pegs off it. She felt the cold plastic clamp her nipple and the warm trickle of pleasure that coursed up through her neck and down her thighs. She saw the desert, the hands of her mother shaking in an alcoholic rage, the sound of her father on an answering machine, the closest she got to him for many years, that disembodied crackle and pulse of humming lines and whispered, breathy urgencies that could only be expressed in the close confines of a faraway telephone booth – she saw all that and then it was blown away, scattered and gone.

He placed the other clothes peg, twisted it so that her nipple seemed almost to blush as the blood engorged it, darkening the already dark skin there. He felt her move, gyrate slightly, though he could sense that in some essential way she was no longer with him, that somehow in her restraints she'd managed to escape to somewhere small and private, and he entered her then, feeling himself ready to explode, the cigarette slowly burning down in the ashtray beside the bed.

'Now that wasn't too hard, was it?' Suze said as he undid the tights and carefully took off her blindfold.

'It was kinda fun,' he replied in that quasi-American accent that she found so sexy in Dutch men, as if they'd all learned how to speak English from movies, giving them a brusquer, more commanding tone than they would have ever learned in pronunciation class.

He lit her a cigarette and then one for himself. She wiped the blood that had begun to dry and crack on his chin. 'Did you enjoy it?' she asked him, placing her hand on his shoulder, feeling the still hot flesh of his urgency.

'I guess so.' He took a drag of the cigarette and lightly placed it in the ashtray. 'Not that I've done this kind of thing before but it's good to try something different.'

And it was, he had to admit to himself, more fun than he'd expected it to be. When he tied her up, he felt as he had with the twins, lost in a world of his own imagining, able to leap whatever barriers.

'But I want to know if you enjoyed it. If you *really* enjoyed it.' She looked at him, suddenly serious.

'No, not really. Not of itself.' He lied, ashamed of the lust that had stirred within him. 'Being with you, yes but this, no.'

She moved away from him. 'I thought all you Dutch boys were into kinky sex.'

'Why do you think that?' he replied. He liked the way Americans managed to generalize and place everything in a box from which understanding could then be gleaned. It made life so much simpler.

'I don't know, it's just the common impression,' she replied, not having really thought about it; but, now that she did, it seemed to make a whole lot of sense. 'You have this legalized sex and drugs industry – I mean hell, Wouter, you yourself run three sex shops.' She smiled, sensing that he didn't find the paradox quite as entertaining as she did. 'And you know, to us foreigners, you Dutch seem so straight and – forgive me – boring, that we twisted Americans have got it into our heads that you must all be perverts of some kind. C'mon Wouter, underneath that prim Protestant exterior something darker must lurk.'

'I don't think that's quite the case.'

'I was just joking.' She grabbed him and squeezed his

30

hand, thinking *God, I wish he had a sense of humour*, but then he'd be pretty much perfect and Suze knew there was no such thing, not for her anyway. She got up, took off the Fibbers and put on Waits, *Foreign Affairs*, sensing the moment required something mellow. They sat and smoked silently for the length of the album.

'I used to go to prostitutes.'

It was later, they were drinking coffee and Suze almost spilled her cup, it was just so sweet the way he'd said it.

'Is there any adolescent boy here who doesn't?' she replied, looking at him, wondering why he'd chosen this moment to tell her.

'Not many, I think. We don't really attach the same kind of stigma to it as you do in your more enlightened land.'

So, he can be sarcastic, she thought – well, that was progress at least, most of the Dutch men she'd met so far had seemed to be severely lacking in any kind of charisma or passion, but damn, did they look good.

'I used to go see these twins, every fortnight or so for about seven years.' He lit another cigarette. 'Hilda and Helena, though of course those weren't their real names. I never knew their real names. They came from Belgium and always worked together. I was about sixteen when I met them.'

She took the cigarette from his hand and pulled two quick drags before giving it back.

'I had gone to whores before, yes, and while it was always fun to fuck someone new, I never really got much pleasure from it after that initial thrill. And then I met the twins and, of course, sex suddenly had many new possibilities. Permutations I had not conceived of, but which they took me through methodically and diligently as if my fortnightly visits were some kind of education, a what-do-you-call-it cor . . . ?'

'A curriculum.'

'Yes, a curriculum to be followed. I never missed a lesson. I would come on a Wednesday evening, pay my money and spend the rest of the night learning from them.'

'Sounds like a great education,' Suze said, wishing life in the States had been that uncomplicated.

'Of course as time went on our relationship grew to be more than that of client and whore. Like a fool I fell madly in love with them.'

'What, both?' she asked, faking incredulity, though she knew that this was the way all such stories ended.

'Yes, both. While they were identical twins in every physical way, psychologically they were two totally different people and I guess that kind of turned me on. The fact that they looked the same but weren't.' He pulled down the bedsheets and moved closer to her. Some sadness had entered his face and Suze was almost surprised, it was something she'd never glimpsed in the four short months that she'd been seeing him.

'What happened to them? Do you still keep in contact?' she asked.

He took another cigarette, lit it, and coughed. 'No. They were murdered two years ago. The police didn't find the killer, they never do in prostitute killings. Someone, a client, had stabbed them both through the heart with a carving fork. Decapitated them and swapped the heads around. The police never knew. It was in the papers, I guess a photographer had got to the scene before the cops. They had different tattoos, that's how I could tell. Christ, they buried them in separate graves with the wrong heads loosely reattached by the coroner. That's what kills me, not so much that they never found the murderer but that to this day they're lying underground with each other's head.'

'I'm sorry,' she said.

'There's nothing to be sorry about, that's life. You Americans apologize for everything, things you have no control over, I do not understand that.'

'I apologized for bringing the subject up.'

'You didn't know.'

'No, I didn't.'

Suze was sitting on the edge of the bed. Her eyes stared into the wall. She knew that if she stared long enough, the patterns would begin to move, shift and squeeze into new designs.

'What's wrong?' he asked. He thought perhaps the story had disgusted her, made her think less of him and, in fact, in the retelling he had glimpsed how it could look from another side and he hadn't liked what he'd seen.

'Your story reminded me of that girl they found last week.'

'The canal killer?' He'd been following the case for the last eight months though it was something that he wouldn't admit to, even to her. Yet, perversely, he felt a twitch of excitement, an uncalled-for snap of charge, every time he opened the paper and saw that there had been another one. In some way, he thought, at least this would bring the issue, the danger, to the surface.

'I just don't really understand it.' Suze shrugged and turned back towards him. She saw that he was smiling. 'Not here, not with all the sex that's legally available.'

'I don't think that's quite what turns this killer's crank.'

She laughed, surprised out of herself. 'Where did you learn that phrase?' she said.

'One of your American TV shows. We get those here too, you know, like serial killers – you export the good and bad.'

She didn't answer him. She was used to his little games and, as an American abroad, she'd learned how she was always a representative of her native country, embroiled in all its horrors and wonders. She'd got so tired of defending herself that she'd given up.

'I once saw someone get killed,' she whispered.

It came out without her planning. It was something she rarely talked about and she was surprised to have found it let loose in this setting, though she knew that there was a bond between their bodies, a sort of carnal contract, that allowed them to explore these things that you never could with someone you really cared about.

'Only one?' he replied, smiling, to show that he didn't mean her any harm. That it was just his way of expressing things. 'I thought you were supposed to have seen something like six thousand by the time you're ten.'

'That's TV. This was real.'

He nodded, as if that made all the difference. 'How old were you?'

'Eight,' she said, and realized that she was going to talk about it. She had promised herself not to. But she had promised herself many other things too – in Amsterdam, none of that meant anything any more.

'I was in a gas station with my parents.' She lit a cigarette and sucked on it hard. 'We were going to the Superstition Mountains for a holiday. Outside of Phoenix. We were buying food and gas for the trip when this man walked in and marched straight up to the counter. My parents were face deep in the soft-drink cooler but I saw it. I saw the attendant's startled look as the man pointed the shotgun at him. Then everything exploded. The sound shook the racks of sweets. I remember screaming. Brightly coloured wrappers

34

rainbowed the floor. The back wall exploded in blood. I can still hear the sound it made. I ran to my parents. There was another blast. More splatter. Glass breaking, heavy breathing. And the man who'd come in with the shotgun collapsed on the floor, the gun shearing away from him and clattering on the linoleum.'

'Shit, you have a good memory,' he said, not sure what else there was to say, not even sure how much of it was true though there was a seriousness to her now.

'I didn't understand what was happening. I screamed but I think I enjoyed it too. To a certain extent. Or maybe I only remember thinking that, maybe that happened afterwards, I don't know. But there was something there. The smell of the gun, that sharp tang following the blast, like a glimpse into another world, the sound and noise and fury, something that was appealing to me, not knowing what it really meant, what it signified. It was spectacular.'

'What happened afterwards?' he asked, finding himself turned on by this side of her.

She moved away from him, looked at the wall, waiting for the patterns to change. 'I don't want to talk about that, Wouter.'

'But you brought it up.' He sounded exasperated she thought, wondering why he was so fascinated though she had to admit it was a fascinating thing, seen from the outside.

'Let's not spoil this moment,' she whispered.

'But this is why you're so interested in Charlotte, no?' He saw her flinch slightly. He didn't like it when she tensed herself up this way. It was like a closing of doors, a folding into herself that left him on the outside. But she liked to talk about Charlotte Salomon. It was why she'd come here. To write about the Jewish painter who died in the poison showers of Auschwitz.

'No, it's not. That's just cheap psychology. I like her art. That's all,' she replied, but even as the words left her mouth she could feel their uselessness hanging in the stale after-sex air.

'And I suppose your work with the Council has nothing to do with it either?'

She smiled, saw that he was playing with her, little post-coital murmurs and teases. She enjoyed him most when he was like this. When the walls of seriousness came down. 'The Revised Council of Blood, it's called. I wish you'd get the name right,' she replied, almost sticking out her tongue but then thinking better of it, giving him a friendly kick instead.

'Big name for a debating society.'

He liked to tease her about it because she never told him anything. It was one of the few secrets they kept. She knew that to speak about the Council would be to betray its basic beliefs. She knew too that he wouldn't understand the full scope of it and that words, uttered from her mouth, would just be a reducing of things, a way to disfigure their intentions.

'It's more than a debating society, I told you that. We have a purpose, a goal.'

'You keep its secrets like they were gold.'

'We all need to keep secrets from each other, Wouter, otherwise life would just be way too damn predictable.'

Like the secrets you have to keep when living with div-orced parents, she thought. You know the ones. Not saying that yes, Mum might be drinking too much because you don't want to hear your father saying again what a worthless, aimless woman she always was and not telling her that yes, Dad has a new girlfriend and yes, she's another of his students and then listening to your mum spill forth her own repressed years and rages. No, secrets were good. They kept the world apart, discrete and manageable. Sometimes the less people knew about each other the better.

That evening she taught him how to fashion stronger knots, how to not let the pegs slip off and how to restrain himself until the final moment. He followed silently, afraid of his own pleasure, but the American girl seemed to enjoy it so he did what she wanted and, while he was fucking her, he pretended that she was one of the twins, untied and loose-limbed, wrapping herself around him – but when he opened his eyes to look at her face all he could see were the badly spaced stitch marks that went around her neck.

3

The detective wanted him to go to Amsterdam to identify the body. He'd made it clear that Jon's assistance would be of great benefit to the investigation. He'd made it sound as if the whole thing depended on his arrival.

Jon put the phone down. His head rattled with blood, pounding in his ears like a fist. He took a deep breath, feeling the air press against his ribcage.

Jake was dead.

That was what the detective had said. Found face-down in a park with a copy of the book that Jon had lent him.

Murder, the detective had said.

He grabbed his lighter and lit a cigarette. There was a high-pitched buzzing in his left ear, a kiss of feedback. His hands were shaking, he was out of breath. The room got darker as if someone had just sucked the air out of it. He drew in the smoke and felt a light coating of sweat form all over his body, sticky and cold.

Amsterdam.

That city again.

It was ridiculous. He had his project to finish. They were launching tomorrow and he hadn't started subbing it yet. The dead screen glared at him. There was so much still to do. There was no way he could go. It was crazy. He knew that if he didn't get it in on time he'd be out of a job. Dave's phone call had made that clear. It *was* crazy. Just pack and go. It terrified and thrilled him at the same time. The same feeling he'd had when peering over the rim of the Grand

Canyon one summer, staring down into the swirling abyss of rock, that wonderful tingling of pull and release, the welcome, wilful surrender to forces outside yourself. But no, he couldn't think like that. He'd promised Dave. He couldn't give it all up just to chase a ghost.

It had been just over a week since he'd seen the old man and yet it seemed as if he'd only left yesterday. He could still feel him occupying certain spaces in the flat, still remember the way he'd had to change the espresso machine filter from a single to a double. The way space takes on a new dimension, a fullness and depth that you were previously unaware of. He looked at the TV but the football was over, he'd missed the final score. There was a straggly, skinny, tired-eyed labrador on the screen, head hanging down, droopy jowls, something terribly wrong with its legs and, even with the sound off, Jon knew this was an animal charity ad.

And then he began to cry. Looking at the dog, feeling as if the whole building was caving in on him, it was something so unexpected, something that he couldn't stop. He felt palpitations rumble and rage through his chest like a rattling train, he tried to catch his breath, his eyes stinging with tears. The next time he looked up the news was on. Fires raged, people screamed and fell to the ground, pride and dignity a luxury they could no longer afford. He turned it off, stubbed his cigarette, burning himself in the process and grabbed his car keys.

He was drunk. He knew this because his ankle didn't hurt that much. Over the limit. He got into the car and tested his foot against the pedal. It seemed okay. So what if they stopped him? So fucking what?

Jake was dead.

He'd thought he could help him. Thought that taking him in might mean something. Jake's death felt like a negation of all that he'd tried to achieve, a lightning bolt from above if you were a religious man.

He missed Jake, more than he ever thought he would a stranger, someone off the streets. He missed him like one misses a dream lover whose perfection is only an index of the dream and whose disappearance when waking leaves you emptier and sadder than any flesh and blood woman ever could. That strange, quiet man had upset every story Jon had made up to explain him and he now understood how it is we look back on things we miss, things that are never apparent in their moment but exist only in reflection, a messy stirring of memory and desire.

He drove up on to the Westway, the great concrete snake that straddled the west of the city, vaulting across housing estates and parks, heading into the black occlusion of night, Townes Van Zandt on the stereo and London passing invisibly by.

In the dark cramp of the car he blamed himself for not having given Jake more money, though he'd tried once and the old man had just refused in that polite yet inarguable way of his. But he should have been more insistent or perhaps just sneakier, slipping it into Jake's clothes when he wasn't there. But what would that have achieved? Was money really the problem? He didn't think so. Jake had never asked for any, even when he was out on the street. At first Jon had thought the old man was still holding on to whatever dignity was left but now he realized that Jake had made it back to Amsterdam and that he'd had money all along.

He clung to the idea that the detective had made a mistake. That it was some other man lying extinguished on a slab somewhere. He wondered if he would have to go to Amsterdam just to ascertain for himself whether Jake was actually dead. Did he really want to know? Maybe it was better to leave the possibility open.

But he knew how remote that was, knew that there was no doubt about it and perhaps the only real surprise had been the Dutch detective.

That and the location of death.

Amsterdam.

But even that wasn't really a surprise.

No, not at all.

At the time, he'd thought it was just a story, a way the old man used to get a point across.

Amsterdam. The place where Jake was born.

It had a seductive symmetry to it, Jon admitted, but was that all?

He hadn't thought about it again, not in the intervening period, and so the question of whether Jake had told him the truth was one that he'd never asked, but which the Dutch detective had nevertheless answered.

Jake had been in the flat a week. He spoke little and always kept his room tidy and clean. He spent most of his time in there, reading, writing, Jon never knew. After the awkwardness of the first night Jon thought it would get better, but the old man stayed the same, accepting food and drink with a nod or a shrug but rarely saying anything apart from the most basic syllabic units, no and yes. The space between them seemed further than the few metres of carpet broken by black coffee table.

Jon had tried to engage him, pull him into dialogue, but Jake had said nothing. The silence made Jon uneasy. He put on music to fill it. He played the old man CDs, asked him what he thought, did he like this one or that one, but Jake didn't answer and Jon fumbled with another CD so as not to drop into awful silence again.

He spent more time outdoors, avoiding the silent accusation that hummed through the flat. He started to wonder if he was losing his mind; perhaps asking Jake to stay had been the breaking point, the first unreasoned act that would bring down the deluge. He forced himself to go back to the flat, entered its unwelcome space, Jake lodged in his room like some autistic monk. He checked to see if anything was missing then made the old man coffee and tea, not sure which he'd prefer. He hid things from Jake, then, in spasms of guilt, put them back in their places. He'd told a few friends and they'd laughed at him and somehow that had reaffirmed his initial act, for it was in their disapproval that he saw the glint of the good he was doing, or at least thought he was.

Those first few days the only thing Jake ever said apart from yes or no was, 'It's a botch. It's all been a botch.' He said it several times, perhaps thinking Jon out of earshot, a steady rhythmic canto repeated to himself, the window, the stale and empty air, and Jon never knew whether Jake was talking of his life or of something else.

'It's my birthday today.'

Jon stared at him, stunned. It was more than he'd said all week.

Jake stood in his bathrobe wrapped tight, always wrapped so tight, Jon noticed, and smiled.

'I thought it would be a good day to go for a walk.'

Jon tried to say something but the words stopped in his throat. He nodded, unwilling and unable to utter anything lest it destroy the moment.

They walked through Hyde Park, watching the skaters and ducks gliding by, the cold precision of September that made

42

everything look as if it were in hyper-focus, carved discrete and sharp by the icy, brittle air. They didn't say anything, nothing much, Jon tried to mention the good weather but the old man just smiled that smile of his, impenetrable as a slab of granite. They walked back to the flat as the rain began to cloak the sky. Listened to a Grateful Dead concert from November 1973. It was the one thing they had in common and though Jake changed the subject every time Jon mentioned a certain show, there was something there, some memory of a different time. Jake nodded along to the November 11th 'Dark Star' and commented on the recording.

'I always had a bad one,' he said. Jon looked at him, unsure what to say. 'Lots of hiss and tape generations. This sounds clean.'

'You should hear the remastered Cow Palace show from '76.' Jon moved forward, encouraged.

Jake nodded. 'Yes, that's a great one. Haven't listened to any Dead for a long time. I feel like a different person now. Different from the one who used to listen to all this. It's strange.'

Jon had caught Jake checking out his CDs one evening. His first thought was that the old man was going to take them and sell them. He was appalled by how quickly the thought had appeared. He made a vow to be kinder to Jake, to not lock his bedroom door as he had been doing the past few nights, stealthily, carefully turning the key so that it wouldn't echo down the empty hall. To stop watching Jake as if he was a thief. He tried not to think about these things. But they came. Especially late at night, lying in bed, in the dark, when he heard the floorboards creak and the careful creeping of tired feet.

When the music was over they sat in silence, staring at the

floor. Sometimes Jake seemed in another world; though his eyes were open they were scanning some wider horizon than the room afforded. It made Jon feel uneasy in his own flat and he picked up a book, something to distract him from the silence.

'When was the last time you were in a synagogue?' Jake asked, making Jon flinch, the book dropping from his hand to the floor. It was the first unsolicited comment from the old man since that morning. He couldn't remember when he'd last been. How did Jake even know he was Jewish?

'I don't know,' he replied shifting in his seat. 'My father was never a religious man.' He glanced down. Jake's eyes bored into him. It was as if he were a machine that had been running on standby only now switching to normal power, unleashing its potential.

Jake frowned. 'We are all religious, one way or another.' He took a sip of scotch. 'You liked your father?'

'No,' Jon replied, surprised by Jake's aggressive tone and by this intensely personal probing. He looked so serene from the outside and yet his voice trembled with a dark and ruinous sonority, a bitter, heavy sound that seemed to fill every space in the flat.

'Me neither. Mine was a bastard.'

He stayed on the Western Avenue watching the dull suburban houses roll by like flimsy backgrounds in a B-movie. He remembered the sculpted tone of Jake's voice, the sound of country boarding schools and old universities, so incompatible with the man's beard and borrowed clothes. The way he'd opened up that evening. And he thought about the way their fathers' deaths had changed their lives irrevocably.

*

44

'Your father changed the name?'

Jon stared at him. He'd never talked about it to anyone. He was scared of people's prejudices. The things they wouldn't say. 'Yes,' he eventually answered, somehow feeling that it was easier for such intimacies to creep out between total strangers. 'Removed the ethnic stain of Rieglbaum and replaced it with the terse gentility of Reed. He said it was something that I shouldn't talk about. He always made me ashamed of the fact.'

'And you still are, I see.' Jake shook his head, gently.

Jon didn't answer. He lit a cigarette. Hid behind the smoke.

'You have much yet to discover.' Jake looked at him, smiled and Jon thought there was a lot of pain in that smile – pain, but also a measure of kindness that he was not used to seeing. His mother had smiled like that.

'I don't think these things matter so much any more.' He wanted to say something, to show Jake that he had his own beliefs, his own opinions.

Jake laughed, a forced, strangled sound. Jon looked away.

'You don't think they matter? You've lived in a room all your life, what would you know? They don't matter until they do and when they do they're all that matters.' He lit a cigarette, letting the words hang in the air. He didn't expect Jon to reply. He continued, his voice hoarse with smoke, but calmer now. 'Those were very different times to be Jewish in, before the war ... before they knew what happened. Very different. You cannot imagine.' Jake marked every punctuation stop with a firm drag on his cigarette, exhaling the smoke with the next sentence. Jon wondered exactly what the old man meant, but he didn't ask him to elucidate, fearing that Jake would think him slow or stupid, an unworthy conversation partner, and fold back into the box of silence from which he'd so recently sprung.

'I suppose so,' he replied, though he wondered how different they really were. His friends were all Christians but here, in the presence of a Jew, he was most uncomfortable and he felt ashamed that it should be so.

'So, what about your mother?' Jake asked.

'She's dead.'

'I'm sorry.'

'Not your fault.'

'Still.'

Jon's cigarette felt dry and tasteless as the memories rolled inside his head like an endless ocean of sorrow and anger. He hated himself for wishing it was his father who had died on that grey, faceless street. That useless, prosaic death. And yet he knew that, given the chance, he could have made that choice without blinking. He blamed him for sending her out, for her death. It disturbed him how Jake brought all that up. It made him angry that he still cared.

Yes, he'd inherited that at least. His father's anger which had shaken his world with all the power of any monster or demon that he could have imagined. And now it was inside him, this anger, breathing through him, as if in some tangible way his father's soul had migrated into his, corrupting it with its bile and hatred. He would flare up like a struck match sometimes and say things, things that no longer came out in his voice, but that of his father's. He hated how he could trace his most hidden prejudices and gripes directly to him. It scared him how strong the influence was, how biological, how inescapable.

'My father gave up on me when the magazine folded. I think in some way he thought I'd failed him.' He felt the need to say it, to make at least this clear. 'He thought I was being too sensitive. Didn't see any place for that.'

'Sounds very much like my father,' Jake replied and they both laughed, releasing the tension in the room, feeling closer, at least in Jon's mind, than since the wet handshake on that first day.

'What was your father like?' Jon asked after a few minutes of silence had elapsed punctuated only by the hiss of slowly burning tobacco. Now that Jake had begun, he didn't want him to stop. And he wanted to know who this person was. Sleeping in his flat. Making strange sounds at night. Accepting everything with a weary shrug.

'One monster father is pretty much the same as another. Your comments were very familiar.' Jake smiled and it was a smile of revelation and conspiracy. Jon found it vaguely threatening.

'You see,' Jake continued, 'the interesting story about my father takes place only after he's dead.'

Jon poured the last of the scotch into Jake's glass and went to the kitchen to fetch some more. It felt good to be making drinks for someone else, good to have to ask them, how many sugars do you take, how strong do you want it? All the little inanities that he'd thought he could live without. Stupidly thought that until, in an empty flat, one night, he realized that it was those very things that made life worth living.

In the next room, Jake put on a CD and Jon heard the first notes of Coltrane's 'Ascension' squawk their way out of his speakers. The room filled with a dense, tight-knit caterwaul, seven or eight instruments screaming and wailing simultaneously, circling around an empty chord, a missing centre, like a flock of lost birds, frenzied and furious, smashing into each other in the massive sky.

'My father had a lot of money. He'd worked in food importation, made his fortune, floated the company and retired to the country.' Jake's voice settled, the terse clip of his phrasing evened out. Jon leaned forward on the sofa, wanting to show his attention, even in this most obvious and empty of gestures, but he also felt the need to at least try to close the physical space between them, the gulf of carpet and air.

'He died of stomach cancer last spring. I can't say I was sad. I'd lost my mother many years before. I hadn't seen him in years. We were not close nor had we ever been. I got a call from the family solicitor. I was the director of a consultancy company. What sum my father might have left me was of no concern but the lawyer said that the main part of my father's testament consisted of a letter. That intrigued me. It wasn't like him to put things in writing. He always believed the spoken word superior, more trustworthy than that which was written.

'I went to see the lawyer. This was about six months ago. He handed me an undistinguished brown envelope, said it was my father's last wish that I should have it. I thanked him and left, not knowing that what I carried under my arm that day would turn my life upside down. I didn't even read it until the next morning.'

'What was in it?' Jon asked, caught up in the old man's tale, the lull and roil of his voice. That special feeling of being told something privileged, intimate, that comes across in the whispered end of sentences and the outbreath of thoughtful pauses. He wondered how something that could fit into an envelope could also ruin a man's life.

'Ten badly typed pages. That's all there was. The old man must have done it himself. It started with an apology. Before the fact. That was just like him. He then wrote of his business interests in 1940, importing food from the continent into England, how he'd set the company up five years earlier with

48

an old colleague from Oxford, a Dutch Jew by the name of Kuper. The two of them had developed the business into a considerable success by the time that Kuper's wife, Martha, gave birth to a son in September 1940.

'The war was on. Disturbing news was leaking from Germany and Austria about the mistreatment of Jews. In Austria they had hounded them down, taken away their businesses, their passports, and paraded them through the streets of Vienna. You must have heard about what happened there?'

'Not really. I was never that interested in history,' Jon replied.

The old man gave him a brief look of such disdain that, for a moment, Jon saw the man Jake must have once been. It was fleeting, only a glimpse, but it scared him. Jon wanted to say something, to make up for his ignorance but he could tell that it would be wasted, that the old man wouldn't fall for cheap platitudes, tawdry excuses or feigned apologies. He felt totally stripped in front of Jake as if each lie he told would come cascading out, trilled with neon and noise, as obvious as a waterfall in the desert.

Jake seemed to be assessing something privately. He stared at a point two inches above Jon's head, then his eyes dropped on to Jon's and he continued. 'They stripped the old people naked and made them do callisthenics in the middle of the streets while the good citizenry threw eggs and shit at them. They forced them to clean the Vienna pavements with toothbrushes and tongues and urinated on them while they did it. These weren't the exceptions, this was the norm. Unlike many other Jews of that period, Raphael Kuper heeded these early warning signs and, when the first deportation of Jews from Amsterdam took place in February 1941, he arranged for his English partner, John Colby, to take his newborn son, Jakob, away from all this horror. He knew that he would probably never see his son again and that he was giving him up for ever, but the alternative was even worse.

'Colby managed to escape on a fishing boat with his wife and landed in England where they claimed the small baby as their own.'

Jake took another cigarette, seemed to draw on it for ever before he resumed as if the story had somehow depleted him. 'So his letter ended. At first, and I think for at least a couple of days after having read it, I believed it was a joke. One last cruelty delivered by him before his death. That would have been just like him, dying and passing on this disinheritance to me.'

'You didn't know you were adopted?' Jon blurted out. It was so strange. He could not imagine what that would do to a person. To suddenly have their history torn apart like that.

'No, it was never mentioned nor alluded to. I always sensed that I was different but I never *knew* that I really was. The realization was, at first, like the feeling of being sucked in by this incredibly powerful drug. My whole sense of identity had been built around my father, my position in English society; Cambridge, where I laughed at Jew jokes along with all the other British anti-Semites. My past had been irrevocably wiped. Worse than that, it had been shown up as a lie.

'I never went back to my work. It wasn't me any more, that suit, that office. Actually, it never was, but somehow I'd tricked myself into believing that it was my heritage, my rightful destiny and so I did it. But that no longer worked. I was nearly sixty, my colleagues were thinking about retire-ment villages and all-day golf but I felt as if my life had just started. I sat in my office and stared out of the window. I delayed calls and cancelled conferences. I couldn't reconcile who I now knew I was with the person I had grown up as. There was a gap between the two that threatened everything. I sat and stared at my office walls. Counted the lines on the wallpaper. It was as if the things that had mattered before I read the letter meant nothing now, as if it had all been levelled by some massive explosion which killed Jake Mk 1, leaving only the scattered pieces of Jakob in its wake.

'I went to Amsterdam. To the Jewish Museum there, the JHM. Almost lived in that place. I spent four months in those rooms trying to find out if it was true and when I knew it was, I came back here. I spent days walking this city that I'd grown up in, finding it totally unfamiliar now, as if I was a tourist, here for the first time, untethered and afloat. I couldn't go back to the world, Jon. I don't know if you understand . . . but that was no longer possible. The streets were a different world. An easier place to hide, to not care, to give up on things. I felt as if my whole life had been a practice run for this moment, a long-winded dress rehearsal with no real purpose or end.'

'How long had you been on the streets?'

'Three weeks.'

'Why did you agree to come here?' Jon asked. It confused him. He wanted to know what had driven him to this, though he understood how easy it was to let go, to disappear, how seductive its promise was.

'Because I'm weak.' Jake rubbed his hand on his forehead, his wrists poking through the thick ring of shirt. 'Because there's a story that needs to be told. That only I can tell.'

'What story?' Jon asked.

'You're not ready yet.' Jake shook his head, smiled. 'Not yet.'

*

That was the last time he had seen him.

No, it wasn't.

He just didn't want to think about the other.

Later that evening, after they'd both gone to bed, Jon had awoken with a tight pain in his stomach, as if it was shrinking, clenching in on itself like a fist. He'd pulled himself out of bed and stumbled to the toilet. He opened the door. Jake stood with his back to him, head down, shirt off. His back was covered in scars. White breaks in the pink folds of skin, zigzagged and broken. Jon took a deep breath. Saw the dark stained tissues on the floor.

'Jake,' he cried out. 'What's wrong?'

But the old man ignored him or hadn't heard. He stood immobile. Jon could hear a low droning sound coming from his mouth and his head was swaying slightly from side to side. He stared at the scars. The separate lines touching and interlocking like fingers. He turned and closed the door. His heart pumping hard. The pain in his stomach gone. And when he went back to his room he made sure to lock the door.

By the time Jon awoke the next morning Jake was gone, his bedding neatly tidied in the corner and the CDs and books that he'd used back in their proper places. The computer on, the day's news glaring at the empty room. There was no note but Jon knew that Jake had gone for good. The arrangement of the linen had a finality to it that made him catch his breath. He feared that the previous night's intrusion had caused the old man's flight, cursed himself for not having knocked.

He turned the computer off. Picked up the pillowcases and sheets and put them in the washing machine. He didn't want to look at them, but couldn't help himself and when dark, cracked patches confirmed his fears he shoved them into the machine and slammed the door shut. He rushed to the toilet. Washed his hands. Used soap, shampoo and body lotion until the smell was totally gone, only pine fresh and morning azure now.

That had been only a week ago, he thought, as he turned the car around at the far end of the Western Avenue and headed back towards the city. One short week. And what had happened in that time? What had happened to Jake? Had he found some new clue to his real inheritance? Or something else?

He felt a deep unrest in his stomach. A clawing and tearing that made him feel nauseous. He'd wanted Jake to stay. He was relieved that he'd gone. Jake's presence had been difficult and yet that had somehow made it feel more worthwhile, this whim, this whatever you wanted to call it that he was doing. He wondered what would have happened if he hadn't walked in on him. What the hell was the old man doing, those scars? The story had been only a beginning. And he wanted to know more than ever, now that it was too late.

There was something about Jake. Something about the old man's silences, his words 'it's a botch', his tired and unrested hands. He reminded him of his mother in some way but there was also a darker resemblance there, the shadow of his father, somehow tempered beneath the beard and borrowed clothes.

He tried to understand the chain of events. It was easier than thinking of what was gone. Had Jake known he was going to Amsterdam the morning he left? Before that? How had he afforded it? He must have had money. It seemed important that he should know. That if he could understand the old man's last movements, it would all make sense. There was no promise of absolution, Jon understood that, but there was the reassurance of maybe knowing why and, perhaps, that would be enough.

He knew that he would go to Amsterdam to identify Jake's body. Work and the project could go to hell. He had committed himself already. When he had invited Jake in, he'd started something that he now knew he had to finish. To forget about him would be just another layer of distance, another way to mitigate the world, another failure to follow through. Using work as an excuse was weak and undignified. The idea of not even calling Dave to tell him was strangely thrilling, like skipping class or stealing an unrequited kiss, and the more he thought about it, the more he knew it was the right thing to do. And he thought about his mother too, how it would be a way to show her the kind of man he'd become.

As he drove, buoyed by newfound resolution, he couldn't get the image of Jake's scarred and torn feet out of his head. He had guessed it was some disease, from living on the streets, but Jake had been out there only three weeks and besides that didn't explain what he'd seen in the bathroom. He'd checked the bin the next day. Felt repelled and sick when he saw the bloody tissues. Relief that the old man hadn't slaughtered him in his sleep. Awareness of what could have happened. And what about the cries that he heard through the walls some nights, assuming it was the old man fighting demons in his sleep? Now all these things became magnified, craving meaning and yet refusing to yield any. Perhaps he hadn't wanted to realize how different they were, how different we all are from the people we pretend to be. He went over everything that Jake had said, trying to remember a telling detail, something that would open things up, explain, make sense of, but all he could think about was Jake's face, the soft lines etched around his mouth, the straggly beard, the way he always wanted three and a half sugars in his coffee – so specific, Jon thought, and laughed, remembering how he too had once been like that until those things, one day, just didn't seem to matter any more. He lit another cigarette, flipped over the tape of *Flying Shoes* and pressed down on the accelerator, enjoying the little sliver of pain that wound around his ankle as, below him, the motorway vaulted the city, past the red brick ugliness of the BBC building, empty basketball courts and the grey columns of council estates towering like accusatory fingers pointing up at the sky.

4

'The fuck-up' they called him. Whispered in corridors and lunchrooms throughout the department. In the eyes of his commanding officers and the unspoken reproaches of the young recruits. In the stories that people tell to ease the tension before a bust, department legends, cautionary tales dragged into gossip, gradually stratifying into myth.

But Van Hijn was used to worse. This was just the latest in a long line of events that had gone only slightly wrong, had at some point sheared away from their original intentions and taken shape as something much less explainable let alone excusable. He wasn't sorry that he'd killed the man. Sometimes you were given a chance and you had to take it – how many more women would he have mutilated? – but he was sorry that it had been the wrong man, that this fiend was still on the loose.

But finding the old man had been a break. A sudden flash of hope in the darkness of the case. A shift in patterns. Experience had taught him that it was these changes that would eventually yield meaning, clues, perhaps even resolution. That he had been given a singular chance to, if not erase, then at least make up for the events in February. The ones that earned him the sobriquet of 'the fuck-up'.

Detective Ronald van Hijn had been the star pupil of his year at the police academy. Even the other students, usually so resentful of these things, had to demur to his obvious brilliance in all fields of police work. His teachers had predicted a bright future, there were whispers of city commissioner and mayor even and, on his graduation, everyone agreed that great things were in store.

It seemed more than a lifetime ago.

As he sat in his office waiting for the Englishman, he wondered about where it had started to go wrong. What had happened? He unlocked the bottom drawer of his desk and took out a joint that he'd prepared earlier in the men's toilets. He was supposed to be giving up. But hadn't he said that at least once a year for the last ten years? It didn't matter. This year he was going to do it. He was getting older, things were starting to go wrong and he wanted to stack the odds as much in his favour as he could. The cigarettes would have to go too, but those were harder, almost a necessary part of the job sometimes, he thought, placing the joint back into the drawer, allowing himself to feel a moment's virtue from this small denial.

The phone rang. It was Captain Beeuwers.

'Ronald. What's this I hear about an Englishman coming to see you?'

Damn. So someone had told him, leaked the news in hope of future appraisal, a remembered payback. 'I called him,' was all he said, wary not to let slip anything more.

The captain was breathing heavily, as if he'd just come back from a gruelling run. 'Ronald, there's really no point in you interviewing him. Let Zeeman do it. There needs to be some continuity.'

He hated how his first name was used to patronize him. His father's son. Still. 'That's why I thought it'd be best for me to do it,' he replied, trying not to let his anger show, not to give Beeuwers the satisfaction.

'Pass it over to Zeeman, Ronald. I promised him this case. You do that and I'll make sure the board awards you the full pension, not the discriminatory one.'

Van Hijn leaned back in the chair. The captain was unusually eager to get him off the case. It had been partly the captain's vote that had prejudiced his pension appeal. He thought about it. Drop the case and triple the settlement. Enough money to go to America on. Retire early. Enough not to have to worry.

'Well, Ronald. I need a decision now,' the captain said, breathy and urgent.

'Goodbye, Captain. I'll see you at the hearing.' He slammed down the phone. Tried to take a deep breath. He could feel his nerves twitch, his body humming and snapping with crackle. The drawer rolled open. He took out the joint, lit it, cursing his weakness, exhaling into the waiting grille of the air-conditioner.

Sucking on the warm smoke he remembered the night of his graduation, twenty years earlier, him only twenty-seven then, drunk with the recognition, the backslaps and the sheer wonder of a whole life still ahead. He'd spent the night with his lover, Elizabeth, telling her of his plans, how he could fast track through this and that division, the whole intricate career path that he'd devised for himself so rigorously and seriously.

He almost coughed on the smoke when he thought about Elizabeth. She'd been his girlfriend since the first week of the academy and he'd loved her with a more insane rush and intensity of feeling than anyone before or since, the kind of whirlwind that swallows you only once in your life and which you spend the rest of your time trying to recapture. They'd married a week after their graduation and had decided to take their honeymoon in California, a place neither of them had ever been to, but whose allure, through movies and media, had gripped both of them since childhood.

They never went.

Jan van Hijn, Ronald's father, had been dead twenty-two years; a hero of the war, a fearless anti-Nazi and freedom fighter in city legend. Van Hijn had walked through the police academy forever in the old man's shadow. People looked at him and noted the facial resemblance to his father, strangers in bars would tell him stories about his dad and everyone treated him with a certain respect which he had grown comfortably accustomed to.

And then the article had come out. Published in *Der Stern* three weeks after his graduation. The article that brought to light newly discovered documents relating to dark deeds that took place in occupied Holland. Correcting the false Anne Frank-fostered belief that the city was good to its Jews, detailing how it had the lowest rate of survival in Europe, only one in sixteen ever made it back from the East or stayed undiscovered in rotten basements. The article that named his father, Jan van Hijn, as the Gestapo's most acclaimed collaborator in the Low Countries.

The facts were irrefutable, backed up by facsimiles that held his father's signature, a shaky, familiar hand that also inscribed his son's books with little quotations, and Van Hijn, feeling sicker and sicker, had read the piece listing the people his father had betrayed, the Jews wrenched out of hiding places and shot or burned alive in their synagogues, the resistance leaders given up.

He tried to remember his father and he couldn't reconcile what he read with the man he knew and yet there was no way to deny that everything they said was true. That he had been both the man that Ronald thought he was and the man that they accused him of being.

That was the hardest thing to grasp, not that he did what he did during the war, any man is capable of that, not even that his legend was what it was, these things happen, Van Hijn thought. No, the single greatest problem that he faced was that his father had been both these men; a loving and generous parent and, at the same time, a seller of men's lives.

People had started gathering outside his house after the article came out. A swastika had been crudely spray-painted on his car. Gangs of neo-Nazis sent him letters and offers of money trying to recruit him to their cause. 'Blood Will Out' they often wrote, he was his father's son and they too saw great things in store for him.

Elizabeth couldn't take it. Her mother had been a Dutch Jew who had somehow survived Auschwitz. The fear of what was inside her husband was too much for Elizabeth and she left. He felt betrayed by her, by his father and by the friends who had stopped calling and who now exchanged only perfunctory greetings with him each morning at work, somehow unable to break the lines of continuity that had been drawn. The fact that he hadn't known about his father did not seem to matter. His father was dead, they couldn't hang him for his crimes, and so they turned to his only son and exacted their revenge on him.

The years passed and people forgot like they always do. But Van Hijn hadn't and he still felt bitter at the way things had turned out; it wasn't so much the promising career at Interpol that he missed, as her, Elizabeth. The way she would make him coffee in the morning and light his cigarette or a half-turn in the late-summer light that would leave him breathless. The way she smiled when she knew he was lying, the little looks and nuances that had been made unavailable to him after her departure.

He stared at his hands. Old and gnarled now though he

was only just past the midway point of an expected life. The nails torn and scuffed, the skin dry and cracked. Once he had been proud of his hands – Elizabeth had called them a musician's hands – but time had left its mark on them just as surely as on everything else. He made a note to get some moisturizer later, to try to care about these things. He stared at his cheap wristwatch. The Englishman was late. He shuffled in his chair. Looked at his notes, the photographs of the dead. He had felt something, squatting down in the rain, staring at the old man, something he'd not experienced for a long time: a little shiver and rush of blood, the coming together of disparate lines. He knew he didn't have much time left.

He checked his watch again. He was looking forward to getting home. A package of videos and CDs had arrived that morning but he hadn't had time to open it. It was better to have something to come back to. He spent most of his evenings watching videos, preferring the passivity of screen people to their real counterparts. He collected and taped films and music with a passion that had been excised from the rest of his life, and his flat was collapsing under the weight of shelving units that held everything from the dark glare of Robert Mitchum to the astounding, inflamed beauty of the young Shirley Maclaine. He especially liked the films made in Hollywood in the late forties and early fifties, with their gritty realism and urgent lighting, their storms and subjugated passions, where the roles of hero and villain became undifferentiated and good men were stretched and torn like canvas by the vagaries of fate and their own small, shoddy mistakes.

5

It was raining when he got on the plane at Heathrow and it was raining when he got off at Schiphol. In between, Jon had read a Zevon interview in *Uncut*, forty pages of the new Kitty Carson mystery, eventually got bored and ended up staring out of the scratched plastic window to his left, sipping a Bloody Mary and wishing for a cigarette, watching the flat and perforated land below slowly coming into view.

As the pilot announced their imminent arrival, Jon finished his drink, tightened his seatbelt and tried to read some more of the magazine. His legs throbbed and he wondered whether it was possible to get deep-vein thrombosis on such a short flight. Almost certainly. Every day there were new ways to die, named and marked, new fears, new anxieties to eat at your content. He tried to stretch his legs as you're supposed to do but that made the pain worse. Like marbles squeezing slowly through his veins. He looked out of the window. Nothing but clouds. Tried to read his magazine again.

The man sitting next to him was asleep and at some point during the flight his head had rolled ninety degrees and was now resting on Jon's shoulder. Jon tried to move but the narrowness of the seats gave him little room. It irritated him in a way that he couldn't rationalize. He felt his fists clenching and couldn't stop them. He looked at the magazine but all the words were jumbled and the more he tried to focus the more they resisted. He wanted to say something but that would have meant waking the man, causing a disturbance and really, all he wanted was a quiet, uneventful flight and so he tried to shrink into his seat, ignore it, look out of the window, think about something else, but it wasn't working.

He'd been feeling like that all day, an unpredictable mixture of sadness and annoyance with an underlying grind of unresolved tension. Even the previous night's drunken drive hadn't helped much. The police hadn't stopped him. The world hadn't collapsed. He'd limped to bed, not even bothering to undress, hiding himself beneath the dark slumberous canopy of the duvet until everything went black.

It had happened while he was making coffee that morning. He'd woken up feeling happy and energized though he didn't know why. He'd got out of bed and immediately a spear of pain had shot up from his ankle, flooding his chest. He cursed himself for the stupidity of it, falling down like that. One unfocused moment was all it took, in that moment a man could lose a leg, a life, so much more.

A couple of painkillers later and he felt ready to face the day. And then, watching the coffee drip slowly out of the filter and dribble down the sides of his cup, he saw Jake's face reflected in the cold chrome and felt as if he were going to suffocate. He went to the bathroom and splashed cold water over his face and wrists, staring at himself in the mirror, thinking about that night, how he'd opened the door as if he were still the sole occupant, and the tissues, the crumpled tissues on the floor, and his unintentional intrusion seemed the kind of deep, dark betrayal that was so elliptical it required sustained and repeated meditation, a perfect smooth pebble to be rubbed for ever. He came back to find the cup overflowing and dark brown liquid spreading across the worktop. He didn't even bother to wipe it up.

Instead he rebooted the computer, spent ten mindless minutes waiting for pages to download, punched in his card number and was told that he'd successfully reserved a seat on the afternoon flight to Amsterdam. He thought about sending Dave an email. Thought about it, then shut down the computer.

He'd felt better at the airport. Slowly smoking cigarettes and watching the screens flicker and flash above him, the endless shuffle and bustle, nervous last-minute gate dashes so filled with purposeful movement. There was something about the way people behaved in airports, he thought, waiting for his gate number to come up on-screen, the way they took on different characteristics more in line with their transient positions. Men sat silently smoking and drinking black coffee while the women prepared themselves for the violence to come, as if the airport were the last vestige of a person you might never return to, as if the act of flight changed something fundamental in the genetic make-up. Perhaps that's why there is so little talk at airports, why glances are rarely exchanged along the long, flowing expressways – themselves rooms drained of dimension – reduced to the skeletal presence of pure perspective. Leaving creates its own space and its own moods. All the unnecessary junk of life is forgotten for a few hours as you stare at the possibilities on the computer screen, the list of departures, of places you could escape to – the past conveniently obscured behind the dream of forward movement, of the new and unimagined landscapes to come.

He could stay here all day, he knew, just watching the people moving, saying goodbyes, crying, smiling, whispering secret words that bring a blush to a lover's cheeks. He felt better here. All that rock and scrape of tension easing, his body melting into the seat. But when the call for his flight came, he took it, knowing that even airports close for the night, leaving you to go back to your life, to the dread and spilled coffee that lies there in wait for you.

At the arrivals lounge in Schiphol he read his name on a sign among a bouquet of cards held by steely eyed chauffeurs dressed in black. He was unexpectedly thrilled by the sight of it in crude black marker on the jagged corrugated piece of cardboard, misspelled of course, an extra H dangling between the O and N, but something of a thrill none the less, the first time.

They drove through the ugly cement suburbs of Amsterdam, massive estates spanning across the flatness. It didn't look like Holland, more like a squalid sector of South London.

'Was this area bombed?' he asked the driver. 'During the war?'

'It was all bombed,' the man replied.

Jon didn't say anything back though he knew this wasn't true. He stretched his legs as far as the front seat allowed, trying to work the kinks out of his blood, the clots and convolutions brought about by being canned and compressed on the plane. He reached for his cigarettes, flicked one out, put it between his lips, sparked the lighter.

'Out! Put it out!' the driver shouted, turning to look at him, the cab swerving wildly. 'Now!'

Jon rolled down the window, threw it out. 'I thought everyone smoked here,' he said, making up his mind not to tip the man.

'You thought wrong. This is my cab. I make the rules.'

'Fuck,' Jon said, making sure the driver heard.

'You don't like it you can get out.' He turned to look at Jon again. 'You tourists think you can do anything here,' he added before turning back and swerving the cab into the right lane.

The rain stopped as they entered the city proper, passing near the central railway station, pulsing and throbbing with backpackers and tourists spilling out on to the streets, the massive elegance of the building dwarfing the bright bustle. They drove across a small bridge, over a postcard canal and into a narrow cobbled street that seemed to hug them as they passed, darkening the day with the alacrity of an eclipse.

Jon could feel his heart quicken, filled with the rumble of excitement that comes on entering a new city, a new country, that wild, swift transformation that shoots through your blood and sits behind your eyeballs. Suddenly you notice everything. The most banal of objects becomes a thing of wonder, the kerbstone, the small telephone lines, the way the roads are named, the shape and tone of the quotidian. He stared out of the window and watched the unfamiliar streets winding around the canals, the people, so unrecognizable from those of London – everything new and compelling, and the reason for his being here was almost forgotten as he let the rush of the city take him over.

The driver stopped outside a pub. He pointed towards a thick, painted oak door. He didn't say anything.

Jon walked into what could have been anypub anywhere. Dark brown walls and red carpets. A small jukebox and a selection of tables. Bad white-boy blues playing. Smoke and the smell of beer. Hunched men sitting in silence, staring into their drinks. It didn't feel like the right place and that sudden burst of hope departed as quickly as it had come.

A tall, precise man with a small blond moustache and curly mullet stood behind the bar, playing blackjack with a woman balancing precariously on a stool across from him. Neither looked up. Jon scanned the room. Everyone else seemed to have melted into their tables, draped over them like stone statues. He felt nervous and his palms began to sweat as he took a deep breath and limped up to the bar. He felt eyes turning to look at him but the more he tried to walk normally, the more it hurt and the more exaggerated his limp became. He'd never known it could be so hard to cross a room.

He caught the man's attention, tried to ignore the disconcerting presence of the highlights in his hair and said, 'My name's Reed, Jon Reed. I think I have a reservation.' Hoping he did. That it would be easy, smooth and hassle-free.

The man with the mullet looked up, went through some internal brain-racking procedure that caused the ends of his 'tache to twirl ever so slightly until finally his eyes sparked with recognition. 'Ah, Mr Reed. Of course. Yes, the detective said you were to be expected today. Come to help us with our serial killer, I hear.'

Jon looked at the man blankly. He thought he'd misunderstood or maybe the man thought he was saying something completely different only he'd misread the phrase book.

'What?' The whole trip suddenly seemed a bad idea, a rush of fake hope and adrenalin worn down now like a cheap pill.

The owner laughed. 'Only a joke, you understand.' He put his cards down and said something to the woman in Dutch, which she seemed to find hilarious, almost falling off her stool, before turning his attention back to Jon. 'Anyway, we have your room ready. Room number 5, it is on the third floor I'm afraid.'

'No problem,' Jon said, trying to sound convivial. Serial killer going around his brain. Jake the victim? Why hadn't the detective mentioned any of that?

'It's just a bit steep, so be careful.'

'What? Oh, the stairs . . . thank you.' He took the key and followed the directions to the back of the bar where a small door led to the staircase.

Jon looked at it. No problem at all. Even with his bad leg.

The second level was worse. Far worse. He paused to get his breath, looked up at the way the angle of the stairs seemed to refute the laws of physics and remembered that Escher had been Dutch. He grabbed the handrail and climbed.

The third set of stairs almost undid him. They seemed to slope towards him. They defied all notions of space and hundreds of years of cold, rational thought. He waited until he could breathe normally again, feeling dizzy, the floor edging away from him, everything screaming Go Back Now. Before It's Too Late.

Jake was dead and that wouldn't change.

He almost did. Almost went straight down the stairs and through the bar. Only the thought of the laughing woman stopped him. He couldn't bear to hear her again. He looked up, sighed, and continued the impossible climb, his ankle screaming in protest, his hand firm on the rail, consoling himself with the knowledge that he'd be home in a couple of days.

6

Van Hijn told the other officers to leave. He wanted to handle this alone. One of the men whispered 'Make my day' as he slammed the door. Van Hijn stared down at his hands and let it go. This was no time to argue. He needed a few minutes of silence. A few minutes of staring at the wall. It was always difficult handling IDs. Thank God he's not family, the detective sourly thought to himself. It was the worst part of the job, introducing people to their own dead.

He had the bookmark. He put it in front of him and rubbed his fingers along the pen's indentations, hard and gouged like the grooves of a record. It was still a string of numbers. They had run it through computers, given it to men who sat in small rooms and saw patterns in things, but it was still only a string of numbers. He placed the bookmark among the rubble of his table, slipping it between a case file and an Eiffel Tower paperweight, making sure that it would not be obscured from Jon's view. He checked the clock above him and waited. He knew that he would have to watch the Englishman carefully, that he was his only lead. It had been a long case and so far there had been nothing. Almost as if the killer was a ghost.

He moved the bookmark an inch to the left, exposing it further, just to make sure.

There was a knock at the door. Van Hijn shouted 'Enter' and watched the small, unassuming figure of Jon Reed shuffle in. He noted the man's limp and the way he tried to hide it, the look of unravelling. He stood up and motioned his guest to take a seat. 'Glad you could come, sir.'

Jon shook his hand. The detective had a firm but gentle grip, not trying to assert its power in the initial squeeze. 'Please call me Jon,' he said.

'Okay Jon, I'm Ronald. I was the one who spoke to you on the phone.'

He called one of the officers in and ordered some coffee. The man scowled and turned away. 'Cigarette?' He held out a pack of Luckies towards Jon.

'Thanks.' Jon took one.

'I hope the hotel is to your liking.'

'It's fine, thank you.' He couldn't help being polite, cowed by authority, by being abroad. 'Stairs are a bit steep though. I sprained my ankle the other day.'

The detective laughed. 'Yes, I see. Still, they say that's the best way to make it better, keep walking on it.'

Jon wasn't sure whether the detective was having a joke at his expense or trying to be sympathetic. He silently begrudged the fact that he wasn't better at reading people. If he had been, would Jake still be alive?

The coffee arrived, fresh and steaming, and they both took cautious sips before continuing. Van Hijn briefed Jon on the basics of the case. His voice was steady and calm and his accent almost undetectable. His eyes, grey-blue and blood-shot, seemed to scan Jon as he spoke. 'We found no wallet on him. We assume it was stolen either by the assailant or someone who came upon the body later. As you know, we also found a small book of poems in his pocket. An old edition of Pound. Unusual in itself. Your phone number and name were written on the first page. It certainly made us wonder.'

Jon remembered the book, remembered giving it to the

old man a couple of days before his disappearance. 'Yes, I lent him the book.'

The detective seemed to be turning this simple notion over in his mind as if it was a wooden box, exquisitely carved and dovetailed, and he was trying to find the small, almost invisible crack that would betray the secret compartment.

'But why do you think he was carrying it on the day he was killed?'

Jon stared at the detective, unsure what to say. There was something fuzzy about the policeman, as if all his edges had been softened by some terrible incident.

'Coincidence?' Jon offered.

Van Hijn smiled and there was a certain quickness in his eyes which made Jon decide to be a bit more careful with what he said from then on.

'Yes, perhaps. There is always that. But why this book? I ask myself this. A book with another man's phone number on it.'

The detective let the words hang in the smoky room. There was nothing Jon could say to this and, as he watched the detective watching him, he wondered whether he was a suspect. Feeling the slight tremble of anger humming through his arms. He'd come all the way here for this?

He stared at the table. The utter mess and chaos of yellowed pages, stained and crumpled, stacked atop each other, lidless pens sandwiched between newspaper cut-outs and the stark edges of photos.

He looked up at the detective. There was a smile on the Dutchman's face.

'How was he killed?' Jon asked, determined not to let the situation put him on the defensive.

'You'll see for yourself soon enough,' the detective replied. He looked down at his hands and Jon sensed a deep sadness huddled around the man like an extra layer of clothing. The same vibrating funk that had held Jake in its grasp.

'We believe your friend was the latest victim in a string of similar murders perpetrated over the last nine months,' Van Hijn finally said.

'A serial killer?' Jon asked, thinking back to the man at the hotel.

'Maybe, maybe not. That is the common consensus.' He took a deep drag of his cigarette. 'I do not think so however, not in the way you might think anyway.'

Jon felt himself edging forward. 'What, then?'

'Well, in none of the cases was there any sign of sexual assault.'

'Were they all men, like Jake?'

'On the contrary, he was the first. The eight other victims were all female, between the ages of twelve and thirty-five. Despite this, there were similarities. The girls had been tortured over a period of several days before their eventual deaths. Your friend showed evidence to suggest the same.' It was the gentlest way he could put it. He paused as he waited for the words to sink in.

'Yes. You see, we found certain dog hairs on Jake's clothes. Those same dog hairs were also present in most of the other victims. The body was found in a similar place. Number nine.'

'Nine?'

Van Hijn smiled, cryptically, Jon thought, as if hiding something behind that pleasantry. 'Well, either he's the ninth victim or he's the perpetrator.'

Jon stared at the detective, unsure what he was supposed to say.

Van Hijn laughed. 'Sorry, that's what we always say. At least, until we find out different.'

'How long has this been going on?'

'Since January.' There was no need to mention the incident. No need at all.

'And you think it's the work of the same person?'

'Not that sure we're talking about a single person here, could be a group of them.'

'A group?'

'The last victim before your friend.' Van Hijn stopped, looked into his coffee and lit another cigarette. 'Have you ever heard of a Judas Cradle?'

'No,' Jon replied.

The detective shrugged. 'An old medieval torture instrument, used frequently during the Inquisition. It's basically a metal pyramid on legs. The victim is hoisted to the top by a set of pulleys and left to sink on the point of the pyramid. Weights are attached to the feet. Death can take up to four or five days.'

'A bit elaborate, isn't it?'

Van Hijn smiled. 'Well, exactly. Not the kind of thing your ordinary killer can be bothered with.'

Jon took a deep breath. 'What about Jake?'

'No, with Jake we are not sure yet but the method of death was certainly not this.'

Jon felt stunned, as if hit by a baseball bat to the back of the head. 'How . . . how can you be so sure that Jake's part of this? He was sleeping on the streets, he could have died a hundred different ways.'

The detective seemed to take this information in. He nodded, thoughtfully. 'Yes, that is possible. However, I don't think so. There's just too much that links up.' He didn't want to admit that the theory he was working on depended on it.

'Tell me about the others.'

'Are you sure you want to know?'

'Yes,' Jon said.

Van Hijn sipped at his coffee, thought about it, how maybe more could be gained by telling him. 'The first victim came to us via the screams of an elderly Japanese lady who was out walking one early morning in the Plantage Parklaan when her dog started getting too interested in what was hiding in the bushes. She was seventeen and we found her in two sections. The dog had discovered her legs. A few hours later we found the rest. But, you see, the body wasn't cut in two, or sawed, it seemed as if it had been ripped apart by bare hands in some unimaginable blood frenzy.'

Jon spat his coffee back into the cup, the taste suddenly sweet and sickly.

'But of course it was a machine that had done it. They found splinters of wood and flakes of leather and hair all over her hands and feet. Then the second turned up. She had been missing for a year. She had been five foot eight when she disappeared. The body we found measured four foot ten. It had been warped and twisted into a horrible convoluted dwarf. Yet her teeth told us we had the right girl. I don't know who first came up with the idea. These things float the halls of police stations, they seem to have no origin in any one person, somehow a conflation of half-thought opinions and late-night lunacy. Someone said that the victims had been tortured to death. That since every other theory had been disproved, let them try Rack and Scavenger's Daughter, let them try to disprove that, and of course, no one could. And by the time the next body was found, a twelve-year-old Surinamese girl ... Well, there wasn't a doubt. She'd been a victim of the Maiden of Nuremberg, one of those sarcophagi with spikes inside, carefully constructed so that they don't pierce any vital organs thus assuring a slow and painful death. We cross-checked all our

74

records, we found certain consistencies. The marks and mutilations made by an Inquisition Chair, a Heretic's Fork, a Garrotte. Once we knew where to look, it was easy. All the victims had been drugged. Rather crudely. Same as your friend. They were all dumped in prominent public places. There was no sexual intercourse. There was a certain stylization in their deaths, a ritualistic element. These were very *visual* deaths. I've seen this kind of thing before. The dog hairs, all of the same type, well, they're what you call the ribbon.'

Jon didn't say anything at first. He stared at the spider-webbed cracks in the ceiling of the interview room. If Van Hijn's phone call had been steeped in a certain unreality then sitting in this dingy room, on a chair that was chained to the floor, made it all very precise and clear. Jake was gone and, down here, he realized it for the first time, not in an abstract way but as something physical, a dead weight of memory.

'What the fuck is this all about?' he asked the detective. All those images spinning up in his brain. Blood and geometry. O-level history, textbooks full of wooden devices with metal and winking eyes, imagining the blood and hair . . .

'You know what snuff movies are?' The detective lit another cigarette, passed one to Jon.

'Of course,' Jon replied. 'Well, I know what people mean by it, I don't know how much of it actually exists and how much is the stuff of urban legend.'

'It exists. Anything that people are willing to pay for, exists. Especially in this town, and snuff of one kind or another seems to be something a lot of people will pay for. Big money, big people. I think these bodies are a form of snuff disposal, if you'll excuse the expression. They need to get rid of the bodies, so they just leave them around the city, knowing obviously what everyone will think initially – it's a serial killer. And it's perfect because they can keep doing this, if there's no actual serial killer then he can't be caught, the bodies pile up, the pressure is put on us but we're following totally the wrong leads.'

'You think they were killed for the sake of filming it.' Jon thought it over in his mind. More blackness swirling. 'Jake doesn't seem prime snuff fodder to me.'

Van Hijn smiled. 'No theory is perfect. But these things happen. I worked seven years in vice, here. Two years under-cover chasing just this kind of thing. Don't let anyone tell you it doesn't exist. Ridiculous. Even if it didn't originally, then just the myths would be enough to make people try it out. What starts as metaphor has a habit of becoming reality. But some of these films, they use extras, the old man perhaps who forces the knife, who knows? A lot of these things are tailor-made. A private exposition of your psyche splattered on to film. And maybe once the old man is finished in his role, after what he's seen he can't go back and no one wants to see an old man die, not for these kind of prices, so, no elaborate torture method, just some routine pain, close-ups, cross cut later with some young thing who doesn't want to get his flesh scarred. Then they dump him. Yet there was a dog present. You can imagine, or maybe you can't, it does not matter . . . you see how these things can so easily happen and perhaps explain a set of events that somehow eluded explanation until now.' The detective coughed, crumpled the cigarette packet in his fist. 'Or maybe Jake was the film-maker and he was killed in a revolt by his subjects, perhaps that is why the torture done to him was small scale and petty and his death quick. Maybe some people only get their kicks thinking they're Henry VIII, have enough money to build some old-time devices, watch and imagine how it was back then, to have power, such absolute power. This is how it begins, you see.'

The detective stood up and abruptly walked out of the room. Jon sat there silent for a couple of minutes, trying not to think about what Van Hijn had said. Desperately trying not to think about it while blood and bone and screams rushed before his eyes.

The detective came back in, flashed a new pack of cigarettes. 'I now need to ask you a few questions about your relationship with Mr Colby.'

'Go ahead.' He caught the detective's gaze knowing that this was the way innocent men behaved. He was innocent, of course, he didn't kill Jake, maybe drove him away, but certainly not murder and yet he wondered if his responses were those of an innocent man, noticing how Van Hijn wrote things down when he hadn't said anything, the smallness of the room that almost seemed to push them together. Medieval torture instruments? It was like something out of a cheap novel.

'You want another coffee first?'

'Okay.'

The detective lit a cigarette and offered one to Jon who reluctantly took it, feeling the insides of his mouth shrivel from the dry bitterness of the smoke. When the coffee arrived he nearly burned himself trying to gulp down the dark liquid, letting it wash away the taste of the smoke. The room of 1,000 cancers.

'So, you and Jake. You were lovers, right?' The detective held Jon's gaze.

'What?' Jon moved in his seat, suddenly uncomfortable. 'No, of course not,' he said, slightly too loudly, hearing it echo around the room. 'It wasn't anything like that.'

'No, of course not,' Van Hijn repeated, scratching his cheek. 'But, I had to ask, you understand.'

Jon nodded. It hadn't even occurred to him but he could see that the detective hadn't totally dismissed the idea and it bothered him; why, he couldn't quite say.

'Did Jake ever say anything relating to Amsterdam or the Netherlands?' Van Hijn asked.

Jon smiled. 'Yes.' A pause. 'It was almost all he talked about.'

The detective looked as though he'd just been plugged in. The weariness dropped from his face, the soft edges appeared to tighten, to coalesce.

'I guess I should start from the beginning,' Jon continued, clearly aware of the power he had over the detective while the story was still untold, determined to enjoy it after being on the receiving end of Van Hijn's sermon.

'Go ahead, please.' The detective motioned, a cigarette jumping between his fingers, his voice dropping an octave.

So he told him. Everything that Jake had narrated that night. All about Raphael Kuper, the war, Amsterdam, the Jewish History Museum and the old man's final disinheritance.

After he'd finished, he took a deep breath, remembering Jake as he did so and, not for the first time, he felt more than just shock, a deep hungry loss had manifested itself through the telling and it filled Jon with all the thoughts of what he could have done to save the old man. All the useless speculation and anger began to rise inside him as he stared at the silent detective and he wanted to reach out and grab him, shake him, hurt him, blame him for everything.

Detective Van Hijn watched. He had learned years ago not to disturb people when they spoke, the slightest comment from him could derail their train of thought, leaving out essential information, cutting off paths, never to be retraced. He'd smoked quietly as Jon told him the old man's story, all the while trying to contain his excitement at this new wealth of facts.

His excitement and terror.

He knew then that he would have to go back through the story, through the things that he'd spent so many years burying, the dark recesses of his past, and it felt almost right, judicious perhaps, that this last case should end where it all began.

Maybe it was just a coincidence, the old man in Amsterdam because of all his history, walking along the wrong canal at the wrong time. In his experience one could not easily discount randomness as a factor in any investigation. Sometimes all the other facts, the ones that seemed most pertinent, the life stories, family feuds, bad debts, sometimes those had nothing to do with the person's demise, they could have had, but something else got there first, something random and quick, though from what he knew of the killer's work, in this case it was anything but quick. But coincidence didn't answer all the questions. Not the marks on the old man's body nor the book in his pocket. So enticingly easy, a name and a phone number. No, there were too many connections already, both forensic and liminal, he could feel it in the tightness of his skin. He turned back to Jon who was silently smoking. He still wasn't sure what to make of him, his links to the case, his involvement. 'Are you ready to make the identification?'

'Yes, I guess so. Let's get it over with.'

The detective tried to smile but it froze on his face. 'It's not pretty, I have to warn you,' he said.

'I never thought it would be.'

7

She stared at the small gouache for hours. Transfixed by its content, what it didn't show, the colours that should have been there but weren't. The utter, blank awfulness of the scene.

A girl sits on a bed in a small room. In front of her lie an open suitcase, some books and a tennis racket. We do not know if she is in the process of packing or of unpacking. Is she leaving this small, drab room or has she just entered it? The colours are dull, broken down and emptied. What was once opaque is now translucent, in fact more like a water-colour than a gouache. Solid forms break apart to reveal what lies behind. And what is that? Nothing, no paint at all. The texture of the paper and that is all.

The girl sits on the bed in her slippers, clutching her hands to her mouth. She looks scared and depressed. Perhaps it is the emptiness that surrounds her. The massive whiteness of the wall behind her, the gaping void on which she rests her feet. The blue wash of her clothes spreads on to the lighter blue of the bed, as if it has leaked. She is literally formless, a ghost sitting in a room bleached of life. Behind her a small painting breaks the desert of wall. A blue figure seems to be bursting from the frame, mirroring the position of the girl, but also satirizing it, so full and expansive while the girl seems to be falling into herself, diminishing slowly. It seems that everything is fading away: the bed, the books, her own form, wrapped and hidden by those arms, holding her face together, almost shaking – a scene of quiet and terrible desolation.

Suze sat in the small reading room of the Joods Historisch Museum in Amsterdam, hunched over one of Charlotte Salomon's gouaches. A self-portrait in turmoil, everything washed away, no longer solid, no longer recognizable.

She spent most of her time in the dusty little room off the main building, studying the 1,300 gouaches Salomon painted in that torrid year in the South of France. An autobiography in pictures with short texts attached to each, the whole work entitled, *Life? Or Theatre?*

She had first come across Salomon in Boston in '96. A boyfriend of the time took her to the Institute of Contemporary Art and introduced her to the work of the 26-year-old German Jew. She'd been surprised to learn that the paintings had been done in 1941. They seemed much more modern than that. The use of textual overlays, the almost cartoon-like narrative which reminded her of Lichtenstein, the freedom of Charlotte's lines, the strictness of the colour scheme, all seemed to point to something produced after the splurge and rant of the abstract expressionists and their militarist theories, more in line with the figurative impulses of pop art and even beyond that.

The phone pulled her out of the tight squeeze of the painting. She picked it up.

'Wouter, hi,' she said, still somewhere far away, slowly, grudgingly, being pulled back to the world.

'Hi,' he said, sounding unusually brusque and downbeat. 'I need to talk to you.'

She looked up at the wall, articles and notes pinned to a small cork board. 'Okay, talk,' she said.

'Not here, not over the phone.'

And she knew then what he was going to say. Almost like all the other times, as if every man learned from the exact same book. 'Tell me now,' she said, trying to keep her voice steady, gripping the receiver to stop the shaking of her hand.

She could hear him cough, get himself ready. 'It's just not working, Suze. At least on my end.' She said nothing, forcing him to continue. 'I just don't feel . . . you know we see each other and everything and it's nice but it doesn't go any further . . . I want it to go further, or at least try.'

She sighed, reached for her cigarettes then remembered she couldn't smoke in here. 'I told you at the start, Wouter. I thought we made this very clear.' She wanted to sound strong, confident. She felt so fucking weak. 'I couldn't spend my life with you, no offence, and to pretend, to set things up as if, it just seems an enormous waste . . .'

'You're too scared to try things,' he countered, his voice rising now, feeling an edge of righteousness. 'You won't give it a chance. You want something perfect and nothing is, so you flit from one thing to another. I can't do it any more, Suze, I can't be just one of the many things you bounce off. If you change your mind, call me.'

He put the phone down and she stared at the wall. She held the receiver, the tone soothing and predictable, constant and true. She took a deep breath, felt the hot swell in her eyes, the blurring of vision, and the more she fought it, the more it pushed forward until she was helpless and her make-up had run down her face and the phone lay uncradled on the desk, humming its one song.

She looked back down at the painting. Wanting to fall into it, sink so deep she would never have to come back up. She wiped her eyes and tried to carry on. There was always Charlotte.

She loved the humour and the irony in her work, the unexpected smiles and sudden, stark epiphanies produced in those small gouaches. The spaces between the words people said, between their bodies and thoughts. So different from the world as it was. She'd studied art history for a long time but had never found any other artist so commensurate with her own feelings, with her own soul. She kept Charlotte to herself, an endless repository of emotion that she could dip into at will. She had the 1981 edition of her works that included 769 gouaches from *Life? Or Theatre?* She read the book like a bible, turning to it for comfort or hope or just to see someone like herself. She knew that she was projecting a great deal on to the artist and her work. She knew she could never be objective. It was too close, too strange.

When the chance to do a doctorate had come along, she'd grabbed it, knowing full well what the subject would be. Knowing she would have to transfer to the University of Amsterdam and do her research there. The complete set of gouaches that made up *Life? Or Theatre?* was housed in the city's Jewish Historical Museum. Or nearly complete. Rumours had spread of a further missing section painted during Charlotte's brief internment at the Gurs transit camp.

She needed to be close to them. Needed to feel that they were real, not just some photos in a book, but real, tangible objects which had a definite size and weight. She liked to press her hand on to the paper, rub her fingers over the blue thumbprints that Charlotte had left in the empty spaces, the indentations and folds, the crooks and crannies of the work. She knew it was the fallacy of the object she had been sucked into. Knew that those small pieces of coloured paper had been touched and held by Charlotte.

'Excuse me, Ms Dean.' The old caretaker had come in silently, bringing a cup of peppermint tea for her. 'We're closing in half an hour. You've been here so long today, I thought you might like a drink.' She looked up from Gouache number 430, took the cup.

'Thank you, Moshe. I get so carried away in here, I

sometimes forget to eat.' She looked at her watch. Could it be possible that she'd been staring at this piece for the last two hours, ever since Wouter's phone call?

The old man smiled, his teeth glinting through the white beard. 'I have some gefilte fish my daughter cooked me at home. You want some?'

She always walked Moshe home, even sometimes when she wasn't studying she would come in at closing time and walk with him the fifteen minutes it took to his flat. 'Yes, that would be nice.' Nice to get out of that room, away from the tempting phone, from the pull of the ringback, the last-minute apology, the hopeless pleading.

'It is our New Year tomorrow. My daughter still cooks me the traditional things, things her mother once taught her.'

They walked past the tourists stuck in their seats in coffee shops and cafés, past the businessmen hurtling through the city on their way to another appointment, past the canals and streets that were now so familiar to her. She held his tired hand as they walked, half the speed she was used to, and tried not to think about Wouter.

When they reached his place, he unlocked the door and let them in. A typically small Amsterdam room, heavy with the smell of dusty books and papers and the old man's unfiltered cigarettes. He brushed away some magazines he'd been reading and placed the small dumplings of minced fish into the microwave as Suze sat down in one of his tattered armchairs.

'You ever eat gefilte fish before?' he asked her as he laid out two paper plates on the table.

'No. Just another gap in my life's education, I guess. There weren't too many Jews in Phoenix, not where I grew up anyway.' She was glad for the talk, the disruption, the emphasis on the small and banal. The room she worked in some-times felt like a glove, slowly shrinking.

'Well you're in for a real treat, young lady,' he said as he piled the little grey patties on to her plate, his bony, brittle fingers laying out the fork and spoon. She watched the precise way he put everything in its proper place and she began to cry, turning away at first, not wanting him to see. But she was unable to hold it in. He slowly stood up, moved towards her and placed his thin arms around hers and held her, like that, until she was done.

'Not something you want to talk about with an old man, I suppose?' he said as he sat back down.

She looked up at him. She wished he hadn't seen her like that. She wanted to appear strong, independent. 'Nothing much to say.'

'But enough to cry?'

She nodded. 'I'll get over it.'

'A boy?'

Nodded again. 'Nothing serious,' she added, more to herself now.

'But you wanted it to be.'

'No. He did. I enjoyed being with him but I couldn't really see us living the rest of our lives together and I thought, if not that, then what's the point in pretending, wasting time like that.'

Moshe looked at her. Hard. Unbelievable to think he was so old.

'But sometimes people change,' he offered. 'Things grow. The perfect man will never come. He will only flower from the less perfect one; if you give him the chance, that is.'

They ate silently, perhaps in respect for the history in those fish cakes. The long nights and empty days that were filled only by the remainders of a religion, the small things that were left when the synagogues were burned and the Torahs spat and shat upon in the main streets and squares of Europe.

She liked the foreign taste on her tongue, the slightly salty acidity that greeted her as she chewed. She liked Moshe too – out of all the volunteers who worked in the museum, he was the one she felt most at ease with. The only one who didn't treat her differently because she was a gentile. Some days when she couldn't look at Charlotte's art any more, she would pack up her notebooks and pens and sit for a while with Moshe, listening to his stories of Berlin before the war.

She remembered him telling her how he'd been a professor of music at the university until the Nuremberg laws came into effect. How he'd fought in the trenches during the First World War. An eighteen-year-old Jewish boy, drafted in 1917, sent in a train to the Western Front, where he spent a year dodging shrapnel, burrowing and hiding like an insect and watching his comrades die. After the war he studied, eventually taking up the teaching post, thinking all the horror was now behind him, happy to spend the rest of his life crouching over books and scores, trying to forget what he saw and felt that year when he had been posted in France.

In 1942 Moshe, his wife and their three daughters, were put on to another train, with sealed-up windows and the smell of death lurking in every joint of the metal, every railroad tie they crossed – heading East this time; to a small Polish village which the Nazis, having problems with the native spelling, renamed Auschwitz, easier to pronounce, the two syllables rolling like honey over German tongues.

They were separated when they got off the train and stepped into the freezing Polish winter: Moshe and his eldest daughter were sent to another line, tattooed with a number and taken to what would be their home for the next two years; his wife and two youngest went straight to the other part of the camp, the one named for the birch forest which surrounded the chimneys that spewed smoke into the sky, day and night, saturating the air with the smell of history.

He'd told Suze how he and his daughter had settled in Amsterdam after the liberation with an uncle of his. There was no blood left in Germany. No house. No university post. Nothing but bombed-out buildings and bitter people scavenging through the once great streets of Berlin.

Eating the minced fishcakes, she wondered how he could live like that. How he could carry on after his wife and two of his children had been murdered. She was sure that in the same situation she would have just folded, crushed by hate and thoughts of retribution. She wanted to understand how one puts a life back together and the difference between that life and the one that preceded it.

'You think about them every day?' she'd asked him.

'Most days,' he'd answered. 'And even when I don't, it's still here.' Pointing to his chest. 'Still with me. It's always with us. Not something we can forget or put away.'

He'd celebrated his hundredth birthday earlier that year and Suze remembered seeing him at the party, his battered face aglow again like a child's. It was as if someone had suddenly wiped the last sixty years from his memory. She'd asked him then why he looked so happy and he'd replied that back in Auschwitz there was a game the prisoners played at night. One man would say 'I will live to a hundred' and then someone else down the block would say 'I will live to a hundred and one' and so on until the Kapos eventually heard them and would come steaming in with blackjacks and pliers, quieting the place back down again.

'Of course we all knew that we would never live to be a

hundred. Maybe you call it Jewish humour, I don't know, but we found it funny back then, saying things like that.

'Words were all we had left, everything else had been stripped away from us, but we always knew that with words we could beat the Nazis, they couldn't steal our language like they stole everything else from us. Our words were inviolable and that was why we didn't mind risking a beating or two for them. I thought about those times and I am so happy to have reached this age, this symbolic age. For me, it means I beat them, whatever they did to my family, to my culture and my people, those words spoken late at night in our crowded bunks, those words survived and became the truth, whereas the words they spoke, their language, crumbled with their armies and is now nothing but lies.

'The fish is good, no?' He brought her back to the present, back to the small smoke-filled room.

'Yes,' she replied and meant it. There was something in the foreignness of the food, in its alien texture and colour that took her away from herself. She had a crazy feeling that if she stayed in this room nothing could harm her. 'I guess I'm just another uneducated American, but hell, I don't mind you know, Moshe. It means there are still things for me to discover, new things.'

'Yes, you are right again, dear, you taste too much too early you become jaded, I think. You believe you have tasted everything, know everything. They were like kids in a sweet shop.' He always referred to the Nazis as 'they'. 'A sweet shop with no adults in sight. They could do what they wanted, try everything. I guess the world was theirs, but it was not our world, not even the world *they* had been brought into but a totally new world, where subtlety and patience were no longer virtues and where appetites could not be satisfied, no matter how much food was on the table.'

He lit one of his cigarettes – unfiltered, an old-time cigarette, Suze thought to herself, smoked in a world before lung cancer and radiotherapy. A survivor's cigarette perhaps, a statement of sorts – if the weight of the Nazi hammer could not crush him then no cigarette could, no cancer to whisk away the world, no Alzheimer's to return to an earlier time, a time when the world was still the right way up.

She helped him clear up the food, throw the plates into the bin, wanting to give him a hug, but she was too embarrassed, as always. 'I'll see you tomorrow, Moshe.'

'Yes, I believe you will.' He smiled at her and though it was a warm smile it was filled with a horribly imaginable sadness that made Suze feel very close to him, feel as though her own little problems were nothing. She almost broke down again but managed to make it out of the flat and into the street where she knew the rain would hide her tears.

8

The room he took him to was brightly lit and painted hospital white. A spear of sunlight spilled through the third-floor window illuminating specks of dust and smoke that twisted through the still air. Along the far wall, Jon saw the bright, gleaming doors with their silver handles, ordered in rows of five, four storeys high, serenely stacked like ovens in a busy pizzeria. He wondered how many dead men and women lay behind those doors as the air-con sputtered like a cracked and collapsed lung and the detective motioned for him to step forward.

'I hope this will not distress you too much,' Van Hijn said. 'We get used to such things in this business, used to them much too quickly, it's easy to forget the effect of seeing a dead body for the first time. Is this your . . . ?'

'Yes,' Jon replied, thinking the detective's question almost funny in these circumstances, 'my first time.'

'Well . . .' He trailed off, lost in his own train of thought, as they neared the wall of slabs. They stopped by the second column and the detective motioned to the third door from the bottom. Jon wondered whether they moved the bodies for viewings, he couldn't imagine anyone having to lean down to identify someone from the bottom slab. How awful it must be for those who came here to identify their blood, the people closest to them, all the time hoping that the face on the slab would be one they didn't recognize, hoping for another chance.

'Ready?'

'Yes,' Jon answered, though he had no idea if he really was or what that word constituted in such circumstances. The whole adventure seemed very prosaic now, brought into stark focus by the sparse white light of the room. The detective wheeled out the slab, exposing the shrouded body. He looked at Jon, who nodded, and carefully pulled back the sheet to reveal the white hair, then the beard of what was once, and in some way still was, Jake Colby.

'Fuck,' Jon murmured under his breath, immediately feeling embarrassed by the outburst. The sliver of hope he'd been clinging to, even after seeing the book, was brutally erased by the old man's face, no different now from when Jon had seen him sleeping.

'Yes, that's him,' he said, trying to compose himself. Feeling his legs sinking into the floor. The warmth of the room enclosing him like a mitten.

'You sure?'

Jon nodded.

'I'll leave you alone for a couple of minutes.'

'Thanks,' Jon said and stared at Jake. He tried not to cry, not in front of the detective, the morgue attendant, all these professionals, but he couldn't help it, he felt his eyes stinging and tried, as surreptitiously as possible, to wipe the tears from his face. This is where it ends up, he thought, dead and on display. He remembered how Jake would always wash his plates and cutlery after every meal, the way he showered regularly now that he could. The tissues on the floor. The night they talked about the Dead. That means nothing, Jon thought, all of that means nothing now, it's just memories and soon it won't even be that.

The detective moved back towards him, handed him a small plastic cup of water. Jon took a sip.

'What are those?' Jon asked, pointing to the old man's cheeks.

Above the boundary of his beard there were three small vertical cuts, about two inches long on both sides. They almost looked like the gills of a fish, Jon thought and tried to suppress the image. Things were horrible enough.

'Exactly what you see. Cuts. Made with an extremely sharp, flat-bladed knife or scalpel. At this stage it looks as if they were made on the day of his death, some healing of the tissue had started.'

'Shit.' Jon looked at the ugly scratches on the old man's face. 'The killer did that?'

'I guess so.' The detective turned towards Jon. 'He had other scars, much older. You knew about them?'

Jon stared at the detective. Something passed between them. 'No. Why should I?'

'No reason. I thought maybe you saw them when he was staying with you.'

There it was again, that insinuation. And now he realized that if he told the detective about what he'd seen that night in the bathroom, how the man would interpret it, the seedy and scurrilous conclusions he'd make. He didn't want to think about the bloody tissues in the bathroom. That was something old men deserved to keep private. He'd thought at the time that the problem stemmed from living on the streets. He held on to that.

'He had a large amount of scar tissue, other marks, burns and cuts and holes that look like piercings . . . you never saw anything like that on him?'

'No,' Jon replied, thinking how we never really know anybody, always afraid of getting too close, creating small walls to cloak what we try in vain to hide from ourselves.

'Look,' the detective said as he slowly pulled back the

sheet to reveal the rest of Jake's body. And the things that lay engraved upon it.

Jon actually did a double take, like in an old Harold Lloyd film – the discrepancy between what he saw and his image of Jake was too large a chasm to cross instantly. He looked down the old man's body, feeling strangely as though he was sneaking a look at a sleeper, an intrusion of privacy no less invasive because he was dead.

Jake's body was covered in an intricate topography of scar tissue, like canyons seen from a helicopter overhead, small black marks that Jon supposed were burns of some sort and holes in the skin, tiny punctures that traipsed over his chest and genitals. His eyes rolled quickly over the expanses of flesh, singed and folded, brutalized in an untold number of ways, the tension between not wanting to look and wanting to. He had to keep glancing back at the face to assure himself this was the man he once knew.

'They did all this to him?' Jon asked, still unable to see that what lay before him was a whole history, a whole lifetime of marking and scarring.

'Some of it. Not all. How well did you know Jake?'

'Not very. Obviously.' Jon stared at the body. His eyes refused to rest on any one spot. He felt sick, looked away, looked back.

'Amsterdam can change a person. I've seen it happen many times. There's something about this city, the idea of tolerance implicit in it, that seems to draw a certain kind of person. The kind of person that can sometimes unravel in this place. There seems to be so much freedom compared to home but people mistake this freedom, it can lead them down dangerous roads, roads they cannot come back on.' The detective trailed off as he pulled the sheet over the old man, finally laying him to rest, at least in Jon's mind, though of course he would suffer more severe mutilations in the upcoming autopsy. Jon wondered what the detective meant and whether he was talking about Jake now or about him. How could a city change a person? Surely it was always there, this thing that becomes amplified in a certain place, this thing that draws you to common streets and vistas. He stared at the detective, not saying anything.

The slab was noiselessly wheeled back into its cubicle and the door shut with a slight metallic ring that bounced across the white tiling of the room as the two men stared silently at their distorted reflections in the gleaming metal door.

'You want to go for a coffee?'

Jon nodded. He didn't want to go back to his empty hotel room. He knew what was waiting for him there. A return ticket, an unpacked backpack. He had done his job. It was over now and a pall of anti-climax flooded his chest.

Van Hijn took him around the corner to a coffee shop. The heady, sweet smell of skunk filled Jon's nostrils as soon as they entered. The stereo system screamed out Dylan, 'Highway 61 Revisited'. God saying to Abraham, 'Kill me a son.'

They sat at a far table in the dark, narrow bar, looking out on one of the canals. Jon watched as people slid into obscured alcoves, emitting thick purple ribbons of smoke, drenched in the thumping rhythms of the music. He looked out at the canal, long, thin barges burning upon the water, the slow inexorable path of progress, and then back at the interior of the coffee shop and the sense of time suspended, held in lieu.

'Pretty,' Jon absently remarked as he poured sugar into his coffee.

The detective snorted, a harsh expulsion of air from his nose. 'Yes, there are some things that are still pretty around

94

here, I suppose. I guess I forget about them, take it for granted you say?'

'Yes.'

'I take it for granted then, seeing so much crime and so much blood, it's hard sometimes to wipe that away with just a charming view or a nice piece of architecture.'

God, he's depressing, Jon thought, looking at the detective as he sipped his coffee. He'd made a mistake in accepting the man's invitation. Moroseness was the last thing he needed now. He hated the way that Jake's body had disgusted him. That it had felt so alien, so unlike the old man who'd stayed with him.

The Dylan track came cascading to a halt and in its place the chug-chug chainsaw rhythm of the Velvets' 'Sister Ray' filled the air around them.

'Are you a literary man, Mr Reed?'

The question surprised him, not so much that it had come from the policeman, but that it had come at such a time.

'Yes, I suppose I am.'

'Good, I like that in a person. Movies too, I love old movies. These are the things we need to hold on to, you understand?'

Jon nodded but he wasn't so sure he did. Wasn't sure he wanted to.

'These are the things that remain.'

A waitress came over and Van Hijn ordered for both of them. A couple of minutes later she was back, depositing two of the largest slices of cheesecake that Jon had seen this side of the Atlantic.

'Cheesecake, I love cheesecake. You know they make the best cheesecake here in Amsterdam?'

'No, I didn't know that.' Jon welcomed the change of subject. He didn't want to think about Jake now.

Van Hijn smiled. 'I'm trying to give up smoking grass. So now I've become an expert on cheesecake.'

'It actually keeps you off the stuff?'

'Yes, funnily enough it works though it does my figure no favours.' He patted the small belly that was beginning to accumulate around his waist.

'But you still come to coffee shops even though you're trying to give up?'

'Of course. Otherwise I would just be avoiding it – that never works. You have to be strong in the face of temptation, that's what it's all about. When I can sit here and not want a joint, even though I'm surrounded by them, then I'll be properly cured. You can't cure yourself of anything by avoidance, that just highlights how addicted you are – you have to confront things before they can go away, no?'

'I suppose. I hadn't really thought about it that way.' Though he hadn't really thought about it at all and was becoming increasingly confused by the detective's scattergun conversation. He wondered whether this was the psychological equivalent of Columbo's about-to-walk-out-of-the-door last-minute question. He reminded himself that he had to be careful. That the detective wasn't his friend, that they had been drawn together by other things and by what each of them thought they could achieve from this.

'They also happen to do the best cheesecake in these places.' The detective smiled, slowly pouring milk into his coffee, stirring with a bovine patience that Jon found admirable and yet somehow unsettling under the circumstances.

They sat silently drinking their coffee. They both sensed what lurked in these silences but neither could find a way back. Like people in cafés everywhere they became almost abstract figures – *Man Sitting Over Cup Of Coffee, Man Staring*

Out At Canal – or figures from seventeenth-century Dutch masters, their occupying the same canvas an almost arbitrary event, their forms occluded and made discrete by their individual sadness, and Jon knew that it was in moments like this, when we don't say anything, that we somehow connect the most.

The detective paid. Jon thanked him.

'So, you going to do some sightseeing while you're here?'

'Hadn't thought about it really. I suppose so. My flight doesn't leave until tomorrow afternoon.'

Van Hijn smiled, then grabbed Jon's wrist. A swift sudden movement. Brought his face up close. 'You're not thinking of following this thing up yourself?' he said, not letting go of his hand.

'No,' Jon replied, though he had been thinking about it, in the morgue, sitting here, wondering what he'd do for the next twenty-four hours.

'Good. It's not your job. Mine, you understand? There are things that you do not comprehend. Things you don't know about this city. It'll eat you up. Don't fuck up my investigations, understand?'

Jon nodded. His wrist was beginning to hurt.

'You want to know what happened to your friend, you let me do it. I don't want you messing around. I don't want to hear that they found you in some alley, carved up, because you asked the wrong person the wrong questions, or even the right ones. Go to your hotel. Visit the Van Gogh. Get on your plane tomorrow. This is what you have to do. Your job here is done. I'm grateful. But that's all there is.'

He unclasped his hand. Jon stared down at his wrist, red and raw. The sudden change in the detective had frightened him and he only nodded, wanting to get away, get back to his room.

'We understand each other then?' Van Hijn said.

'Yes,' Jon replied.

9

He sat in his hotel room and listened to the rain outside. It sounded so different from London rain. More percussive, denser somehow. An all-encompassing drip and drap beating on the roofs of the houses and swallowed by the dark canals. He stretched out on the bed. Feeling tired, still shaken from the previous day, the cold morgue, the unsheathed body, Jake.

There was no reason for him to stay. His job was done. Jake had been positively identified. And yet he couldn't stop thinking about what he'd seen. The wounds and injuries, that grotesque tapestry of pain. Though he'd identified him, at some deeper level he hadn't quite recognized the old man, as if the corpse on the slab had been a twin brother, identical in outward appearance yet with a wholly divergent lifestyle. He found himself wondering whether Jake's story was even true – if there was so much he didn't know about the man then nothing was certain.

He'd woken to the sound of a Swedish couple in the room next door fighting and screaming. He lay still and tried to focus on the words they were saying, staring at the ceiling, hearing another couple break up, the fury and exasperation of their words transcending any language barrier as the screaming rose in pitch and the door finally slammed.

The next thing he heard was a toilet flushing nearby and a group of Australians laughing boisterously in the hallway. He knew that as long as he could listen to these ghostly voices, these invisible lives lived out behind walls, he wouldn't have to think about his own situation, his own life.

Maybe it was only meeting Jake that had awoken him. It sometimes seemed as if he'd lived the last few years in an insulated silence, only the sound of his own voice to quell his fears. Of course Jake had reminded him of his father, but more than that, he reminded him of the father he never had, the one he'd always wished and prayed for.

He lit a cigarette and tried to focus on the sounds from outside his room, to pick up a conversation, the fragment of a goodbye, but he could hear only the whistling of water pipes branching through the walls. It seemed that his fellow residents were all out, braving the rain and hitting the galleries and museums, canals and coffee shops. He checked his watch. His flight was at five. He had most of the day. He could stroll around unplanned, he could check out the Rembrandts at the Rijks. But he knew it wasn't going to be any of those things. He found his city guide and marked out a route: the shortest distance between the hotel and the Jewish Historical Museum, the place that Jake had talked so much about.

Jon had never had a bar mitzvah, never eaten chicken soup except out of a can, didn't learn Hebrew or fast on the Day of Atonement, ate pork all his life, went out with a Catholic girl and never once thought of visiting Israel. He'd hidden behind the fence of his name and had effected a passable imitation of an English gentile for most of his life. Of course, his father had achieved more than a passable imitation and Jon, in this at least, had his father as a role model for the years to come. The word 'Jew' did not come into the Reed household, as if even the mention of it might infect the child and cripple him in what was gradually becoming a harsher world.

As he walked across the crowded squares of Amsterdam,

so filled with bustle and steam, the crisscrossing of trams and bicycles, the small runnels gouged into the road, Jon remembered the incident when his father, being questioned as to whether or not he was a Jew by Polish officials at a remote border post, had replied 'Absolutely not.' Until then Jon hadn't really thought about such things; his relatives had strange accents and even stranger foods but that seemed a throwback to some time before the year zero, or so his father had always insisted.

That day at the border crossing, the young Jon found himself surprisingly shocked at his father's reply, so much so that he quickly rolled down the Mercedes's window and blurted out 'He *is* a Jew' at the border guards. His father had subsequently been taken into a small hut where, he later told his son, the guards had stripped and searched him. He would never let Jon forget that moment, saying 'I hope this teaches you a lesson' many a time after recounting the horrifying events that occurred within the customs shack. Jon was sure that the incident had taught him a lesson, but as to what the lesson was or whether there was a moral to glean from it, he didn't know, and in the following years he made sure not to allude to this mysterious part of his heritage that had caused his father such undue punishment and humiliation.

Jake's story had awakened in him a long lost sense of, well he couldn't really call it Jewishness, never having experienced or been taught what that was, but more a feeling of a curious membership of some esoteric group. He remembered that the only time he'd felt any Jewish identity was when he was being abused. Called a Yid or a miser, watching the other boys rubbing their noses and singing the praises of Adolf Hitler. It was no more than if they'd mocked the colour of his hair or the way he slouched, there was nothing behind the naming but the will to hurt, yet it still rankled and made him wonder why there was so much hate directed against this attribute that he'd unwillingly received at birth. Consequently he'd never considered himself Jewish. Though the insults still hurt, he knew that they really weren't directed at him, that the kids had somehow got it wrong, had got him mixed up with someone else.

The rain stopped as he wound through the thin, clasping alleys of the red-light district, avoiding the hustlers and early-morning wrecks. Out of an alley he emerged into the sudden explosion of space that is Nieuwmarkt. He had to stop, take in the space, the open vista stretching across the square. Out of the dark huddle and into the light. He lit a cigarette and stared at the Waag, the weigh-house that looked like a medieval castle, almost arbitrarily located at the centre of the square. He looked around. It was early, the city, sleepy and slow, was still shuttered and shrouded in the aching movements of waking. The cobblestoned and unadorned square was empty, stretching beyond the Waag and to the tall buildings on the other side. The castle with its round medieval towers, its slitted windows and garrets, seemed an afterthought, as if to compensate for the massive emptiness of the square. Here he could breathe, see the sky as more than a strip painted between roofs. He enjoyed standing around, no one to hassle him here, only a few feet from the district but also in another world.

The Jewish quarter lay to the east of the Waag, a long boulevard that wound down to the museum. He sat in a café, only just opening, the waitress bleary-eyed and tired, and ordered an espresso. He wanted to delay things for a bit. He knew the museum was waiting for him. It was the only link he had left to Jake. And though the detective had been pretty clear, he knew that this was something he had to do. Besides, it was a museum, he could be going there for a thousand other reasons and by late afternoon he would be on a plane, heading back, the detective none the wiser. He sat and smoked quietly, watching the people slowly passing by and feeling no desire to return to London.

Back home, his days always started exactly the same, a slow trudge to the bathroom, coffee and a cigarette, a CD playing. Then he'd go downstairs, check the mail, back upstairs, boot up the computer, download his emails, browse the web, maybe buying a book or CD and by then it would be time for lunch. So the days disappeared in a pleasant routine that masked any surprise or shock, making them go quicker, filling up with things that didn't matter. The last year had gone by frighteningly fast. Was that just getting older, he wondered, time telescoping down into number of years left, or something altogether different? It scared him that he'd begun to worry about time running out. He'd always thought that would come after his fiftieth birthday.

He got up, paid and crossed the great, empty square. Checked his map and headed down St Antoniebreestraat.

Jake had stretched out the days they'd spent together, filling up the usually vacuous time with silences and gestures, smiles and mysteries. Why hadn't he missed all that before? Or had he and just not realized it? The latter was probably more accurate, some things are so essential a part of your life that you never pause to think about them until they're gone. And even then, for the first few months, years, you just feel the hollowness of something lacking and you ascribe it to other things that are missing in your life – your wife, success, self-confidence, money. It takes a long time to realize it isn't anything as earth-shattering as that, that it is in fact something very small and easily replaceable. It was good to be nudged out of those old patterns and routines that he now glimpsed might actually be the cause rather than the symptom of his malaise. And yet, when the old man had left, he'd slipped right back into the same old habits like an alcoholic remembering the sound of the cap breaking open. Amsterdam had blasted all that, exploded those cigarettes and mail checks into pieces, so that although he'd been away only for a couple of days, it already felt like years and those routines almost the movements of another man.

He lit a cigarette and watched as a couple of teenagers walked past him, holding hands and smiling as if the world didn't exist. Or maybe it's exactly because it does, he thought, maybe that's it. He continued walking, waiting for the Jewish Quarter to appear in all its imagined old-world grandeur and seediness. But it was gone. The street was lined with small shops selling cuddly toys, books, magazines, small items that you know you don't need but kind of want anyway. Above lay apartment blocks, the whole street one long promenade of sixties' pastel-coloured buildings. Balconies and small windows. Clotheslines and TV aerials. People slowly emerging into the day. He remembered reading how the whole quarter had been torn down. Replaced by this prefab apartment complex that stretched from Nieuwmarkt down to the Waterlooplein. He'd been hoping for clotted doorways, old grimy steps, the smells of cabbage and coffee, bullet holes in the stonework. But, staring up at the cool, calculated planes of these dwellings, he could have been anywhere and he tried to not let this disappointment cloud his day.

There was no reason to go back for the moment. None at all. London always depressed him in the autumn with its grey skies and grey people trudging through the clogged and sticky streets. He knew that he needed a change and, in London, ensconced in the cocoon of his flat, he could never drag up the sufficient amount of will and excitement to make such a decision, to say 'Fuck it' and get on the next plane out of there. There were always reasons for not doing it, for putting it off or ruling it out.

He remembered the building opposite his flat, the dole office, and how he would sometimes watch the glum men and women queuing up, slowly wasting their time, inching forward, knowing that if it hadn't been for his father's death and the resultant inheritance, he would be just like them, waiting his turn even now. Sometimes at night they forgot to turn off the LED signs and he could see from his window, as he sat on the sofa, the clear red illumination that said PLEASE WAIT. For months he had seen the sign lit up in that empty hall across the street and if he'd needed any confirmation for the life he was leading, he would stare at it for a few minutes. Now that he was finally away, he knew that the waiting was over, that you can delay and defer your life only for so long.

He checked his watch. The flight was getting closer. But first he had debts to pay. To the old man and perhaps also to the religion he'd been born into. What had happened to Jake? Over and over again, it rang through his head. What the hell could have caused a man like that to do such things to his own body? It seemed almost unimaginable to Jon, a shocking reversal of all that he thought was given. The bloody tissues on the floor. The scars and skin, like something out of a horror flick. And he thought about what the detective had said. Snuff films. Torture. Sex. Wondering if Jake really did all that to himself, if it wasn't something else, someone else.

He crossed the canal and headed towards the museum. Everything around him was new, the demolished medieval buildings of the Jewish Quarter nothing but unremembered ghosts. Everything modern and shiny. The massive buildings, the streets uncobbled now, the great white expanse of the

Operahouse. He came to a stop by the black granite monument that stood at the edge of the land, almost dangling between the confluence of the wide, raging Amstel and the quiet Zwanenburgwal, the place where the city spills open. He stared up at it. The inscription in Hebrew and Dutch. The way the black reflected the scuzzy sun and the swirl of the canals behind it. It looked like a monolith from the film *2001*. Some pre-natural signifier stranded here in another empty square, the sterile, dead concrete fields of the Operahouse stretching out in every direction, bounded only by the restless canals and the memory of what used to be.

The Jewish Historical Museum had once been four separate synagogues, greatly frequented by the many Jews of Amsterdam. After the war, there being not many Jews left, the buildings lay empty until the 1980s when they were converted into one composite structure that now served as Amsterdam's memory of its Jews. Four synagogues, from the ancient stone of the Grote, built in 1671, to the stark brickwork of the Nieuwe, built a hundred years later, to the functional spaces of the extended gallery appended in 1987. All together now. Linked by a feat of architecture even more impressive for the fact that it was almost invisible. Four synagogues, merged and buttressed, under one roof, a sort of homogenizing of past and present, the kind of thing this city was so good at.

He remembered Jake telling him about the place, animated, the closest he'd got to enthusiasm. After learning about his father's will, the old man had come here to see what records he could find about his family, his real family, and he'd described it to Jon with all the reverence of a new husband describing his wife's body. Jon wondered whether the detective had already been there, already questioned the people. It didn't matter. As long as he didn't bump into him . . . and even then, he could just say he was sightseeing. He had his own investigations to make, parallel but not congruent with the detective's. He felt a hot buzz of expectation shoot through him, a quiver of curiosity, now that his search for Jake was becoming less abstract.

Jon entered the museum. An old man, positively Methuselean, sat at the counter, collecting fees and handing out guides and brochures.

'I'm looking for a friend of mine,' Jon said, surprising himself. He'd meant to lead up to it, start talking about something in general and narrow it down. The old man looked at him as if he didn't understand. Jon described Jake, his beard and purpose. The old man's face betrayed nothing.

'He came here a lot. I was wondering if you remember him,' Jon said, disappointment making his voice sound thin and desperate.

The old man shook his head. 'People come and go all the time,' he said in a wheezy, old-century accent.

'I know that he came here quite regularly. He was looking for his family, his history.'

'We all are at some level or another.' The old man refused to be drawn.

'Is there anyone else who might have seen him?' Jon asked, hope slipping.

'No.'

Jon didn't believe him. He must have seen Jake. Unless Jake's whole story was a lie. Unless there was no revelation, no Raphael Kuper, no history.

The old man looked at him, stoic as a rock – Jon knew he would never tell him anything he didn't want to and he felt himself go weak. Another failed attempt, another bust.

Perhaps the detective had been right. Perhaps it would be better if he just went home. He smiled, gave the old man the entrance fee and set off into the cool, high-vaulted spaces of the museum.

He walked by the Torahs and scriptures as if they were alien relics, the strange backward language and tradition into which he had been only partly initiated. Nineteenth-century Passover tables, neat, exact and somehow sad, ensconced in their glass cages. The sun slanting in from above, illuminating great, huge, frazzled Bibles, mysterious marks etched into the parchment. He wondered how the old man had felt walking into this cool, reverent space, through the corridors and rooms of a history that he'd only recently discovered was his. Of course Jon saw the parallels but he'd always known he was a Jew, even when he was desperately trying to hide it – more so then – and Jake, well, Jake had suddenly been drowned in the knowledge at such a late date. He wondered if Jake had felt Jewish or only an impostor while gliding through these rich and detailed rooms. Jon felt stranded between the two.

He slowly and painstakingly read every piece of printed literature tacked up to explain the exhibits. He stared at the black ribbed shofars, like artefacts from an alien civilization, the gold menorahs, elegant and out of time. He knew that in this place he was a gentile, someone who needed interpretive guides for the objects on display, a stranger with no sense of God or belief, only a nagging curiosity as to what the objects were, their material meaning and function. He stared at the Tefillin, the small black boxes containing Bible verses that the reverent fastened to their left arm and forehead, straps of leather going round the skin like snakes. He understood little of the ritualistic artefacts on display, not having partici-pated in such ceremonies, not knowing even what they signified in the minds of believers. He felt a little ashamed at his ignorance and was glad that he hadn't told the old man at the counter that he was Jewish. What if he'd asked him some innocent question? He would have been shown to be the impostor he now felt, someone who'd lost their right to claim their hidden heritage.

In the next room were ancient, gloomy canvases filled with huddled men from previous centuries. Even the bright halogens of the modern age were not enough to illuminate the darkness that surrounded them like soup, enclosing them in some terrible secret, so dark that it was hard to make out individual figures. Next to them lay fake Torah scrolls, made out of plastic, with a video monitor at their centre where the text should be. He stopped and stared, watching on the screen the old, liver-spotted hands of a man painstakingly scratching the strange figures that populated the scrolls, that mysterious writing, the dead traditions.

In the next room he saw the photos of people herded out of their houses and into the streets. Saw the misery and fear in their faces and knew he'd reached the Holocaust section. He'd never really thought about the Holocaust, not until Jake had told him his story, had always seen it as just another chapter in the book about the Second World War. Of course he'd studied it at A level along with everyone else, watched the Laurence Olivier-narrated documentary and felt sad, perhaps even a little thrilled and disgusted at the same time, as did every young boy of his age. But that was all just 'history', something to be learned, something gone, the elusive past.

He wondered how Jake had felt, walking through these rooms. Had he cried? Had to leave? Jon didn't know, would never know, and that made him feel sad as he looked at the faded sepia photograph, tired black and white faces lined up against a wall, the words '*Juden*' and '*Schwein*' scrawled in primitive graffiti behind them. He stared at their faces and wondered whether Jake had done that too, maybe trying to see some facial resemblance, some signifier of himself.

There were countless documents on display here, letters of transit, faked postcards from Auschwitz, children's identity cards, different types of yellow stars and bills of receipt for human cargo. The neat handwriting on the latter made him feel queasy. He wondered what it would be like to see your own name on one of those bills, a record of your slaughtered family, up for display now to anyone who paid the entrance fee. There was a certain intrusion of privacy inherent in such exhibitions, even if the people were all dead.

He came back to the first photo he'd seen, the one of the men lined up against the wall, and it seemed especially cruel to have fixed their images as such, their faces smeared with fear and anxiety. Surely these were once proud citizens who would have been aghast at the idea of being displayed in their moment of weakness.

The photograph had its own narrative thrust beyond and across the scene that it presented. The look on their faces and the abject way in which they stood against the paint-splattered wall told a story beyond that moment, no less horrifying than if they had chosen the next shot, the inevitable mound of bodies and smiling officers. These men died in their best suits, Jon thought, in the middle of the day and in front of a camera. In front of a fucking camera.

When he had seen all he could, he walked back into the enclosure that held the Torah and sat on the stool staring up at the impossibly delicate object, suspended in a room by itself, a quiet place to get away from the densely displayed horrors of the other hall. He tried to focus on the fine detail of the finials with their ornamental bells like tiny Venetian spires, the gilded, etched mantles and crowns, but all he could see were the faces.

There were so many sad faces in those photos, in that history, so much injustice, hate and cruelty. Any one face displayed the whole terrible fate; of a people, for sure, his people even, if he could let himself think in that way – but more than that, the fate of those that perpetrated those actions and also the fate of those who viewed these artefacts. The beauty and exquisite silence of the room could not temper the anger which he felt burning itself through his body, as his chest got tighter and his palms began to sweat. He took three deep breaths, felt giddy and then got up and went straight through the Holocaust hall and into a small adjoinment that was filled with colour and hope.

He looked at the series of gouaches, the portraits of the woman and the man, the long discursive rambles that were superimposed on to the images, the bright and ebullient vivacity of it. He'd never heard of Charlotte Salomon before and he spent a long time going from one gouache to another, letting their colour and space soak into him and burn away the image of the men. Some of them were so funny, a sharp and focused irony at work in the tension between what was shown and what was said; in the words that dwelt in the empty spaces of paint. Others spoke of a terrible loneliness, inherent in the minimalism and nuance of the composition, but even here, there was *something*, this awful past transformed through art into something else. Something that existed now.

It was a good way to finish, he thought, a good way to leave the place. The paintings had made the image of the men fade slightly. His anger too had subsided. He didn't know what the paintings had to do with the Holocaust, only that Salomon had been Jewish; perhaps the curators had put up these works as a necessary adjunct to what came before, a way of dissipating the ugly information that had soaked in. He hoped it was so at least, feeling that the paintings had indeed refreshed him, put that other photo in context, though in context of what he didn't know.

At the end of the exhibit, on a small table, was an old leather-bound book of comments. Jon stepped up to it, wanting to write something, to make concrete his feelings but nothing came and instead he began flicking through the previous pages, reading the comments of other men and women who had passed through here. He deciphered handwriting that would flummox a cryptographer, skimmed through messages of hope and fear, and that was when he saw it.

The old man's name, Jake Kuper, and above, a small paragraph.

He could hear his heart ricochet inside his chest.

Jake had been here.

The story must be true. The trail alive.

He read the three short sentences that his friend had written about Charlotte. He'd hoped they would cast some light on Jake's own history but they were pithy and dry as dust. Terse descriptions of the beauty of her colours. The sadness of her life.

Instinctively Jon reached down and ran his finger along the rough edges of the paper, feeling the indentations that Jake had pressed into the book. Everything left a trail, from the most insignificant life to the most famous. We cannot erase our history, like snails we only manage to smear it behind us, leaving others to follow, make sense of, come to terms with. Jon's finger rested on the word Jake. Everything was there and he felt a sudden understanding that it was left to him to follow the trail, to recreate Jake from his leavings.

He closed the book and checked his watch. He had just enough time to make it back to the hotel, pack and get to the airport. He took out his ticket. Checked the flight schedule. Yes, plenty of time.

He looked once more at the paintings, sadness burning his heart, then walked out into the street, the sun all dazzle and glitter. He threw his plane ticket into the first bin he came across, watching it flutter and spin to the bottom. All around him couples embraced and kissed, the darkness of the past conveniently hidden behind the grand old walls of the synagogue, like Amsterdam's Jewry, a petrified relic from another time.

10

The sun streamed all over her face. Suze felt its warmth and almost cried. It reminded her of home, that wild, unbroken country that now seemed not merely a continent but a whole world away. Another place and time.

She checked her watch. Dominic was late.

He was always late. Fashionable or otherwise, he never made it on time. She'd arrived at the café half an hour after they'd arranged and now she thought maybe she'd missed him, maybe he'd actually got there on time, waited and despaired. But that was not like Dominic, he would wait – he'd wait for her until the city crumbled around them, until the land sank under the water and the last boats left.

But maybe, just maybe, the urgency in her voice had made him come on time, wait, get pissed off, wait another five minutes and finally leave.

She lit a cigarette and watched the sun hide behind the tall buildings that marked off this area from the enclosure of the District with its medieval proportions. She felt better here in this old continent, buttressed by leaning walls and serpentine streets, than in the great oceanic swells of desert in which she'd been raised. To her left the city rushed on; yellow streaking trams, bicycles, so old-fashioned and somehow definitively European, rolled by, threading through the accumulating crowds, shaking off the night.

But the sun made her feel uneasy, refusing to be an unambiguous delight, taking her back to those mesas and plains, the drenched daylight of her youth, lived in the unblinking heat. The priest at her mother's funeral collapsing, sun-stroked and heavy, on to the ground, the silence that he seemed to draw with him, as if his fall had sucked all the words and emotions out of the mourners' mouths. It had been so hot that day. Trust Mother to die in August. First summer vacation from college, first day back, filled with words and wonder and wanting to talk so much. A haemorrhage had taken her in her sleep. And a week later, her father, dead in a car accident, skewed and burned with his latest lover on some god-forsaken highway in Idaho. A fearful symmetry she was just beginning to grasp. As if that shot, heard and seen twelve years before, had only now reached its target, a long, slow and deliberate trajectory that had taken all this time to come to its conclusion. And so: counsellors and more counsellors. Lawyers and heavy doubt and sudden wealth and through it all she couldn't wait to get back to college. To sink herself into paintings, into the dark canvases and obdurate theories that promised to swallow the past. It was the only thing that made her feel better, the swell and sway of other people's lives.

And was it really only the sun that made her think about these things? Or something about yesterday, Wouter's stumbling phone call? Or was it the face of the dead girl that stared out from her TV set that morning?

She saw the dog first. Then Dominic following behind, gently loping along as if he wasn't already fifty minutes late, smiling when he saw her, though she'd seen that he'd noticed her earlier, when she was looking at the dog. She smiled back.

'Sorry I'm late. I had something to finish. Lost track of time.' He stood beside her, blocking out the sun. His thick Yorkshire accent dry and sleepy. 'Drink?'

She only then realized that she was sitting at an empty

table. 'They do those super sickly sweet guava juices here?'

'They do. I'll get you one,' he said, watching the curve of her ankles as she crossed her legs. Sighing.

He started walking towards the door, then turned, as if suddenly remembering something.

'Oh, wow!' she said taking the magazine from him. The dark maroon gloss of the cover soft and sexy under her fingers, the embossed letters *(An)Aesthetics – a Periodical*, slightly raised, reflecting back the overhead sun.

Dominic smiled, all was going well, he could feel it. 'It arrived from the printer's this morning. And another thing . . .' He reached into his pocket. 'I saw it second-hand, cheap. Thought you'd like it.' He handed the book to her.

'Oh my God, how did you know I wanted this!'

'I saw you admiring it in the university bookshop.'

She felt herself go red. 'But it's just come out. It's so expensive.'

Dominic smiled. 'I found it second-hand. It was dead cheap.'

'Thank you. That was so kind of you.' She suddenly felt a rush of affection, a deep fist in her chest. She grabbed his hand, squeezed – it felt as though there were no bones under the layers of flesh – said thank you again, kissed his cheek, genuinely touched that he'd thought of her, though feeling guilty too for never having done anything so kind for him.

As she waited for him to come back with the drinks, she carefully opened the magazine. She loved its smell. The smell of new things, of recent printing, paper and ink and oiled machines. She saw her name on the masthead, 'associate editor', she liked that, previously she'd only been a contributor but Dominic had recently given her more of the editorial work as he'd been so busy. It was their third issue. In small, almost invisible lettering at the bottom of the cover were the words 'produced by the Revised Council of Blood'.

It was Dominic who had formed the group. She'd met him during her second week in the city. He'd sat across from her during seminars and, even that first time, she could not ignore the way his eyes would settle on her as they scanned the room, always looking away when she caught his stare. And yet she liked him, despite his obvious and painfully occluded attraction to her, or maybe because of it, she wasn't sure. When he told her about the Council she'd been thrilled, there was something about its mystery, the way they met weekly in a rented basement in the red-light district, the air of being part of something secret. She knew it was silly, this attraction, but she couldn't help it. And the Council was useful for her work. Dominic had formed it as a debating group, to hammer out a theory of representation. A *moral* theory of representation. Of course they never agreed and she sensed that it seemed silently to frustrate Dominic that they couldn't come to a consensus. She knew it was the nature of these things – language and theory showed everything to be so slippery that even their own foundations were always being put into question. She liked the fact they disagreed. It was more exciting.

They looked at the impact of photo-journalism, the saturation of atrocity photos, newspapers once full of breasts and beaches were now routinely filled with mutilated corpses, the inner workings of rape camps and dream-like cities made of skulls. They wanted to know what this meant. How the aesthetisization of images made them anaesthetic, drained them of their power to shock and outrage.

Dominic firmly believed in the power of these images to politicize. Suze, having seen people discussing wallpaper shades over coffee-table books of the Holocaust, wasn't so sure. Charlotte had chosen to show something else. This was what held her and the Council was a place where she could discuss her ideas. The journal, subtitled *Periodical*, was an organ through which they could publish essays or critiques relating to their concerns. They printed 500 copies and usually sold them all within the quarterly run at bookstores and coffee shops throughout the city.

She saw that this issue was mainly devoted to a forty-five-page piece by Dominic entitled 'The Seduction of the Banal: The Utilization of (Imagery) in Life (is) Beautiful as Process in Revisionist History'. He always used (seemingly random) parentheses, except the word (is) which was routinely enclosed and therefore put into question. She flicked through the introduction, more parentheses, a sentence that she knew she'd have to read three times to get the sense of, something about the Italian film, a withering remark . . . she scanned the rest, feeling the onrush of a mega-migraine. Forty-five pages! She couldn't believe it. There was something horribly pretentious about it all. She hoped Dominic wouldn't ask her opinion.

She saw him navigating the door with the drinks, smiling. She knew what he wanted from her and she knew, just as surely, that it was something she could never give. He was so different from Wouter and yet both were men with whom she enjoyed moments but couldn't envisage sharing a continual stream of time with. She thought about what Moshe had said. Even if he was right, and she was willing to concede that maybe he was, even then, there was something about men who desired possession so much, with the attendant labelling and identification, surname and marriage certificate, that made her skin crawl, not in any metaphorical sense, no, like ants slowly inspecting your skin, that kind of crawl.

She could never be with Dominic and yet she couldn't

help liking him, the way he always edged around his infatuation, never coming out and saying it as American boys did, keeping it, like a special locket, just to himself. It made their relationship easier, for her at least. It kept the unspoken hanging. And that was good. She knew he didn't have many friends in the city and she felt it necessary to make known to him that he wasn't alone. And she enjoyed his company, his passion, especially when, momentarily, he would forget that she was the girl he was in love with, and relax, be himself. But lately she'd felt a new tension between them, as if the air was suddenly charged. There was something in Dominic's face she hadn't seen before, a tightening, a resoluteness that worried her. He'd begun to miss meetings.

'How's the work going?' He placed the drink beside her, sat down.

She jumped, smiled, annoyed that he'd caught her unaware. 'My work?' She put the glass to her lips. She'd been so lost in thought she wasn't sure what he was referring to. 'It crawls along. Like most things.'

Dominic nodded. But they both knew they weren't here to talk about that.

They sat and sipped their drinks, each unwilling to break the silence, to utter her name, the dead girl.

Suze had seen it on the morning news. She didn't fully understand the fast-talking presenter but her face and name needed no translation. She felt her stomach drop through the floor, the room spin around her. She'd immediately called Dominic. She'd needed to talk but now, as they sat staring at the unburdened tourists that strolled past, she didn't know what to say. That yes, death had finally affected her so? That yes, it had taken the murder of someone she knew? That all they talked about in the Council was a lie?

'I'm so sick of it all.' It came out of her, a surprise, and she looked to see if Dominic had heard but, oh god, he had and was now looking worried and anxious.

He put his hand on her leg. She tried not to jerk back though her body's natural reaction was exactly that. She couldn't say why his touch should have that effect on her, that it was only an innocent gesture, a measure of reassurance gladly given. She froze as his hand rested upon her knee, trembling slightly, trying not to show what she felt.

'We have to carry on.' He smiled but she could see that he was just as nervous about the position of his hand as she was. 'It doesn't change anything.'

She swung her legs away. 'It changes everything, Dominic. She was just a dead girl until today. Today she's someone we knew.' She felt herself shaking but understood she would have to control it in front of him.

'It's just a coincidence,' he said, trying to sound calm, inching his hand towards her again.

'Nothing is a coincidence,' she replied.

Beatrice had been a member of the Council. No one had seen her for a few weeks. Everybody thought holiday, no one believed murder. Not until this morning when the police had finally revealed her name, splashed across countless newspapers and TV sets in the faint hope that it would yield some further clues and in the safe knowledge that it was what the public wanted.

Suze moved back. 'You can't think that.' She edged her chair further back. 'You know what happened – how can you say it was a coincidence?'

'You think it was because of the Council? The work she did?' He leaned forward, bridging the space between them.

'You think it wasn't?'

Dominic shook his head. A headache was crawling its way up his neck. 'Stupid, dumb luck, or bad luck. People aren't killed for writing articles, discussing theories.' He tried to sound reassuring.

She looked at him. His eyes steadfastly refused to focus on hers as always, bounced up and down until they found a neutral point to rest upon. She didn't believe a word he said. 'The TV talked about how she was killed.'

'She's not the first,' Dominic replied, thinking back to the preceding victims, their faces paraded. Their faces always with us.

'She was someone we knew.' She thought this plain fact was enough to explain itself.

'And that makes it different?'

She looked at him; as usual she couldn't read the signs. Was he teasing her? Or being comforting? 'Yes, that makes it different. It's no longer a set of words and I know that's the point, Dominic, but . . .'

'You don't sound like you believe that any more.'

She noticed that he was grinding his foot into the floor, small violent circular motions.

'I'm not so sure what I believe any more. I know that I can't talk about all this horror, look at these kind of images, discuss and debate them. Not in the same way. I can't look at them. The idea of it makes me sick. We were just playing around. I feel it's my fault she's dead.'

'Your fault? Don't be stupid, Suze.'

'I'm not being stupid.'

Poor boy, she thought again, the more comforting he tried to sound the more patronizing he ended up being. She quickly scolded herself for always thinking the worst. His intentions were good and that was the main thing, had to be.

'When they reported the second victim I wanted more,' she said. 'I told myself this is it. A serial killer. Right here in Amsterdam. That particular method of killing. I thought this is what we need. Horror. A wake-up call. Something more than cartoon violence, something more than images on the screen. I read the papers every day, wanting more, another victim, a death more horrible. You understand? I couldn't believe how it tied in with everything the Council was talking about. I thought this would make people realize the horror of what they routinely take as entertainment.

'And then more came. And I was happy. I know that's a terrible thing to say but it's what I felt. Not happy that they were dead but now that they were dead I was happy it was in this way. I thought having it splashed across the newspapers would create something positive. In February when the police had the suspect I hoped they'd got the wrong man and when the next girl was found I felt a surge of excitement. But now I'm asking myself how did I even think like that? How *could* I? Did I really want more people dead just so a point could be made?'

Dominic leaned back in the chair. 'Which is why we need to crank it up a notch,' he said.

Suze looked at him blankly. 'We need to stop. Didn't you hear what I've been saying? Stop and reassess our motives.'

'We can't stop. *They* won't stop. Killings will continue. Our fascination with them will only expand. It's up to us to show people the true face of murder.'

She realized what he meant. 'You're going to use Beatrice.' She caught his eyes. Watched them shift, then light up. He smiled.

'A friend passed me the police photos. Not the smiling graduation shot on the front pages. The after shots.'

'Get rid of them.' She grabbed his hand and squeezed tight.

'No.' But he didn't pull away.

'Please, Dominic. It's gone too far. I know your intentions are good but I'm not sure this is the solution any more.'

'People need to see what the word "murder" stands for. They need to see the blood, skin and bone that make up this word. The pain and loss and never-againness. I thought you understood.' He shook his head, unclenched, stood up, called his dog Bill to his side. 'This is the only weapon we have. We don't have guns, we have images. You'll see. I've got something special waiting. Something that will make all this talk academic. We need to take it to another level. We need to take it as far as it can go.' He turned from her before she could answer him. He didn't want to hear. She would see when it was all over. She would understand the necessity of it. Then she would move across a table and place her hand in his, smile and say, 'I should have known all along.' He wanted to share conversations with her that no one else understood, to hold her when memory ripped through her soul like broken glass, to stop her shaking and make her smile. But he could never say these things to her. His own fear was like a gag slowly working its way down his throat. But this would all change very soon. And then they would be joined and the world would melt away from them, fall off the edges, vanish altogether.

She sat and watched him disappear into the flux of itinerary-chasing tourists, lost now, just another floating ghost.

She lit a cigarette and leafed through the Breugel book, quickly getting drawn into the vertiginous plains and imposs-ible towers of his work, wanting her thoughts to be com-pletely engulfed, submerged, silenced and squeezed out.

It was only when the coffee was done, the cigarette too, that she noticed the price tag on the inside front cover, the full price, the name of a new bookshop, and she wondered had he really found it second-hand or bought it new and forgotten to take off the label? She looked up, not wanting her head crammed with such thoughts, with so little kindness and she pledged to try harder. Feeling better already, filled with the instant absolution that making a promise bestows, she got up, tucked the book under her arm and was quickly swallowed up by the tremulous masses.

He sat amid his machines, shiny, humming computers and insect-like chipboards, the transferring equipment, the black editing boxes and the old film projector that his dad had given him on his sixteenth birthday – the only time it seemed to Dominic that the old man had actually thought about what he was buying his son, rather than the token, sometimes wildly inappropriate, present that was the norm.

He thought about his meeting with Suze, all the things left unspoken, the silence in their lives which neither of them could break. Would she leave the Council? When he'd seen the paper that morning, he knew that things would change, that they could not continue as they had done. But while for Suze it seemed a severance, for him it was an indication that they were right. That things had to be brought out into the open. The world was always darker when it lay hidden behind words.

He thought about the body in the canal. The feel of dead hair. The slurp of the water swallowing it up.

He looked through his CDs and picked out Willie Nelson's *Red Headed Stranger*. The opening bars of 'Time of the Stranger' crept into the room and then the lone, high voice filled the space around him. Sometimes every song on an album told you about yourself. Dominic listened quietly, thinking about Suze.

Later, the dog came and curled at his feet.

'Come on now, I went and bought this especially for you so I want to see you eating it,' Dominic said as he picked up the two cream cakes off the table. 'That's more like it.' He smiled, watching the dog lap up the cake and, in one gulp, swallow it. He stroked Bill a few times and muttered some words. There was an awful smell in his flat these days. He knew he'd been letting himself go. But it was almost over now. And someone was coming. The old man had said so. He had an idea where this person would go. It was visible from his window. He rigged a small cam to the outside of his window ledge, facing the enclosure. Routed it so that it appeared as a self-contained square in the top right of his computer screen, overlaying the Work. He sighed, lit a cigarette. It was almost finished and yet why did he feel so apathetic towards it? He should have been thrilled, scared yes, but overjoyed too . . . instead he felt numb and he tried not to think about Suze or about what they'd said. How it was him who should have felt guilty for the girl's death and not her. He smoked weed and listened to Hüsker Dü until his brain stopped humming, and when he fell asleep that night it was Beatrice who kept him company until dawn.

II

Van Hijn walked through the rain which had picked up and was slung almost horizontally by a brewing north-easterly wind that had wrapped itself around the city.

He didn't want to do this.

Each step seemed to take for ever. He had a sudden urge for cheesecake and he stopped at a small patisserie and had one slice of chocolate and one slice of banana. He felt better immediately though he knew he'd suffer for it. He'd eaten too fast again and that telling first shot of pain would soon come, then the full heartburn and indigestion double-whammo.

He stood outside the piercing parlour and waited for his stomach to settle. He smoked two cigarettes. Checked his watch. The Englishman should be on his way home by now. That was good. If Jon Reed fucked up in some way, they would blame it on him. Take him off the case for good. Immediate suspension. He had a feeling that Jon was searching for something beyond his friend's death and it worried him. Another thing to get stressed about. He looked out at the canal. It calmed him, he loved the open view here, so different from the District. There was something in openness, in unrestricted vistas and vast spaces that made you feel as if your very self was expanded. He turned back, feeling better. The rain continued regardless. Umbrellas jostled the sky like spears in an Uccello painting. He took a deep breath and stepped inside.

'Good afternoon.' The blonde receptionist smiled.

Van Hijn smiled back. Maybe this wouldn't be as bad as he thought.

'Afternoon.' He flashed his badge. 'I'd like to talk to the piercer, please.'

'Concerning?' Her smile hadn't changed. She wore nurse's whites, was older than she'd first appeared. Her hair spilled like honey on white shoulders and Van Hijn noted how she held herself more like a work of art than a human being, delicately poised in the space she occupied with a certain measure that seemed to betray deep character. For a moment Van Hijn was speechless. He looked down at the table. Small printed leaflets and photocopied disclaimers. A half-eaten sandwich.

'Just routine questions. Could you get him, please?'

She nodded, a smile still lurking somewhere in her face. Van Hijn watched as she went into the room behind her. He felt for the photos in his pocket. Twenty Polaroids.

Images of scarring. Images of burns. Images of holes.

Jake's body. In little pieces.

Whatever his friend Jon might have thought, it was obvious to Van Hijn that most of the damage done to Jake's body was self-inflicted. He'd been a detective in Amsterdam long enough to recognize the markings. The city was a bright, shining light for these moths of the night, slamming themselves against the fire, trying to find that one perfect moment of stillness. He could feel their urgent desire to break free of things the world held dear. He knew it in himself, the need for separateness, the constant cigarettes, weed, needles and hooks of their own. We all gradually kill ourselves, he thought, we all, moment by moment, do things that make us less and we accept this, even cherish it. And yet we continue.

The woman came back through the door.

'The piercer?' he said, feeling slightly annoyed.

'Yes.' She sat down in front of him, a lithe, heart-quickening movement that quashed all his anxiety and annoyance with the flick of her heel. 'My receptionist told me that you wanted to ask me a few questions.' She smiled, watching the surprise on his face. 'I'm sorry, it's not your fault, there's not too many women working in this business. Don't worry, it's just a way to pass the time, I don't even take it personally any more.'

'I'm sorry, I shouldn't . . .'

'Forget it. Take a seat. I'm Annabelle, what did you want to know?'

He sat down. He wanted to sink into the chair. Let it gobble him up. How stupid. How fucking thoughtless. He couldn't believe it. He would have to try harder.

'A case I'm working on. The victim had numerous scars and markings that I think were self-inflicted or, at least, willingly inflicted.'

'Piercings?'

Van Hijn nodded. He reached for the photographs. The phone rang. She picked it up, began speaking.

He stared at the small parlour to his left. Tiled white. Sloping away. Spotless. A chair at its centre, a drain in the floor. What a strange way to make a living, he thought, then smiled, people probably said the same about him.

He flicked through the photos while she spoke on the phone. He wondered how Jon could not have known about Jake's self-mutilations. Their relationship intrigued him. Why would someone take in such a seriously scarred man? But if Jon hadn't known? Still, it was hard to fathom, especially with the old man dead with that book in his pocket. Perhaps it would have been better to ask Jon to stay, keep an eye on him.

'Sorry about that.' She'd put the phone down, was staring at him. 'I used to have a receptionist but then we got divorced. Have to do it all myself now.'

He didn't know what to say so he showed her the photos. She sat down and looked at them slowly, like an old woman seeing her grandchildren's holiday snaps, except the kids are so small that she has to squint, to make them take form out of the blur. She made little sounds – like appreciation? Van Hijn couldn't tell.

'Definitely.' She was nodding. 'This man's like a walking textbook of body modification. Very impressive.'

'Ever seen him before?' He handed her the face shot.

'I'd recognize those markings before I recognized a face, but no, never seen him. I definitely would have remembered.'

He felt a slight sinking, familiar as hell. 'Anything else you can tell me?'

She looked back at the photos. Took one out. Pointed. Her nails were painted a deep blood red. Van Hijn looked from them to the photo. 'This. This is from suspension.'

'Suspension?' It was a new world. One of many that existed congruent with our own, occasionally touching or leaking in. He looked at her and wondered how she'd got into this – the former husband, a lover, something else? Was he just being prejudiced again? He wasn't sure, wasn't sure at all if he'd wonder the same thing about a man.

'From flesh hooks. Big in Native American ceremonies. Big in modification circles too. The true test of a person, if you will.'

'So, not everybody does this?'

'No, not at all. Most people come for ordinary piercings. That's what I do. Nose. Lips. Ears. Belly. Some pop star's done it and there's a rush. That's how it goes. But that's just the surface of the culture. The bits that have filtered out. It's all fashion. Your friend in the photos was doing it for entirely different reasons.'

'Sexual?' Van Hijn thought about the way the female victims had been tortured. The time and care that had been taken in their mutilation. It was a good bet that the perpetrator had enjoyed himself and it made him wonder again about Jake's involvement. He remembered what he'd said to Jon: either Jake was a victim of the same killer as those girls or he was the killer himself.

'Sexual is only a small part. That's what almost everybody thinks but it's way deeper than that.'

'What kind of man would do this to himself?' Van Hijn asked.

'Women do it too, you know,' she said, sharply. 'You ask what kind of man, but in most non-western cultures they'd ask the opposite. In a lot of places it's the norm.'

'But this was someone who grew up in western Europe.'

She shrugged, as if conceding the point. 'I don't really know is the answer, all I'm saying is that it's perhaps not as unusual or unnatural as you think. What I do know is that this is many years' hard discipline and study.' She pulled out a photo from the stack. 'This man's body is like the Michelangelo of modificationists.'

'Or the Jackson Pollock,' he said, swallowing her earlier comment with a grin.

She smiled. A wide, open, unaffected sweetheart of a smile. 'Or the Jackson Pollock.' She pulled out another of the photos. Pointed to a small rippled bit of flesh from Jake's chest. It looked like satellite imagery of a mountain range. 'See those marks?'

Van Hijn nodded.

'Play piercing. The skin gets like that. Like old leather.'

'Play piercing?'

'Just making holes. The holes seal up and they do it again. They're not interested in the piercings, just the act of piercing. Not many practitioners who'll do that. I won't. Too destructive. People want to do it, they can do it themselves as far as I'm concerned. There's no skill in play piercing.'

'So, it's a whole different level.'

She nodded. 'A whole different level.'

'You don't by any chance know of anyone in the city who would do this?'

'Most likely the man did it to himself. Otherwise try Rijn's in the Jordaan or Quirk's by the Old Church.'

'The Old Church?' Van Hijn could feel his heart beat at his ribs. Pressure in his ears.

'His place doesn't have a name but it's below the Skull & Roses tattoo parlour. You know where that is?'

Van Hijn nodded. 'I didn't even know there was a piercing parlour below there.'

'One of many things you don't know, I'm sure.'

He was wondering how to answer her when the phone rang again. Van Hijn reached for it. 'Hello, Bone Palace Piercings, can I help you? Mmmm? I'll put you through to the piercer, just hold for a second, please.'

He passed her the phone. She was smiling. She mimed 'Thank you', nodded once and took the mouthpiece. 'Good afternoon,' she said as Van Hijn turned and moved towards the window. He pulled back the screen a touch. The man was still there, waiting on the other side of the street. He'd been following the detective all day. Van Hijn thought about taking a back door but there was no point. Better to find out who it was. He turned, waved to Annabelle and walked out into the rain.

Jon lit a cigarette, picked up the guide book and forced himself to read the dry descriptions of architectural interest. It was no good, the words didn't mean anything. Didn't connect. He looked at the photos of gabled façades and saw the scars on Jake's cheeks. The receipts for human cargo so neatly written out. The men staring into the camera that will be their last witness on earth. The unavoidable persistence of the past.

He put the book down. Rubbed his eyes and checked his watch. The plane was taking off about now. The thought made him smile. He stared out of his window, the small sliver of canal that the view afforded, the milling, spilling rush of people in the street below. He needed to get out. A walk. The room was closing in.

The detective had mentioned where Jake's body had been discovered. Jon had found the place on the map. The only spot of green in the whole area. Had to be that. Right by the Old Church, smack in the heart of the red-light district.

Outside it had stopped raining and the dark sky had cleared to let a smattering of stars through: tiny, bright points that seemed extremely flimsy and dull as he made his way down Warmoesstraat. He passed two bicycles chained together so closely that he felt he was intruding on some intimate scene. The streets were gradually filling up, teenagers, backpacked and stoned, strolled around, cops, dealers, tourists lost or scared. It amazed him how crowded the city could become, how the small streets managed to hold everyone.

He'd been chewing painkillers all day and was starting to become immune to their effects. It was as if a sharp knife was being ground into his ankle every time he put too much weight on it. He used his umbrella as a crutch, preferring to get wet than risk the embarrassment of falling over. The streets were still soaked and the pavements were pockmarked with small craters and water traps.

Soon his mood was distracted by the bright flickering neon and bustling streets of the red-light district. He stopped in a coffee shop – the first one he came to that wasn't shaking with dance music – found a seat, a small table by the window, watching everyone go by. He bought some grass and rolled a joint. Tourists walking the streets stared at him and he realized how he'd become a tourist attraction, safely pinned behind the glass front of the shop, the strange feeling of doing these things out in the open. He smoked the joint and listened to the second side of the first Springsteen album on the house system. To his left was a message-board. Handwritten pieces of paper pleading for jobs, accommodation, money, hung like discarded dreams. One of the pieces had a photo on it. A young man, goateed, with long hair and lost eyes. Jon squinted to read the text. 'Please come home, Carl,' it said and the shakiness of the handwriting, the slop and slack of the letters seemed to make it all the more poignant. 'Les has had a breakdown, Denise loves you. Daddy forgives. Please come back to us. We love you.'

There was something there, in the language of public facsimile, the syntax of cliché and nuclear family, that almost undid him. He turned away. What had happened to him that he could be so easily moved by such things? He stared back out of the window. By the second joint, the whole place seemed more comfortable, the pain had gradually subsided to a gentle throb and he felt himself sinking into the barstool.

He still had no idea as to why Jake had come back to Amsterdam or what had made him leave the shelter of a warm flat. Had it really been because of his intrusion that night? Jake was gone the next morning and it had been the first thing Jon thought of. Or was that just the catalyst? Underneath Jake's polite manner, Jon had felt the rippling of something much deeper and he wondered whether Jake had come back here to purge that shadow self, or to indulge it.

Sitting there, he began to feel paranoid, sensing that it was not just coincidence that everyone in the place was of North African extraction but him. Young men played pool and smoked reefers, their faces sharp as daggers, others huddled around tables, shrouded in serious discussion, their arms agitatedly flapping about. He realized that it was one of the few times in his life when he really felt Jewish, here among people who probably would have stuck a knife in his heart had they known. And he thought, isn't it funny how being alone in a strange city can make you detach from yourself, make you see yourself in a way you never can when you're with a group of people, as if watching from across the room, another vantage point, the obvious stranger.

He got up, not knowing whether they were staring at him because they'd guessed or just because he looked scared. He resented the fact that something so random as his faith could leave him dead in a bar-room toilet, a knife in the heart, but nevertheless he acceded to it and left, feeling their cold eyes penetrating him even when he'd turned the corner and was back in the mêlée of tourists and whoremongers.

He walked through the narrow, winding streets, aware of the way his limp drew the same kind of looks that having 'child molester' tattooed on his forehead would have. Marking him out as a freak. His money belt chafed at his stomach, so full and bulging. He'd debated whether to leave everything in the room. But he didn't trust that. Better to carry everything with you, feel it scratch up against your belly, know it's there.

He tried to make sense of the map but it was like a picture drawn by someone on a very bad acid trip, all squiggles and concentric circles that, on closer inspection, were irregular as hell, an upside down fingerprint, and yet he felt a growing certainty that he had to see the last place that Jake had lain.

Men sidled up to him whispering 'Coka, Ecstasee' in strange and disturbing accents, sex-show barkers called out, promising a night unlike any other, hustling here and there, surrounding him with noise and light, dream and desire. The steady flow of people shunting down the streets. The bright lights spelling strange, incomprehensible, possibly compounded words and those that just said SEX and GIRLS and made everything clear.

He hadn't been to Amsterdam since he was fifteen. A two-week holiday with his parents that had felt like a prison sentence. He couldn't remember much about it apart from the arguments his parents had all the time. It was the summer before his mother's death, when the altercations between the two of them were fierce and frequent and no longer kept hidden from 'the child'.

He remembered the visit to the Anne Frank house, his mother's half-hearted attempts to teach him something about his culture and history. His father's scowls and impatient foot tapping. It meant nothing to him then and even now, like for many others, Anne Frank existed in his mind only as an easy-to-swallow metonym for the Holocaust. A beacon of light that illuminated all the horror.

Now, at the age of thirty-five, he felt like a kid on his first visit to Disneyland. The magic fucking kingdom. The garden of earthly delights. The place of dead roads, where leaving is no longer an option and all dreams are accounted for and fulfilled for the smallest of prices. Sex and drugs on the surface and everything that congregates around them, the bottom-feeders and vampires that buy and sell lives as if they were prison cigarettes.

He walked around stunned, drawn by the procession of delights as he turned through the winding streets of the District, buzzing on weed and excitement. The closeness of the streets held him, their illogical design intrigued him, leading him further into its heart then looping around, always back to the same place.

He stopped in front of a sex shop, drawn by the bouquet of dildoes in the window, strange brutal things of all shapes, colours and permutations, that seemed more like instruments of torture than any kind of pleasure devices that he could imagine. Not so unusual for Jon who, while enjoying girls and fumbled moments as much as anyone, never really found that sex was the great big thing that mitigated all the horrors of life as everyone else seemed to think. Not to say he didn't enjoy it, he almost always did, it was just that it was nothing special, no fireworks, no moving earth, none of the above.

It was eleven o'clock and the streets of the District were packed and pulverized by strollers, drug dealers, husbands holding on tightly to their wives, sneaking surreptitious glances at the girls preening and pouting behind their windows, businessmen and drinking buddies on a lost week-end and cops walking their beat. Jon let himself flow with the mass of people, unaware of where he was going and not caring too much either, happy to be entertained for the time being by the sights and smells, the movable feast of flesh and neon that decorated the streets. There was a tightness to the roads in Amsterdam that was entirely lacking in

London, a sense of clustered communality that he found strangely comforting.

He walked along a narrow alley, only about three-foot wide, with rows of windows on either side. He found himself sneaking glances, too embarrassed to catch the eyes of the women, avoiding the staccato beat of fingernails tapping on glass that tried to entice him. People walked slowly, surveying the girls, checking out their figures and wondering whether to lay their Euros down. Comparison shopping. Jon watched it all, thinking about Jake, wondering if the old man had spent his time walking these streets too.

He went to the nearest bar and ordered a coffee. He took out his last few Euros, paid. Then went into the toilet so he could take more out of his money belt.

It was gone.

All gone.

He checked and rechecked, undid his shirt, looked down his trousers, tried pockets and crevices, all the while the inevitability of it zooming up inside him. He cursed in the empty toilet. He wanted to scream. Hit something. How the fuck . . . ? He gathered himself, walked back into the bar, trying to keep a straight face, not sure if they'd heard him cursing in there.

Passport. Credit cards. Cash.

All gone.

He sat and sipped his coffee and felt as though the ground had swallowed him up. The coffee tasted like mud. He couldn't breathe. It had suddenly got so hot. He had perhaps 50 Euros left, that was all.

He tried to tell himself that it was all replaceable. A matter of a quick phone call. But that didn't make him feel any better.

'Hi there.' A young man, pony-tailed, Deep Purple T-shirt,

sat next to him. 'Thought you looked like you wanted some company.'

Jon stared at him. Had he seen him before? 'Fuck off. Leave me alone,' he said.

The man said something in Dutch, got up and walked back into the darkness of the bar.

Jon felt bad about it. But he didn't want company. Not now. He lit a cigarette and tried to think about something else as the house stereo blasted out the closing gasps of *Dark Side of the Moon* and moved seamlessly into the first Beatles album. The music disgusted him. He left.

His head felt loose, clouded by smoke, failure and loneliness, his ankle was playing up again and he knew that he looked an open invitation to violence. So he tried to appear straight, to open his eyes wide and look as if he meant business. He didn't know if it was working but at least it was something else to think about.

'You want coke? Coka? Ecstasee?' A gnarled old man, the shade of weak coffee, approached him, 'Coka, my man?'

'No.' He tried brushing the dealer off but found he couldn't muster up the right level of confidence to do it.

'I can get you a girl too. Blonde. Very nice. Big.' His hands traced the shape of a pair of breasts.

'Why would I want a girl off you?' Jon replied tersely. 'I can get my pick round the corner.'

'Yes, that is very true, sir, but they only give you fifteen minutes, twenty if you're lucky. This girl you can have for good.'

'No.' Firmer this time. Hearing the adenoidal weakness in his voice, wishing he had a stronger tone, something brusque and boardroom businesslike. He took out his map. 'That's not what I want. I want to find this,' he said, pointing to the small red dot that he'd marked on the paper.

The dealer flicked his lighter and viewed the map in its quivering glare. 'Two lefts, then right.'

'Thank you,' Jon replied, taking the map and folding it into his pocket.

'You sure you don't want a girl?'

He found the park easily enough, though it was stretching the definition of a park to call this tiny enclosure of hedges and grass that. It lay between a canal and the Old Church. Apartment buildings looked down upon it, their lights like winking eyes. There were fewer people here and those who passed had an urgency to their manner not seen elsewhere. A few window-girls beckoned him but he ignored them. He walked towards the green space. He couldn't think why it was there. Like an island breaking up the asphalt. It was too small to be enjoyed as a park and too big to be just some place for dogs to do their business.

Jon walked up to the entrance, a gap cut between the hedges. Inside it was dark and cool like a walled-off room or a city within a city. There was nothing to show that a man had died there. No police tape, no sign. Death lasts a few minutes and then things go on. Jon tried to imagine Jake lying here, dead or still dying, knowing that this patch of sky would be the last he'd see. He took a deep breath, felt the past few days stick in his lungs.

That's when he heard it. Something in the bushes.

A faint rustling. Breathing?

He looked around, saw nothing but arboreal shapes.

Then another sound.

And he saw him.

The man just stood there, off to the side, enmeshed in the foliage, looking at him.

Jon stopped breathing. He lit a cigarette, his hand shaking, the lighter failing, and in the spark of light he saw the man again, standing behind the main ring of hedges, watching him.

'Who are you?' Jon shouted. 'What the fuck do you want?' His voice faded into the wind. The shape didn't move. It didn't say anything. Jon walked towards it. There was a flash of light, sudden and terrible, and then he couldn't see. He pushed his arms in front of him, clawing the rough edges of the hedgerow. Panic and blindness consumed him. A sudden terror.

Then light began leaking back into his eyes, blurred and watery. He heard the man walk away. He tried to follow but stumbled straight into the hedge, cursing himself. His heart could be heard all over Amsterdam.

He'd walked back into the main canal ring, got lost trying to find the hotel, found himself instead going in circles, the map absolutely no use. He saw the dealer who had directed him to the park. The man smiled, exposing a black hole and one crooked tooth. Jon walked faster. His ankle screamed. The weed was wearing off and it throbbed like a racing heartbeat.

He stepped into the Sex Palace, a large department store of sex and fun. There was a peep-show, video booths, private booths, self-charging cards from a machine, a pornucopia of illicit pleasures. He changed his last note at the desk and stepped into one of the many video booths, thinking that at least this way he could drop out of sight a while. Gather himself.

As soon as he closed the door the light came on, like in an aeroplane lavatory, and he sat down in the plastic armchair that faced the screen. In front of him were numerous buttons, levers and joysticks – it looked like the flight capsule of the space shuttle – and it took him a good few minutes to find the slot for the coins. The screen flickered on and Jon was greeted with one of the most disturbing, and in his state, frankly horrifying things that he'd seen in his life up to then.

There was a blonde woman and a horse. All the things one heard about as a kid but never really imagined were true, urban legends for frustrated fourteen-year-olds, whispered in school playgrounds and assembly halls across the country. He tried the button pad and joystick on the console, finding that the buttons switched through the channels while the stick allowed you to fast forward or rewind to pertinent scenes. It seemed he had struck a band of animal channels as he flicked through horses, dogs, cats, hamsters and scorpions, all in the throes of copulation with a selection of pretty women.

'You got any normal sex channels in there?' he asked the guy at the change counter, a pimple-faced youth reading Balzac.

'There are over a thousand channels, mister, I'm sure you'll eventually find something you like.' He looked up from his book, 'Just keep flicking, I can tell you like to watch.'

Jon didn't feel like going outside. Not yet. The choice was more animal favourites or the peep-show. He chose the peep-show. Actually, a hexagonal structure of booths placed around a small revolving stage where a girl would strip, dance and press her parts against the viewing screen while the timer in the booth counted down the money. He watched as she did some kind of intermediate callisthenics on the stage, then moved up towards the occupied booths and pressed the soft flesh of her labia right up to his screen, leaving a smeared residue of sex on the glass. He could see the ghostly shapes of other men, across the stage, hunched, moving, twitching, staring. Inside, the booth was pitch black and weirdly comforting as if the closeness of the place precluded any wayward thoughts, anything but the viewing itself. He stood there watching for about five minutes, the strange theatricality of it taking his mind off more serious matters.

When his money ran out, he fished in his pocket for some more change which he then managed to drop on to the floor in the process of negotiating the coin slot. As he bent down to pick it up, he felt the cold, sticky substance that coated the floor and squeezed itself between his fingers and he knew immediately what it was. He left the booth, money still on the floor, swimming in that saline sea, and headed out of there feeling dirty and disgusted with himself.

He walked back to the hotel, thinking about the incident in the park, the lost wallet and passport. Totally freaked. Knowing the weed wasn't helping. Jumping at shadows, at anyone who strayed too closely into his path.

Had he stumbled on some sex deviant? Something else? He was pretty sure that what blinded him had been a camera flash. That someone had taken his photo. He didn't know what that meant. He didn't want to guess. The only thing he knew was that he couldn't go home yet. That there was something here, in the streets and canals, the faces of the people, the buildings and the flash of the camera. Something that had found Jake too. Something that would not let him go.

13

Van Hijn spent the afternoon going around the relics of Amsterdam's Jewry. He had a photo of Jake and an uneasy sense of the past coming to assail him as he trudged through the rain from the Anne Frank Huis to the Hollandse Schouwburg to the Joods Historisch. He had shown the photo, asked the right questions but no one seemed to remember anything. The sight of a pretty blonde at the Hollandse made him feel a bit better and he went for lunch at a small restaurant by the Plantage Parklaan.

At the Joods Historisch he was told to return later by an American girl. She told him the old man who'd know would be back then. He thanked her, wishing he was fifteen years younger, and wandered around the museum, happy to get away from the rain for a while.

As he stared at the photos and letters, pinned behind glass like rare butterflies, he felt an overwhelming sense of despair and dread and he had to turn away so as not to embarrass himself in front of the tourists. He was crying, his chest wrenched by the onrushing past. As he looked at the faces of the men and women boarding the trains, he wondered whether his father had sent them this way. Was he even in one of these pictures, wearing Nazi uniform?

He hadn't thought about it all for so long, had left it there, somewhere in his memory, clouded over by days and years that passed, by alcohol and weed, music and films. It had stolen his youth. The ages between twenty-five and forty when the world is yours, when everything seems possible and imminent. His father had robbed him of that, after his death, and he now felt only a sort of detached bitterness towards the man who had always cuddled him before bedtime.

That was the hardest thing. His father had always been so gentle, so kind to him – a measured, respected man who would sometimes, out of the blue, surprise Ronald with a present or the news that they were going off on holiday that very evening. How can he have been that person and at the same time the one who sent these people to their graves? And why had he made himself into the opposite, into a war hero when he could easily have slipped back into anonymity?

Van Hijn knew that these questions had no answers. He had spent years asking them, over and over again, all to no avail. It was as if the article had stolen his father from him, leaving him bitter and frustrated, cheated of the completion that he needed to continue his life. He had gone on the best he could but there was always a hole in his past, a disjuncture that continually threatened to rip the present apart. Only by forgetting, by persuading himself that he didn't care, had he been able to carry on. And now it was all coming back to him, because of that damn tramp and it probably didn't even have any bearing on the actual case, the man was murdered plain and simple. Part of the snuff ring or an actor used once and easily disposed of.

He was dying for a cigarette, dying to get out of this enclosed space that pressed itself around him. But that old question came back, that chestnut that had haunted him like a koan throughout his thirties: why had his father done it?

Had he done it because he was a weak man, a coward who realized that collaboration was the only safeguard? Or was he just ruthless? Maybe he didn't care about the Jews, maybe he saw in it only a way to attain power, to climb to the top of the pole? Van Hijn was tormented between the two, between the idea of his father as a gutless collaborator and the idea of him as a machiavellian schemer. Which was worse ethically? To do something out of fear and cowardice or to do it out of greed and ambition?

He saw the old man was back. Though 'old man' was an incredible understatement. Van Hijn was sure he'd never seen anyone that ancient. The man looked far more of a relic than most of the objects on display.

Van Hijn showed him his badge.

'I was wondering what you were looking for,' the man said.

'You were watching me?'

'I was. Eating my lunch and watching people go round. You were looking for something, I think, not a tourist.'

Van Hijn felt slightly taken aback. He'd assumed a doddering fool when he'd seen him. Didn't expect to have the tables turned on him.

'You're surely too old to be sitting here doing that,' he said.

The man laughed, a slow descending release. 'Too old? What, you think it's better I sit at home and stare at the wallpaper?'

'Forget it,' Van Hijn replied, taking out the photo of Jake. He placed it on the table in front of the man. Moshe took the photo gently in his hands. The detective watched him smooth thin, brittle fingers over its surface.

'I read about it in the newspaper. Very sad.' He put the photo back down as if holding it for too long was somehow wrong.

'So you knew him?' Van Hijn suddenly felt a surge of adrenalin. That old familiar feeling.

Moshe nodded. 'I don't know how well you could say I

knew him but, yes, he used to come here a lot. Often we talked.'

Van Hijn moved closer, sat down on the chair by the man. 'What about?'

Moshe shrugged. 'What do old men talk about? Our pains, the things we missed, fear. What else is there?'

'What was he doing here?'

'Looking for his family, at first. Then he used to come and help out.'

'Help out?'

'In the archives. We have many manuscripts, unlabelled texts, unknown footage – we don't have the resources to hire anyone to catalogue it. Jakob helped with that. He used to come almost every day. We'd talk for a bit, smoke a cigarette or two, drink coffee and then he'd go down to the basement and watch all those films and videos. Sorted through documents we had.'

'Films? What was he up to?' Van Hijn moved closer to the old man.

'Up to? Why do you think he was up to something? I think it is obvious why he would want to do that, no?'

Van Hijn nodded though it was not all that obvious to him.

'You know, when he first started coming here, I asked myself the same question. He didn't look Jewish. Came every day and just wandered round staring at the displays. At first I thought he was one of those people.'

'What people?'

The old man looked at him, a sad and elegant face, Van Hijn thought, unscathed by age or life. 'You know there's nothing we can do. We set up the exhibition to remind people, to leave a memory of those that are gone. But we cannot control who comes and sees it. Many come from the other side. They too appreciate the way we've handled things – but you can see it in their eyes. Pride.

'They see the exhibition, the constantly running films of the transportations from Westerbork, the dark rust-smeared trains that clawed their way across Europe to Auschwitz. They read the statistics, the lists of the dead and they feel a warm glow inside. It is like church for them. They watch with pride and awe as handsomely dressed officers corral the streaming mass of people into the cattlecars, appreciating the logistical genius of the whole thing, the scale and purpose of it. They see the museum as a shrine to a better time. For them these are the artefacts of their glory. You can see it in their eyes. And what can we do? We can't stop them. Can't only allow Jews in here.'

'And Jake?' Van Hijn didn't like the direction in which the conversation was heading.

'At first I thought he was one of these people – to my shame.'

'And you have no idea why anyone would want to kill him?' It was the old stock question and it felt tired and useless as he said it.

Moshe shook his head. 'Not more than anyone else,' he said. 'Do you mind if I keep the photo?'

Van Hijn saw the man's left hand, wiry like a bird's foot, gently resting on the photograph. 'Of course,' he replied.

Moshe smiled, took the photo and placed it in the breast pocket of his shirt.

'You know, someone was asking about him just yesterday.'

Van Hijn had got up, ready to leave. He snapped back, sat down. 'Tell me.'

'British. Quite young, very polite. Asked about him. I didn't say anything of course. You can never tell who you're talking to.'

Jon.

Van Hijn felt a smudge of irritation. So, he hadn't listened. Had gone ahead and tried to investigate. They read three detective novels and think they can do better themselves. And yet, he also felt a curious appreciation. He hadn't thought Jon would go against him, had believed him too weak, too stuck in his own problems. This new information made him smile, not quite sure exactly why, but smile none the less.

'One has to be careful. Especially these days,' Moshe continued. He stared up at Van Hijn. A pause. 'I assume you're aware of the films currently up for auction? That you're investigating this?'

Van Hijn shook his head. He had no idea what the man was talking about.

'Maybe it is something that would be worth your while checking out?'

'What films?' He got closer to the old man. Tried to control his breathing.

'These things, you know, there's always rumours they exist. No one believes them and yet they do at some other level. Well, it seems this time they're true. Someone's put up for sale on the Internet 49 reels of concentration camp footage; 8 mm.'

'Real?' It felt as if the chair couldn't contain him.

'Apparently so, though my knowledge is limited.'

Van Hijn stared at the old man. It all came rushing in. Nine months of fruitless leads coalesced around this point. Finally he had more than a feeling, more than a hunch. The snuff films were out there and he wondered, had he set this in motion? It was almost too symmetrical. He realized that until this moment he hadn't really believed it himself, the theory about snuff, had only accepted that it explained more than a serial killer. But now he felt the cold, dryness in his mouth, the uncontrollable heartbeat. He leaned forward.

'Okay, okay. You want to follow this up. Go here.' Moshe took out a small pencil and wrote an address on the back of a museum welcome card. 'Go and see these people. They know more about this than me. It is what they do.'

Van Hijn took the card, looked at the address, South Amsterdam, placed it in his pocket. 'You've been very helpful, thank you.'

'No need to thank me. You find these films, make sure they don't get into the wrong hands, it'll be me thanking you.'

He got home just before the rain started again. His head buzzing with the things that the old man had told him. He'd had a sudden attack of nerves on the way out, wondering whether Moshe had recognized him – his photo had appeared in countless newspaper articles after the *Der Stern* piece. It wasn't just paranoia and he hated feeling guilty for something which he hadn't done or even had knowledge of. He decided not to think about it. To think about Jon instead and what he really knew about Jake. Whether he'd told him the whole truth. What was he doing here and had he actually gone back on his flight?

Van Hijn could now see that there were layers and layers to this case, stretching back to the first murder, layers whose existence he'd only just been afforded a glimpse of and yet which had possibly defined the shape of events so thoroughly as to have wiped out their own traces.

He was dying for a joint. Something that would stop the tangle of thoughts. He nearly went for it but then recalled the toffee cheesecake that he'd bought that morning; sweet sticky toffee, dark, almost loamy chocolate, crispy pecans and thick, sugary cream. That would be better, he decided, though over the last few weeks he'd begun to feel his waist pushing up against his trousers and he knew that substituting cheesecake had its own pitfalls.

And then he remembered the box set.

He'd been too tired to open it yesterday. Had forgotten about it during the course of the day. Now he felt a giddying sense of excitement as he picked up the heavy grey Amazon box and ripped open the packaging to reveal the Harry Smith *Anthology of American Folk Music* box set.

For the last ten years Van Hijn had developed a growing obsession with early American folk and country music, dark, scratchy voices from the twenties and thirties. Those massive box sets produced by the Bear Family, chunks of history, bound and annotated, complete and chronological, a riposte to the history he himself knew, the fragmented nonsensical blur of the past.

There was something about the music of that period that seduced him, something about the quality of the recordings. The crackles and surface noise like history snaps, situating it in a time before magnetic tape. It was music that sounded as if it came from a totally different world, saturated with tales of murder, adultery, crime and soul-selling. Often sung by a lone voice over minimal accompaniment, it embraced a certain darkness and narrative sensibility that made it quite unlike anything else. It was music that scared him, left him shivering sometimes. Music that had to be played in the dark. Alone.

There was something about the dip of oblivion when the needle drops down, Dock Boggs' haunted voice pleading, *Oh Death, Please spare me for another year* or the impossibly high, lonesome sound of Roscoe Holcomb singing 'Omie Wise.'

He had in fact stopped listening to most other forms of

music, finding them all lacking the depth and substance that he found in early American folk music. These CDs were like spaceships jetting him off to other worlds, distant and different from his, worlds of stark brutality and compromised choices; whalers, coalminers, bank robbers, murderers, union men, adulterers and yet, sometimes it seemed as if this tradition and these songs were nothing but a blueprint for his day-to-day work, for the moral composure of the early twenty-first century.

He lay back on the sofa, drink in hand and listened to the first CD. Every now and then he would exclaim 'Fuck!' or 'Yeah!', if there was a particularly choice turn of phrase or vocal quirk that caught his heart. Does this make up for all the shit I go through? Does this make it all worthwhile, even the things I saw today, he asked himself, and pouring another whiskey, just as Mississippi John Hurt launched into 'Frankie', he thought, yes it does. Yes it does.

Because it has to.

14

The room was strangling him. Boxing and battering him. But it didn't move. He knew that. It only felt as if it was crushing the space slowly, surely, contracting and compacting until it would reach his body. The view was no good. It was too small and too dark. The rain covered up the sky. The room became every room he'd ever inhabited. Each one getting smaller, darker. A life lived in small rooms. A life barely lived.

Rooms of rage and rooms of gloom, where the ceilings hung down like an overattentive mother, rooms filled with doom and headaches and the fear of going out, of leaving your room, rooms full of sleep and bad memories and the solitary sound of your heart exploding in the emptiness.

He was waiting for his credit card. The replacement. They'd assured him it would be there in the morning. It wasn't. So he sat and waited, and he understood that this was a test, the last attempt of gravity to pull him back to London, which itself sometimes resembled a small room with many dark corners. But if this was a test, he was determined to pass it, to fight the lustrous pull of an easy life, a quiet life. And it somehow seemed easier, here in this city, with its canals and constant rain, its strange layout and soft feel, easier to fight all that, to step away from it.

The card arrived just after lunch, though of course he hadn't had anything to eat having waited all morning and as soon as he'd signed the papers he was back out on the street, drifting unavoidably west. He wondered about his passport, most probably already sold – what shadowy twin had now been born, carrying his name and vital statistics, had they passed each other in the street or would they cross sometime in the future, one mistaken for the other?

The sun hit him as he entered Nieuwmarkt. He was still amazed by the explosion of space and he began to understand how the city trembled to a rhythmic dialectic of concealment and revelation, how every dark, imposing street eventually funnelled out into big empty squares from which the only exit was to crouch back into another small street, darkened by tall buildings, until that too ended in another grey, concrete square, another opening.

He took a different route this time and found himself in Wertheim Park, walking past the rich foliage and shrubbery of the gardens, and he looked at the great greenhouses, the reflected sun, the silky canal water and he felt good. Smiling. Not knowing why, not questioning it, just, damn it, smiling, that was all.

He wanted to go back to the museum and yet felt a momentary trepidation. What was he scared of? The past? Surely there was nothing there that could harm him any more, he thought, not even his father could do that now. So what else?

He wanted to question the old man again. He was certain that he knew something. Jake had been more than a ghost. He'd left his mark on that page, had walked through those rooms. Jon cursed himself. He'd been too meek the first time, taken no for an answer too easily. Absolutely typical his father would say, but his father was just a dream now, no need to listen to him. No, this time he would assert himself. This time he wouldn't leave without finding something out.

He stood across the road from the museum, watching a party of schoolchildren lining up, bored, chewing gum, gabbing and swaying, waiting for the day to be over. He took a joint out of his pocket. That would make it easier, he knew, easier to not be so hesitant and accepting. He watched the schoolkids clumsily entering the museum, fourteen-, fifteen-year-olds. What did they take away from this, he wondered, smoking the joint, feeling things slot into their proper places. He crushed the butt under his shoe and was about to cross the road when he saw Van Hijn coming out of the museum.

A scowl on the detective's face, that long droopy face, emerging from the front entrance, black raincoat swirling around his heels, and Jon slipped back into the doorway of a house, hoping the detective hadn't seen him.

Jon stepped out, about to cross the road when he saw the other man. Emerging from behind the museum, following Van Hijn. A tall man who moved too fast for Jon to notice his features. The man looked behind him, making sure perhaps, then set off after the detective. Jon watched and waited until both of them, pursuer and pursued, were gone.

'How are you today, Suze?' Moshe took her bag and smiled.

'Good, you?' She didn't want to tell him how she really felt and she knew, deep down, that talking about things only made them worse, brought inchoate feelings into the world, made them concrete and real and far more terrifying than if left unspoken.

'Great for my age!' he said and they both laughed, uneasily, drawing surprised looks from the few people who'd got there early.

In the small back room she carefully leafed through some of the gouaches, trying to imagine what it had been like for Charlotte, exiled in the South of France, remembering her life on to paper. She found it awe-inspiring that Charlotte could have created these thousand or so paintings from memory, there was such a wealth of detail and setting, each painting quite often being a compression of several story lines running across the page like those early Mannerist paintings she'd so admired in her first-year studies at Berkeley. The paintings were so populous, alive and electric and yet there was also an economy to Charlotte's work, an uncluttered sense of space and peace that was perhaps only the result of her knowing that time was running out.

Suze was beginning to see in Charlotte's art a way of working through her ideas. For such a long time she'd thought she'd failed. She was so scared of that. But Charlotte was not going to let herself be the straw-woman Suze had set up to expound her own ideas about political representation, the need for brutal images, for the artist to comment directly on his or her times – no, Charlotte evaded that with the skill and subtlety of her work. That had been a fairy-tale, Suze now recognized, a childish assumption on her part, reductive as hell, which had blinded her to the most important aspects of Charlotte's work: the light streaming in through the windows, the stunning Côte d'Azur colours and small exchanges that people managed between themselves, the shared moments of peace and hope – after all it was those things that had initially spoken to her, drawn her into Charlotte's world – unaware still of the hideous fate that awaited her.

She'd almost given up on finding the lost sections. She'd spent too many days going through old documentation looking for clues, a mention here, an allusion there. And she had found the clues; they were always there to find. In a way she'd felt like a detective, searching for the missing section through the traces left, and perhaps that had been the seduction itself, not the actual lost paintings but the foraging for them, the unravelling of the past, the accumulation of data. She'd let herself get sucked in, distracting her from the real work at hand, from coming to terms with what was there rather than trying to understand it through what was missing.

The old man wasn't there. A sign said please deposit the entrance fee in the box. He walked around but there seemed to be no one in charge, no one to show the photo to, only bored security guards who didn't look Jewish. He felt a punch of disappointment, a low swinging feeling like finding out you hadn't passed the exam you were so sure you had.

So he walked up to the small enclosure. Looked at the self-portrait of the artist and thought, I could have fallen in love with her so easily. He stared transfixed by the painting and then, walking around, by the others, slowly being introduced to Charlotte's circle of characters, picking up her rhythms, the dense nature of the work, littered with allusions to things he only remotely knew, foreign tales and dramatizations that added to the mystique that he found so pleasing.

He came back to the self-portrait and stared. Her lips were so beautiful, her mouth so elegant, so intelligent. He moved closer to the painting, noticed the smudged fingerprints and it suddenly made it all so immediate, intimate, these left-over signs that now were all that was left. He wanted to touch the paper there, press his thumb against Charlotte's. Feel the actual grain of the paper and paint.

Her eyes were staring at him. Whichever way he looked at the painting, they seemed to follow him around, a proud and resigned sadness drooping the right eye ever so slightly, a portrait of indecision, worry, fret and anxiety. He moved closer, wanting to see the swirl of her lips, the full bottom lip sensuous and sexy, and he got closer, wanting to fall into the painting, to drown in her lips, her nose, moving nearer, seeing small details otherwise unobserved, edging forward, was that a mistake or had she intentionally left that part . . . closer still, the eyes drawing him in, yes sadness, sadness and pride mixed together and those fine eyebrows so delicate he could almost count the individual hairs, and if he could just get a bit closer . . .

The sound of the alarm ripped him out of his reverie.

A shrill, piercing repeating tone that bounced around the high walls of the synagogue, getting louder, the space between pulses narrowing, loud and petulant, screaming, screaming, screaming and the men coming towards him, the security guards.

He didn't move. Didn't turn or run though he knew they were coming for him. That he'd got too close. Tripped the alarm.

He tried to smile but they grabbed his arms and though he protested, said it was an accident, they pulled him through the museum, in front of all the schoolkids, awake and excited now, the trip suddenly better than they had expected, all gawping at him being carried away.

She'd been watching him staring at the Salomon paintings. He stared so intently that she couldn't help but watch him. She traced his reactions, the way he smiled. He looked like a man falling away. And then she'd turned, walked towards the entrance, but Moshe was at lunch, she'd forgotten, and returning, acceding to the darkness of the small room, the limits of the page, she'd heard the alarm buzz through the museum, watched as everyone woke out of their staring slumbers, looked around, tried to isolate, see where the trouble was.

And then she saw him, being led away by the two guards, looking dishevelled, scared and lost and she knew that she had to do something.

'What happened?' She stopped in front of the guards. They knew her. Smiled at her in the mornings and wished her well at night.

'Nothing to concern yourself with,' the taller man said, his hand gripping Jon's arm, holding him like you would a toddler who has a fondness for straying. 'Just the usual.'

She looked at the man. His eyes refused to meet hers and she understood his embarrassment, the public spectacle that was being enacted here.

'What are you going to do?' she asked.

'Take him outside. Tell him not to come back.'

'Let me do it.' Though not quite sure of her motives, she felt better for saying it, taking the man's arm, feeling the guard's grip loosen.

'You sure?'

She nodded. 'Don't worry,' she replied and looked at Jon, his face lifting, his eyes meeting hers. She smiled and saw him smile back.

'You okay?' she asked as the security guards peeled away and returned to their posts.

Jon stared at her. Surprised that she was an American; her Dutch had deceived him. He nodded. 'Are you going to chuck me out too?' he asked.

Suze laughed. 'No. I thought maybe you needed a coffee, some cake, sugar, you look a little woozy.'

Jon smiled. 'That would be great.'

She offered her hand. 'I'm Suze.' Was she blushing? He couldn't tell under the artificial light. 'That's with an E not a Y, my dad was a big Dylan fan.'

She spoke so fast that he didn't know what she was talking about but he smiled back, introduced himself.

'I saw you looking at the paintings,' she said.

'That's what got me in trouble. I wanted to sink into them.'

'I know,' she said. 'There's a gravity there, most people don't see.'

'I think so,' he answered, his heartbeat pounding like a drum track.

'I'm doing a thesis on her.' She pointed at the self-portrait behind them, nervous, wishing she hadn't said that, was she trying to impress him?

'That sounds fascinating.' He bit down on his lip. Had he just said that? Christ, he thought.

They sat in the museum coffee shop. Empty apart from a cleaner hunched over a mop, another woman organizing food behind the counter. The place smelled of coffee and bleach. He sat at a table and waited as Suze went up to the counter.

'I'm sorry for what happened,' he said as she came back, balancing a tray, putting it down.

'Don't worry about it. The alarms get tripped all the time. Gives the security something to do. Here.' She placed a small plate containing a round whorl of pastry in front of him. 'Specialty of the museum. Get your blood sugar back up to normal.'

He took the cake, set it before him, waited a couple of seconds, then broke its surface with the edge of his fork, releasing a steaming vapour smelling of almonds and butter, long days and endless afternoons.

'Wow,' was all he said, juggling the piece in his mouth, trying not to burn himself, thinking of mouth cancer, voice-boxes and how her hands, holding the coffee cup, were so delicate and precise that nothing else seemed to matter. Only the warm, delicious taste of the cake and the sight of those hands.

'So, what are you doing in Amsterdam?' she asked and he almost told her the truth – almost.

'Just another dumb tourist,' he replied. 'The sights, the weed, the museums.'

'You knew about her before?'

Jon shook his head.

'But you liked it?'

Jon looked up. 'Yes. I don't really know what to say. I'm not very good at describing such things. Who was she? Tell me about her, I don't know anything.'

Suze smiled and he realized he'd said the right thing. First time in a long time.

'She was a Berlin Jew. Good family, father a surgeon and war hero, nice house. The Nazis came into power. The family stayed on even though they lost their posts and livelihoods.'

He leaned back and lit a cigarette, listening to her talk; he loved the way she spoke, the hard, cutting rhythm of her syntax. He'd always had a fetish for American accents, some peculiar after-effect from watching too many films perhaps, but had never really known any Americans. He stared at her short-cut brown bob and green eyes framed by delicate silver glasses, and sipped slowly on his latte as she continued.

'Eventually her father sent her to the South of France, near Nice, where her grandparents had fled to earlier in the war. It was better than Berlin. There she did all her paintings. In one year she sat alone in a small hotel room in St Jean Cap Ferrat, while Nazis marched all around, and painted over a thousand pages of her autobiography.'

'She painted all that in a year?' He found it funny how she preferred to talk about Charlotte than about herself but he also understood that it was a way of holding back the world and for that he had great sympathy.

'Yep. All from memory.'

'And then what?'

'And then what,' her face visibly sagged, 'and then what happens in all these stories. She met a man, they got married and she got pregnant. That's all we know. Not the how they met, kissed, cuddled – there's just an old certificate. It was 1944. The Nazis were losing the war and trying to kill as many Jews as they could before the inevitable surrender. Charlotte and her husband were put on to a cattlecar and taken to Auschwitz. They got off the ramp. Charlotte was pregnant, so the doctor on duty that morning sent her straight to the gas chamber. She was twenty-seven. No more art, nothing. The gas chamber and then the furnace, shaved of hair and fed to the fires.'

'Christ.' He thought there would be a happy ending despite the fact that he knew there were no such things in these stories, even Anne Frank had found only one way to escape the Nazis. The story depressed him and they sat quietly, not talking much, staring out into the street.

'I saw those paintings as really hopeful when I was in there,' he finally said. 'I'm not sure I'll be able to see them in the same way again.'

'I'm sorry for that but you would have found out sooner or later.' She wanted to put her hand on his, but she didn't, not quite sure why.

'I suppose so,' he replied, thinking back to Jake and wondering whether finding out was really all it was cranked up to be. It didn't seem to bring much joy or hope most of the time. But he didn't want to think about Jake, not now, not with a pretty girl across the table from him. The pills were working, the pain in his ankle was minimal and it was a sunny day.

'What first got you into her?' he asked, noticing again how beautiful her hands were, long fingers ending in the smudge of red nail polish.

'Same thing as you probably, the humour, the vivacity and sheer vision of the work. Also as an art historian, shit – she was doing things other artists wouldn't do for years to come, not until the seventies maybe. The whole nature of private and public art, the mixing of styles and genres, the endless allusions to literature and music. I don't know about you, but I believe everyone has their own special artist, the one that clicks for them more than any other and I guess Charlotte was the one for me.'

'And it didn't depress you knowing what became of her?'

'Sure it did. If she could do that in a year, imagine what she could have done in a lifetime. You know she was so young and it was such a waste,' she sipped her coffee, 'but it was also that very facet of her work that both intrigued and depressed me.'

'How's that?' He was struck by the passion that exploded from her when she talked. He could sit here happily listening to her all day.

'Well, on the one hand, it was a beautiful reassertion of the importance of Jews to German cultural life while on the other – listen, am I boring you? I sometimes go on about this and not realize that . . .'

'No, carry on. I want to hear more.'

She smiled, opening up to him, feeling herself expanded in this dialogue. 'Well, as I was saying, on the other hand it seemed, to me at least, to be a wilful refusal to face up to or represent the horrors and atrocities that were going on at the time. Your people are being killed wholesale and all you can

162

paint is your own little family history. I used to get so angry at her . . .'

'And now?' He loved the way she stared him straight in the eyes when they spoke and he didn't want her to stop.

'And now I don't know any more, now I suspect she knew exactly what she was doing and that she was right to do it.' She looked at him, feeling something swim between them, not necessarily understanding, no, not yet, but at least an acceptance of its possibility. 'That girl that was murdered last month.' She chewed on the end of her cigarette. 'I knew her.'

Jon didn't know what to say. The non sequitur jarred him out of the cosiness they'd fallen into. He felt a definite chill. But he didn't say anything about Jake. Instead he let the silence pull them together.

They sat there all afternoon as people came and went, and spoke about Charlotte, Amsterdam and about each other. While she talked Jon felt himself lighten up, as if ten years had just been taken off his life. It took him away from why he was there and that felt good. Now was no time to talk about Jake. He didn't want to go into that. The sun was too bright. Later there would be rain, but not yet. She in turn told him about the desert, the long star-smeared nights and jagged mountains that still haunted her. She told him about her father's death, about her mother screaming at her in the middle of the night, accusing her of everything but mainly of draining her gin, leaving her dry. He didn't say anything about his mother, another accident, not wanting to diminish Suze's story in any way, leaving it for later, presupposing, already, that there would be a later. He understood that there were areas that had to be left unspoken, that sitting over a coffee can sometimes be the most fragile of things, easy to splinter or shatter with too many revelations and he knew that he too had to keep certain things hidden.

They sat and talked more, eating chocolate cake and listening to Steely Dan on the house stereo, watching the day fade, until Suze said, 'I've gotta go, got a meeting to attend.'

'Can I see you again?' Jon asked, surprised at himself, finding it much easier to voice such things in a foreign city.

'What are you doing tomorrow evening?' He noticed her smile, then turn half away as if embarrassed.

'Nothing, I'm a tourist, remember?'

'Want to come to a concert? I'm going anyway, but I'd be happy if you could come.'

'I'd love to,' he replied, a little too quickly.

'Okay, it's at the Paradiso.'

'Sounds great.' And he gave her the phone number of his room and she gave him her mobile number, saying she'd call him with the exact time.

She stared down at him, hesitant, not wanting to screw anything up, trying to read his expression. He looked up at her. She leaned down and planted a small kiss on his cheek.

Jon watched her legs sashaying as she walked back into the gloom of the museum's elegant, dead rooms and wondered, had she just chatted him up? Had that really happened? God, he hadn't been chatted up like that for so many years. It felt fucking great, he thought, listening to the clicking of her heels fading into the distance, feeling as if anything were now possible.

He walked back to the hotel, all thoughts of the past fading quickly like the light, and when he got there he saw the message from Van Hijn.

A small, scrawled note jotted down on a ripped-out piece of paper. 'I see you're still here,' it said. 'You should have taken my advice.' Then, below, 'Meet me tomorrow.' The time and place of a film. The unspoken assumption that he'd done something wrong. He crumpled the note, tossed it into the waste-bin. How the hell had the detective known?

++++++++++++++++

Grandmother threw herself out of the window today.

The sun was brilliant like all the days before and the sea quiet, like it knew what the hours would hold. We knew it was coming. Grandpapa had joked about it often enough. I had seen it in her eyes, in the way her breath slowly escaped her mouth as if loath to do so, in the distant echoes of her speech, her faded skin, the weight of the collapsing world. She went towards the window and cast herself down.

We sat in the small courtyard of L'Ermitage and ignored the blazing sun. I did not even feel it against my skin, I who had always burned so quick. Grandpapa stared at the small tree in the middle distance, its branches twisted and dying, turning black, turning in on themselves like witches' fingers coiling. Its roots had come through the ground and now spread like spiders around its weathered and broken bark.

'Today was a day I always knew would come.'

'Shut up, Grandpapa.' I turned to look at him but his eyes were fixed yet on the tree. 'You couldn't have known that this would happen, none of us could have.' Though I knew that this was not the truth, I also understood that in its own way it held as much truth as anything else for whatever we think we know about people, we're always wrong, surprised or disappointed, depending on what the case may be.

Grandpapa laughed. I looked away, towards the sea, the smell of it still a new pleasure recently discovered. 'My darling, if only you knew.' He coughed into a small handkerchief, which he then folded neatly in four and placed back in his jacket pocket.

Suddenly his head snapped around, as if it were a weather-cock caught in an unexpected gust. His eyes looked deeply into mine. 'They all killed themselves, all of them, all the women in your family. It is only amazing that she lasted so long.'

I sat there dumb. Staring at his unblinking eyes. My mother had died of the influenza, my aunt of the same. 'Grandpapa, the sun has got to you. Today is not a day to be sitting out here.'

'Listen, Lottchen.' He raised one spindly arm, so like the branches on the tree, and pointed at me, a gesture he hadn't used since I was a child and his shadow long and endless. 'You too will succumb. You all have done. Your mother, my dear girl, threw herself out of the window, your aunt too, my only other daughter. The women in Grandmama's family have always done it.'

'You are crazy, Grandpapa.' I felt the heat all of a sudden then, as if my arm had brushed a raging fire.

'No, it is you who is crazy. Mark my words, Lottchen, you too will follow your inheritance.'

'No!' I stood up. My legs nearly buckled. My head spun. I could hear the sea rushing and breaking but the sound was inside my head. 'No, I will not,' I screamed at him, the old fool, and ran through the courtyard and up to my room.

The sun here is different from the sun I knew. In Berlin it was scared, occasionally showing its face between the blocks of apartment houses and shops, but mostly it hid behind dull shapeless clouds, smearing an ugly greyness over the city and everything in it. Here the sun makes all discrete, every object its own. I look around the room, the light spilling through the high window facing the courtyard and I see every piece of furniture and every object so clearly that it is like a dream. The pencil balancing on the table there is so sharp and beautiful, its hexagonal planes reflecting mirrors of light across the old burnt wood of the table. In Berlin I had forgotten how to see. I walked through the streets blind, concerned only with where I was going, rarely looking at anything but the air in front of me. Here everything announces itself. Is of itself. Here there is light and beauty and difference. Here the world is shown as it should be, cleared of all the dust and grime of cities, refreshed in the late evening sun that slips behind the sea like a promise from the lips of a lover. Oh, if only Alfred could see this. My sweet Alfred, my one love, would understand me. His eyes would see what I saw just like back in Berlin where our bodies melted into each other like paint running on a canvas.

Where is my sweet Alfred? I think about him most. I would gladly take Berlin with its greyness and death if I could be with him there. But I do not think he is there. Maybe in Amsterdam where I believe my father is, where Paula is. I fear for Alfred, he is so sweet and useless in the eyes of others, no one sees his passion and fire. It is only the newness of this place, the light, the surroundings, which make it bearable without him. I feel that he is like one of my lungs and that without him I will not live long.

I look at the sea and roads here. The roads so narrow and slight, as if ashamed to be conduits for such a modern load. There is an excitement in new places, a quickening of the heart; it appeals to everything we have lost. It tells us that all is not gone. That we can see again, that the light bouncing off a bicycle standing by the side of a fence can be more beautiful than anything man has ever or will ever create. But there is also sadness. We take our losses with us.

Everything left behind. Everything unknown. I will not surrender to my inheritance. I will not prove the old man right. I must do something wildly unusual or I will go crazy.

+ + + + + + + + + + + + + + + + + +

15

It was so strange to be out of the District. To see the other world that existed congruent to the one he knew so well. The everyday shuffle of commuters, last-minute cigarettes outside glass-fronted office blocks, new buildings constantly going up, a surprise at every corner, unfamiliarity at every corner. The old city slowly giving way to the new, its body marked and scarred but painted over, a palimpsest which the past kept pushing against, at every turn and step, in the ghosts and phantom limbs of demolished buildings and renewed façades.

For the past seven years Van Hijn's life had been bordered and circumscribed by the small yet all encompassing boundaries of the red-light district, *his* District, and he felt a sudden moment of release, as if the area were a prison so well designed that only on escaping did you even realize its true nature and function.

He found the address that the old man of the museum had written down. Another remnant from a previous century, he thought, walking up to the splintered doorframe, the rusted buzzer.

No name.

He pressed it. Heard something like an amplified insect whirr, looked up to see a small camera mounted high above, away from the hands of intruders, tracking its way towards him.

He put on his best smile, serious yet unthreatening – he'd once spent time in front of a mirror perfecting a vast array of smiles that conveyed many things – and held his badge out towards the dead eye of the lens.

He heard a small click and the door opened. A young man, black frizzy hair, Lennon glasses, dark polo-neck and trousers, stood smiling.

Van Hijn didn't know what he'd expected, another Methusalan perhaps.

The man shook his hand and led him inside. 'Glad to meet you, detective. Piet Pretorius. We can talk upstairs,' he said, in almost perfect Dutch, but not quite; Van Hijn noted a touch of Afrikaans there. 'Moshe at the museum told me you might be coming.'

'Oh.' He hated it when the element of surprise was gone. This man had had time to think of what to present of himself and his organization, what to say, how much . . . yet if Moshe hadn't called, the door might not have been opened at all. 'He told you why I was coming?'

'Yes.' The man stopped, turned around, creeping closer. 'You understand most people will never know about this, let alone see it. We are not a public information group or a resource for policemen. Some things can exist only in the shadows.'

Van Hijn nodded and the man continued down the hall. It had once been a wide passageway, wide for Amsterdam where every building had a width tax levied on it, but was now narrowed severely by hundreds of white cardboard boxes stacked on both sides, each seemingly on the point of toppling and setting the whole thing off in a chain reaction. As they passed, plumes of dust spun like dirt devils from the tops of the boxes. Van Hijn walked carefully, inhaling the deep, rich aroma of old books and paper gone yellow and musty. It was somehow comforting.

The man stopped when they reached the fourth floor. He

stood before a black door. Metal, Van Hijn reckoned, pretty much unassailable. He watched as another camera picked up their faces and then a slow whoosh of hydraulic release and the door opened.

It could have been any office. Van Hijn stared at the small partitions, people locked behind computer screens, each in their own cubicle, the giant hum of machinery like static saturating the air. A sense of purpose and dedication surrounded them like smoke. Some turned and watched as he walked past and he noticed how young they were, staring at him with light-drained eyes. They reached a cubicle at the far end of the room, by the window, and the man motioned Van Hijn to sit.

'Welcome to AYN, detective. As you can see we are not a big organization and our resources are limited but I will be happy to help you in any way you wish.' He flicked on the computer screen and a leather-jacketed Snoopy ran across the desktop, back and forth, a cute grin on his face.

'I don't know how much Moshe told you about what we do,' Piet said.

'Nothing.'

'You know about the Internet, detective, about auction sites?'

Van Hijn nodded.

'Well, when these auction sites were first set up, at the same time another group of sites were encoded and put into motion. Sites for selling things that can't be sold on Ebay or Amazon. A lot of these sites just sell bootleg CDs, films on video months before they've reached the cinema – harmless, really. But there's a small group of sites that sell items of, shall I say, special interest. Several of us noticed that the Internet suddenly provided an incredibly easy, risk-free and profitable place for the dissemination of these items. Some even thought the Internet came into being because of this very need. Regardless, we track them here.'

Van Hijn watched as the man keyed in some commands. 'What kind of items?'

'Yes, you're interested, of course you are, everyone is. The organization was founded in the mid-fifties when this type of memorabilia started appearing regularly at auctions, in the backs of military magazines. Then came the Internet and suddenly it seemed the whole world was flooded. We started out monitoring only items that had links to Nazism or other anti-Semitic content. The collapse of the Soviet Union inundated the market with newly "unearthed" souvenirs that had been taken during the fall of Berlin and slept, silent and cold, for that long Russian winter. There was so much. Of course, Hitler's skull and hairpiece, his teeth and shoes – these things hold a certain allure. People who might not even believe in that man will want his relics. People will collect anything and the more illustrious or infamous its history the more it's desired. We tracked who the buyers were, the sellers, we made lists and drew up charts. Certain patterns kept emerging. There were a few groups who were buying the majority of the stuff. There were groups that were interested only in certain things – in Holocaustiana for example.'

'You track only anti-Semitic objects?' Van Hijn understood how something like the Net could be the breeding ground and habitat of rumours and myths that externalized our darkest folds, and how its very structure was similar. The snaking, sinewy lines reaching out, spilling information, the constant cluster of numbers streaming in.

'No.' Piet shook his head. 'We track anything of the sort. Hairpieces and underpants – all that stuff, we leave. We're primarily interested in film. There is something about film, don't you agree? Something that makes us forget we are watching it. That takes us somewhere else. We believe in it more deeply than in the other plastic arts. I think we may even believe in it more deeply than in our day-to-day lives. A few years ago a sudden glut of video footage from the Yugoslav wars hit the market. Home-made videos from the rape camps near Manjaca and the concentration camps of Omarska. There were streaming real-time previews available. You could test before you bought. It seems that in every regime, everywhere across the globe, people have filmed the worst atrocities and of course it makes you wonder why. People don't film stuff unless they want to watch it repeatedly, or preserve the memory, or disseminate it. You see what we are dealing with here? We are talking late-night entertainment. There are parties organized. Strict non-copying regulations. These items have to remain scarce, you see, or they're not quite the same.'

Snoopy kept walking across the screen. All ones and zeros, Van Hijn thought, whether it was a cute animated beagle or rape footage, it was just numbers to the computer. 'Moshe mentioned something about reels of Nazi film.' He thought it best to keep to himself what he knew, what he suspected, about the nature of these films. That they weren't the holy grail that Piet and the others sought. That they were something else altogether.

Piet turned to look at him, his fingers still tapping on the keyboard. 'Yes, there has been a somewhat unnatural amount of interest since that was posted. Enough to suggest that this might be the real thing.'

'The real thing?' He felt his heart speed. A tremor. But these people were always looking for the real thing, he understood their excitement and he wondered how good the fakery had been to convince them. Had Jake been used to add 'authenticity' to the footage? Was he a victim or an assailant? He knew he would have to watch these films, that inside them lay the answer to the murders of the last nine months.

'For many years, ever since the end of the war, there were rumours going around that there was some surviving footage that the Nazis had taken inside the camps. Of course it is well documented that many things were filmed but they were, if nothing else, extremely assiduous in destroying a lot of this stuff before the Russians came. But this was different, rumours of footage of the medical experiments, actual footage of Mengele working in his lab. Can you imagine that? Even I, a Jew, have to confess a certain desire to see that. To actually see this man, these things. Like all rumours it had its moments of intensity and then of silence. Every few years someone would claim to have found such reels but they always proved false.'

'And what makes you think they're genuine this time round?' Van Hijn said, still suspicious.

'I don't know. I've been doing this job for ten years. It feels like it could be true. You sense these things. How words will suddenly give you a certain chill. We'll see in the next couple of days.'

'What happens then?' Van Hijn asked.

'The preview goes online.' The man clicked the mouse. Snoopy disappeared and a single HTML page took its place. Van Hijn read the scant paragraph of information that announced the forthcoming auction of 49 reels of highly collectible 'home movies' shot during the Nazi regime. There was a time and date for the auction and a further statement that a small preview of the footage would go online at the site's address in a week's time. This would be the only preview. The footage was believed to have been privately shot at different concentration camps across the Third Reich during the years 1942 to 1944. Thirty of the 49 reels were in colour. There was no further information.

Van Hijn leaned back and lit a cigarette. A few faces turned his way, expressed disapproval and then hunched back into their monitors. The room vibrated with the low, lulling hum of processors firing, printer keys rattling and the pling–plock of keys hammered by young, agile fingers.

'You mentioned that you track the people who buy these things,' he said, trying to find somewhere to flick his ash, settling on his palm.

'There are a lot of groups whose mandate is the search for such artefacts.' The man handed him an empty CD case, pointed at his cigarette. 'Have you heard of SPAR, detective?'

Van Hijn shook his head. This was a new world to him, existing behind the bland plastic of hard drives, humming in the wires as it crossed continents and oceans, like the perfect spy.

'We have reports that two of their members, one male and one female, arrived here in Amsterdam late last night.'

'What . . . why?'

'They are after the films. The 49 reels. Their presence here in the city leads us to suspect that we might be dealing with the genuine article.'

'So the films are here,' Van Hijn said, more to himself than to Piet.

'Yes, in Amsterdam. That's where the site is based at least, we have strong reason to suspect that the films are also in the city. It would make sense.'

'This SPAR you talked about . . .'

'The Society for the Preservation of the Achievements of the Reich.'

'Achievements?'

'Yes, detective. The society was founded about a year

after the unconditional surrender. There were people who believed that what they had achieved in those twelve years since Hitler had come to power was something that had to be preserved for future generations; for a time when people would appreciate these things again. Their aim was to retrieve as much of their history from the hands of the invaders as possible. This is just one group, the most prestigious you could say, but there are a thousand smaller groups, harder to track, almost invisible.

'They tour the newly renovated concentration camps with their interpretive signs and maps of death. They salute the artefacts of their history, the crematorium doors and barbed-wire fences. They collect and stockpile bars of soap and lampshades made from the dead. They tape the documentaries that appear on every television station, endlessly watching old footage of generals and officers striding through the Fatherland, the whole world theirs for a short space of time. They cruise the Internet and bid on a succession of items from embossed plates to Bormann's skull to darker things, things of more worth. They believe that their time will come again, that the Thousand Year Reich wasn't just a rhetorical one, and they collect and save these things so that when the time does come, their children will have a link to their past, a sense of history and pride in the achievements of the Reich. It will be their inheritance.'

'And these people are here, in the city?' He was starting to understand how this tied up with the case, the old man's past, Jon's story. Obviously SPAR believed the films to be real too. If only he could see them, he thought, catch a glimpse of one of the victims, then he would know.

The man nodded. 'Yes, we have information from Frankfurt – we have a sighting at the train station last night. They are here. Not only them but others too. Such a thing as this collection does not appear every day. If it is what it purports to be then certain groups will do anything in their power to get hold of these films.'

Van Hijn shifted in his chair. Outside the light had disappeared and the rain began a steady tattoo on the windowpane. 'Can you track the films?'

'That is not our job, detective. We track only the buyers, those interested – we compile lists and databases – the rest, I think, is up to you, no?'

Van Hijn nodded, though it was not so much in agreement with Piet. He was thinking about Jake Colby, what the old man of the museum had said about his interests in film, and thinking about Jon too and why he'd decided to stay in the city. He had a sudden flash: Jake perhaps finding the films, the real films, in the museum's dusty basement. Someone had killed him for them. It didn't matter if they were real or snuff; either way, Van Hijn was now convinced, they had led to the old man's death, the deaths of the girls. Either someone had known and murdered Jake for the films or they had somehow convinced Jake to act out his history on film, to recreate the horrors. And why? It seemed money was the motivation as usual, the auction, the frenzy, the belief and need for belief in the reality of these objects. Van Hijn held down a smile, inappropriate in these surroundings. He checked his watch. Late. He was supposed to meet Jon half an hour ago.

He gave Piet his card. 'I want to see the preview when it goes online. Call me.'

16

The next day Jon awoke burning with the spark and pulse of infatuation. That flush of feeling, the reeling madness that occurs only once and only before you know someone too well. It was crazy, he knew, and it had never happened so fast. That was strictly for fiction, and yet he didn't want it to go, it felt so good.

He'd thought of nothing but Suze the whole previous evening and now all he wanted to do was sleep through this day so that the night and concert would come quicker. It was nice to have something else to think about, something other than . . .

But first he had to meet the detective. That damn detective.

How had he known? Had he been checking, suspecting that Jon was somehow tied up in this? How ridiculous it seemed, truly paranoid, but the note had unnerved him. He'd almost forgotten about it all, well, not quite, but at least had muted its clamour and now here he was again, the room shrinking, the walls sucking the air out of his lungs.

He ate breakfast at what had become his local Chinese; a rough, basic place with shared tables and a small, fat-splattered menu. The food was good however and Jon ate it with relish. Thinking about the way she'd kissed him excited him and his heart lurched suddenly, making swallowing difficult.

He'd been surprised that morning when he'd noticed in the mirror the definite beginnings of a beard. Had he not looked in the mirror before? No, that was silly; just hadn't noticed it or remembered to shave, that was all. His ankle was getting better and he needed only two pills this morning to relegate the pain to the back of his mind.

As he drank the last bitter dregs of tea he checked his watch, saw that he still had an hour to go and ordered some more.

He hadn't seen the detective anywhere. So he sat in the dark, stranded in a foreign cinema, watching the opening credits of a German film, subtitled in Dutch, Herzog's *Heart of Glass*. He made out the title and the movie contained very little dialogue, so he had no problem in following its visionary landscapes as they oozed across the screen. He almost knew what the film was about but it didn't quite cohere and he liked it left just like that, balancing precariously.

'Mr Reed.'

He turned around and saw Van Hijn walking towards him, coming out of the same cinema. He felt a burst of anxiety and wondered why he'd come. He looked around to check if there were others, if this was a trap, an arrest, but he couldn't see anyone and he relaxed slightly, still lost in the film.

'Mr Reed, hello.' Van Hijn's smile was cold, his eyes distracted, looking behind him. Jon remembered what he'd seen outside the JHM, the shadowy man, but he wasn't sure if he wanted to tell the detective yet. They shook hands.

'I was late.' A statement rather than an apology.

'That's okay, I enjoyed the film. My kind of thing.' He felt a curious mixture of dread and relief. Despite all his fears, the detective made him feel better.

They walked down the cinema's steps, past the crowd of queuing strangers – chatting, nodding heads, speaking into mobile phones, finishing cigarettes – and the posters of movie stars, all bruise and bluster, fire and steely eyes staring into the distance. The detective took out a pack of Camels and offered one to Jon. 'I thought you'd be back in London by now.'

'I thought so too.'

Van Hijn stopped and stared at him. A hard, fixed look that carried the years in its gaze. 'I told you that this is no longer any of your business.'

Jon shifted, wanted to continue walking but the detective's stare held him tight. He thought about telling the detective that he was just enjoying the sights, a tourist nothing more, but Van Hijn's eyes made it clear that he knew. 'I don't see the harm in me . . .'

Van Hijn cut him off, grabbing his arm. 'You don't see. That's exactly it. You can't see. This is not your city. You do not have access to the right information. You walk into the wrong area and start asking questions, I'll be staring at your corpse tomorrow morning.'

Jon looked at him. Wrenched his arm away, making Van Hijn flinch. 'You can't stop me. There's nothing you can do. I'm going to do what I need to, whether you help me or not.'

Van Hijn burst out laughing. Jon reeled back, surprised by the older man's reaction. 'What's so funny?' he said.

'Nothing. Nothing at all.' Van Hijn composed himself, hunched back down into his crumpled shape. 'Let's go for a coffee. You want to follow this through, I can't give you my blessing but I can give you some information that might be of help.'

They sat in the Four Way Street, a Crosby, Stills, Nash and Young-themed coffee shop. Squeezed into a small table behind an enormous air-brushed rendering of David Crosby, walrus moustache and all. Each wall of the coffee shop was decorated with similar representations of the other members of the supergroup, though you could make this out only as the clouds of smoke parted and cleared and Van Hijn liked to think that it was a rather apposite metaphor on the group's existence.

'You ever hear the one about the unreleased recordings?' he asked Jon. 'It's a Zappa skit. Frank's rapping about this and that and all these objects he's going to tempt this girl with and among them are the four unreleased recordings of Crosby, Stills, Nash and Young arguing backstage at the Fillmore East.'

Despite himself Jon laughed, amused at the way the detective's mood had changed, as if something lodged between them had suddenly given way.

'The cake trolley's coming round. Then you'll see why I brought you to such an ostensibly horrific place.'

'I was wondering about that.'

'Well, wonder no more,' Van Hijn said at the exact moment that the creaking trolley came to a stop parallel to their table. The waitress smiled and Van Hijn indicated with three quick jabs what he wanted.

'Liquorice cheesecake.' The detective pointed to a slowly oozing black globule on one of the plates. To Jon it looked like a seabird drowned in crude oil.

'Only place in the city you can get this delicacy. High calorie count but what the hell, I've had a bad morning. Only way to make it better.'

Jon nodded, agreeing in principle but not at all sure about the object in question which seemed to be dissolving rapidly, covering ever greater expanses of plate.

'You said you had some new information, detective?' he asked, hoping the policeman wouldn't force him to try some of this 'delicacy'.

Van Hijn looked up. 'Call me Ronald, please.'

'Oh no.' Jon shook his head. 'Detective sounds much cooler. I've never known a detective before.'

Van Hijn grinned, tore apart three sachets of sugar and upended them into his drink. 'You want a piece?' he asked, smoothing his fork into the liquefying mass and wrapping it around it like spaghetti.

'No, I'm fine. Really.'

'Okay, but you've got to try it before you go back to London.'

Jon let that hang.

Van Hijn glanced up from his drink. He looked tired, tired and worn out.

'This morning has been particularly crazy, I hope you will excuse me. Okay, yes, the coroner made his report. Your friend Jake died from a speedball, heroin and . . .'

'I know what it is,' Jon replied, shocked. It was almost too prosaic a death after all the things he'd imagined. 'Self-inflicted?'

'No. That's not the way it looks. He didn't show any other signs that he'd ever injected anything. And I told you, those other girls were injected with heroin too, same type, the forensics think. Another link.' Van Hijn stirred his coffee. 'There was something else on him.'

'What?'

'When we found him, apart from the book. Or rather, *in* the book, there was a bookmark. I was told not to mention this to you originally. I don't suppose it matters now.'

Jon leaned forward, almost unable to get the words out of his mouth. 'A bookmark?'

'A piece of paper really. I wasn't sure if you knew about it. There was a string of numbers on it, handwritten. It was being used as a bookmark; we don't know if the numbers have any connection with the book. They don't seem to.'

'What numbers?' Jon asked, dying to see anything that might shed some light on events, anything written in Jake's hand.

The detective took out his wallet. He reached into one of the side pockets and extracted a small strip of photocopied paper. 'We thought it could perhaps be a bank account or code for some locker or retrieval area. I've been keeping it in my wallet. Looking at it from time to time, trying to understand what it refers to.'

Jon stared at the paper, obscured in the detective's hand. 'Is it possible that it doesn't refer to anything?'

'Possible, probable even, but if I accepted that then I'd have no job to do. I have to give it the benefit of the doubt.'

Jon nodded as the detective passed him the piece of paper. He looked at the photocopy, smudged and folded many times in different directions, in and out of wallets and pockets, scarred and tattered as Jake's body had been.

'Maybe you're some kind of mathematical genius, maybe you can see what it is.'

Jon looked at the string of numbers

827723169

'A combination maybe?'

The detective sipped his coffee. 'I wish it was that simple. We've had the number run through some serious computers, trying to find out any pattern or relationship to a conforming set of numbers, but came up with nothing, or with so many results and possibles that it means the same thing.'

'I'm sorry I can't be of any help.' Jon pushed the scrap of paper back across the table. He felt his chest tighten, felt himself useless again. Crosby sang in the background about how he almost cut his hair.

The detective handed the slip back. 'You keep it, maybe you'll think of something. I've got so many copies of the damn thing anyway. Don't know if it's of any relevance at all.'

Jon took the paper and folded it into his wallet, his new wallet. He wanted to tell the detective about his pick-pocketing but it seemed so self-pitying.

'I read about Beatrice's father's suicide this morning,' he said instead, thinking about Suze and what she'd told him about Beatrice. Thinking how everything here comes back to death.

'Terrible. Things like that, shit.' The detective rubbed his forehead, speared a chunk of cheesecake and chewed on it hard. 'Somehow he'd got hold of photos of his daughter. The press, no doubt. If you'd seen what had been done to that girl, Jesus, Jon, much worse than anything you can imagine, much worse than Jake, they all were. Christ, I just wanted to rip the heart out of the motherfucker who did this to her. I can't believe they gave him those photos, no parent should ever have to see that.'

'I thought you experienced this kind of thing day in day out,' Jon replied, enjoying the detective's outburst. He was usually so laid-back.

'We see a lot of homicides, a lot of people shot or strangled or poisoned for money or for love or for lack of love or for a million other reasons. I can understand that. I can take it in as part of my normal routine, it makes sense to me on a big scale, it can fit into the way I view the world. Then something like this comes along, every victim more dis-figured than the last, as if he's gearing up for something and Jesus, you know he didn't even rape her. He had her for three days, did everything he could to her while she balanced on the point of the cradle, burned most of her skin off, cut holes and marks into her flesh – fuck . . . you know, this girl, Beatrice De Roedel, she had so much going for her, twenty-six years old, everything ahead and then some beast comes and takes it all away . . . just because he can and because that's what he enjoys.' Van Hijn was shaking. He'd spilled coffee on the table and it was racing towards the edge where it trickled down on to the floor. Jon could swear he could hear every drop as it splashed the tiles below his feet.

'You still think it's the same people? The snuff makers?'

'Yes,' the detective looked pensive, 'but maybe I'm wrong.' He stared up at Jon, wondering how much he should tell him, still unsure of the Englishman's involvement. Did he know about the Nazi films?

'Why?' The spilt coffee irritated Jon. He wanted to wipe it off but couldn't face reaching over the detective. Why didn't Van Hijn notice it?

'Things have changed. I thought the girls had been butchered for the sake of filming it. I still believe this. I think the evidence refutes every other possibility. I thought your friend was a victim of the same perpetrator. I still do, but things are more complicated.'

'How?' Jon asked, feeling the pulse in his fists, oblivious now to the coffee and the gauzy air around them.

Van Hijn shrugged. 'There's a collection of Nazi films up for auction at the moment. You know anything about that?'

Jon looked at the detective, unsure what to say. 'What kind of films?'

'From the camps – Auschwitz in particular, I think. You could call them snuff films but that seems somewhat of an understatement.'

'And Jake, you think he was somehow tied into this?' What would Jake have been doing with such films? How would he have got hold of them? The museum? Jon's mind reeled.

'There are two possibilities here. One, that these films are indeed what they purport to be and that Jake discovered them in the basement of the museum. Somehow others found out that he possessed them and killed him for them. This, I consider the less likely version. I don't think those films are real. I think they were made right here in Amsterdam, this year. They needed Jake, used him in some form and then disposed of him. I am sure that we will identify Beatrice and the others once we can get hold of these reels.'

17

He arrived early at the Paradiso. Way too early. He sat, nervously excited, like a teenager on a first date, drinking scotch and trying to calm his nerves, alternating between thinking how ridiculous it was to feel like this and following the surge that shook his chest when he thought of Suze.

What Van Hijn had told him was still rattling around in his head. Those numbers. The talk of films. It didn't make any sense and neither did the snuff disposal theory that the detective was espousing. Jon was becoming more and more sure that Jake's murder hadn't been random. Something had made him go back to Amsterdam, a place that had held only bad memories for the old man.

His thinking was distracted by the fact that Suze was late. She'd said ten o'clock and it was already quarter past and he was beginning to feel stressed, aching for a joint to calm his nerves but not wanting to appear too stoned when she arrived.

Three middle-aged men came on stage. They sat down and picked up their instruments. Two of them had unspeakably distasteful mullets, short and severe at the front and rolling down to soft, trussed perms that spread evenly out across their shoulders. They began to play what sounded like a very bad translation of Irish folk music, guitar and bouzouki reels, ham-fisted instrumentals, the three of them skipping in and out of time with each other, then segued smoothly into a medley of Toto and Boston covers.

'Jon!'

He turned around and there she was, resplendent in a maroon dress that stopped just above her knees. He felt his heart skip a beat, his palms go clammy.

'I've been looking all over for you,' she said.

'Been sitting here all the time.'

'Shit, this isn't the right hall, I forgot to tell you to go upstairs. The concert's up there.'

'You mean we don't get to see these guys perform?' He smiled, the tension now dissipating.

'Unfortunately not. The Handsome Family are just starting up, c'mon.'

They went out of the hall and up the stairs into a much smaller, more intimate room, loosely filled with expectantly whispering people. They stood next to each other, close but not too close, every now and then brushing up against shoulder or arm, then quietly retreating.

Jon pulled a ready-rolled out of his pocket and lit it, letting the smoke sit deep in his lungs before exhaling. He hadn't wanted to get stoned before she got here but now he didn't care. He knew how much he needed it, how much he needed to be here with her. He felt his whole body gripped by the smoke, relaxing and expelling all the nervous tension that had built up during the day.

The band came on and began to play their mournful music, a deep, lonesome sound, rich with the American vernacular, playing strange early-century instruments over the faithful tap of a drum machine. Charley Patton and Jimmie Rodgers slipped in and out of the programmed heart of the beat merging decades in a single sad chord. The singer sang of dead poodles and suicide attempts, incarcerations in a mental institute and boys stoning swans to death. A Rohypnol George Jones on a country death trip. His wife played the autoharp, its weird angles and ancient resonance not lost on the people watching, her beautiful, sad eyes setting the whole scene on fire.

Jon looked at Suze as she stared at the band, enthralled. He noticed the way her ears looked, the round dimpled nuzzle of her flesh. He so much wanted to kiss her and felt frustrated that he didn't have the courage to just do it. Right here and now.

And yet, as the music washed over him, he felt such a tremendous surge of possibilities. The moment when it all comes together in terrifying clarity, a feeling whose familiarity had gradually slipped away from him over the years and he was amazed to feel it here, in this small room, above and enclosed from the pulsing city below.

That evening she took him back to her flat and they sat on the sofa talking about stupid things, pointless things, full of drink and dope, a radio channel emanating cocktail jazz in the background. He didn't make the moves, was too scared or too stoned or something. She had to initiate it, edge towards him, and then, all of a sudden, he grabbed her and she saw the surprise in his eyes and then felt him move himself against her, his lips, warm and moist, pressing against hers and then everything went black, black and soft and beautiful.

Afterwards they sat on her balcony and watched the sun come up over east Amsterdam. The slow gathering of people in the square, the setting up of café tables and shop awnings spread to shelter from the rain, the restful motions of ordinary life.

Suze watched him from the corner of her eye. He was quiet, which was fine by her, she hated men who, after sex, could do nothing but talk and talk, about the most mundane things usually, thinking that sex somehow bonded them in a way that allowed them to bore her with their lives. Jon just sat and stared at the street, smoked cigarettes, and she appreciated the way he seemed to know when silence was more sexy than sound.

They spent the next few days in each other, floating through the streets of Amsterdam, eventually ending up at her flat every evening. Wild days full of disarray and promise, first flushes and unexpected thrills. Days of talking and talking and walking through the streets and yet more talking. Days full of history and days where only the moment existed.

She took him around the city, showed him the houses along Prinsengracht and explained what the gables and curlicues signified. She told him the history of the city, its establishment at the place where Dam Square now stood, where the Anabaptists were burned at the stake in 1576, its mercantile foundations and autonomy from Church and rulers, money the only governing factor, leading to tolerance, the welcoming of Inquisition-fleeing Jews, the proto-capitalist freedom of the free market, leading also to portraiture and still life instead of the agonized Jesus that writhed and squirmed on altarpieces from northern Germany to the dwindled tip of Italy. Rembrandt and the Golden Age, the decline into decadence and loss of empire, the dark days of war, hunger and betrayal, the post-war Amsterdam squatters and hippies, Provos chanting nonsensical Dada poetry, the sharp crack of billy-clubs and free bicycles, civil rights and the commercialization of criminality.

They sat in coffee shops and talked for hours over a single cup. They went to movies that neither would have ever thought they'd want to see, did stupid things – all these moments that suddenly take on new meaning when shared, like laughing at bad films together or at the way people marched like cattle out of the trams and into the glass-fronted office buildings that welcomed them like the doors to a slaughterhouse. A whole new world revealed only in conspiratorial closeness.

They talked about poets they both liked, finding each other's tastes so similar that it was uncanny; yes Lowell and Cummings but Berryman and Eliot too and don't forget Jarrell's crazy rhythms or the restless, unstoppable energy of Pound.

'I can't believe it,' he said when she mentioned how she spent days reading biographies, sucking up the facts of these poets' lives as if it were the only nutrient that would sustain her. 'I used to love reading all that stuff too,' he said.

She looked at him. 'Yes. Berryman selling encyclopedias door to door, Joyce passed out in the gutter, Eliot and his breakdown, Pound in his Pisan cage. I love all that. I used to read their biographies and it made me feel somehow better.'

'Better because their lives were so much worse than yours?' Jon asked.

She sipped at her coffee, shook her head. 'No, it was more than that, I think. Just to know that these people could be so fucked up and yet produce such beautiful poetry, sentences that could stop the world dead. To know that was somehow a release.'

He nodded, understanding totally. 'Lowell punching out policemen. Erickson working in a comic shop because he felt he had nothing left to say. Auden dying in his slippers. They're great stories.'

She looked up and the late-evening sun managed to catch her eyes in a moment of perfect stillness, Jon held his breath, and then just as quickly the moment was gone.

'Do you still write?' she asked.

He looked at her not sure what to say. He'd told her that

he'd written and edited a music magazine once but not what had happened. 'Not for a long time,' he finally said.

She seemed to take it in the way she did most things, turning it over in her mind, a few seconds of reflection, allowing it to show itself in its full aspect before replying.

'I have a feeling I might start again soon.' He couldn't bear the silence, the waiting, as if that space held a judgement upon him. He wanted to sound positive, to expand himself in her presence. 'Amsterdam seems to have pricked my senses, I've started making notes.'

'Notes?'

'Just basic things. Simple things. The way the street curves around the canal. The colour of the railings in the early-morning light. It's a start.'

Sitting next to her, he stopped seeing himself from across the room as another man, instead feeling inside his own body, present and alert, a part of the moment. The dread of the past few days, the fear, guilt and paranoia, was mitigated by her body, her mouth and tender lips. And, in what she didn't say, in the spaces she left blank, he found a mystery just as involving as that surrounding Jake, yet with promise of a better resolution.

She told him more about Charlotte, took him to the museum's archives and showed him the whole collection, narrated the story of the Jewish girl as if it was her own and in a funny way, Jon thought, it probably was.

He told her about Jake. They sat in her flat one evening, listening to Steve Wynn sing about burning the cornfield down and he showed her the photograph that he'd borrowed from the detective.

She stared at the grainy face and he thought he saw her twitch as she slid it back across the table and apologized for not being of any help. 'I'm sorry, Jon.'

When she spoke, he heard the whole of America, the endless ribbon highways, diamond deserts and great flat plains, Mickey Mouse and Richard Nixon, Marilyn and Gacy – and, although he'd never been there he knew it intimately from a youth filled with American books and lyrics.

Whenever he mentioned Jake again or his search here in Amsterdam, she would tell him to forget the past, that it wasn't doing him any good and then she would go quiet and he liked her like that, stripped of all the trouble that seemed to sit so heavily on her. All he wanted to do was take her in his arms and brush away the sadness, erase it from her life.

There were a couple of Council meetings over those days and Suze went to them, leaving Jon watching television in a language he didn't understand. When she came back they would make love again and then walk the deserted night streets of the city. One morning he asked her.

'The meetings?'

'Tell me about them,' he said.

She shifted on the bed, turned towards the table, picked up a cigarette. Jon had quickly learned it was her way of keeping separate, of distancing him and he wondered, not for the first time, distancing him from what?

'Well, it grew from the seminars we were doing. Several people wanted to explore further the meaning of the atrocity image, the shocking hungry face or burnt skin.' She placed the cigarette in the ashtray and cuddled up to him, pressing her face into his stomach. She knew this was safe ground. 'We wanted to know if these images can be used to politicize people – does seeing the inside of a rape camp make you want to do something about it? – balancing that against the entertainment value of the image. We all stare at car crashes.

It's pointless to deny it. Why do we do it? That's the question. Is it merely titillation or something more extreme?'

'Seems to me like maybe it fulfils certain desires and needs in us that we haven't been able to fully articulate as yet,' he said. 'Perhaps it's a reaction to the good life we've kidded ourselves into believing we're leading.' He watched her. She made no remark. 'Why call it the *Revised* Council of Blood? Seems a bit sensationalist considering your credo.'

Suze propped herself up, looked away. He knew she was hiding something. She turned back and began speaking as if reciting from a school textbook. 'In 1566, following a frenzy of iconoclastic destruction in Amsterdam, Phillip II of Spain sent the Duke of Alva, the Iron Duke, to the city to punish the protestant heretics. The duke arrived in Amsterdam and immediately formed his own death squad, the Council of Blood, which carried out his orders with relish and abandon. Mass executions became an everyday occurrence; the skyline of the city silhouetted by dangling corpses and bodies floating in the canals was a commonplace sight, so much so that the city was nicknamed "Murderdam" during the period. We thought it sounded good.'

Always that attempt at levity, as if she wasn't quite convinced of her own seriousness or had had it challenged too often to take it for granted. 'What does the group actually do?' he asked.

'We talk a lot. We also produce a quarterly journal, containing essays, that sort of thing and run a website. Nothing that sinister really, just a bunch of boring academics who can't get enough.'

'I never once said it was.' She was hiding something, he could tell from the rhythm of her speech, the way it kept tumbling over itself.

'No, but everyone always thinks that when they hear words like council or group. Everyone's obsessed with the idea that there are myriad secret cabals existing just under the skin of their lives, always there but seen only in flashes.'

'I thought it was just Americans who believed that.'

'You Europeans are just as bad.' She got closer to him and began kissing his neck. End of conversation, he knew, right there and then. He moved his body into hers and let her drape and fold into him, erasing all the words they said, couching them in delicate silence.

'Tie me up,' she said, handing him the stockings, the clamps, the instruments of her subjugation. Jon stared at them as if she was holding a dead dog.

'What?' he blurted. What the hell was she talking about?

'Do it,' she said. 'Please. It helps me relax. I need it.' There was such naked honesty in her reply that he gently took the objects from her hand.

As soon as she was all tied up, he began to laugh, unable to help himself, it just looked so funny, like something out of a home-made porno mag. She didn't mind however, even joined in, and after he'd managed to suppress his giggles, he did what she wanted.

And that was the strange thing, Jon would come to think later, how easily he'd acceded to it, how without question he'd followed her. For there was a problem he could sense, something, perhaps just his own up-tightness, which made the whole thing wrong. And yet, here in Amsterdam, like everything else, wrong had been turned into right, and he began to wonder why he didn't protest more loudly, when it was still possible, at the beginning of things. Why this thing which he would have abhorred back in London had a strange seduction to it here amongst all the noise and glitter. And did he in some way enjoy it too, the mute bound body beneath him?

She started to miss seminars, to neglect Charlotte, finding herself having so much fun with Jon, not wanting to spend any time away from him, from his legs and stomach, his Botticelli mouth and circumcised cock. She kept asking herself the same questions. Was he just a reaction to Wouter? To being alone again? But the answers never came for he seemed to exist in a different world, somewhere more serious. She'd never thought she'd go for an Englishman, way too cold and unadventurous she'd always assumed, and Dominic was a good example; but Jon was different. He didn't seem so much of a fool like the rest of them, constantly having to prove to themselves that they were men. She liked his indifference to that, to all the rituals of possession and infatuation that seemed to solidify so quickly around some people.

But she was scared when he talked about Jake. Scared for him and for her. She didn't know how much he knew. What Jake had told him and where it would lead. Christ! She wanted to scream. She meets someone she likes and … better not to think about it. Better to forget it all.

18

They'd been in the city an hour and already they were arguing. Karl stared out of the window at the grey wash of canal. Why think it would be any different? Just because they were here to work? Was that it? How deluded he was becoming.

'It's fucking typical, isn't it?' Greta glared at him. He would remember her like this, he knew, not smiling, no. He didn't even bother going for the bait any more.

'I mean, *of course* you have to go alone. *Of course* it's not a woman thing. How many fucking times, Karl? Jesus, I really hate you sometimes.'

He let her burn herself out. No, it was nothing to do with that. She was seeing slights in every little thing now. It had reached that point.

'I'll be back before dark,' he said. 'I don't suppose it'll even take that long.'

'You bastard,' she hissed.

He hit the streets feeling as if his stomach, head, arms, whatever, were going to erupt. As if something in her tone could boil his blood. Fuck. And it was no holiday this time. Though when he'd mentioned it to her, said the word 'professional', she'd spat it back at him in the guise of denial and outright fucking lying. But she did know how serious it was. Dieter had left no doubt in their minds back in Frankfurt.

They'd always worked together, he and Greta, even before they'd shared each other's beds. Dieter, the local chapter head, had recruited both, him from a battered and defunct East German anti-Communist group and her from the university of Munich. The early nineties, the fucking wall, the burst dam and the ensuing flood of bad haircuts and cheap denim. Yes. Those years SPAR grew from a dwindling cadre of dying oldsters to the strong and vital corps that it was today. The twenty-first century had them in mind.

They had worked together first. Then they had tasted each other. It was encouraged that cells should be small and self-sufficient. It was perfect for a while. Now it gnawed at him like a fucking toothache.

He went into the McDonald's situated at the next corner. Straight to the toilets. Christ! He hadn't meant to get fucked up at all here in Amsterdam. Then why had he taken all that coke across the border with him? Stupid fucking question, he knew. His first major job, Dieter had smiled, said the time comes but he'd also emphasized how important the films were to SPAR – and how essential it was they retrieved them – fuck-ups would not be tolerated. The originals. Oh yes. Two jagged lines and he bent down, the smell of urine, disease and detergent entered his nostrils first followed by the reverse avalanche of powder. Whoooosh. Fucking right.

He snorted, stared at himself in the mirror. That was better. He felt like he looked now. Not scared. That was the thing. And Greta knew it. How terrified he really was. She'd picked her moment to fight and – stupid stupid – he'd told her he had to go alone to the piercer's because that was the way it was, a woman could upset the balance, but really he'd just wanted some time away so that he could retrieve his courage from the wrap in which it was kept. That, and well, fuck it, he had to admit, now that the stuff was flowing through his blood, that it might be nice, on the way back of course, to step into some lady's window and well, hell, he still had a lot of powder.

*

199

He leaned down and sniffed a mound of coke off his credit card, then buzzed the unlabelled buzzer. Really, he hated this. When he'd joined the society he'd had dreams of organizational leadership. Maps and movements. Tracking items. The important stuff. Long-term strategy and five-year plans, that sort of thing. And yet every fucking time they gave him leg work, potatohead work. Like now. He should have been back in Berlin, or at least Frankfurt, co-ordinating. Not this fucking errand that any idiot could do. Immigrant work. That was what it was. Punishment for being born in the Sudeten, a fucking Czech to all intents and purposes though his parents had been German. So, everywhere he went, they looked in his face and saw the slav, the slave . . . but maybe, he thought, taking another long snort off the card, maybe this time, these items – yes, retrieve these and then refuse to hand them over until Dieter promoted him. Karl smiled. Felt better. Warm rush through the veins and the thomping whack whack of a heart all ready for action.

Some greasy fucking kid opened the door. Looked at him like he was some kind of . . . Karl didn't quite know what. 'Where's Quirk?' he asked.

'He went out for cigarettes,' the boy replied.

Karl walked past him and sat down in the waiting room. His feet tapped the tiled floor to an imagined beat. He flicked through the raggedy magazines. Where the hell was the old man?

Dieter had directed them to Quirk. Quirk was a well-known sympathizer, a useful source of information. Was in at the ground floor on this one, Dieter had said. A little cantankerous but what the fuck, he's useful, right? Winking at Karl, handing him the small, bland business card.

'Yes?' Quirk said.

Karl looked up. Quirk didn't even bother to smile. The

fucking kid hung around like a cold sore. 'What was it you wanted?' The old man was thin and gaunt but with all the muscled tension and tightness of a well-trained hound. He stared coldly into Karl's eyes as if nothing could mean much to him any more.

'Let's talk in there,' Karl said, feeling the coke rush down the back of his throat, coating it in numbness. Anmotherfuckingtarctica.

Quirk nodded once and led Karl into the piercing gallery. The old man locked the door behind them, then felt for the knife he kept on his belt. The German was shaking, looked whacked out on drugs. Piercing was getting to be a dangerous profession these days. 'Yes, what exactly is it you want?'

'An address.' Karl smiled. He felt good now. In control. Thinking about his promotion. 'Dieter sent me.' He watched as the old man visibly relaxed, moving his hand away from the blade that Karl had recognized glinting in the harsh, white light of the room.

'Ah, yes. He said there would be two.'

'My partner was sick.'

'Ah.' Quirk moved away from Karl. He could dispatch the German right here, he knew. The room was soundproofed. Karl had surely underestimated his speed. They all did. He'd know about the blade but only once he felt it breathe cold against his throat. Then Quirk would have the films all to himself. It felt so tempting he had to bite his lip, hard pain to distract him. So tempting, only the one of them, like a fucking pleading to do this. But no, he couldn't however much he wanted to. Because others would come. Of that there was no doubt. Dieter would know almost immediately and how long would Quirk last? Not long he knew, not unless he went on the run, but what was the point in having the films if you couldn't watch them? He wanted to scream.

They come all the way from Germany and think they can just pick them up like that. The films should belong to him, after all . . .

'Come on, old man, I haven't got all fucking day,' Karl said. He wanted to hit something, hard. He wondered if the old man would let him punch the boy.

'Fifty-five years and he says he hasn't got all day. You stupid young fuck.' Quirk turned round. His mouth was ringed by a thin layer of white stuff. Karl noticed the old man was shaking. 'It's a fucking wonder you don't rush out of your own skin, so eager to have it all now, right this minute. Well, you'll have to wait. Because it's not so easy. It doesn't work like that. I will know in the next few days.' He smiled, enjoying the scene now but the German didn't look too disappointed. Well, fuck him. 'Come back in a couple of days. Once the preview is up, it will be easier. The possibilities will narrow, you see. I will have the address then.'

Karl thought, well, that's not such a surprise after the fucked-up way the whole day had so far gone but what the fuck, more time in Amsterdam. Dieter said it might take them a few days, wanted them in place early. More time to argue; well, fuck that too. 'You got a toilet I can use?'

Afterwards he told Quirk he'd be back in a couple of days. More assertive now, not feeling so cowed by the old man's rudeness. Feeling better, as he entered the daylight again and the girls all tapped their nails against the window for him and he smiled at them like any tourist would until he finally saw one that looked sadder than the rest and as he walked around the circuit a few times he invented a history for her, eastern European, that was easy to see. And the story came easily, as it always did for him, this whole elaborate scam that co-opted her from the cold bosom of mother Latvia, promising her a waitressing job, a guard at the museum, promising anything and then chaining her and feeding her drugs and letting men fuck her every which way they wanted. Kept like a slave. The years ahead. Her life – that's what he riffed on. The cruelty and disappointment. The sad fucking waste and how it glowed from her fucking eyeballs.

And she was the one he picked.

19

On the eve of their first week together Jon and Suze took a canal boat cruise, enjoying the tacky anonymity of being inside a group of tourists, slowly sliding past the streets, watching everything from a different level, relaxed by the swell and roll of the boat, the dark, smudgy pit-pat of the tunnels.

'Tell me more about the Council,' he said as they passed by the sex clubs and neon lights of the District. He was fascinated by the parts of her life that were still a mystery to him, by her youth in Arizona, the Sonoran dreams she'd feverishly recounted and the nights when she lay awake, inscrutable and all the more beautiful for it.

'The Council? I've already told you.'

'You haven't told me much. What made you get into it?' He could hear the canal water lap against the boat, slurp, slurp, slurp, and he realized that this was the only time he felt Diamonds are Forever or the sense of being submerged in an Alistair MacLean book. The real Amsterdam experience as the side of the boat so judiciously declared.

'Just happened to deal with things I was using in my thesis. It's a good place to talk, share stuff, work through your own ideas.'

'But why are you so fascinated with violence?'

She turned away from him then, inched along the canal boat's seat. He grabbed her hand.

The boat swelled and rocked as they entered the sea, the Ij, in all its uncaged wildness, even the driver dropping his mobile phone, alert now, and as Jon looked up and out he could see the whole city fall away. Suddenly there was only the horizon and the swell and torment of the waves breaking against their boat. 'Why?' he asked her again.

'What do you want me to say? Because I find it thrilling? Appalling?' She breathed out. 'All those things and more. Am I really so unusual?' She lit a cigarette, drawing angry looks from the other passengers. Her voice softened. 'When I was eight I saw a man killed,' she said and told him about the incident at the mini-mart. 'My mum began to drink after that, my father to spend nights away from the house. I don't think it was the actual fact of what we'd witnessed but there was something about that day – something I think my parents could never recover from.'

He moved closer to her, felt her breath on his cheek. Her hand trembled on his knee. He remembered the breath of his mother and his body felt as if it had just exploded, a huge force entering and then, just as abruptly, leaving him. 'And you?' he asked Suze.

'I didn't think about it for years. It never seemed to affect me. Perhaps now I know better. Perhaps not.' She didn't like to talk about it. She wanted everything to be perfect between them. To be normal, and yet he seemed to have a knack for poking at those spots she thought were most hidden, and it frightened her. She wondered: if he knew everything would he still sit so close to her?

'And so the Council fits into all that?'

'I don't know. I guess so. I hadn't really thought about it.' Though Jon could tell that she had, but he kept it to himself, aware that any stray thought could lead to the discovery of a chasm too wide to cross.

She laughed as the boat rocked gently over the canal, black and shiny like silk. 'You know, we originally had this naïve idea of resuscitating the image.'

'Resuscitating it from what?' He knew she was changing the subject but he went along with it.

'From its current invisibility. You know the basic idea that once you reproduce a certain image a number of times, its power weakens until finally it becomes blank, impotent? You know how the first time you saw a starving Ethiopian it really got to you and by the time that image is on a Benetton poster it's lost all its shock value?'

'Yes, but if we didn't see the picture in the first place we wouldn't even know there was such a thing as a starving Ethiopian kid, not in real terms, we might hear about them but surely it's always the image that brings it home.'

'The reality signifier?'

'Something like that.'

'Well that's exactly where the Council was split. There's a faction which believes that no matter how short-lived the shock value of the image is, that it's still a powerful and important tool, a very necessary tool in making us aware of what these things actually are. While others were totally against the representation of more horror arguing that – somewhat like American Indians believing a photo of them stole a part of their soul – these images of atrocity are actually draining those actual things of their meanings.'

'And you? Where do you stand?'

'I don't know, I agree to some extent with both viewpoints. It's not as simple as saying which side you're on any more. The sides aren't there, only the areas in between. It becomes a moral question. How do you represent violence? Can you do it in a way that doesn't glorify it, a way that will bring home to an audience just how sickening and brutal it really is? That will cause them to abhor it? To want to do something about it? That's the objective, to try to do it in a way that will educate and hopefully eradicate the very violence that's represented.'

They passed by what seemed a city of bicycles or, maybe, a graveyard. Jon craned his neck at the sight, hundreds upon hundreds of bicycles stacked against each other like people crammed into trains, four massive levels stretching up to the dull sky, metal and brass blinking in the muggy light. 'What about images from the Holocaust?' he asked her, thinking about what the detective had said, Jake's visits to the museum, his obsession with the footage there. The films. Thinking also about his own reactions to those images, the way they made you shrink a little bit, the way they took something from you.

'The Holocaust somehow stands outside. I don't know why and it's dangerous to claim uniqueness, though of course, every historical "event" is always already both unique and symbolic, but there's something about those images, those living skeletons and piles of bodies, naked women and children shivering in a pit standing on top of layers of their dead. Something about the way the images are so professionally composed.'

Jon listened to her and watched the walls of the canal slowly move across his line of vision. He understood that her passion was a product of the pain and sadness that engulfed her, her method of trying to reason her way out of it. He knew then that he wanted to be with her more than anything else, that it was stupid and childish and that that made it even better. What was it the detective had said about the things that remain?

'You know, funnily enough it was the Holocaust that brought us back together as a group.' She took the cigarette he offered her and crouched down into the wind to light it before continuing. 'One of our members found this book in a secondhand bookshop in the south of the city. It was a Holocaust memoir by a former Jewish prisoner-doctor called

The Garden of Earthly Delights. No one had ever heard of it before.

'It began by quoting Dante. The author, Dr Chaim Kaplan, recounted how in the middle of the journey of his life, in a dark forest on the edge of Byelorussia, he was arrested by roving SS guards and put on a train, destination Auschwitz. And it was even better than Dante. It was well written and more explicit and horrifying than any other books about the camps I'd read, which was quite a few, due to my research on Charlotte. The Doctor told of his time as a "volunteer" for medical experiments; there were things in that book no one else talks about, the trade in dead human flesh among prisoners, rape and sex slayings, long technical passages describing how they turned bodies into soap. That book changed everything for us, it really galvanized and centred us as a group.'

'How?' Back to the Holocaust, Jon thought, watching the sights drift by, always, in this city, leading back to that.

'I think it showed us that the only way was through representation, that the fear of wearing away the image like a bar of cheap soap was something we had to confront, to confront and break through. That we had to use images as bullets. Bullets to be fired into the heart of apathy. There was such courage in that book, such heartbreak and sadness – but most of all there was the relentless necessity of telling. The desire for memory, in the form of words and images, to be kept and retold down the ages. We all felt swept along by the book, it affected us very deeply, it was a terrible and necessary book.' She looked at him aware that she'd said too much. That it was too late now.

'Necessary?'

'So that people know what happened. If you don't think

the bogeyman exists, you never get the chance to fight him. That's what my mother always said.'

The canal boat came to the end of its trip and they silently alighted along with a group of elderly American women in shell suits and sneakers, chatting and smoking cigarettes in the night air.

'We traced the author.' Suze hesitated. It was too late to back out now, whatever the consequences. 'He was still alive. Living here in Amsterdam.'

'How'd you find him?' Jon leaned forward, stopped walking.

'Dominic, one of the members of the Council, managed to trace him somehow through the Internet. He invited him along to meetings.'

'Did he come?' He was holding her arm. Squeezing. He noticed it now.

'Yes. He was an old man, still had a thick German accent. His eyes were like the eyes of a goat, no feeling or empathy – that always scared me. I said to myself, it's because of what he's been through, but still, I never liked sitting next to him. He would nod his head and listen to us talk. Answer questions, very polite and reserved, an old-school gentlemen, I guess, but those eyes . . .'

'And?'

'And that was it really, he came a couple of times and then we never saw him again.' She wanted to move away from the subject, from where it was inevitably leading – she hadn't even thought about it recently and now it was coming back, like a nightmare that refuses to die in the dawn, magnifying in the bright light of day. She knew that she should tell him everything but she couldn't bring herself to. What would he think of her then?

*

Jon didn't think much about Jake during that time, didn't even look at the slip of numbers in his wallet that the detective had insisted on him keeping, and it wasn't until Suze read the newspaper article one morning that it all came back. A short, terse column which recounted in cold, functional prose the victims of the supposed serial killer. A round-up of facts, easily digestible nuggets of death, sparked by the celebrity funeral of Beatrice's father.

Jon made Suze read him the full article, her halting translation releasing the sentences one at a time, letting them sink deeply into his mind.

When she finished, she put the paper down and sipped from her drink. He could sense her fading slightly from him, nothing much, just a slight reduction.

'I need to go and see her,' he said, suddenly convinced.

'Who?' But it was obvious. 'Do you really want to do this, Jon? Have you asked yourself whether it can do any good? What it'll do to you?'

'It doesn't matter,' he said, though he knew it did, and he'd felt the slight shifts in him from the moment he'd arrived in the city, shifts that now opened up new and hungry spaces. 'I need to see her.'

'I don't think it's a good idea,' she said, but she could see that his mind was made up and that she could only do further damage by trying to make him stop. She bit her lip and remained silent.

20

His pager had beeped an hour into the first film; he'd forgotten to turn it off again. His day off. *High Sierra* and *In a Lonely Place*. Double Bogart. A light lunch. Some cake for the movie. The rain kept at bay for a while. And then his pager had gone off.

He called the number.

'AYN Technologies.'

'It's Van Hijn,' he mumbled.

'The preview's just come online, detective. I think you should come and see.'

He'd seen the Bogart film four times before. So it was no great loss, and now he felt a curious excitement at the news as he hurried through the drenched streets.

He'd thought it would be awful. Intolerable. This dredging of the past, all the history that he'd purposefully forgotten, but instead he felt a huge relief, to be able to move through that history without collapsing under its weight. To accept that it was never past, that it would always be here, a part of him, a part of the city.

As he swept through the rain he had a sense that someone was shadowing him, glimpses when he turned a corner or stopped to light a cigarette, an old instinct that had never left him. It wasn't the first time he'd felt this and he walked in circles, doubled back and bluffed, used side doors until he was sure that he was alone.

'You made it here quickly,' Piet said, standing behind the inner door.

Van Hijn smiled, smile number 46, humble yet interested, not giving away too much, and followed him inside.

Unlike the time before there was no buzz of concerted effort, no sequestering or hunched concentration, everyone was gathered around the large computer monitor on Piet's desk watching a flickering black and white stream.

'It was posted half an hour ago.'

'Is it real?' Van Hijn asked.

Piet nodded.

The others left them alone. Van Hijn sat down facing the monitor. If it was real, then he was wrong. Totally and utterly wrong. His theory fucked. He felt the floor sink, as if he'd stepped in mud. The screen was blank. The Realplayer was on.

'It's only a minute long.'

Van Hijn was about to say something when the screen flickered and an image began to take shape. He sat and watched the segment and when it was over he motioned for Piet to run it again. He did this four times, each time couched in silence, watching the film unfold, these horrors imagined but unseen until now.

'Is he really doing what I think he's doing?' Van Hijn asked, pointing to the officer in the foreground.

'You have a keen eye, detective. Yes, he is.'

'Christ!'

'Christ had nothing to do with it.'

'Begs the question, doesn't it?'

'So they say.'

Van Hijn watched the clip again. He kept his face a mask though what he saw on that screen turned everything upside down. It was one thing to read and hear about these events, but you never really got it, no, not until you'd seen it. He turned away, stared out of the window, trying to flee from their spell, the mesmerizing allure of filmed evil, of rare history.

'Quite a piece, huh, detective?' Piet leaned over and clicked the mouse a couple of times. The film disappeared and in its place Snoopy bounced across the screen.

'And there's no doubt?'

Piet shook his head. 'No doubt at all. Manny over there.' He pointed to a small dark man hunched over a computer. 'He ran the film through his software, blew up certain bits. Here . . .'

He clicked twice. The screen filled with what Van Hijn recognized as the top corner of the previous footage. The operating table out of sight. A man walked quickly across the frame, disappearing off its edges into the blackness. It took him only a second or so to cross the room. In the normal footage he was just a blip, a smudge in the background while all eyes were pinned to what was happening on the table. Now Van Hijn could see the man's face, turning slightly to acknowledge the scene in the foreground, a smile breaking the strict geometry of his face, for only a second, before he disappears.

'You recognize him?'

'He looks familiar, that's all,' Van Hijn conceded.

Piet laughed. 'Familiar? That, detective, is perhaps the only footage we have of Mengele at Auschwitz.'

'Mengele.' The name hung in the air, heavy and poisonous, between them. The name that was almost a metonym for all the horrors of the camp. The name of the man who sterilized women with Barium.

'Doesn't look so evil, does he?' Piet said, clicking back to the screen saver. 'It's no coincidence that this piece was chosen for the preview. Not just for its gruesomeness you see, though prospective buyers will want to know that this footage is of the import that is claimed. No, it wasn't very hard for us to spot Mengele.'

'The film carries its own provenance.' He felt deflated and yet strangely exhilarated at the same time. So, perhaps Jake had found the real films. Had been murdered for them. There was what the old man of the museum had told him. Jake rummaging in the basement. Jake being obsessed by the filmed documentation of the time. The timing of the 49 reels' appearance and that very visual texture of those eight dead girls.

'Exactly. This is what we've feared all along. That these rumours are true. That these films exist.'

'How many people have bid on it?' He leaned back, wanting to get away from the humming claw of the computer.

'Forty-four so far. Current high bid's around $110,000 though it will get far higher in the days to come. The web counter shows over a quarter of a million hits already.'

'People are watching this segment?'

'All over the world.'

'How? I had to come here. You said it couldn't be accessed without knowing a string of passwords.'

'These things get out. They spread faster than is imaginable. One person sees it, cuts and pastes the link and passwords, sends it to thirty people on his list, a little note attached, check this out, they watch and yes, perhaps they're horrified, disgusted, can't believe what they're seeing, that anyone would put this kind of thing up on the net, and yet they'll still pass it on, what do you think of this, they add, distancing themselves from the source, each of them to another group of people. It grows exponentially and with the kind of speed that was once unimaginable.'

They sat and talked some more and then Piet took him to

a large room off the back. Inside he showed him some of the things that AYN had successfully bid on. 'These are things no one wants apart from as souvenirs – Naziana – that's why we could afford them. The real stuff, the important stuff, is far beyond our means.'

He showed him plates embossed with the Berchtesgaden logo. 'Heroes of the Reich' playing cards. Van Hijn shuffled through the deck. They were all there: Eichmann, dark and scrawny, Himmler the junkie, Goebbels the gimp, the hook-nosed and hunchbacked Brunner, below them their attributes and scoring. Lampshades with nipples. Mengele's spectacles. The rug from the bunker that Adolf reputedly chewed on in those last days. Faked postcards, train time-tables, a bottle of amphetamine tablets that belonged to the Führer.

Van Hijn picked up a paperback book. There was a stack of them to his left. All identical. A thin, faded book with a barbed-wire fence on its cover. 'What's this?' he asked.

Piet turned and looked at the detective. '*The Garden of Earthly Delights*. It's a Holocaust memoir. But one that is very popular among collectors. Quite rare now,' Piet said, gnomically. Van Hijn took the book, checked behind him. Piet had already walked on. The detective slipped it into his jacket pocket.

'This is only a small and insignificant part of a greater whole.' Piet stopped at the far end of the room. 'But in my years here, I don't think there's been anything as significant, or as dangerous as these films on auction now.'

Van Hijn knew what was implied. Go and find them. Bury them here or somewhere else. He knew it was what he should do. Do what his father had never had the guts to. That preview had been enough. What if the whole collection was aired on the net? Or kept in a vault somewhere for a time when its true 'merits' would be appreciated? He also under-stood that behind the films lay Jake's murderer. That he had seen this whole thing upside down until now. The films were the crux and once he had them the rest would follow.

Piet turned towards him and Van Hijn could see that the man looked uncomfortable. 'I'm really sorry.'

'Sorry? What are you talking about?'

'It was us, detective, who found out about your father. Years ago, it was our first big scoop.'

Van Hijn stood stunned. The floor had collapsed. He felt himself spin away from his body. He grabbed on to the door handle. Felt the world split. Everything twist.

'I really am sorry.'

'Did you sell the story?' He didn't know it but he was shouting, his voice trembling on the edge of hysteria. 'Did you sell it?'

Piet nodded. 'Not me personally, of course, but yes, we did. How do you think we can afford to keep buying these items, taking them off the market?' He sounded as reasonable and rational as a teacher explaining something very simple to a slow student. Van Hijn turned around. Slammed the door. Ran down the stairs until the breath pushed against his chest and his lungs felt heavy and ready to explode.

Outside he stood and watched the rain. There was a strange smell in the air, an acrid chemical smell but he didn't pause to think about it. All he tried to do was breathe. And that was suddenly the hardest thing to do.

+ + + + + + + + + + + + + + + + + +

SUMMER, 1940. GURS TRANSIT CAMP, THE FRENCH PYRENEES

One stupid syllable, like a sob that gets stuck in the throat.

Gurs.

Today is like any other. The sun shines. But we are not allowed outside. Not today.

It has been four weeks since they brought us here. Took us from Nice and put us on unwindowed trains. Nearby are the mountains, those beautiful impossible peaks, and though they are not the ones Friedrich saw and painted, I am sure that if I were to climb their glacial sides, I would come upon a chapel perhaps, standing like a jewel in the middle of the rock.

Four weeks and I do not like the women I have to share this room with. There are six of us here and we speak four different languages and we are all scared and not sure of each other though our bodies are constantly touching, scraping against one another for there is no room to move and you can only stand at one point in the middle of the room where the roof is kind enough to arch itself.

And it is so hot.

Summer is here and the windows do not exist.

At night I hear the rats running below our feet, sometimes even feel them as they cross my body, but I do not move lest waking, I might turn from something to cross into something altogether different and when I feel the flick of their tails, I want to cry and scream but I know there is no use.

Today we must clear the mud.

But there is always mud up here in the mountains. Every night brings with it rain and the earth turns soft and untrustworthy beneath our sleeping feet. Anna, who sleeps on my left, fell over today as she was carrying the laundry. The mud ate her up but no one stopped what they were doing. Soldiers held her down but we turned away and later that night there was slightly more room to move.

On my first day here they separated us. Grandpapa went to the men's camp and I was sent here. Why do they put me here? I am not like these women. They are not like me. We speak different languages. We know different things and yet they say we are the same. What makes them think we are all alike?

Everyone paints. Whenever there is some time that is not filled with work, people paint. They use polish off their shoes and mud and flowers to mix colours and I feel ashamed because I do not feel like painting.

Today three women were moved into our barracks. There was very little room but they were so crumpled that they took the place of only two and, even that, only barely. Like me, they spoke German. That night they told me about a camp in the East that all the Jews were being sent to. I listened to what they said and then translated as best I could for the rest. They told of horrible things, of ovens working day and night and a camp the size of a small town. The poor things were so distressed. They had cigarette burns all over their bodies. They'd escaped, made their way to France and then, like me, were rounded up and sent here. It cannot be worse than this place I told them, and they laughed like madwomen and we knew that their stories weren't true — that some awful thing had happened to them and that this was a metaphor they used.

*

I started drawing again. I found a small piece of burnt wood and I began to draw upon the walls of the barracks room. Then I traded my day's food for some paper. I drew the mud and the women with their backs bent like threshing machines and I thought about that story of the camp in the East. It couldn't possibly be true. I cannot believe the world could hold such a place. And even if it was true, what could we do? Is it really better to know these things if it only leaves you impotent? Are we damned by what we know and can't change? I decided not to think about it. I decided to stop painting. I looked on what I'd done and there was so much anger in those pieces of paper, so much pain that it scared me that it had come from my hand. That was not what I wanted to paint. I didn't want this ugliness, it has no place in the frame. I almost burned the drawings but it would have been another thing gone into smoke and something held me back, something told me to keep them close, to remind me of what was outside of my work.

I couldn't believe it. They woke me today to tell me that I had been given a pass. That I was to accompany Grandpapa back to Nice. The other women looked at me as if I had just hidden the last piece of food. I tried to say something but there was nothing to say.

Grandpapa hadn't changed. He was complaining all the time. We had been freed and all he did was moan. I hated him then.

There was no way to get back but to walk to the nearest town. Grandpapa complained.

'What's the use?' I screamed at him. 'Why tell me? It's not my fault. I can't do anything about it. Just stop it.'

Later we talked about going back. How the world would be. He didn't tell me anything about what had happened to him at the camp and I said nothing of my own experiences. He never even asked what the pieces of paper I had under my arm were.

'Grandpapa,' I said, as we came to the top of another hill. 'I've come to feel that one must piece the whole world back together again.'

He slowly turned to me. 'Oh just do it, kill yourself too, so this yakking of yours can finally stop.'

We didn't say anything else to each other. We walked up and down the hills, the roads, this place so far away from anything I knew and then it happened. I looked up and saw the sun bleeding into the horizon, slowly oozing across the peaks above us, Grandpapa disappeared and the hills suddenly melted, the world fell away, as if it was nothing but a wrapper, discarded and useless now, and I said 'God, my God, oh is that beautiful' and I knew then exactly what I had to do.

+ + + + + + + + + + + + + + + + + +

He ate breakfast at the Chinese, thinking how nice it would be to have slipped into that most desired of lives, the uncomplicated courtship, the girl who seemed to vibrate on the same pulse as you, the effortless roll of an early relationship.

In Suze there was a promise of something better, of dreams fulfilled and warm evenings spent, dripping dawn kisses on bathroom floors. All morning his head had been filled with her movements, with her canyon eyes and long, desert silences.

But there was something else there. Some terrible sadness that seemed at times to overwhelm her so deeply, and all he could do was look helplessly on. And yet that too had its own seductions, however unwilling he was to articulate them. He wondered about her fondness for being tied up, for pain, this thing that had appeared so sudden and strange, and he thought about Jake, the marks on his body, the things Van Hijn had said. What was it about this city that drew pain junkies to its streets and coffee shops? Perhaps it was the way people minded their own business. The little pockets of freedom that had opened up here, on the shoulders of Europe. Or was it something else, something in the nature of freedom itself, in that long look into the abyss, the seductive blackness of space?

He finished his noodles and looked at the map again. Took a sip of tea, trying to ignore the little-girl Chinese pop music that seemed to be coming from every part of the restaurant. He'd got the address of the dead girl's mother from the phone book. He'd wanted to ask Suze but he understood that some things were best left unsaid. And there was something else, something about her these past few days that disturbed him. The way she seemed to turn away from questions and mutter to herself, the look on her face when he mentioned Jake.

He'd re-read what there was about Beatrice in the English-language paper, her academic achievements, her charity work; the golden girl it seemed, perfect newspaper fodder. Her life had retrospective tragedy written all over it. Curiously, he felt some connection with the girl's mother, some intangible community of murder.

He walked through the quiet residential streets of the quarter, through the waves of trees and flowers, so absent everywhere else in the city, and past the tall austere houses, their width adjusted to the rate of tax, their windowsills like mouths drooling over the canal. And it was almost like another city, the postcard one, the perfect one, poking and breaking its way through the dark slumbering stew of the District.

The house he stopped in front of was wider than the others, better looked after, a strict protestant ascension in its timbers, in the restrained urges of its gables. Yet, like the rest of the neighbourhood, it seemed a remnant from another time, something so out of place in the early days of the new century that he almost didn't go in, afraid that it would suck him out of the present.

As he climbed the stairs towards the door, he passed by two stone dogs that stood sentry on either side of him – sad, cold objects, stoic and useless as they guarded, silent in the rain. He pressed the buzzer.

The door didn't open. A frail voice somehow came through it. 'Yes?'

'Mrs De Roedel?' Jon tried to sound as comforting and unthreatening as possible. 'My name is Jon Reed. I would very much like to talk to you.'

'Please go away, whoever you are.' Despite the weakness of the voice there was a tremor of urgency, a charge vibrating below the words.

'Mrs De Roedel, please. I'm a friend of detective Van Hijn's.'

'Are you from the police?'

'No. I'm from England,' was the only thing he could think of and he immediately felt stupid for saying it but it seemed to have done the trick. The door slowly opened revealing a tall, elderly woman, dressed in the style of the fifties, staring at Jon with piercing blue eyes. She looked at him for the briefest of moments, then said, 'Come in, please, Mr Reed.'

He smiled and shook her hand. 'It's Jon. Thank you.'

From the outside the house gave the impression of being small but when he stepped indoors he was surprised at the sense of space that had been achieved. Decorations and ornaments filled the place, ancient mementoes from the empire, Indonesian swords and crisses, tall, elegant spears sprouting butterflies of iron, flags from countries that no longer existed. Animal heads, wide-eyed and pinned to boards, stared down at him as he followed her into a large room with an ornate carved table in the middle and two facing sofas. He stared at the paintings, large canvases filled with busy people drenched in colonial summer and, on one wall, portraits of family members, proud and elegant in their heavy wooden frames. He took a deep breath, feeling small and speck-like, wondering whether anyone had managed to paint Beatrice in time.

'You didn't tell me what you wanted, Mr Reed.' She sat

down opposite him, her frail figure hardly disturbing the velvety sofa.

'I don't even know what I wanted.' He hadn't prepared a speech or really thought about what he might say to her and now that he was sitting here, he felt strangely lost for words, an intruder in this woman's life. 'My friend was killed just over a week ago. The detective thinks that it's linked with . . .' He stopped and looked down, 'I'm sorry Mrs De Roedel, I shouldn't have come, I'll go now if you want me to.'

She stood up and Jon knew he'd fucked up again, she was going to tell him to leave. He'd stepped over a line, imagined similarity when there was none. He stood up too.

'No stay, please, Mr Reed. I was just going to make a drink. Would you like one?'

'Yes. Thank you.' He sat down, feeling embarrassed and watched as she went into the adjoining room.

He studied the massive canvas hanging opposite him. So large, it dwarfed the room. India. The compound in the centre of the frame was a colonial structure. He saw the neatly plotted crops, the strict geometry imposed on the crazy land, everywhere people working, dark-skinned, turbaned figures setting up tents, chopping wood, carrying huge, impossibly heavy pieces of cloth, the Dutch on their white horses looking on from above and in the distance, a great ship, manned by so many slaves he couldn't count them, setting off from the channel, searching for more lands and bounties, the cycle endless and terrible.

He looked down, stared at the gnarled swirl and heft of the table. There was a quietness to the house that Jon had yet to experience in Amsterdam. It seemed that wherever you were in this city, you could hear the crowds, the rain and police sirens through the walls – here he heard only his own shallow breathing and the distant hiss of a stove-top kettle announcing its readiness.

She brought in a small tray with assorted pastries and cakes and put it down on the table in front of him. She poured the tea into his cup and then into hers and offered him a slice of cake. They sipped their tea politely, not saying anything to each other, caught up perhaps in the beautiful stillness of the room.

'Tell me about Beatrice,' Jon said, finally breaking the silence.

She carefully put her cup of tea down, her hand shaking, looked up at him. 'What can I say to you, Mr Reed? With all respect, how can I tell you?'

'I don't know, just tell me anything you can. I know only what I read in the papers.'

She sighed and Jon thought she wasn't going to say anything. He twitched in his chair.

'She loved her father so much. He couldn't take it when he heard what happened. He disappeared for two days and came back to me crying. I had never seen him look like that. He begged me for forgiveness, I thought he meant about Beatrice, and so I gave it to him. He left that night.' She coughed into a small handkerchief, excused herself and continued. 'You know, when she was twelve, we were on holiday in Italy and we were walking along the beachfront. As we passed by the pier we heard this terrible noise coming from underneath it. Beatrice ran to see what was going on before we could stop her and my husband followed.

'There was a man beating his dog. He was cursing and berating him at the same time as he was slashing the poor beast with a belt. My husband quickly took Beatrice in his arms and joined me and we left the beach. All the way back to the hotel Beatrice was crying in the car. "Why didn't you *do* anything, Daddy? Why didn't you stop that man?" just over and over again, crying so violently that my husband was overcome himself and had to pull the car up to the side of the highway and I sat there and watched them both hold each other, silently trembling for about ten minutes before we could resume our trip.' She wiped the tears from her eyes. 'I'm sorry Mr Reed. That must seem like a horribly sentimental thing to tell you, but it was all . . . all I could think of.'

'It's okay. Thank you for sharing it, Mrs De Roedel,' Jon replied, moved by her tale despite himself. He went over to her sofa, sat down and held the old woman in his arms, feeling the hard knots of her bones against his and the saggy flesh that gave as he pressed up to it. She cried in his arms, shaking and sobbing and he held her, watching the light slant in through the blinds, until she was cried out and she apologized to him, wiping her eyes with the small initialled handkerchief.

'You know, I grew up during the war. I remember when the Canadians liberated the city and people shot all the remaining Germans on sight. There were bodies everywhere, young handsome boys in SS uniforms and the city kids, kids of my age, picked through their pockets and kicked them in their faces as they lay there in the mud. Older men came and mutilated the bodies and no one cleared up. They left them like that for a few days, a horrible sight, Mr Reed. I remember walking past the body of an SS man, we knew them from the skulls on their uniforms, and I saw that his groin had been cut out and I began crying. My father who was with me, just looked at me angrily. "Stop crying," he said, shouting really, "you should be rejoicing. What you see there are devils – devils who have been defeated, this is a happy day, Elaine, remember it for one day you will know." And I really thought then that the worst was over. I really thought that nothing would cause me such pain again.'

Jon let the story have the necessary space it needed to settle. They sat in silence for a minute or two, Jon staring at the painting, the old woman at her hands.

'Mrs De Roedel, was there anything strange that you noticed before Beatrice's disappearance?' He hadn't meant to be so abrupt. It was too late now that it was said. He tried to look apologetic as he watched her gather herself together like a sleeper rudely awakened.

'The police have already asked me all that, Mr Reed. I'm afraid there's not much I noticed. I told them what I knew.'

'What was she involved in before her disappearance?'

'She was a student, Mr Reed. She did what all students do. She studied hard, she went out to parties, she got drunk.'

'Can I see her room?' Now that he was here he was determined to get what he wanted, not to shrink like so many times before.

The room was like that of any young woman caught between the suspended days of her youth and a future now unrealizable. There were faded posters of pop stars and movie idols, books neatly arrayed, CDs and small trinkets. Make-up cases and mirrors. The small accretions of a life, a personal history externalized in the way we fill up space. Nothing sadder than a room that no one will return to, Jon thought, as he looked around.

He saw it immediately. Almost hidden. Sitting on a small stool by the bed, partly covered by a tasselled Indian shawl. A black, plastic projector. An 8 mm projector.

'What's that?' he asked Mrs De Roedel, hoping she wouldn't sense the breathless excitement in his voice.

She seemed to have drifted off and her reply sounded as

if it was coming from a detuned radio. 'Oh, I think that was a present from a friend of hers. She was working on some project that involved all those old films.'

Jon's heart catapulted inside his chest. It filled his throat. 'Are any of the films here?'

'No. She said the humidity in the house ruined them.'

'Who was her friend?'

'I don't know, Mr Reed. I'm afraid I never kept track of these things. Someone from her classes, I think. A man. Twice he left messages with me, that's all I know.'

Jon stood still as he watched the old lady retire downstairs telling him to take his time.

He stared at the projector. Controlled his breathing. Checked the reels but they were both empty. He felt disappointed though he'd known there'd be nothing there. He wondered if there was a link between Beatrice and Jake, something outside of their common deaths – the equipment seemed to suggest it. Of course Van Hijn would say it was circumstantial and there was probably no point in telling him, he'd just berate Jon for having disturbed the old lady. But Jon knew that there was more to it than that. Had to be.

He walked around the room, looking at the law books on the shelves, those long words seemingly without vowels that the Dutch were so fond of. Anthologies of American poetry. A collection of Thackeray novels in English. Swinburne. Whitman. Romantic poets. And he didn't even notice it the first time, his eyes slipping easily over the many coloured spines. It was only after he'd turned around that it registered. He looked back at the bookcase. And there it was, innocently nestled among the greats of Victoriana.

The small, unassuming spine. *The Garden of Earthly Delights*.

He pulled it gently out from between Wordsworth and Shelley. Dr Chaim Kaplan subtly embossed on the front. A photo of that most famous of barbed-wire fences. A small book: 126 pages. He looked behind him. Slipped the book into his pocket. Went downstairs.

Jon sat with Mrs De Roedel until it got dark, listening to her stories of the old days in Amsterdam and eating the cakes and pastries that she kept insisting he have. She'd talked about Beatrice fondly, as if she'd merely gone off to university rather than for good. She never once mentioned the husband, father, suicide.

'It's getting late, Mr Reed, you're probably dying to go.' She reached her hand across the table and put it on his. 'Thank you for staying with me, listening to my boring stories. You can't know but it means a lot.'

'I'll stay longer if you want.' He took her hand. 'I've got nowhere to go. I like being here.'

'Then come again sometime but I've tired you enough for one evening, I can see that.'

'I will come again. I promise. Thank you for your hospitality.'

'You can't flatter an old lady.' She smiled and for a moment Jon could see the woman she'd once been, the face behind her face. 'But you've made a pretty good attempt,' she added.

Jon left her like that, sitting on the sofa, staring at the portraits on the walls, herself like an undiscovered Vermeer caught in the fragile beam of light.

Once outside, he walked furiously through the rain-beaten streets, moving with such force and determination that even the hustlers stepped out of his path. All the way back to the hotel he couldn't stop shaking.

22

The Skull & Roses tattoo parlour stood at the end of a long alleyway that led from the Old Church. About a minute's walk from where Jake's body was found, Van Hijn thought, a coincidence most certainly, but in his years as a police officer he'd learned to take coincidences seriously.

His stomach felt bad. It always felt bad when he was about to do something he didn't want to. It had been feeling bad a lot lately. A dull, twisting pain that sat heavy and solid as a stone in his lower abdomen. The cheesecake he'd just had didn't help. Neither did that faintly chemical smell that seemed to be following him around these days.

He'd been to three parlours already. Shown his photos, got non-committal sighs of appreciation, but no positives. None of them seemed to be lying. He wanted to go home. Stupidly left this one for last.

He descended the stairs leading to the basement. There was no sign, just a black door and a small plastic buzzer.

'Yes?' The voice came from behind the door, muffled and impatient.

'Detective Van Hijn. I need to speak to Mr Quirk.'

The door opened and a teenage boy, long hair lank and matted, stood there staring at him as if he'd never seen a man before.

'I assume you're not him,' the detective said as he stepped past the boy and into a small waiting room with its sickly pastel plastic chairs and magazines adorned with chrome and flesh.

'He's working. If you don't mind waiting, I'm sure . . .'

Van Hijn stepped up to the boy. 'Get him,' he said.

'I can't disturb him in the middle of a . . .'

They both heard the scream.

It came from behind a white door at the end of the waiting room.

Van Hijn pulled out his gun, his stomach crying out. He swallowed, heard the second scream and ran towards the door.

It wasn't locked and he charged in, gun pointing, shouting 'Stop! Police!'

It was only then that he saw what was going on.

In the middle of the room was a chair, somewhat like a dentist's, and on it, stripped to the waist, a teenage boy.

The old man he assumed was Quirk stood beside him holding something in his hand. The boy's nipple was clamped into the device and was stretched out, about four inches from his chest. There were tears in the boy's eyes as he looked towards the detective.

'What the fuck are you doing?' the old man shouted, letting go of the clamp, the boy screaming again as the skin quickly sprung back.

Van Hijn looked towards the boy. 'Are you okay?' he asked him. The boy nodded dreamily. 'What's going on here?'

'He was piercing my nipple,' the boy said, suddenly ashamed.

Quirk couldn't help but unleash a smile. 'What, you think I was torturing him or something?' he said to Van Hijn. 'They always scream, you know.'

Van Hijn lowered the gun. Another stupid mistake. It seemed that he was making more and more of them recently. His stomach was trying to claw its way into his chest. He saw a door behind the piercer. A closet? Instrument cupboard? He noticed the thick new padlock on the outside, smelled the heady mix of ether and ammonia that saturated the room. 'You Quirk?' The old man nodded grudgingly. 'I need to ask you some questions.' The piercer looked so much like William Burroughs it was disconcerting and he found it hard to meet his gaze.

'It can't wait?'

'No.'

Quirk put down the clamp. Walked towards the detective.

Van Hijn gave him the photos. The old man looked at them. Shook his head.

'Never seen him before,' he said, his accent breaking through for the first time. Been here a long time, Van Hijn thought, almost undetectable. 'Look again,' he said.

'You think I'm blind? You think just because I'm old I can't see?' He threw the photos at Van Hijn. The detective let them flutter to the floor.

'No, I just don't think you looked closely enough. Pick them up and look again.'

Quirk stared at him. It would go either of two ways, Van Hijn knew, and his hand slipped back down to his gun just in case. The moment hung between them. And then Quirk bent down, retrieved the photos, flicked through them again. 'No.' And gave them back.

There was not much else Van Hijn could do. The old man was worried about something, that much was certain, but it could have been any shabby secret. 'Thank you for your time. I'll be back,' he said.

'I'm sure you will, detective.' The old man's smile was as thin as a paper cut and just as unpleasant. 'I'm sure we'll see each other again. Now if you'll excuse me I have work to get back to.'

As Van Hijn left the room, he counted his steps.

*

Outside, the rain seemed to have got worse. He pulled out his small torch, flicked it on, relieved to see that it was working. Groups of men passed him heading for the window girls. Even in this weather, Van Hijn thought, as he circled the building twice.

Yes, there was definitely something wrong. Something that didn't add up.

He circled it again, counting his steps this time.

The basement he'd been in seemed to be smaller than the perimeter of the first-floor premises. Impossible, he knew. He paced around again just to make sure. Same number. The ground floor was stretched out about ten feet longer and five foot wider than what he'd estimated the basement area to be. Even if he'd been slightly mistaken it wouldn't account for the disparity.

Of course he knew all about them. Hidden rooms were a part of the city's legend. There was even a house you could visit that hid a whole Catholic chapel behind the swivelling occlusion of its fireplace. And of course the much-visited Anne Frankhuis, many more throughout the old quarter, priest-holes and last resorts, the small cramped refuges of the hunted and hated.

He walked through the rain, buzzing on the new information, heading back towards his flat. A video, Woody Allen perhaps, something to take his mind off the day, to ease the welcome respite of night. Wipe the whole thing clean. Something to make up for all the horror he'd seen on that computer screen.

The piercing parlour would need to be staked out, the architectural incongruities reported, but that could wait until tomorrow. Tomorrow was a monster, flashing its teeth, gaping and hungry and he wanted to put it off for as long as he could. He knew that he had to get hold of those films.

That the key to the tramp's murder lay there, and more, for he knew that all these deaths were linked. He thought about Jon and what he was hoping to find. Whether he'd find it, and if he did, would it be what he thought he was looking for. Or just what he'd been running from.

They caught up with him three blocks from his flat. He was so distracted that he didn't notice them until it was too late. Too late for his gun too as he felt his wrist being pulled away and then the clear, sickening sound of it breaking, the pure, hot dagger of pain that shot through his body. The rest became a blur as he landed on the cobblestones and felt the needles piercing him. He furiously scrabbled about, trying to protect his side with his hands but the needles still found their way in. There were always gaps to be exploited, prodded, entered. He could hear laughing and what sounded like the pitter-patter of his blood trickling on the stone. He tried to stand but found that there was nothing left in his legs. The pavement swallowed him, hard and cold and wet. The stars twinkled unnoticed above and eventually he was left on his own, the crumpled form of a man, leaking, dimming, falling into the black night that he'd spent so long running away from.

23

'Use the clamps.'

'Do you want me to?'

'I just said so, didn't I?'

'Okay.' He reached over and picked up the plastic pieces, almost like office stationery he thought, and placed them gently on her nipples. Then he kissed her, pulled her bottom lip out with his teeth and bit down on it, not hard enough to draw blood perhaps, but hard enough to draw a moan from her.

'Let them snap shut,' she said.

So he did and watched her nipples whiten and the skin of her breasts warm. 'Twist them,' she cried out as he was fucking her and he did, enjoying the way she moaned and writhed under the pain. 'More,' she said and he dutifully twisted them again, watching the small drops of blood escape the plastic and dribble down her breasts.

'Tell me about Beatrice's mum,' she said, getting out of bed and slipping a Richmond Fontaine CD into the player.

'No.' Jon stared out of the window. The visit with Mrs De Roedel had left him drained. He couldn't really explain the rush of feelings he'd had in that antique house and wasn't in any mood to try.

Suze sat up on the bed. 'What do you mean, no?'

'I mean, I don't want to talk about it.'

'Why?'

'Why? Because I don't want to.'

'Fuck, Jon.' She got up off the bed, cranked the music up, way up, turned away.

'What's the matter with you?'

'With me? I just wish you'd tell me more. You keep everything so close to your chest, you don't ever tell me how you feel.'

He got up, exasperated by her tone, by the things she wanted from him which he found so hard to surrender. 'I don't know how I feel, Suze, not really. I put it into words, it's something different, no longer what I feel.'

She snapped her head back towards him. He could see she was crying. 'You're just like my parents.'

'I'm not your parents.'

'No, but you close yourself off like they did. After that day, they never said what they felt.'

'Perhaps it scared them too much.'

'All the more reason to talk about it.'

Jon got up, moved towards her, took her hand, felt it limp in his. 'Sometimes talking just disfigures things.'

She pulled her hand away. She felt unreasonably angry and she knew that it had to do with Beatrice's father's death. Dominic had sent him the photos after all. That stupid boy. Killed him almost as surely as someone had killed Beatrice. She spat out a piece of tobacco from her mouth. 'Excuses. I heard them all through my adolescence. Mom, Dad – they never said anything, let the silence devour them, they never thought about what it was like for me.'

He felt a terrible sadness in her words, a world that was closer to his than even she thought, and he took her by the waist and pressed himself so close to her that their mouths were unable to speak, to do more damage.

*

'Want to do some mushrooms?' she asked later.

'Mushrooms?' He hadn't done mushrooms since he was sixteen and they hadn't left any pleasant memories, being sick, yes that was it, no transcendental visions only the cold hard kiss of marbled reality.

'Let's do some mushrooms and go out on the town.'

'But it'll be hell, it's Friday night.'

'All the more reason.' She pulled the sheets off her and moved towards him, 'C'mon, Jon, let yourself go, have some fun.' She grabbed his cock which was semi-hard and began playing with it while he thought about all the bad things that could happen to him if he took mushrooms on a Friday night in Amsterdam.

'It tastes like shit,' he said, sipping the foul lukewarm tea that Suze had made, unable to quite believe he was doing this. He wondered if he was still trying to impress her in some way.

'Just hold your nose and down it, if you don't like the taste.' She drank her mushroom tea, then lit a cigarette. Upended a wrap of white powder on the CD case. Chopped it with a credit card into two lines. Richard Buckner was singing about distance, love and alcohol. 'This'll get us started.' She bent down, snorted the line, handed Jon the rolled-up note, watched him do the same. 'We've got about half an hour of normality before the 'shrooms kick in, how do you want to use it?'

He tied her up. He was so sick of it. It took all the spontaneity out of sex, this endless preparation, this setting up and marking off. But he didn't want to argue, afraid of what schisms it might yet open up between them. And he kept telling himself it was nothing, just rigmarole, something he should be able to accept. He tied the final knot, looked down at her. She was smiling.

'I want you to rape me, Jon.'

He stared at her, not sure he'd heard right. 'What did you say?'

'I want you to go out, come back in. Pretend you're a burglar. Come upon me like this. I want you to fuck me, Jon, rape me.'

He pulled back, swung to the side of the bed. 'You're fucking crazy,' he said. He could feel the coke running through his blood, the sense of power and decision it gave him.

'Jon, please.'

'No. There's no fucking way, Suze. This is already too much. I hate doing this. I do it for you but it takes a lot out of it for me – but that, what the fuck, are you crazy?'

'Don't you think most women have a secret fantasy of being raped? Every woman adores a fascist, the boot in the heart, the brute leer, didn't you ever read that one?'

'No, I didn't and maybe they do, I don't know. I just can't do it, Suze, might as well ask me to burn you. How do you think we can go on after that?'

'It's only a game,' she said.

'It's never only a game.' He got up, turned the CD off. Leaned down and untied her arms. 'I'm going out. I need to be alone.'

'But the mushrooms. You can't go out alone, Jon, not with all that inside you.'

'You think it's any better here, tying you up, having you pleading with me to rape you? I think I'll take my chances outside.'

The street was like a river of bodies, merging and coupling, flowing slowly down towards him. The faces were all blank like the discarded early sketches of a painter, half-conceived souls that oozed through the alleyways and across the canals as he tried to swim past them.

There was a strange smell in the air, heavy and chemical, and every cigarette he lit tasted of meat. He felt ready to burst, to hit anyone who got in his way, who tried to fuck with him. He didn't know where he was going, didn't care. He moved out of the way of a pack of elderly tourists marching towards him with all the power and precision of a Paulus Panzer attack. His nausea had disappeared and the early feelings of disorientation replaced by a warm fuzziness that felt like something better. Even the pain in his ankle had finally gone.

Everyone was eyeballing him. Everyone looked mean. Hate filled their eyes and had etched their faces into grotesque grimaces like gargoyles he'd once seen in France. He concentrated on the buildings, trying to understand where he was, what he was doing. He felt sharp twinges of pain and he wondered whether his liver was about to go or whether it was his kidneys or his blood that was wrong. He tried smoking some more cigarettes but they still tasted of meat and after a drag or two he had to throw them away. A man turned to him and began saying something but it sounded like the voice of the teacher from a Peanuts cartoon and he tried to relay to the man that this was so but he'd forgotten where his mouth was.

The buildings were falling down. Obscuring the sky as they huddled together over the dwarf streets. Everything went black as the melted habitations formed a canopy over him. Darkness came. A medieval darkness. But he could still feel the rain and he wondered how it had got through the shield of houses. Everything moved slowly but he knew that when it came, it would come fast and out of nowhere.

He walked back through the busy shopping canyon of Kalverstraat, the only one going against the flow of bodies, and he saw that the zombie-like stream of consumers was trying to show him something. As the people passed him, they turned their arms around so that he could see them. Old ladies and young children showed him their numbers; a group of mentally retarded kids passed by, their smiling marshmallow faces looking up at him as they too exposed their camp tattoos. And he didn't want to look. Knew what he would find. And when he did look, he saw the numbers, messily etched out on his own wrist.

He kept checking his pockets, certain that they'd been perused, felt and emptied, but miraculously his new wallet was still there. The Doctor's book was also in his pocket. He'd forgotten all about it, or perhaps had not been quite ready to read it yesterday. He stopped in the street and stared at the cover, flicked through the yellowed pages. He thought of the book as a wound: writing the slow, sinewy movements of the scalpel through the white pulpy body but, he sensed, it was also a way out of the wound. Both one and the other and always at the same time, continuously pushing and nuzzling like two bloodied hounds in a fight to the death. He stared up at the engorged street, slipped the book back in his pocket. The pain had now moved up to his neck and he was sure that he was about to have a heart attack.

He passed a coffee shop near the Rijksmuseum and heard the sound of the Grateful Dead spilling out, Jerry Garcia's guitar lines like the tentacles of some prehistoric sea monster reaching out of the place, snapping and coiling, wrapping themselves around him in the street. He felt a deep empty ache in his stomach, a memory of that autumn day listening with Jake to the Dead. It seemed almost another lifetime.

He went inside, sat at a table, managed to order a drink, his eyes focused on the speakers above.

Jon sat listening to Garcia as the guitar emerged, roaring through the mix, and the bass came rumbling, hungry and fast, quickly behind it. Then everything exploded. The Dead had slowly built up a wall of noise that unleashed the *Tiger Jam*, Jerry's unique circular feedback noise solo, peaking in intensity, the man picking more notes, cleaner and faster than anyone else had ever done.

As the song came cascading down, the spaces between the notes becoming elastic, Jon tried to remember which version this was. He knew that Jerry had used the *Tiger* only over a small stretch of years and he tried to slot his mind back into position as the Dead effortlessly segued into the fast polka step of Marty Robbins's cowboy death ballad, 'El Paso', and he realized then that this was none other than the legendary Creamery benefit at the Veneta County Fairgrounds, Kesey's place, in Oregon, 27 August 1972. The ultimate performance of 'Dark Star' according to most Deadheads, a swelling apocalyptic maelstrom that was unique to this performance.

The waitress had been watching Jon staring emptily at the speaker, when he suddenly leapt up, sprung like a jack-in-the-box. She watched as he frantically emptied his pockets, throwing cigarette packets, tissues, crumpled notes and a paperback book on to the table. Poor tourist got pickpocketed, she thought, and went back to her work.

He nearly had a heart attack when the wallet wasn't where

it was supposed to be and then he remembered that he'd moved it around different pockets just in case anyone had been following him and noted where it was. He upended the whole thing on the table, pulling out receipts and banknotes until he found the small strip of photocopied paper.

827723169

It was so fucking obvious. It had been staring at him all along, hidden in plain sight.

8/27/72 – 3/1/69

American dates, of course.

8 – 27 – 72

The Dead at the Veneta County Fairgrounds, Oregon.

3 – 1 – 69

The Dead at the Fillmore West, San Francisco.

All classic performances. All part of his collection of live Grateful Dead CDs. Back in London. The ones Jake had listened to.

He walked up to the waitress, asked her where the phone was. She smiled, pointed. He dialled Suze's number, hoping it would be the answering machine, hoping he could just leave a message and not be drawn into anything more.

'Jon, I'm so glad you called, I'm sorry . . .'

'Suze, I have to go to London. I can't talk now. I'll call you when I get back,' he said, and hung up the phone before she could reply.

II

'I just awaken the barbaric, the prehistoric demons,
to a new Godless life.'
– Werner Herzog

'I have talked to you about the difficulty of being Jewish, which
is the same as the difficulty of writing.
For Judaism and writing are but the same waiting, the same
hope, the same wearing out.'
– Edmond Jabès

24

Boarding the plane, hung over, wishing he was back in bed, he wondered again, what exactly did he think he was doing? Buckling himself into the miniature seat that pressed and prodded him from all sides, it seemed he'd made a dreadful mistake. Everyone else on board was smiling with the initial rush of holiday adrenalin or the warm smugness of finally going home. But for him it was neither of these things. Not coming or going but somehow still suspended in the spaces in between. Secretly dreading his return to London lest he end up staying.

It was stupid to think those numbers meant anything, that they would somehow clear everything away like a quick wipe to the inside of a steamed-up windscreen, and all the way to the airport he'd been having second thoughts, big bad doubts about his hallucinogenic satori. He'd left the café immediately after calling Suze, checked out of the hotel and headed for the airport. It was only at Schiphol, with twenty minutes to go till his flight, that he realized he'd left *The Garden of Earthly Delights* on the coffee-shop table. It made him feel terrible. Beatrice's book and all for what, for a string of numbers, a flash of fake insight.

But the old man had liked the Grateful Dead and the bookmark with the code had been in his book after all.

He felt that he needed this, so as not to give up hope and consign Jake's death to being just another unsolved murder. There were too many of those, too many bodies without stories, both here in the present and in the texts and photos at the Jewish museum.

He knew that the detective would probably give up soon enough or be transferred to another case. If and when the killer was caught, all that mattered to anyone would be how many he'd killed, not who, just the bare statistics. Not much would be said about Jake, nor about Beatrice, and murder would just be the word MURDER, nothing behind it at all – no screaming, pleading, crying, torture, rape – none of the gritty stuff, the small, horrible details that make you choke and curse humanity. No, none of that, just the fact that he killed this number of people and where does he rate in the taxonomy of killers, the Nilsen ratings, above or below Dahmer? Manson?

The plane took off and Jon began to sweat, hope and failure swirling in his mind. He drank two Bloody Marys and looked out over the English Channel, a small smudge of grey, thousands of feet below. He scratched his emergent beard, enjoying the strange feel of hair on his skin. Maybe it would be good to get out of Amsterdam for the weekend, he thought. Maybe it was Suze, maybe that was the real reason he'd decided to fly back to London.

Getting away from her or from himself? Or from the part of himself that opened up in her presence? He'd enjoyed making love to her the other night, bound and tied, enjoyed it too much perhaps, and though she'd asked for it, he knew that he too was getting a certain pleasure from inflicting the soft hurts which she so deeply desired. The whole thing had made him uneasy.

And then she'd come up with that request. And he wondered, if he'd surrendered to her desires would there be any possibility for them? Or was it his reluctance to step into that arena which precluded a future? He thought of her Colorado eyes, her little-girl stare which always made him laugh and the small, serpentine smiles that crept from her mouth at the most unexpected of times. Why the hell couldn't she just be normal and not want to be hit, tied up? Why does everyone want what's so bad for them?

Stupid question, he thought, stupid fucking question. Better he should think of those eyes and that look of hers, keep that in mind.

London was perversely sunny for October and he stood for a few minutes, eyes closed, outside Terminal 4, just letting the weak winter sun bathe him with whatever heat it had to give. He took a taxi home, trying to avoid making any conversation with the driver as they inched along the M4 early-evening rush.

Cruising through Chiswick, Jon felt the anticipation growing in his stomach, and he tried to tell himself that it might all be for nothing, trying not to get too worked up, too excited – after all, what the hell could Jake have put inside a double-CD case?

He paid the driver, picked up his mail and went straight to the flat. It looked smaller somehow as he turned on the light and watched the dust scatter through the air. Smaller and darker than he remembered it to be, and he suddenly felt a crushing sensation as though someone had just stamped on his ribcage. The flat was so empty and it was only now that he realized it, like walking out of a smoky room, coming back, and only then smelling the smoke. He stood there for a few minutes feeling everything draw away from him. He looked at the sofa where Jake had sat and he felt furious for having let the old man go. He wanted to scream at the room for not telling him. For not realizing what he'd meant to him while he was still alive. The dumbest of mistakes, used to prop up countless Hollywood movies and he'd fallen for it.

'I'm not going to let you slip away this time,' he said to the empty room. 'I'll follow it through.'

He went to the kitchen and poured himself a scotch, ripped open a pack of Marlboros and sat down facing the television. He picked up the framed review, *that* review, which took pride of place on top of the TV. Stared at it, skim-reading the derisive paragraphs. He unclipped the frame, pulled out the cutting and crumpled it in his fist. It gave so easily, he was surprised. He put the empty frame back in its place then smoked two cigarettes, letting the anticipation course through him, watching the black screen.

He got up and went over to his CD cabinet. It had originally been a shallow cupboard but Jon had removed the door and mouldings and put up shelves so that it became a neat indented bookcase for his live Grateful Dead CDs. He had about 200 of them, live concerts burned on to disc from across the group's history, mostly triples, this being the length of an average Dead show.

He took out the two concerts. The boxes didn't feel any heavier or substantially different. He'd somehow thought that when he got here, he would know immediately. He prepared himself for the worst.

He opened the cases. Everything looked normal. As it should be.

A dizzying rush of disappointment swept through him. What had he thought Jake had left anyway, the name of his killer? The thing that would make his death okay for Jon?

He'd wanted something, yes, some magic talisman that would explain and absolve everything, and instead he'd followed a bad trail, the old man probably just jotted down his favourite Dead concerts while waiting for a bus, nothing more. Jon stared, deflated, at his reflection in the CDs, his face coming back thin and far away. And that was when he noticed it.

He'd always used one type of blank CD for his recordings. Discs 1 and 3 were of this brand but disc 2 was a TDK. He'd never used those.

Excitement bubbled up in his brain as he frantically opened the other case and found that the Fillmore East set also had an anomalous second disc sitting on top of the original.

He sat staring at them for a while, not quite knowing what to do, or not quite daring, just staring at this face that stared back, bearded and dull – his own – and he thought that maybe he should just leave, get back in a cab, back to Amsterdam. He wished he could settle for not knowing, consign the past, bury it, forget it, fuck it.

He took the first rogue disc and put it into his CD player. He watched the tray withdraw and the machinery humming as the laser tried to read it. He could hear it spin at some impossible speed, the light plucking the information from its surface. He lit a cigarette. Took a deep breath.

Nothing happened.

It kept spinning. There was no display. There didn't appear to be anything on it. He cursed silently and then, of course, he realized.

He took the CD out and walked over to his computer, waited while it booted up, then placed it in the CD-ROM tray. He listened to it whir and buzz and watched the black screen.

The cursor went into its swinging ape 'wait' mode, the media player window popped up, and Jon watched, absolutely stunned, as Jake's face appeared on the screen in front of him.

25

'I made my first cut at the age of thirteen, in the safe locked-up spaces of my rooms, with a sewing needle I had taken from my mother's bureau. I put it through my left nipple. Slowly, measuredly, I let the needle feel its way through to the other side. It took half an hour for it to come out the opposite end, but by the time it did, everything had changed and I knew that I had somehow inadvertently stumbled upon my true self.

'I began to explore my body in this way from then on. Always in the privacy of my rooms, when Mother and Father were out on one of their many social engagements. I would lock the door, set up my needles and pins and enter another world.

'Of course, a psychoanalyst will tell you that it was a reaction, a reaction to the overbearing controlling impulses of my father and the dull, grey childhood possibilities of the late fifties and early sixties in England. But it was more than that, more than they could ever imagine – a special door through which only I was allowed.'

Jon listened as Jake detailed his father's final disinheritance, Raphael Kuper, the whole sad story.

'I hated my father, let me say it again, I hated the old man more than I loved or cherished anything in this world and my life became structured by this hatred. Its walls were my walls, its breath the breath stuck in my throat.

'By the time of my teens, my father had become one of the largest importers of food from the continent, using the connections he'd made before the war. Money and influence crowded him like bats fluttering all over our ten-bedroom home.

'I always knew that I was destined to follow him into the business, into the wheeling, dealing, expense-account trips and boardroom battles that filled his life. From as early as the age of thirteen I felt that this was not what I wanted to do or to become. Perhaps like all children of a certain age I was seduced by the allure of doing something different, of changing the world in some way. A couple of years later I realized that what I really wanted to change was myself.

'It started with small things – little burns or scratches on my thighs and torso, small black and purple marks of independence on secret parts of my body. After yet another argument with him I would run up to my bedroom, strip off my clothes and take back my body. The pain took away that other pain – it was cleaner. It was mine.

'If you've never experienced this then you don't know. And you will never know. You will sleep until the big sleep slumbers down upon you. You will never wake up. Never feel the world, move only like a weakened, bitter ghost through it.

'There is something pure and fundamental about letting a sharp, silvery blade ripple across your flesh, watching the first burst bloom of your body creeping across the skin, feeling it in your stomach, your balls and your heart. Feeling on fire for the world. Feeling the world in every last spasm of pain and heartache and hate and sweetness that it contains. It can take so many years to learn that one is dead. You still don't understand? Think about it. How when you step inadvertently on an upturned plug suddenly the world is right there, electrically and immediately sprung and sprayed in your face, and for a few seconds everything is clear and motionless, suspended in tremulous space. This is what happens. This is how it begins.

'Thus, I experimented voraciously through my adolescence, with fire, with constriction, with scarification.

'Perhaps you find this weird, inhuman, un-understandable, so far from your experience of reality that all you can do is dismiss it in a frightened glance. Perhaps people still do, but you must understand that it is only the smallest of differences between that and those other lethal methods of forgetting – alcohol, tobacco and sweat. We all kill ourselves in little ways every day. Paradoxical as it may seem, I do believe it's what keeps us alive. We need to remember our bodies. We are thirsting for it. We have lost our bodies, forgotten them, tossed them away, discarded, bedraggled, meaningless, reduced to function, to nothing. We need to get back to them. We are aching to feel them. Put the needle in. Try it. Once. Then judge. Feel every rotten, pulsing, pain-drenched, sizzling little atom in your body. Remember it is yours.

'After a few years of various improvised techniques and routines, I began to enjoy the pain, to see that it held something for me that other so-called pleasures did not.

'I don't like using words like transcendence, they carry too much religious baggage, but a transcendence of sorts it seemed, entirely secular and yet infinitely repeatable.

'Even when I started, pushing sewing needles through my flesh, I felt that something was happening to my body and mind, something unexperienced before, a world that I had not even imagined was suddenly displayed before me. I realized who I was in the most intimate and sensuous way, in the trailing wake of memory awoken out of slumbrous vein and artery, cortex and bone, the remembered body alive to itself for the first time, itself for the first time.

'My father – predictably, inevitably – wanted me to take over the business from him and so when the time came to think about university, I was told that I was going to Cambridge to study law and woe betide me if I didn't get myself accepted there or if I happened to have any fanciful notions of other possible paths. I didn't argue. Not with him.

'When I got there in the beginning of my nineteenth year, I found that my course covered enough things of sufficient interest to me to balance my father's holy triumvirate of company law, tax law and international trade law.

'I settled into Cambridge comfortably and rather quickly to my surprise. It was as if being physically further from him had stripped away the residue of years sitting on my chest. I wrote infrequently and came down to London only for Christmas.

'My father had been raised an Anglican but I believe that after he reached the age of fourteen, religion didn't mean a thing to him. Once he started working he realized that his brain had little space or time for what could not yield results in the short term. However, he felt it his duty, for reasons that I could never quite figure out as a child, to instruct me in the ways of our Lord and to make the token gesture of presenting us on the church steps every Christmas Eve. I went with him, uncomplaining, somehow closer to him then – in the shadow of something we both did not believe in – than I had felt at any other time.

'I pursued my studies like any earnest young student but I also pursued my undercover curriculum. You see, until I went to Cambridge I was just a novice, a child eagerly experimenting with no form or history, just whatever was to hand. I felt it rather than anything else, I had an instinctual notion as to where to put the needle in or how tight to tie the waistband. The university libraries proved exceptional places of learning. In the Anthropology department I read about African tribes who practised scarification, Polynesian tattoo initiations and other esoteric rituals duly recorded for "scientific interest" by awed, bespectacled Victorian explorers. They did not know that they were in fact writing a manual, a do-it-yourself guide for the second half of this century. Across the countless anthropological texts and essays lay a fragmented bible of the pleasures of the body, pleasures achieved only through steel and fire.

'For every hour I studied statutes, I gave an hour to Sioux hanging ceremonies, for every tort there was a slice of flesh, a pierced membrane, a new world entirely strange and yet impossibly familiar.

'There were only a few people in the area at the time who were pursuing a similar course to mine. Sometimes we would bump into each other at certain lectures or performances though we never really got together and spoke about what lay beneath our clothes. There was an imperative secrecy about everything, as if that was part of the force that kept us entranced. We never shared anecdotes, compared notes or piercings. That kind of community wasn't to form for another ten years or so and even then . . . it's only in this past decade that things have become more organized. Information is now widely available on the Internet. Where once I had to scour through dusty volumes in Cambridge's silent libraries, now any fourteen-year-old-kid can learn how to pierce his scrotum in twenty-two different ways by clicking a few buttons and, should his mum burst into the room, he can deftly flick the screen back to *Grand Theft Auto* and she'll think everything's perfectly all right. It makes it easier for kids now. They can see that they aren't the only ones, that there are others out there and that what they perhaps thought was sick and ugly about themselves is in fact a form of art, a form of freedom.

'I never stopped experimenting. I wore tight constricting waistbands under my cloak, sat in lectures with a hundred clothes pegs carefully hanging off my flesh. I read all the literature I could and tried to copy the ancient ceremonies and rituals depicted there. It gave me strength, a deep power that was all the more satisfying because I knew that I had nurtured and developed it myself. It was perhaps the only thing in my world at the time that I could truly call my own.

'I continued with my practices after I left university. I also became a businessman. I wore a pinstripe, shaved and shined my shoes every day. I set up delivery contracts and supply networks, negotiated and expanded our field of interests. I became quite feared, a man of action and all that. My father was impressed and, on reaching his fiftieth birthday, he set me up in my own business, relieved that I had finally seen sense and "grown up". I diversified and accrued more money. I learned how to hang from horizontal flesh hooks for hours at a time. I flew across the globe, signing contracts and buying stock. I always went to see the "natives", sat in on tattooing sessions and scarification ceremonies.

'As time went on I began to meet more people with the same interests as me, computer executives in California who would perform Olgalga hanging ceremonies on their weekends off and housewives who cut a scar on their thigh every time their husband beat or humiliated them.

'I always wanted to be different from my father. I hated everything he stood for and by the time of my adolescence I hated every minute spent with him. He was always cold, always businesslike and he poured the hate that had drowned his heart on to me.

'He hated everyone, thought everyone was about to rip him off or cheat him in some way and he always looked for ways to screw that person before he himself would be screwed. He brought down companies large and small, shook hands with prime ministers and then planted stories about them in the press. He was a nasty man in every sense of the word. I cannot find anything to mitigate him. I have tried because your father is your father even if he is a monster and I sought some way to understand him, to break through the cement wall that he'd placed around himself and, if not to agree with him, at least to see why he did what he did.

'So, as you can imagine, it was the all-time ironic kick in the balls when he died and left that testament. It seemed to me that I had spent my entire life trying to be different from my father and suppressing and hating the parts of me that I felt were like him and then, finding out that he wasn't my father, not the biological one anyway, that was a hell of a thing.

'I had always been scared that I would turn out like him, that genetics would out. At the age of twenty-seven I had a vasectomy. I wanted to be certain that I would never have children, never do to them what was done to me, and now I found out that I had fought all my life not to carry on the family line, only to discover that my family line had in fact been wiped out wholesale some fifty years previously.

'It also opened up another part of my "father" that I had never thought him capable of. I couldn't imagine the man that had made so many people's lives a misery as the benevolent rescuer of a Jewish child. It was tempting to reassess him on that basis but I knew that the reasons for what he did would remain for ever buried and obscure and that it was not to be the mitigation that I had searched for all that time.

'I rarely turned up for work after that. I delegated and disappeared. Cashed in my chips, as they say, sold my options – all too aware now that I had only one option left. Everything I'd known about myself had suddenly been overturned and I felt an impostor in a suit, walking through the thirty-first-floor office that bore my name, which wasn't even my real name, on the door.

'I sat in my dead father's flat and read everything I could about Amsterdam during the Nazi occupation. I had Foyle's deliver all the books they had about the period and I immersed myself in them.

'I knew my family name. It was Kuper. I'd gone through my father's documents and found out who his partner had been before the war. I scoured through indexes and compendiums of the dead and the surviving. I didn't find anything and I knew that the next step was to go to Amsterdam. To be once again in the city of my birth and of my first death.

'I had been reborn an Englishman, the son of a wealthy business-man and a trusted part of the Establishment. My father's testament proved only what I had intuited ever since I was thirteen. My difference, the way my parents always seemed so alien to me, the way the rest of the world seemed strange. These were things I knew as a child, knew them so deeply inside myself that I never doubted them.

'I found a new freedom when I lost my father. I was no longer part of anything, I was anything I wanted to be and I felt a glorious relief that I could never communicate to anyone else – a delightful, unimagined awakening of freedom.

'I went to Amsterdam. I visited the places of the past. I began my search. There was a website on which you could look for survivors of the Holocaust. I tried. It came up empty.

'I watched hours of testimony in the basement of the Jewish Historical Museum. Hundreds of hours of videos and scratchy celluloid filled with survivors telling their own stories. I learned all the things that I had shamefully avoided during my life. We weren't taught about it in school back then; the idea of Holocaust Studies had not even crept into historical academia.

'I had caught up on my ignorance in London, had read everything, the building mountain of horror and fact getting higher with each book. But it wasn't until Amsterdam – when I really came face to face, so to speak, with the victims – that I felt it personally and unbearably.

'When I had read my father's testament, the fact that I'd been born a Jew had meant nothing compared to the liberating force of the knowledge that my father wasn't really my father. Here in Amsterdam I felt it all hit and tear through me like a slow and jagged piece of glass.

'I watched the footage of the deportations from Amsterdam to Westerbork on the small, constantly running TV set at the Hollandse Schouwburg. Black-and-white flickers of another time. Families dressed in their best suits looking around dazed, waving to people on the trains, wondering where the windows are. A lazy Sunday afternoon feel about the whole thing that could have been created only through a massed tissue of lies. The soldiers indolently lolling by as if park rangers and there, in the corner of the screen, a last handshake, a partial awareness in a drooping mouth quivering, while soldiers walk by chatting so unconcerned by the meaning of this whole scene and finally the train bucks and glides into the horizon, diminishing, till only a speck and then, not even that. I watched it endlessly and I scrutinized the faces of those being deported. I wondered whether I would see my father, a face I would recognize, some genealogical signifier. Of course no such thing happened but I was entranced by the footage and I sat, all day sometimes, watching it as it looped its way through, forward and back again, and each time I looked at someone else in the crowd, focused on another fear-filled face climbing into a railway car. I was born into this, I thought, this was a part of me.

'When I had read the books, I had been shocked and moved by the numbers, the organizational wizardry of the Nazis, their cruel and demonic bureaucracy – but when I stared at the black-and-white faces I saw myself in the sluggish movements of dead men and women, in the pieces of film that outlasted the lives that had been burnt on them.

'I had been in Amsterdam for two months and had found nothing but other people's deaths. Then one day I got an email. An American professor who was writing a book on Dutch Jewry had uncovered some documents relating to my family. He had seen my posting on the net and wanted to meet.

'He was tall and suitably professorial, a voluminous mane of hair balancing gently on his head, and he brought with him one of those large, wide black briefcases that salesmen use to carry their merchandise in. We had coffee opposite the Stedelijk and he showed me photos of my mother and father, sepia-drenched prints from the thirties, a wedding photo with a swastika hanging in the distance. There were family trees and pages from the backs of Torahs listing the dead.

'I stared entranced at a photo of my father. A thin, hooded-eyed man, who looked not at all like me, standing proud by a large store, his clothes impeccable and his hair greased down smooth in the fashion of the time. I would not have recognized him. It was strange to look at that photo, to think that this was once him, for a split second of time he had been caught and that was practically all that had remained.

'The American professor gave me the briefcase. "It belongs to you anyway," he said and handed me his card. He promised he would send me a copy of the book when it was finished.

'There had been approximately 127 members of my branch of the Kuper family in 1939. It was the year of a golden jubilee and the whole family had gathered together in a country house, outside Amsterdam, to celebrate. There were photos of kids playing in the river and adults sitting on old-fashioned deck chairs, smoking cigarettes and reading the German papers for news of the imminent war. It was the last time the family was together.

'By 1943 they had all been sent East, died of hunger or were living like rats, hidden in some occlusion in a house somewhere, in constant fear of the inevitability of being exposed. A Holocaust census report from the fifties shows that none of them survived.

'One hundred and twenty-seven people. I could not believe it. I looked at the numbers for Amsterdam Jews. Over 105,000 deported, under 5,000 came back. A bad percentage even by wartime standards.

'Things become hazy here. I started drinking. I smoked drugs, snorted them, never cared what they were as long as they were strong. I felt fuzzy and undefined most of the time, felt like I was fighting the very clothes that kept me warm. I woke up screaming every night. I tried not to sleep and then the demons came in the daytime. They followed me around the city. I could feel their festering breath on my neck, hear their mechanical footsteps and insect shrieks as I passed by the canals. The city became drenched in evil, in history, in all that had happened on its streets, and I realized then that the past does not exist. Because to call it past is to betray its touch. Everything that has happened is still with us, some of us, one of us, all of us, and together we are the past, carrying it on our shoulders, imprinted in our psyches, the personal parental hells and the ones that take place in the dark, in disused fields and pits and crematoria. A wiser man once said, if all time is eternally present, then all time is unredeemable. And maybe he was right. And maybe he was wrong. Maybe we can escape the clutch and clamour only by sinking ourselves further into it, accepting it as part of our eternal and terrible present.

'But I was telling you a story. Forgive me. Yet it all comes to the same end. I was stuck in hell. I could literally feel the spin of the planet below my feet, the onrush of people and buildings, the terrifying speed of the present, dissolving into past. It was only in alcohol and drugs that the world stopped for the briefest of moments. Soon four months had passed and I hadn't even realized. I would wake up and drag myself to a bar, sit there and read survivor testimonies until they closed, or snort some Ketamine and spend all day going through the films at the JHM. Even my body was no refuge and, though I still practised the routines and modifications that I had all my life, they were now drained of pleasure, no more useful to take me away than an out-of-date travelcard. I tried more extreme forms but they too yielded nothing but blood. The people I was staying with tried their best and without them I would never have made it past that terrible summer.

'One evening I was sober enough to understand them when they spoke to me. They said they wanted me to meet someone. They wouldn't let me demur and they took me to their meeting hall. They called themselves the Revised Council of Blood. Just another bunch of kids desperately trying to make their reality more romantic. I understood them. That night they introduced me to their new member, a frail old man, older than me. He was extremely gracious and well spoken and he introduced himself as Dr Chaim Kaplan.'

26

Jon paused the CD. Scanned back through the last few seconds. Played them again. Jake had definitely said what Jon had thought he'd said.

The Revised Council of Blood.

Jon looked at the flickering, paused image of the old man, thinking, she hadn't told him anything.

Not a fucking thing.

He'd told her enough about Jake, even shown her the photo. She must have known. And he felt betrayed, deeply betrayed – not only by Suze's silence but by the old man as well. He felt resentful that Jake hadn't told him this while he was still alive. Why had he gone through the whole charade of hiding the CDs? And what for? So he could detail his life? Spew street philosophy and garbled autobiography? Perhaps that was all Jake had meant to leave, a testimony of survival not too far removed from the survivors' testimonies that he'd viewed in Amsterdam. Either way Jon felt cheated. It didn't explain anything.

He lit a cigarette and wheeled his chair back from the computer screen. The body stuff had disturbed him, or, more accurately, it had disturbed his image of Jake, his memories and perceptions of the old man. Even though he'd seen the body that day in the morgue, and before that in the bathroom, he'd still refused to assimilate fully the information that he'd been given. Now that it came directly from Jake's mouth, it was a deluge, unstoppable in its implications. Was this really the same man who'd stayed with him? It made his skin crawl. And, of course, he thought about Suze too.

He should have guessed there was a connection, that pain freaks huddle together. There was something about the city, its subconscious, the dark alleys of its most forbidden dreams. Something like a kind of psychological gravity that pulled all these people together. And what about him?

He hadn't wanted to upset what they had by talking to Suze about it, not that day, and then they'd had that argument and he never had a chance to ask her about Beatrice. But now he knew, there were no doubts left, only questions as to how deep her involvement was and whether she had assisted in Jake's murder. Perhaps the detective had been right from the start. Jake could have been the killer. He had a fondness for pain, that was obvious – had Suze and Beatrice stumbled on to this fact, plotted to kill the old man? Succeeded maybe, but only after Beatrice had been silenced? No, that couldn't be right, Jon reminded himself, Beatrice had been killed while Jake was staying in his flat. But maybe he'd had an accomplice.

It was all too much, too much to think about, to digest and assimilate. He wished that they hadn't had that argument, it would make things more difficult when he saw her again. And he wanted to. That was the damndest thing. He wanted to so much.

Despite all the problems which now seemed as far away as that enchanted city itself, despite the words they'd bounced off the walls of her apartment, despite all that, he still wanted her. And now there would be this between them too. Another barrier, another obstacle.

There was a certain dangerous disassociation in what Jake had done, and in what Suze was doing. Pain was perhaps the most basic reflex and to be able to withstand it, to take pleasure from it, showed a strong capability for disassociation – the same capability that Jon had seen in the faces of SS men as they killed babies with rifle butts to save on ammunition.

His car was still there, unticketed, unclamped and untowed – a modern-day miracle in central London. He needed to drive. He had no desire to get back to the computer even though he knew there was still a lot of footage left. It had made him feel sick and depressed. It had made the old man's death even more poignant and pointless, almost unbearable. Jake had been killed twice in his mind. Once when the detective had called him and again now, for he had to accept that everything he'd thought he'd known about Jake was a lie, or if not that, then only the smallest fragment of a hidden whole. The Jake on the video was not the man he'd known in those two weeks and it was like suddenly finding that a stranger has been occupying your bed – a cold sweat and short breath kind of feeling. He stuck an Uncle Tupelo tape into the machine and turned it up to the max to drown out the sounds of life around him and the questions inside him.

It felt strange to be driving again. The early-evening rush hour had dwindled down to a few cars and the motorway was clear. He drove up and down the Westway for a couple of hours until he stopped thinking, until all that existed was the road ahead of him, the music in his head and the metronomic ticking of the car's engine.

He ended up in the West End. He parked the car, spent an hour in HMV, browsing blankly through the shelves, returning with a couple of CDs under his arm.

But he didn't feel like getting back in the car. Didn't want to roll up the windows, drown out the world, keep moving. Suddenly that was the last thing he wanted to do. He took his tape machine and several tapes that were lying around. He left the car there, aware that it would be towed away first thing the next morning, and walked into the quivering mass of Piccadilly Circus.

He walked slowly, watching the young backpacked tourists standing still for photos, smoking and playing bongos, strolling around bedazzled by coke signs and speeding buses, black taxi snakes winding down Regent Street, coffee bars on every corner where once pubs used to stand filled with chattering happy people, stopping for a few minutes in the warmth and light provided, filling up on the smell of coffee and fresh cigarette smoke before heading back to their lives, cramping into tubes and standing on buses, keeping hold, never losing balance, traumatized and pulverized by the time they finally reached home.

He stopped in a pub off Oxford Street whose walls were dark with cigarette smoke and exhaled lives. His ankle felt much better. Almost back to normal. He drank a couple of whiskies now that he no longer risked being breathalysed and went back out into the late-evening rush, watching a group of women, beautiful and elegant as they crossed his line of vision, smiling and giggling. He felt so damn jealous. Why can't I be that happy, that carefree, even some of the time? And as he walked past them he made a vow to try not to think of all the things that were missing. That was always the first, irreversible step. That, and thinking things would only get better. That was why the women were laughing. They existed only in the moment.

He turned back and headed for them. They were waiting at a light. He grabbed the redhead who was standing nearest to him and kissed her. He thought she would wrench herself away, kick him in the balls, scream rape – but she didn't do any of these things. The light had changed and her friends were staring silently. Jon hadn't even really seen her face but he could feel her warmth and life pound through him. Then the lights changed again and they uncoupled, staring at each other with bemusement and a gentle affection that held their smiles in place.

27

'I'm going to tell him when he comes back.' Suze slumped back into the soft embrace of the sofa.

'You can't.'

'I'm sorry, Dominic, I have to. I can't stand it any more.' She got up, reached for her cigarettes on the table. 'I just have to. It can't go on like this.'

'I don't think it'll be of benefit to either of you,' Dominic said, creeping slowly into his corner, trying somehow to get a hold of this situation, understanding he was failing.

'With all respect, I don't really think it's any business of yours.' She regretted having come.

He leaned forward. She could see the muscles around his mouth twitch as if they were pulled by invisible cables. She felt a shiver. 'If only you knew, Suze.'

'Knew what?' She was so exasperated by the little teases that she'd once found romantic. Now it seemed to her that he enjoyed the obfuscation and mystery, somehow got off on the power of things untold.

'I don't think I can tell you, Suze. I'm not sure you'd understand.' He leaned back. Bill brushed by him and settled at his feet. 'Especially if you're going to talk to Jon.'

She stared at him and for the first time she felt frightened. She sensed that there was something terribly wrong about the room, the smell, the cramped lighting, something she just couldn't place. How well did she really know Dominic?

She'd come over to his flat with a bottle of wine and a bag

of grass, needing someone to talk to, having spent the last day under the bedcovers, trying to think of all the ways she'd fucked up, or of how she'd do it differently if it was hers to do again. Jon walking into the museum, her seeing him. The truth from the beginning.

But it didn't help, this constant chewing over of what was already done and she'd called Dominic, asked if she could come round. At first it sounded as though she'd woken him from some monstrous Rip Van Winkle slumber – he was so far away he sounded like a radio signal lost in the ether – but he'd quickly got himself together, said, sure, come round. Yet there was something in his tone that almost made her not.

His place was a mess but she didn't care. She snuggled down on the sofa and began drinking, knowing that this was the only way she could really say what she felt. And though she knew it was probably the wrong thing to do, she'd told him about Jon, watching his reactions like a lab assistant peering into a microscope.

He hid it well. But not really well enough. She told him how they'd just met a couple of weeks ago and how she was really missing him. She told him of the fight they'd had though not why it had occurred. Sex was something she didn't feel comfortable talking to Dominic about, but everything else she told him. And she found that in the telling a deeper desire was revealed, as if she'd held back from accepting it these last few days, afraid of where it might lead. She spilled out her heart, spilled a bottle of wine on his carpet, told him she'd never really felt like this before, apologizing all the time for her state, for the carpet and for coming round at such an ungodly hour.

He had to listen to all this, saying, no really, it's no hassle, no, the stain won't even show, it's perfectly okay, slowly numbing himself with wine. Every so often he disappeared into his bedroom, coming out a few minutes later, his face ashen. She wondered if she was doing the right thing, something was very wrong here, but now that she'd started she felt she needed to finish.

And then she'd mentioned Jake. That Jon was here looking for the reasons behind the old man's death.

'I was so scared, Dominic. I didn't say a thing. That we knew Jake, nothing. He showed me his picture and I pretended that I'd never seen him before. I was so surprised at my willingness to enact this deception. I was so scared.'

'Why, Suze?' He looked at her, knowing then that she would never be his, that their lives were destined to pass by each other, touching only at the periphery.

'Why? Jesus, Dom! Jake's dead. Doesn't that mean anything any more? Two people from our group are dead. The same fucking killer. Doesn't that scare the shit out of you? Make you think?' She looked at him but he was gently stroking the dog, his eyes hooded and downcast. 'I just couldn't tell him.'

'Because you wanted to fuck him?'

'Dominic!' She felt like punching him. 'No, that wasn't the reason at all. I just liked him, you know, I thought perhaps there's something here. I haven't felt that for a long time. Yes, Wouter had just chucked me – I wasn't even thinking about that. He just looked so helpless that day, I had to save him from the security guards. And everything, at first, was so easy with him, so untroubled. And when he mentioned Jake, it was too late. I knew that if I told him, yes, I knew Jake, all about the Council – then those things would always stand between us. They would be there from the very start. This is how it begins. You know that. Nothing would proceed as normal. Everything totally fucked up.'

'But you knew it would come up. You couldn't have thought you'd keep it hidden from him for ever?'

She shook her head, she could tell that he was enjoying this. 'I just thought if we had a couple of weeks to get to know each other, then I could tell him. And it wouldn't matter so much. I didn't want our first few days together to be stained with that. I don't know why he's so obsessed with finding what happened to Jake, he knew him even less time than we did, but I could see that it was something that would pull him down. And I didn't want him to know what had happened. Our involvement in all this.'

'Why?' Dominic tried to appear as cool and collected as he could though inside he felt a terrible ripping. He could feel his heart thumping away and he was scared that Suze would hear it. He thought about what was in the other room and how he'd saved it just for her. How it was all just for her.

'Because there can only be sorrow in it. For him. For all of us. You know, I'm not very good at gauging people usually, but with Jon, well . . .'

'Are you scared of what he might find?'

'I just don't want this relationship to fuck up, not this time, and I know if he started digging around, uncovering all those ghastly skeletons, well, I don't know if that's the Jon I want to be with.'

'Then don't mention it. Don't mention anything to him.' It would be better that way. Better for her and better for his purposes too. Things were moving fast and he didn't need anyone disturbing the flow. Not until the weekend. Then everything would be different.

'I have to, Dominic. I have to do it before he finds out for himself.'

She got up, went to the kitchen, kicked past the doggy

bowl, empty film canisters, data CDs and ashtrays that littered the floor and poured herself some more wine. 'The ironic thing is I don't even know anything,' she said, spilling some of the wine on her shirt, little roses arcing towards her breasts.

'Maybe you know more than you think.' Dominic smiled, exposing the dark hole of his mouth. He passed her a recently rolled joint. She took a deep drag and felt her lungs sizzle. The room began to spin. She'd thought it was weed but she could taste the crack on her tongue and she took a deep breath to stop the spin of the room. She felt herself losing control.

'What the fuck are you talking about? I wish you'd just be clearer. You knew Jake better than anyone else. You introduced him to the Doctor. I always knew there was something wrong there. I was so stupid not to see it. It was only when I heard about Beatrice and then I tried to deny it, to deny that we were in any way involved – but it's no use. You can't deny things. You can't keep them hidden. I'm such an idiot for thinking I could but I think I've learned now.'

He snorted. 'Even if it means Jon will never speak to you again?'

She wanted to say that she wasn't sure if he ever would as it was. After that terrible fight, when they were both not themselves and yet somehow managed to show more of themselves than they had previously. But she didn't tell him. Didn't want to see the subtle smile of satisfaction that would suddenly appear on his face and just as quickly be erased.

'Even if it means that,' she said.

He moved towards her. She was drunk, didn't see it coming. Before she knew it his head was resting on her lap. She was too far gone to try to move away. She began to stroke his hair. 'What happened? Dominic, please tell me.'

His head moved slightly but remained on her lap. 'I wish I could, Suze, I really wish I could. Next week. Next week it'll all be over.'

She hadn't expected him to say anything and so she was not disappointed. She knew that he had introduced Jake to the Doctor. But perhaps, she now saw, perhaps there was more to it. She understood that the Doctor had created a terrible schism in the group in the few meetings he'd attended. Something, she now thought, they would not be able to repair. They'd found it shocking for a Jew, a camp survivor, to talk the way he'd done and yet, when researching the Charlotte work, she'd come across similar testimonies – not many and often under-emphasized, existing in appendices or in miniature at the bottom of the page as part of a footnote – of others who felt a certain sympathy with the Germans. She'd heard about the Stockholm Syndrome but this was different. This put into question everything they believed in as a group, for if witnessing such horror only made you a part of it then what was all their work for?

She felt his hand, cold and smooth, reach under her skirt, his head still as a stone on her lap. She tried to move, to slide ever so slightly out of his reach but his hand kept creeping up, raising goosebumps on her legs.

'Dominic,' she said, looking down at him, frightened now, as his hand rested upon her panties and he swivelled himself up from her lap and in one swift move placed his lips upon hers. She could feel his tongue probing her mouth and she put both her hands on his chest and pushed him away. He reeled back, fell off the sofa; she heard the dog grunt, then saw Dominic coming towards her.

'No.' She realized she was on the verge of screaming, slipping into hysteria.

'I want you so much,' he said. She understood that somehow she had caused this, she'd not been strong enough to voice her feelings early on and now it had come to this.

'Jon's no good for you, Suze. He'll leave as soon as you tell him about Jake. Please, we could have such an amazing life together, I know.'

'Stop it, Dominic.' She eyed the door, calculated distance, speed and likely obstacles.

'Why? Am I making you uncomfortable?' His tone had changed, sarcasm thickening those northern vowels, and he moved closer towards her. 'And you hate that, don't you? Hate having any kind of confrontation, anything that will make you feel less than good. You lied to Jon, you lied to me just to make your life easier. How do you think it feels hearing you talk about him like that?'

And she realized he was right, or partly right or not right at all, but still it was the way he felt and therefore had as much validity as anything else. 'I'm sorry, Dominic. I should have been more sensitive.' She knew she needed to say this, that things were quickly moving out of control. 'I hide from things, I don't mention them, but I'm trying, Dominic, I'm really trying.'

He turned from her, walked towards the bedroom. 'Please, just go. Get out of here. Before anything happens,' he said and disappeared into the other room, shutting the door behind him. She grabbed her things and left.

When she was gone, he went to the hollowed-out niche he used for the video camera. He first made sure that the front door was locked, that she wouldn't burst in, having forgotten her cigarettes. Then he took the camera and wired it to the TV. He rewound the tape. Rolled himself a joint and stretched out on the sofa. The weed was good. His mind was spinning instantly.

Yet what he saw wasn't good. Not any more. Not for a long time now. Not since the touch of the body. That slimy, cold clasp of dead flesh. The sound of it hitting the canal water. Its slow descent into the blackness. Shit. He had to stop thinking about it. He rolled and sparked another joint. Blew the images from his mind. Turned on the TV. Set the tape to play, to replace the images in his head with ones more desirable.

She'd been sitting dead in the eye of the camera's lens. Centred perfectly. If he'd staged it, he couldn't have done a better job. He was glad he'd set the zoom right.

Suze's face danced on the screen, alternately crying, smiling, angry and appalled. He lay back and butted the joint. Slipped his zip slowly down and felt the hardness raging underneath. He stared at her as she mutely retold her story and he came, shuddering, almost falling off the sofa. He wiped up, stopped the tape, put the camera back in position and smoked another cigarette.

Later, he sat on the bed and began to think about Jon and his place in all this. He needed something else to think about. He felt as if his chest had collapsed, one of those bombs had sucked the lungs out of his mouth. The whole room folding over him. The work of the last few weeks, all the time since Jake had died. He ground his foot down into the floor until the pain made him scream. Then he felt a bit better.

Bill walked into the room, came to rest by him. Dominic buried his face in the dog's soft fur. If Jon was so intent on playing the detective, well, there were ways that he could deal him in, make him part of it. Of course, he already was – he just didn't know it yet. He should have told Suze, he knew that, told her that Jon was in danger, that they all were, everyone linked to the group, to the doctor. But something held him back. Of course she suspected but not the full extent of things. Not how far they'd gone. He knew she was scared and he liked her like that. He stared up at his computers, the flickering screens, the editing boxes, the projectors. Jon would have to be careful, and if the time came, and he was almost sure that it would, then Jon would be pulled into this, used as a buffer. After all, Dominic thought, he wants to know, he wants to be a part of it. It's the least I can do.

28

The next morning Jon woke up alone in his apartment. It was another sunny day and his head felt as if an entire jazz band had taken up residence inside it. He barely managed to make himself some coffee, spilling the grounds all over the floor, suck two cigarettes and take a couple of painkillers before the pain became too much. He lay in bed, his head pounding, and thought about the night before. He couldn't remember what he'd done after he got in. It didn't really matter, was probably best left forgotten anyway.

When the pills had shaved the edge off the pain he went straight to his computer. He'd had an idea last night, miraculously still remembered it this morning. He recalled the day Jake had gone, waking up to an empty flat, the computer buzzing like an unwanted friend. And then it had struck him. The computer shouldn't have been on.

He smoked a cigarette while it booted, watched the icons lining up in their usual positions, a Giant Sand record wheezing in the background. He hit the Explorer button, scrolled down to the History folder.

Clicked.

Double clicked.

Worked out the exact day that Jake had left, clicked again.

And there it was – a list of fifteen or so pages that Jake had visited that morning. It had been there all along, like the CDRs, waiting for him to discover it.

Jon started going through the list, clicking on the links, making sure he wasn't online, making sure he got the same page that Jake had viewed and not an updated one. We are all our own detectives, he thought, here on the net, we all become that.

Sites detailing body-modification conventions.

Ebay. Items no longer available.

The Heathrow webpage, details of flights to Amsterdam.

But nothing that would have made Jake return, nothing Jon could see. He kept going through the pages, slowly scrutinizing every word, just in case it was the smallest of things that drove Jake back. But there was nothing, absolutely nothing.

Jon leaned forward, lit another cigarette, breathed out his frustration. And then he realized. He hadn't looked at it because it was his default home page. But now he could see that Jake had linked from it. He followed the trail of addresses. Brought up the BBC News front page that Jake had looked at – linked to the Northern European news section, linked down from there, and there she was.

Beatrice. Unnamed, unseen, but lurking between the words flickering on the screen. A small paragraph related the discovery of another body thought to be linked to the current string of murders that had been taking place in Amsterdam since January. Jon read and re-read the article. The short detailing of Van Hijn's blunder in February. The killing of the suspect who happened not to be the suspect at all but another freak, a rapist with a collection of mounted nipples. But it had been Beatrice, the ghost of her lurking in those tense, brittle words, that had drawn Jake back to Amsterdam. Which means he must have known. Must have had some idea at least. Though she hadn't been named, he knew that Jake had recognized her. There was no doubt about it in his mind, though why Jake went back or what his involvement was, Jon still hadn't figured.

He saved the pages into his files. Turned off the CD though Howe was still singing about being stuck in the desert, comfort eroded by the dark night. He loaded the CDR and fast-forwarded it until he reached the place where he'd stopped the night before. He didn't feel so bad towards Jake this morning and when the old man's face appeared he felt a deep, thrusting sadness engulf him.

'Dr Chaim Kaplan.

'I should have known really. Should have known that this frail old man would become the pivot on which my new life turned. I sat in on a few of the Council meetings, watched him, noticed how the group obviously revered the old man, deferring to his opinions on a wide range of things.

'I kept drinking, taking more and more drugs and walking around the city, always finding myself at a monument to the war dead or some neighbourhood my family had once walked through. I visited the old house that had been detailed in the tax records. A grand nineteenth-century gabled monster in the lush green calm of the museum quarter. I stood there and watched a young family as they arrived back from some kind of weekend trip. Father and mother and three small children all gaily unloading the accessories of their lives. They joked with one another and promptly carried everything into the house, laughing and smiling. A couple of hours later, I saw them having dinner in the front room, and I watched transfixed as the man slowly carved the roast and served it to his family. There was such a sense of peace in that room that I would have given up my life, right then, for a few seconds of its warmth.

'I was staying with a friend of mine, a member of the Council. He left me to my own devices and was as gracious a host as one could hope for. He kept insisting that I should go and see the Doctor, that I should talk to the old man. That there were connections between the two of us that I had only guessed. He told me so many times that finally I said yes. And I admit, I was intrigued by what I'd heard and seen of the Doctor. His survival from the hell that had sucked my family down. The sense of him being a last link in that awful chain.

'The Doctor lived in a small, fifth-floor walk-up apartment just off the Rembrandtplein. The common parts of the building had once been elegant but were now faded with years of neglect and the whole place had that shabby European feel of something grand gone rotten.

'The old man opened the door and asked me in. He was always polite, always the gentleman. It gave us a connection in those early meetings, an entry port into each other's lives. We were both from a generation that still held on to those virtues of politeness and a stiff, respectful formality and, even though the Doctor was over twenty years older than me, he still seemed closer in many ways than people twenty years younger, a generation I don't really understand.

'We talked about nothing at first. Comments about the weather and state of the city. Sometimes we would talk over some of the ideas we'd heard at a Council meeting, or about an article in the day's paper. We were really only skirting around each other for the first two weeks. Afraid of what lay in the past, what lay waiting. We played chess a lot, a silent game of unspoken friendship, sipping the Doctor's exquisite coffee and eating his delicate Austrian pastries.

'One night, I believe it was a holiday, we'd got very drunk on expensive schnapps and smoked a few joints. The old man was really loose. I'd never seen him like that before, it was as if the alcohol and drugs had taken thirty years off him.

'That's enough of me talking though. My story ends here and this is where his begins. I wanted to preserve some things in their original state. Things that would soon be gone. After he had told me his story, I went back, I borrowed a video camera and turned it on him. I made him tell it again. Naturally, he was glad to.'

The screen went blank and Jon lit a cigarette, shaking in anticipation. He fast-forwarded. Still nothing. Feverishly, he reached for the second CD, almost snapping it as he shoved it into the tray, and waited.

An older man's face appeared, slim and gaunt but filled with life, with a certain animation that is absent from most elderly people. He took a silver case out of his perfectly pressed suit and extracted a thin, unfiltered cigarette. His hands were small and delicate like a woman's, extremely clean and manicured. He put the cigarette to his mouth and took a deep drag that made his cheekbones even more prominent – almost a human skull, Jon thought, if he didn't have that fire in his eyes. He began speaking in slightly accented English, in a stronger and deeper voice than his body had suggested. 'What, you want me to talk about my childhood, my doggie and all that stuff?'

'No.' Jake's clipped, English tones came from some place off-screen, 'just tell me some background.'

'Okay, background you want.' The Doctor took another distressingly deep drag off the cigarette and continued.

'I was born into a comfortably well-off family in 1922. My father had been a surgeon in the Great War and had lost a leg at Passchendaele. It was always given that I would follow in his footsteps and I had no objections to this. But you know the rest. You know about the Nuremberg laws, all that. My childhood, adolescence, all that means nothing. That was a former life, perhaps not even mine. My life started when I got on that train, or more precisely, when I got off the train.

'I arrived in the winter. The Polish air was cold and bitter and snow lay thick and sleepy over the ground. You know the way snow can muffle sounds, well, when I got off the train, I felt like I had stepped into some Dali-esque world, some soft, soundless place.'

'What was it like?'

Jake's voice was calm, interested but also trailing a wisp of uneasiness mixed with impatience.

'Tell me about Auschwitz.'

The Doctor stared at the camera, laughed.

'Yes, everyone wants to know what it was like. The more terrible a thing is, the more they want to know. Think they'll understand it.'

The Doctor laughed, turned his head to the left, staring at his invisible inquisitor.

'Yes, all right, I will try to tell you. I remember that it was bitterly cold that morning, a sort of visceral cold that I had not previously experienced. The kind of cold that you can feel in your teeth, that makes you aware of every part of your body, its discomforts and sudden exposure. On disembarking I had lined up like the rest. When they asked me what I did, I told them I was a doctor, and they sent me to a line where we waited for our tattoos. The next day Dr Werner, an SS man, informed me that I was to be his assistant. He took me to the "Ramp". Showed me how it worked.

'It was an incredible thing, you could hear the screaming before you heard the trains approach. The endless procession of blinkered cars that came to a stop at the large ramp. You ask me what it was like? If only I could take you there and show you, it was a unique place and a unique moment in history.'

'Tell me. I need to know.'

Annoyance was creeping into Jake's voice.

'Well, you could hear the Jewish band playing soft Viennese waltzes in the cold February air as the figures were unpacked from the train. Guttural shouts of "*Raus! Raus!*" and a mass of slow dejected movement spilled out, hurried along by clubs and whips. The soldiers beat and kicked those who didn't move fast enough, the elderly, the sick and the young. The band continued playing as prisoners threw the corpses out of the train. Withered skeletons draped with a thin layer of flesh like greaseproof paper. You could see men in striped burlap, shaven-headed, sunken-cheeked ghosts that slowly went around collecting the newly arrived group's luggage and belongings like obedient bell-hops at a seaside resort town.'

The Doctor leaned back, continued.

'The crowd are told to stand still. A handsome, immaculately dressed officer with a gold rosette in his lapel tells them in a soothing southern German lilt that their troubles are over, that here they will work and here they will live. They have merely been relocated. He promises them that they will be kept together; families, the old, the sick, the newly born. They listen to the lachrymose nostalgic sounds of the band and they believe him. Anything else just wouldn't make sense, after all, would it?

'They line up as they are told. Those who do not are shot, or beaten to death by smiling soldiers. The officer makes his way down the line, humming a jolly melody that was popular back in the twenties. With a point of his finger he signals either left or right. A quick, almost invisible, movement. The old and the sick, the women and the children go to one line, the healthy and strong to another. He tells them that one line is for those that can work and that the other is for those whose duties will consist of "housekeeping". The people duly follow his finger, placing themselves on either side of the ramp. You can see that the logic of this affair begins to dawn on some of the prisoners, they smell that strange heavy burnt scent in the air and they can see the massive, red-brick chimneys that silently spew black smoke into the February sky. And, if you look closely, you can see them trying to make themselves look taller, more confident – smiling, as the Angel of Death passes them by.

'A hunchback and a midget are taken to one side. The officer with the gold rosette questions them and then orders the soldiers to take them to the hospital. The healthy and young are marched away, towards the barbed wire and the barracks in the distance. The other group heads for the building with the chimneys. They follow silently as the guards shout orders at them. Some of the older ones stumble and fall. They are shot with one bullet to the back of the head or clubbed to death for expediency. The majority of the group take no notice, they believe the SS are shooting at troublemakers, they do not want to believe what they hear. It would have grave repercussions for the rest of them.

'They stop in front of the brick building. The dashing officer tells them that before they can go to their camp they must first be disinfected. He takes great relish in pronouncing the word.

'They are led across a small cinder path, down some iron steps and into a massive room. They see the sign at the entrance that says "Baths and Disinfecting Area" in four languages and they feel relieved. The two hundred selected people crowd into the room. It is whitewashed and brightly lit and it augurs well. There are wooden benches along its length and hundreds of individually numbered hangers, the type you might see in any municipal swimming pool or sports ground. They are told that they will have to take off all their clothes before they can go into the showers. Old men look at each other, girls blush – after all that has happened they still have some dignity left. But the second order is more menacing and the barrels of the guns point at them, so they slowly take off their clothes. The SS officer puts a great emphasis on the need for them to tie their shoes together and keep their belongings tidily bundled. Some of the older men laugh at this latest example of German fastidiousness as they knot their shoes, little knowing that pairs of shoes so neatly tied are easier to collect for the home front. The officer informs them of the necessity for them to remember their numbers so that they can pick up the right set of clothes when they are finished with the disinfecting baths. A huge, collective, sub-vocal sigh of relief goes through the huddled, cold mass of women and children, the old and the sick, the rabbis and intellectuals.

'A large oak door opens at the far end of the locker room and they are ordered to go into the shower area where the disinfecting will take place. They slowly walk into the large room, stumbling, not really wanting to be the first in, some helping the elderly step through, others carrying the large number of babies and small children who are to be disinfected. The room is once again brightly lit and they look up at the shower-heads in the wall, not knowing that they are dummies, unconnected and dry. They notice the free-standing square columns that line the length of the room. Each column has many small perforations but they cannot begin to guess what they are.

'Meanwhile, an International Red Cross van arrives, and two young SS unload silver canisters of gas from it. The canisters have written on them in large letters, "Poison: For the Destruction of Parasites". This is what passes for humour.

'Down below, the group stands silently as the door is closed. There is a strange atmosphere in the room and all the long-standing fears that they had managed to keep buried all this time suddenly rise up and fill them with dread. A boy cries in the corner, his voice sounding metallic and already dead as it bounces off the tiled walls of the shower room. Babies begin screaming as the lights go off.

'Then they hear the water hissing through the shower-heads but they feel no moisture raining down upon them as the room begins to fill up with Zyklon B. A mad scramble ensues. The gas starts at the bottom and works its way up. They are trying to outrun it but the bodies they trample on to get there only go to show that there

283

is no escape, only perhaps a minute or two of respite. The screams reverberate all around the chamber as people climb on to the bodies of the dead, fighting and scratching each other, trying to reach higher ground. Screaming and shouting and crying and praying and shitting and pissing all over their own dead bodies.

'The SS doctor in charge opens the viewing hatch. He looks into the shower room and sees the familiar pyramid of corpses at the far end. He is, by now, used to this strange sight, having witnessed it hundreds upon hundreds of times during his stay at the camp. He motions to an officer who turns on the electric ventilator. Twenty minutes later, twelve Sonderkommando wearing gas masks come in and hose down the mountain of corpses stuck together by sweat and shit and menstrual blood. They carry them to the elevators and send them down to the ovens.

'In the bright and whitewashed incineration room, the Angel of Death floats by on the way to his lab. He does not seem unduly concerned by the overwhelming smell of the burnt flesh nor by the backlog of bodies stacked up, waiting their turn in the ovens, like pizzas in a busy restaurant.

'The men from the Kommando bring the new bodies to the dentists and hairdressers, the only place in the camp where these services are available. The hairdressers take the corpses and expertly shave off all head and pubic hair. They place the hair to one side, from where it is collected and sent to a factory in Leipzig that makes amazing things for U-boats out of it. Then, one by one, the good Jewish dentists extract all the gold fillings from the mouths of the dead. They use a lever and a pair of pliers; men once renowned professors of dental medicine at all the leading German universities now prise apart the jaws of the dead, their dead, and extract gold filings, bridges and other shiny things. They put the gold into a bucket containing an acid that melts away any pieces of flesh or bone that might still be clinging to the metal. They also take off any jewellery or ornaments which they throw into a small area to their left that by the end of the evening will be an Everest of gold and sparkling jewels. One man's job is to insert his fingers into the vaginas and rectums of the dead looking for hidden valuables. That is what he does all day long until, he too, is sent the same way these corpses came.

'Fifteen immense shiny doors line the length of one wall. Members of the Kommando open them and orange spears of fire spill out, as three by three, the bodies are put into the blazing ovens and sent into the sky. When the ovens have cooled, the remaining ashes are swept up, loaded into a Red Cross van and deposited into the dark and turbulent waters of the Vistula.'

The doctor lit one of his cigarettes and took two quick drags.

'That was my first day at the camp. It was quite an education as you can imagine.'

'And how did you feel?'

'What kind of question is that? It was a long time ago. Now all I have is memories, what I felt then is lost, gone for ever.'

'But your people were being killed?'

The Doctor turned from the camera, looked towards Jake.

'My people? My dear Jakob, you are making the very same mistake that the Germans made. You think those Romanian and French and Polish peasants were my people? That I had anything in common with them apart from a birthright? That is plain stupid. I felt closer to the Germans than I did to most of the other prisoners. That is not to say it wasn't a terrible thing. It was. But you get used to things. I can't explain it to someone who wasn't there. You think, how can anyone get used to that? But you'd be surprised what people get used to when they haven't got a choice.'

'You were there for selections?'

'Yes. It was better that I, as a doctor, helped with these. But there was no order to it, only the pretence of order, I found that out soon enough. Sometimes we were told that everyone on that day's train would have to go straight to the gas chambers. The camp was overfilled and Jews were streaming in at an amazing rate from all corners of the Reich. Sometimes we had to do what was necessary to keep the ecology of the camp stable. Other times it was the Goebbels Calendar.'

'The Goebbels Calendar?'

'Ach, it was the man's twisted sense of humour. Ever since the mid-thirties, the days of Jewish holiness and festivity were designated by Goebbels for the grandest of actions. The Day of Atonement was always a big one. Many ghettos burned on that day. Many deportations and executions. In the camp we had to make extra selections and everyone newly arrived was not given a tattoo but marched straight to the chamber.'

'And you never objected?'

'What, you think I could have changed all that? You think for one minute that I wouldn't have been walking the same path to the shower rooms if I hadn't co-operated?'

'But this way they win.'

'My dear Jakob, either way, they won. That was how it was. For them, the ramp was the cornerstone of their philosophy, you could see the awe in their eyes. I think for the Nazis it was almost a transcendent moment, not in any cheap religious way or anything, no, it was something much more spiritual; they really believed that they were reaching into the essence of the *Volkische*, into that deep well of ancestral history and memory. That they were diving down to where the water was clear, where it had not been polluted and poisoned, and I too have to admit that there was a certain seduction to it. They saw us, the Jews, as the rotten appendix threatening to burst and spill its poison all through the Fatherland. Once they believed that, the rest followed. What starts as metaphor soon becomes reality. That is how it begins.'

The Doctor coughed, looked away from the camera.

'You know, after a few days of acclimatization, I really understood that I had found my place.'

'Your place? What about your people? How the hell can you say that?'

'As I told you, there was little choice and besides, I was a doctor before I was a Jew. That was how I saw myself.'

'How long were you there?'

Jake sounded exasperated, or was Jon just reading that into his tone because he wanted to?

'Until the end. There was a lot of work, important work.'

'What exactly did you do there?'

'Each doctor had his own area, his own special field of research. They were allowed to use whatever means were necessary and there were a lot of means at their disposal. One thing you all have misunderstood about the Nazis was their quest for knowledge. The Führer was nothing but the shadow of your own enlightened, rationalist selves. Only with complete freedom can breakthroughs be made. That was something I could agree with them on, something I had always believed.'

'But their premises were all wrong.'

'Not entirely, my dear Jakob. Maybe nowadays they seem politically suspect – you might say so – but that does not, in any way, demean their value as tools for the gathering of knowledge. You see, they had ultimate freedom and only through that can you discover new worlds and new things.'

'And what was your particular line of research?'

'I was helping with a series of experiments for the SS. With their usual dry humour they called them "terminal human experiments"!'

The Doctor stopped to laugh. Was he doing it just for the camera, Jon wondered, not at all sure if he wanted to carry on but compelled to do so.

'I had been interested in the human reaction to pain ever since I'd first picked up one of my father's dusty Victorian anatomy books. The SS were interested in finding ways to make the extraction of information more efficient. These were experiments in resistance to torture. Of course by then the Jews were all ghosts, not really worthy volunteers at all and we tended to use the Russians, who were a stronger and fiercer race by far. They had captured three million Russian soldiers in their first campaign on the eastern front and a great many of those ended up in Auschwitz, in fact, the gas chambers themselves were road-tested on Russian POWs.

'We exposed them to varying levels of pain. We tried different instruments, different techniques, and we noted down the results. They were then typed in triplicate and one copy was always sent straight to Himmler, this field being of particular interest to him.

'I remember one day we were told that Himmler was coming to visit us. Dr Werner was scared, he'd spent all morning shouting at us prisoner-doctors – we'd heard that at Sobibor, the camp commanders had organized a special show for Himmler. They had selected the forty prettiest Jewesses in the camp and then stripped them and put them in the gas chamber. There was in all gas chambers a viewing slit; usually doctors would use it to ascertain whether the people inside were dead, but the viewing slit had other uses too. When Himmler arrived, they took him to the gas chamber and let him watch the Jewesses slowly die in there.

'Werner didn't know what we could do to top that but he needn't have worried for Himmler was fascinated by our work here and was a gentleman to the end.'

'And Mengele?'

'Ah. That name. How many times have I heard it to describe evil?

288

Spoken by people who had never met the man. Let me tell you, he was the most erudite, well-dressed and polite human being I ever knew. Nothing like the monster you have invented to explain the horror – you need that monster, no? But that was not him.

'Some of the guards feared Josef almost as much as the prisoners did, but when you saw him playing with his children, the ones he was working on, and you saw him pass them chocolate and sweets, there was such a warmth and empathy about the man. Not for nothing did the prisoners call him the Angel of Death. He was death to them but he was also an angel, fallen down and still capable of a certain amount of grace.'

'But you thought less of his experiments than you did of Werner's?'

'Yes, Josef was one of those men who become obsessed by an idea, a set of words and theories, and then mould the world around those ideas, warping it and reducing any medical breakthrough that one might have stumbled upon. Of course in Auschwitz it worked, the place itself was a tear in reality you see, so he could do what he wanted and he could always find the specimens to prove his theories.

'He was obsessed by the genetic and eugenic theories of the time. Werner and I worked on real people with real premises. He endlessly collected and gathered twins, freaks, anything that could go to prove his theories that genetic corruption will eventually out and manifest itself in physical features. Really, that was, I think, a slightly too literal take on the Führer's work, but you know Josef found many hunchbacks and cripples and other proofs of his theorem among the millions that passed through that railway spur, so who knows, huh?

'I remember he became obsessed with eyes once and one day I was sent to collect something from him. I went to his work area which was right next to the crematorium. The other doctors worked well away from that place but Josef seemed to like passing the raging ovens with their sickly sweet smell, the mounds of hair and teeth and valuables, on the way to work each morning. I think the place inspired him, he felt at the crux of the New Order right there in that crematorium. So, I go in to see him and he has this wall with eyes pinned up all over it. Maybe a hundred or more eyes, pinned like butterflies to the wall. I asked him what it was in aid of and he said, "So that we can see, my dear Kaplan, so that we can see." It was the only time I had known the man to make a joke. But I was too scared to laugh. There was always a sense of unimpeachable dignity about him that made you take his work seriously however much you objected to his premises.'

'What did other doctors do? Were they all involved in experiments?'

'Pretty much so. That was their role in the camp. It is why so many of us prisoner-doctors survived. They needed us. There was a lot of work going on around the whole sterilization issue. They felt they were paving the way for the new civilization, for a better time. Clauberg was in charge of that What were the best and most efficient ways to sterilize masses of people? They tried everything, had prisoners come in, sit at a table and fill out an innocuous form. While they did this we blasted their genitals with X-rays. There were some horrible swellings and abnormalities from that. Other doctors believed in surgical castration as the only safe way to achieve total sterilization and would have contests to see who could perform the fastest castrations. Dering, another prisoner-doctor, a Pole, used to carry around this small wrinkled tobacco pouch that he had made out of a scrotum, an off-cut from the day's work. Mengele sterilized a lot of women, used barium and God knows what else. Many died of course but that is a small price to pay, no? In this, I think, we all came together. Nazi and Jew. In those rooms all that mattered was science. Ideology and politics were left at the door. They even almost treated us as equals.

'You have to understand that Auschwitz was a spasm, long delayed, resulting from the Enlightenment. A reaction to that time and the way it had shaped our world. Human beings cannot stand too much order. You look shocked when I mention scrotum sacs but you would be very wrong to think that these people were psychotic, that's just the easy answer, eh? So, you see none of them was psychotic, whatever you may think – remember "National Socialism is nothing but applied biology" – they didn't see themselves as outside of society; on the contrary they thought they were the very fabric of that society. And perhaps, to a point, they were right.'

'Right about what?'

The words struggled from Jake's mouth. The Doctor smiled.

'We were so stupid. The majority of us walked ourselves right into our deaths, still smiling and hoping and believing in the Nazis. At the crest of their glory they could kill twenty thousand Jews in twenty-four hours . . . which they did, of course.'

'They walked themselves to their deaths? What about all the soldiers pointing the guns?'

'Yes, yes, but there were so few soldiers really compared to the number of Jews processed, they could have fought back. They would have suffered heavy casualties but they would have disrupted the whole machinery – look at the Sonderkommando rebellion – but no, they walked into the gas chambers and the cattlecars before that like obedient schoolchildren. You know when people say this and that about the Holocaust, how its uniqueness lay in the skill and efficiency the Nazis brought to killing, the mechanization of death – they really don't get it. What made the concentration camps unique was not so much all the horror that occurred there but the fact that millions of people marched themselves to their own deaths with hardly a whisper. That was what was so special about the place. You would see them, silently trudging towards the spewing black chimneys, smelling their kinfolk in the air and yet they still didn't believe it, just followed the orders and marched into the shower room.'

'But you never fought back yourself. You were just like them.'

'Perhaps so, Jakob, perhaps I am more of a Jew than I know. But I understood what was going on. My decisions were based on fact. The majority of the prisoners refused, until the very last moment, to see the reality. They died because of their refusal to face the horrible truths that were staring them right in the face, that they could smell. Also, a foolish and suicidal belief in the inherent goodness of people – remember Anne Frank, still believing, writing that thing in her diary about the goodness of Man, even as they wrenched her out of her hiding-place and sent her to Belsen. Right until the end they refused to believe that the Nazis would really just be killing them for the sake of it. To have accepted this would have been to have let go of all the assumptions and beliefs that their world-view rested upon, it was too much to give up, even on the price of death.'

The camera moved and tracked the Doctor as he looked towards Jake.

Jon's heart jumped a gear.

There was another person in the room.

Someone doing the filming.

Someone else.

The sound of Jake's voice brought him back.

'So you think it was their fault?'

The camera tracked back towards the Doctor.

'I don't think blame comes into it, I don't think that works at all. There are an infinite number of factors that make up any event and the event is only such because of those factors, take away one, shift emphasis and you have a different event. But I do think the Nazis saw it as a confirmation of their beliefs. The fact that we did not fight back, that we accepted and believed, that just reconfirmed why they were doing it all in the first place.

'I remember one morning I was on ramp duty, this was late in the war. I was going through the line, most times you could tell, it was an easy decision, left or right. I asked this girl what she did, she answered in German that she was a draughtswoman, she also told me she was pregnant and could she stay with her husband. I said, "Of course", and motioned her to the line for the showers. When I had finished and the ones who'd survived the selection marched off to Auschwitz 1, I went back along the line and saw the strange German girl again. She was motioning to me so I went over. She took something out of her jacket, I thought she was going to try and bribe me with gold, they all did – but no, she took out a sketch book full of these dark and tormented drawings with texts overlaid on them. Horrible, anguished stuff. She thought because I was a Jew like her that I would somehow understand. She asked me if I could give this to her husband, she told me his name, I think she had guessed her fate by then. I said I would and took the sketch book.'

'You ever find her husband?'

'I never tried to. That wasn't the point of the story.'

The Doctor lit another cigarette. Jon noticed how he seemed to have lost years since he'd started speaking. He wanted to leap into the TV set and strangle him. Couldn't understand why the fuck Jake didn't. Jake's voice echoed off-screen again, calm and collected. There was a frightening lack of critique in Jake's comments. Jon couldn't believe he was so docile and calm. Could it be that he was in such awe of a man who had actually survived that to criticize him seemed a sort of betrayal? There was a certain reverence in Jake's voice when he spoke to the old man, almost as if *he* was Jake's father, his real father, finally found.

Jon leaned back, smoked a cigarette, watching the paused image of the Doctor. Too many things clouded his mind, too many questions that led to further questions. Too many decisions, Suze, Jake and all the other ghosts that haunted

Amsterdam. He stubbed out the cigarette, set the film back in motion.

'What happened at the end? How did you escape?'

'I didn't escape. There was no escape from that place, no earthly escape that is. By the beginning of January 1944, the Red Army was closing in. On the seventeenth they entered Warsaw. We knew that they would be in the camp in a few days. The orders were to evacuate. To evacuate and to destroy all evidence. That morning I accompanied Dr Werner as he went into the infirmary and performed his final duty at the camp. The patients looked at us with a strange expression as he shot them in their beds. They did not know the Red Army was but miles away. Those that could walk were gathered together by the Kapos and would follow them to Germany, there were still camps there, work that needed to be finished. I suppose I was one of the lucky ones they thought they needed back in the West.

'We marched across huge deserts of snow, stretches of white dotted with the dark smear of bodies. All the way there were bodies, Jews shot on the marches, those that weren't strong enough to make it. There were thousands of corpses on that road, twisted and frozen in place.

'We passed the skeletons of villages and towns, bombed and burnt, as we headed towards the border. Smoke billowed and twisted from the black hills. Not much had been left to stand. The churches were gone, their spires, brick and rubble strewn on the streets, everything pocked and cratered like a moonscape and I knew then that I was seeing the new Europe, that below me lay the future and that something would rise from this rubble, something new and tainted.

'We met with others, sometimes marching with them at night through dangerous territory. I remember one morning the most amazing sight. Me and my companions were coming down from a low set of hills and we could see a march in the distance, a group of twenty or so small figures, holding hands, walking two by two, slowly making their way through the snow. We climbed a ridge and viewed them through our binoculars. They were all Mengele's twins, what was left of them. They had broken out and were marching themselves to freedom. No one said anything. The Germans let them pass.

'The next day I was on a train bound for Buchenwald. I was there until the Americans liberated it. All hell broke loose that day. Young American soldiers, eighteen and nineteen, came face to face with the piles of bodies that the Germans hadn't managed to burn, with the living who were not really living any more. They went berserk. They cried and cried and hugged those that were still alive. Can you imagine that, Midwestern farmboys putting their arms around Jews, crying wildly? Well, that's what happened, at least, at first. Then they went round and hanged any Germans they could find. They got the prisoners to pull out all Germans that were pretending to be Jews, their fat faces hiding behind the striped burlap. The Americans let them torture them for days. Their screams filled the nights. It was a horrible scene. I was held in an internment camp for several days where they questioned me, processed me and then they let me go.'

'Was that when you wrote the book?'

'No. I moved to a small village near Munich. There was never any question of going elsewhere. Germany was where I was born, where I received my education. I could not go to Israel, the United States – these were as foreign to me as the South Sea islands. I was a German, a Jew, yes, but always a German too.

'I set up a practice and, when the old doctor died, I became the town's doctor. I was Dr Kaplan. No one ever commented on the fact that I was a Jew. No one talked about the recent war. There were many things that were left unspoken in those years. I lived there through the fifties, watching the country grow back, the buildings going up, memories fading away or consigned like unwanted toys to a dusty attic somewhere. I was bored practising medicine in a small town. I had to deal with coughs and flu and children's diseases. You can imagine how it felt after being in Auschwitz. I saw that my life was gently petering out and that I would have to do something about it, something wildly unusual, or be dragged down. So I began writing the book. I would write between patients and at night in my small house. It took me three years.'

'Let me tell you a final story . . . you know people sent me a lot of correspondence in those days after the book came out and one thing I remember to this day. I got this letter from an Israeli. He had fought in the war of independence, '48. He told me the guns that the Israeli army used to keep their statehood were all stamped with swastikas and iron crosses. Wehrmacht guns were going cheap in Europe I guess, but the point is the State of Israel was won with Nazi guns, the same guns that had been used to kill the nation of Israel.'

The image blacked out and the CD stopped. Jon tried to access it to see if there was anything else but that seemed to be the end of the recording even though it obviously wasn't the end of the conversation. He punched the monitor screen, glad of the pain that spread around his knuckles. He then lit a cigarette and thought about what he'd seen, thought about the Council involvement and, most of all, about Jake.

Jon had found it disturbing not seeing Jake's face, just hearing his voice off-camera, cool and academic. He had wanted to see the old man's reactions to the Doctor's speech, thinking maybe that would help him understand. What was the purpose of this? Did Jake see Kaplan as some lost, missing father? Someone who had gone through all the horrors that Jake had himself escaped? Did Jake merely want to record the vile old man's reminiscences or was he trying for something more? Jon would never know. And who was the third person who filmed the event, the ghostly presence behind the camera, silent and unwavering? Jon had his suspicions.

He smoked another two cigarettes and drank half his bottle of duty free. He punched the wall a couple of times. When he was sufficiently drunk, he began going through all his Grateful Dead CDs, opening each case to see if there was another TDK left by Jake, another ending to the tale. He spent all night going through his discs, leaving them scattered, uncased, on the floor, but all he found was his hangover, and in the morning he packed his bag, put Jake's two discs into it and ordered a black cab to take him to Heathrow.

III

'A small hole was punctured on a temporal latitude marked 1945, and through that hole rushed the black future, curving around on the horizon like a boomerang and then threading the present.'
– Steve Erickson

29

'You were lucky, very lucky.'

The face smiled down at him. He tried to move but found that his arms had been strapped to the bed. His mouth felt dry and rancid, his body soft, his mind unclear.

'Nothing important damaged, just surface wounds. Looks a lot worse than it is.'

The doctor smiled. Van Hijn tried to smile back but he couldn't move his mouth. He watched the doctor walk away. Tiredness overcame him and he fell into a restless and haunted sleep.

He awoke in the middle of the night. He couldn't breathe. He pressed the button for the nurse but no one came. He heard far-off screams from another ward, the rattling and scrape of metal beds being wheeled along the grey corridors, muffled voices speaking behind doors and the ever-present bleeping of the machines that he was connected to, like a facsimile of his heart.

At some point his arms had been freed, or perhaps they had always been so and earlier he just couldn't move them. He slowly and carefully touched his side where he'd been punctured, but all he could feel were the rough edges of the gauze that covered most of his abdomen. He noticed that his stomach was flatter than he remembered it. Small pleasures indeed.

'Nurse, I need some cheesecake.'

The nurse looked at him as if he were a child who'd just asked to see the Wizard.

'It's three in the morning, detective.'

'I need cheesecake,' he repeated, trying to sit up, but he felt everything drain from him and he collapsed into the bed.

'The doctor will see you in the morning,' she replied, turned, and left.

He didn't think about what had happened. Not at first. The last thing he remembered was making his way to the flat. Next, he woke up in the hospital. They told him that he'd been attacked on the street. Stabbed with a small dagger. He'd lost some blood. No organs were touched. The doctor said it was a miracle. Van Hijn the human sieve. He knew what he'd have to face when he went back to work, the catcalls and jokes, he was used to it by now but that still didn't make it any easier.

'Hi.'

He looked up. It took him a few seconds to focus. Another few seconds to recognize her from the first piercing parlour he'd been to. Annabelle. So different out of her white smock. She looked elegant and beautiful as she placed the flowers beside his bed.

'I read about it in the papers, thought you might appreciate some company.'

He tried to smile and this time almost succeeded. It hurt but it was worth it. He knew that it would take too much effort to talk. He wanted to tell her how happy he was to see her, to see anyone, but nothing came. She sat with him, holding his hand. They watched the day collapse outside. She read to him from a James Sallis book that lay by his bed. It wasn't his and he had no idea how it had got there but he was content to listen to her soft voice, to watch her face darkening in the twilight. He fell asleep to her words.

*

'Detective.'

He awoke to the pit bull-like visage of his commander, Beeuwers, a stout and solid man, immovable as a stone monolith and with about the same sense of humour.

'We caught some kids. Junkies. Stiletto blade on them. Your blood type. Thought you'd be happy to know.'

'It wasn't kids,' he managed to say.

Beeuwers shook his head slowly. 'You don't even remember where you were when the attack happened, detective. Don't worry, we have them in custody.'

'It wasn't kids.' He tried to get up, felt Beeuwers' hand like a weight settle upon his shoulder. 'Who found me?' he gasped.

The captain smiled. 'One of Zeeman's men. Lucky for you. Blood was leaking out pretty fast from what the doctors said.'

Van Hijn remembered the phantom that had been following him the last few days. 'You fuck.' He groaned. 'You had him tailing me, didn't you? All this time?'

Beeuwers stared at him like a parent trying to make a child understand something very, very simple. 'We had to make sure that the case was being investigated in the proper way,' he said.

Van Hijn wanted to scream. All the information he'd collected, the leads and dead-ends, all this had been typed and handed to the captain, laughed over in meetings. Discussed and filed. He was glad that he hadn't put his real ideas down on paper.

Beeuwers smiled, so sincerely that Van Hijn knew he was in for some bad news.

'You're off the case, detective. You need to rest, recuperate for your hearing. We have something less demanding for you. I'm sure you'll find that Zeeman will continue ably enough.'

Van Hijn stared at him. Wishing he could get up out of the bed and strangle the fucker.

Beeuwers patted his shoulder. 'Not my decision. Higher up. They don't think you're getting anywhere. They don't think it's good for you, this case. You know they still hold February against you.'

'The man was guilty,' Van Hijn said but he knew it was futile. All the decisions had already been made, stamped and double stamped, and approved and, as a courtesy, they were telling him.

Beeuwers nodded, enjoying the scene tremendously. 'Perhaps next time we should let the courts decide that.' He put one hand, thick and meaty as a prime piece of steak, on Van Hijn's shoulder, squeezed it, not a friendly squeeze but full of grip and irritation and ire. 'Take a few days off. Relax. Forget about all this. We have some good men on the case. Go away some place, Ronald. Wait for your hearing somewhere else.'

'I don't want to.' He felt utterly helpless, like a small child in the shadow of his father, lying in bed, hardly able to talk, unable to move. He knew that this was it. That somehow the attack had only justified their opinions and that the pension hearing would not go well. He closed his eyes. Tried to remember Annabelle's face. He heard Beeuwers talking but he no longer listened to what he said. Finally the chief grunted something and the door slammed.

Then darkness came, and with it, at last, silence.

30

Climbing the four floors up to her apartment rather than waiting for the lift had been a bad idea and it took Jon a couple of minutes to regain his breath before ringing Suze's doorbell.

He'd booked himself back into the same hotel, reassured by the presence of his familiar room, its paint-peeled walls, grudging view and memories of previous residents. He'd wanted a few days to sit and think. To try and trace the connections, work through his feelings towards Suze. But he found himself here, on her landing, barely two hours after arriving back in Amsterdam, breathless and filled with anger, longing, hope, dread and affection, not knowing what to make of any of it, only knowing he had to see her.

'Jon, you're back!' she said, opening the door wide.

'Why didn't you tell me, Suze? Why the fuck didn't you tell me?' He hadn't meant to be so aggressive, to confront her so early, but it spilled out regardless.

She looked at him and she saw that he knew. That it was too late. All her good intentions meant nothing now. She went towards him. He moved out of her reach. She could feel the tears trying to push through but she managed to hold them back.

'I'm so sorry, Jon, I should have told you; believe me, I was going to,' she said, afraid that this was the end, knowing how phony she sounded, how weak.

He just looked at her, his face empty. His jaw was clenched tight and his eyes were cold and hard.

'Why, Suze? Why did you lie to me?' He moved past her into the room. He didn't want to have this conversation out in the hall. 'You knew about Jake's death all along and you never said a thing. You never even fucking told me you knew him.' He sat down on her sofa, lit a cigarette.

'I swear to you, Jon, I know nothing about his death. The first I heard was when you mentioned it.'

'Then why didn't you tell me you knew him, why keep it a secret?'

'I was trying to protect you.'

'Protect me?'

'Myself too.' Her hands covered her face. 'Oh God. I know I should have just told you, let you follow your own instincts.' She moved towards him. 'I didn't want anything to break us up, to come between us. I could see what you felt for Jake, don't doubt that. I don't know what happened to him. I really don't. I know he was mixed up with Kaplan. I know the Doctor came and sat in our group and infected us all with his disease. Things have been fucked ever since. I didn't want you to step into that circle, Jon, you must believe me. I didn't want you to be infected.'

'I wish you wouldn't try to protect me.' He stared at her, trying not to let his other feelings show, the ones that told him to take her in his arms, hug her, kiss her.

'I can't help it, Jon. I saw what it did to my parents. The way they drew away from me after that, the way they slipped off the face of the earth. I was almost happy when they died, relieved. At least now they wouldn't have to pretend to be dead any more. There's things we shouldn't know. Things we can't deal with. I just wanted us to have a chance. Something outside of all this terror.'

He wanted to tell her that he wasn't like her parents, that he hated others making decisions for him, but he kept his mouth shut and slowly edged along the sofa until their bodies were touching, folding over each other. He took her hand and held it and they didn't say anything else for the next few hours.

She was the first to wake. She stumbled over to the sofa and covered him in a blanket. She went outside and bought milk and eggs, her mind reeling, her heart lurching. She cooked him breakfast, watched him shuffle the food around on his plate.

'Tell me what you know about the Doctor.' Jon sat on the sofa, looking at her. Outside the rain swelled and crashed on the pavements. The sun had given up hours ago.

'I don't know much. Only that Dominic found him. Told him how the group had admired his book. Asked him to attend a meeting or two. I never spoke to the old man. I didn't like what he did to us, the way he split us apart. You have to understand that when we all first read the book it was amazing. It gave us focus and inspiration as a group. When we met the man himself it was a whole different matter.'

'I know, I've seen the video Jake made of him,' Jon said, stubbing out his cigarette, flicking his tongue across the dry, bitter expanse of his mouth, watching her surprise.

'How well did you know Jake?' he asked, bitterly aware of the irony, the memory of the detective asking him the same question, his reply.

'I met him at the museum. We talked a bit some days. I told him about the group and he expressed an interest. He came a few times and that was it. I never really knew him beyond that. I always found him very unapproachable, as if the man you saw was only a cover for someone hiding underneath. When you told me what happened, I felt so guilty. I felt as if I was the one to blame. I'd introduced him to the group.'

He took her hand, slipped his fingers through hers. 'Blame doesn't come into it, Suze. I don't know why Jake was killed but I don't think it has anything to do with you.' And he told her about the 49 reels that Van Hijn had mentioned.

'You think that's why?'

Jon nodded. The films had gone up for auction just over a week after Jake's death. There was no doubt in his mind.

'I think if we got to see them, we'd understand why,' he said. 'What was he doing at the JHM? You must have seen him enough to know.'

She thought back to those days, the way she'd avoided Jake. 'He was always in the basement going through all the footage. It's a mess down there. There's hundreds, perhaps thousands of reels of film and video that have been sent in to the museum. They're kept in crates. No one ever has the time to go through them.'

'The detective thinks that Jake was looking for something. The existence of these 49 reels seems to suggest that he found it, but I'm not sure – maybe Jake was just going through all this footage educating himself.'

She shook her head. 'No. You're right. He was definitely looking for something.'

'Why do you say that?'

'Just the way he went through them now that I think about it. There was nothing random about it. I think he was looking for someone in those films. He used to stop them and get right next to the screen, scrutinize the faces there.'

'You think he was looking for his father, perhaps?'

'Maybe. Or maybe he was looking for someone else.'

*

'What's wrong?' She'd woken to find him sitting on the edge of the bed, smoking a cigarette.

'Nothing.'

'C'mon, tell me.'

'I don't know, I just feel terrible. Like a whole house of dread is sitting on my chest. I woke and couldn't breathe. I thought I was fucking dying.'

'Jon.' She moved towards him, sat down, began to roll a joint. 'You can't let it take control of you like this. You can't let it affect you. It's history.'

'This is what you were so afraid of?' He looked at her but she turned away, concentrated on the joint she was rolling. He understood why she'd done it but he also knew that not to know would have been worse.

He tried to light a cigarette but the lighter was damp. He threw it across the room, watching it shatter into its component bits.

'Jon!' It was all coming true. Everything she'd feared had transpired and she was so unsure as to what she could do to stop it. She wanted to run away, forget it all, but she knew that she'd spent her life doing that.

'That fucking tape that Jake made. The Doctor's story. All that stuff – I still can't believe it. The way they gave those madmen complete freedom and they just ran amok with it.'

'I know, Jon.' She moved closer towards him. 'I was like that for a long time after I read about what had happened to Charlotte. It filled me with so much anger.'

'How did you deal with it?' he asked. He liked it when she was riled up like this. Liked the fire and passion that he saw in her. The way it deferred his own thoughts.

'It wasn't all that bad at first. I felt more awake, more in control ... there's something about anger that's very liberating. I went with it. Indulged it. Read as much as I could, tried to drown myself in the horror, as if that was the only way out. It took me some time to see what it was doing to me, how it was eroding my capabilities to love and distorting my view of Charlotte's work. I looked to her then. I thought if she could live through those times and manage to contain her anger then I should damn well be able to. And that was when I really began to understand her work. When I let go of the rage and the need in me for her to comment on her times, I realized that she was doing so in the only way she knew how, by telling her autobiography, her whole family history between the pages of *Life? Or Theatre?*'

'But isn't the anger necessary? Isn't that what makes us human?' He was shaking. Trying to hide it.

'Maybe it is necessary and it's surely unavoidable but that doesn't mean it's useful or healthy in any way. Where do you go from there? Revenge?'

'Sometimes that feels like the only goal worth anything any more.'

'Revenge isn't worth a thing. Alois Brunner, the SS head who personally sent Charlotte on her way to Auschwitz. Well, he wound up in Syria after the war, teaching them how to torture prisoners, how to kill Jews. In the eighties a letter-bomb amputated both his hands. You think that's compensation for anything? Those hands that did nothing but point people towards their doom against Charlotte's? The hands that painted those pictures?'

'How else do you react? At least anger is a positive reaction, a conscious revulsion. Otherwise what happens, do you become like the Doctor? Accept it all?'

'No, you don't have to. You can't let it eat you up. You can react in other ways. Charlotte did.'

'By painting her life story?' It was easier when they were

talking about lives other than their own. He could forget about all the things she hadn't told him. 'Why?'

'Because it was the only way she could react as a Jew to what was going on around her. Anger might have just succeeded in getting her killed. The whole period leading up to the war entailed a series of actions against Jews that slowly stripped them of their identity and heritage. The Nuremberg Laws put them outside of society, of the German society that they'd always felt a deeply enmeshed part of. They had their jobs taken, they were forced into ghettos. They became aliens to themselves. I think that's why so many trusted the Nazis until the very end, they could not accept that people from their culture, their own country, could ever commit such atrocities. It would be an acceptance of their own capability to do such things. The Nazis weren't monsters on the whole, but educated, cultured Germans, the very same people the Jews thought themselves to be. Charlotte's work is full of quotes from Goethe, Schubert and Schiller. It's a deeply German work, steeped in tradition and allusions to the past. It was the only way that Charlotte could reassert her identity. The only way she could take back control of her life. I saw that there were more important things than anger and protest – when you lose yourself, when you've been stripped of all your identity, the only thing you can do is build it back up again, page by page, painting by painting. With the world in fragments around her she had to sustain her own narrative, where there was no meaning or continuity, she had to create it.'

'But maybe if more people had got angry about the Nuremberg laws, Germans and Jews – I wonder if things would have taken the same course.'

'Who knows? Who knows what really happened when it comes down to it, what a single one of these people felt?'

He moved closer to her. Felt the heat of her hand in his. The ugly shadow of the Doctor darkening both their lives. He held her as tight as he could.

'I think this Dominic you mentioned was there, when Jake filmed the Doctor,' he said, letting it out finally, the last secret.

'Dominic?' She thought back to the previous night, the ugly scene that had left her wandering the empty streets for hours.

'You said he got the Doctor and Jake together. I think he filmed the testimonies. There was someone else moving the camera, someone other than Jake.'

'It wasn't Dominic,' she replied, aware finally that there was nothing left to hide. 'It was Beatrice.'

He mouthed the words but nothing came out. Took a deep breath. 'Beatrice?' He hadn't contemplated that. It came as a shock but, as he thought it through, it began to make sense. The films that her mother had told him about. The projector.

'She was working on some project with Jake. I didn't know what. They'd become quite close. She was so headstrong, she really wanted to take on the world. When they announced her name, I suspected it had something to do with all this. Christ, Jon, that's why I didn't want you to know – it was too close to me. I'm so fucking scared. What if I'm next?'

He hadn't thought of that but now that he had, he realized she was right. Two members of their stupid group had already been killed. 'Beatrice,' he repeated. The golden girl herself. 'Dominic is involved somehow, more than just introducing them, I'm sure of it.'

'Leave him alone.'

'Why are you protecting him?'

'I'm not,' she said though she realized that she was, but

it wasn't something she could explain to herself, let alone Jon.

'I want you to contact him, Suze. To set up a meeting.'

'No.' She had no inclination to see Dominic again, not after what had happened. If she called him now he'd see it as a sign of her surrender, an apology for not sleeping with him last night. She was beginning to see another side of him. One that scared her. Of course he would apologize but it would still be there between them and maybe next time he wouldn't stop. 'I can't do it.'

He stared at her and there it was again. The gap that had opened up between them.

'You don't understand.'

'I think I do,' he replied. Why was she protecting Dominic? She moved towards him and he backed away. Dominic, Dominic, Dominic – he was sure the answer lay there.

'Let's go to bed,' she said.

'And tie you up again?' He got up from the sofa, moved towards her.

'There's nothing wrong with it.'

'Yes there is, Suze! Yes there is!' he shouted. Before he knew it, his hand was raised, crumpled into a fist. Heading for her face. Her perfect smile.

He took a deep breath. Relaxed his hand. Just.

'Go on, hit me. I deserve it,' she screamed at him.

He moved back, away from her, holding his fist as if it was an unreliable gun.

'You like it, don't you?' She moved towards him, he kept his back to her. She pulled him around. 'It's not that you *don't* like it – that's what scares you so much, isn't it? That you just might like it too much.'

'No!'

'Liar.'

They stood there, a few inches apart, breathing hard, the air dense with their words.

Jon looked at her. It had been clouding his mind for the last few minutes. 'If that's what you think then there's no point in us carrying on.'

The words hung in the air like cigarette smoke, heavy and cancerous. She stared at him, taking in what he'd said, the stiff angle of his jaw, the tightening of his body.

'But, Jon, there's no point hiding from things. You need to accept whatever it is you feel.'

'So do you, Suze, so do you.' He looked at her and, for a moment, almost gave in. He remembered how much hope he'd seen in her eyes when they'd first met and it was all but drained now. Maybe it was a lie, he thought, maybe all we saw in each other was a lie, created by our need and nurtured by our refusal to see anything but that.

'I'm sorry. It's better that it happens now than a few months down the line, a few years. Years that we'd know we'd wasted. I can't do this any more. Can't keep pretending it's all okay, nothing wrong, just another quirk. Can't fucking do it. I've wasted enough of my life up to now. Jake woke me up. I'm not going to make the same mistakes again. I'm not going to waste my life.'

He turned before she could answer, out of the door, down the stairs, his lungs burning, his mouth tasting dry and bitter. Outside, the sky exploded, the open spaces of Nieuwmarkt suddenly drowning him in unwelcome light. He turned left, not knowing where he was going, not caring, wanting more than anything else to get lost, to stumble and hide in the streets, covered up and anonymous, to be where the world couldn't touch him, where it was far enough away and so unreachable as to become a dream.

++++++++++++++++++

WINTER 1941-2. ST JEAN CAP FERRAT

I can't get this damn song out of my head.

This stupid melody that has been following me like an underfed cat through this small room.

I am now a habituée of small rooms. My space is defined by their leaning and cowering walls. By the light they allow in, by the measure of the world that leaks in through their curtains, the world which I so longed to touch and that now lies like an unwanted dishrag, filthy and stinking, hidden in the darkness below the sink.

There it is again. That song.

I miss my records. They are in Berlin. I could not take them with me. But yet, they are with me, here in my head, my constant companions when everything else has fallen away. But I do miss their covers, the feel of the cardboard and smell of vinyl. I miss these simple things most of all. More than I miss Father. Am I wrong to be like this? Is something up with me? Am I just like the rest of them in my family? What is wrong with me that I go from utter despair to ridiculous happiness? I do not have answers to these questions. This is not the time to think about such things. This is the time to be sitting in small rooms.

I tore up the things I made today. I hate them. Hate the way I can see myself in the folds of the paper. No one will ever see them. What is the point? Who am I painting for? I spent all morning and made three pieces but no one will ever see them. Perhaps I should burn them. Perhaps Duchamp was right and the art is only in the making, everything after, commerce. But still, I wish someone would see them. Hung up in a small gallery somewhere, nothing special but they need to breathe, need to get away from me. I hate it. Hate it all.

Today I painted seven pieces. I woke and the sun was streaming through the window. I felt its heat like a hand on my bare thigh. I made myself coffee and hummed a tune. The one I couldn't get out of my head. The tune suggested an idea, the idea an image, the image a set of words.

They can all go to hell.

There is such freedom now that there are no rules.

No one will see these paintings. I have no one to paint for but myself. There are no rules any more. I can do what I want. And what I want to do is something wildly unusual. My thoughts cannot be contained in the old forms. They are too rigid, too reductive. They are not the world as I see it. They are poor and empty. They are no longer relevant. We desperately need new forms. The world is not the world.

I had to move away from Grandpapa. I couldn't stand to be in the same town as him any more. He drowns me with his hatred. Makes me feel physically sick. Being near him, I am overwhelmed by a paralysing stupor. I can't think when he is around, can't paint. It is no wonder Grandmama killed herself. I believe I would have done it much sooner had I to live with the old goat.

Here I cannot hear his shouting. I have my own room. The hotel is small and no one bothers me. There are more Italian soldiers and they do not look at me in the same way as the German soldiers. Yesterday, I was walking in town when a young Italian whom I had seen a few times before (and was sure had seen me) came up to me. I began to move away, scared, I had heard the stories – but he smiled and I knew that a smile like that could not contain anything bad.

He handed me a package. Winked and was gone. When I got home, I opened it to find a salami, two tomatoes and a small bar of chocolate. I began crying. I couldn't help myself. I held on to the chocolate like it was a lover and cried my heart out.

The paintings are going well. I have lost count of them. One day, I will sit down and go through them, put them into some kind of order. I think I got the numbering mixed up, or I changed my mind. But first I need to finish. To see the whole thing before I know the shape it will have. I have less materials now. I only have three colours I can use. I do not know how much time I have left.

I can hear that awful man ranting on the radio every week. That awful man I once was so enamoured with. I remembered Alfred showing me the *Draft of XXX Cantos* that had recently come out and his face as he read to me from those startling stanzas, the fire and beauty and generosity of the man that wrote them, the blinding, brilliant supernatural rhythm of his sentences. And now he is on the radio, ranting from Rome, screaming about credit and usury and about how a certain people should go to hell. And yet, I still remember the beautiful lines he wrote and I pretend that this is a different man, not the poet but a lesser man and I close my eyes and think of other times.

Yesterday German soldiers were in town. The hotel landlady said it would be better if I stayed in my room. She promised nothing would happen. I crawled under the bed. I lay there, curled up until night. I waited for the knock on the door though I knew that was only for theatre. That in real life there was no knock. That these people didn't need to knock.

317

I was too scared to get up and go to the bathroom. I was afraid my shadow would give me away. I tried to remember songs and hummed them, careful not to let any sound slip. I do not know how much longer I can stand this.

I am desperately unhappy. I spent all day hiding under the covers again. My old despair got the better of me and threw me back into a slow death-like lethargy. If I can't find any joy in my life and my work I will kill myself. I feel so hopeless. I have time enough to work and yet I can't. My happiness is at an end. I have no one to talk to. The sun has been stolen from me. From deepest sunny brightness to greyish darkness. I am sinking in despair. I am scared to get out of bed. It is a winter such as few people could have experienced. Extreme torpor, unable to move one finger . . . I am ill, my face always red with dull rage and grief.

+ + + + + + + + + + + + + + + + + +

He couldn't get the song out of his head.

It had joined him on the walk back from Suze's. No particular reason, not even a song he'd listened to for quite a while. And yet there it was, constantly humming just under everything else.

He'd fallen asleep to it, trying to remember the words, the order of the verses – anything to forget about what had happened earlier between him and Suze.

The morning brought with it sunshine, and the song, like an elusive lover's name, came back and filled his head during breakfast.

'The silver one, please,' Jon said and watched as the shop assistant tallied up his purchases, twenty or so CDs and a portable on which to play them.

He'd been too long without music. Too long with other people's choices, never what he would have liked. He spent all morning browsing the aisles of a record shop on Kalver-straat. He thought it would be the same. Some refuge in the familiar. But there was difference here too, and he spent hours going through the racks, picking up old favourites – Springsteen, Dylan, the Dead, Miles – checking for European bonus tracks, bootlegs, things he couldn't find back home. And of course, that song. The title track from Tom Waits's *Blue Valentines*, the one that had been going round his head.

He sat in a café enjoying the wide luxury of the square, so unlike the Amsterdam he was used to, with its clustered streets and cloistered bars. Walk ten minutes and it's a whole different city. Turn a corner and you're in another world. It was only now that he began to realize how much a prisoner of the District he'd become, how it had shaped and warped his vision of the city.

He drank his coffee and looked at his CDs. He refused to think about Suze. Every time she came up (and she came up quite a bit) he tried to remember the track listing of a particular album. Diversionary measures.

He popped *Viva Last Blues* into the personal. Plugged the earphones right in. Took a long toke on a joint as Will Oldham's ravaged voice started singing. Within minutes, he realized that a massive smile had taken residence on his face, making his jaw hurt, his lips ache. But he did nothing to remove it. The sun would be out only for so long. This was the time to enjoy it. The time for other things would come later.

He spent the next couple of days locked in the private world that a Walkman provides. Where everything becomes detached; the world silent and impenetrable. Something viewed from the outside, like a television with a broken speaker or an old silent movie.

He began to walk, in whichever direction he desired. Every morning from the hotel, making sure he was out of the District before its weight could surrender him. Make him prisoner. On the first day he walked west, into the Jordaan, stared at the seventeenth-century workers' houses and small shops, the unmistakable stench of the poor areas, the constant rhythm of the city, the way the land seemed to pulse up at you in the form of bridges, both a connection and a disconnection, a link and a break. It was as if the streets were nothing but an elaborate Rubik's Cube, constantly shifting, from the wide open Mojaves of the empty squares to the sweetheart of the sudden darkness that surrounds you in the smaller streets. He walked south, into the great commercial district, past skyscrapers and smoked-glass office buildings, the new face of the city, reflected endlessly in its mirrors and distortions. Walking, walking, walking, all the while soundtracked by the music pumping into his head, leaving no room for wayward thoughts.

He watched the people swarm and ebb. Dressed in suits and rags. Women so beautiful it broke your eyes. Men tall, cold and professional. Bikes skidding across his line of vision, trams hurtling, cars puttering. There were so many ways to get run over in this city, so many crisscrossing lines of travel.

He noticed how he looked at women differently after having been in the District. He didn't like it, but he kept doing it. Strange what shapes this city wrought upon you, what subtle shifts and changes – as if everything was up for sale, whispering in its alleys, 'Everything is yours for a price.' Or maybe the city had only made him realize that this was the way he looked at women. The way all men do.

On the second day he walked west, into the old Jewish Quarter, though there was not much left of it but tourism and commemoration. He read the multilingual plaques, looked at the stern monuments, their obsidian darkness a metaphor for all that had occurred. The city itself was like a textbook. A palimpsest of history, seen in its gables and arches, the length of its canals, the monuments and squares that described the spilling of the city from its centre into the farthest reaches of the old marshland.

He sat in cafés, music affixed to his ears, and watched stoned tourists stumbling about, serious strollers, the whole mess of life, so colourful and different here. In London he had stopped noticing. Here the world was born anew, each small facet worthy of contemplation, even the taste of the coffee or croissants, the way the lights of the restaurants danced upon the roiling surface of the canals at night.

It was on the second day, in the Jewish Quarter, that he began to realize he was being followed.

It wasn't much. But attuned as he was, alert as he was, he noticed the same man (had he seen him yesterday?), the same man always there when he turned or stopped to light a cigarette. Always too far for him to see the face. Only the long black trenchcoat he wore, the battered biker boots and constant cigarettes.

Jon tried to ignore him. Not to let fear get the better of him. But it was there. Shooting through his veins. He remembered what Suze had said and he wondered if he was next. If this man had previously followed Jake and Beatrice too, staking them out, getting their routines down.

He walked through the long streets, so much quieter and sparser than back in the District, every now and then stopping, looking behind him for a flash of black that told him the man was still there.

He began to walk fast, as if something urgent was pressing down upon him. He took as many turnings as he could find, tracing squiggles and asymmetric loops that he hoped would be hard to follow. He didn't even stop to light cigarettes now, just kept backing and double-backing, walking through alleys and then turning on himself only to see the swish of black behind a corner, the spiralling cigarette smoke creeping from a blind alley. He began to run, carefully sidewiping other pedestrians, frantically looking behind.

Every time he stopped, he saw the man, getting more brazen now, not even hiding. And was that a smile on his face?

Then the man started running towards him.

Jon sprinted across the canal, down an alley, heart beating

hard, sweat breaking out cold and clammy, hearing his pursuer's footsteps clicking on the cobblestones behind him. Before long he realized that he was back in the District.

He ran past the girls behind glass, the small-fronted cafés, not knowing which way he was going, thinking maybe that's better, maybe that's the only way you can lose someone. He doubled up an alley and stood in a small square. High visibility. He got out of there quickly, looked back, didn't see anyone.

He didn't stop though. He kept running through the alley until he nearly slammed bang into the man in black.

He stopped just in time, slunk into a nearby doorway and watched his pursuer scanning the square.

Jon smiled, watching the man's head rotate, searching for him. He got his breath back. Still he couldn't see the man's face.

The man in black turned round.

Jon leapt into the doorway's niche hoping he hadn't been seen. He could hear his heart beat thick and fast through his body. He waited for the man to find him. To finish it all.

But he didn't, and when Jon summoned up the courage to look he saw the man disappearing into the square.

He quickly propelled himself out of the doorway and into a group of sightseers, all the while keeping his eye on his pursuer, now walking towards Nieuwmarkt. Jon pulled away from the tourist pack and stood at the head of an alley. The man in black turned left at the end. Jon ran the length of the alley, came to a stop, saw the man walking down some stairs into a basement below a tattoo parlour. He waited a couple of minutes and then walked over, pretending to gaze at the window display. He stared at the photos, canvases of flesh still inflamed from the needle, pinned under the flashbulb explosion of the camera. He thought about Kaplan's story about the wall of eyes. It made him feel dizzy. The window display of flesh made him sick.

There was no sign on the door of the basement, only a buzzer. Jon smoked a cigarette and waited across the street. His pursuer still hadn't come out. He checked his watch. Took his wallet out, found Van Hijn's card.

32

Jon and Van Hijn sat in the back of the Hieronymus Bosch patisserie, staring out over the canal and the busy tramways of Damrak. One wall of the establishment had been covered with an immense reproduction of the artist's famous triptych and Jon stared at the ugly deformed creatures that populated the mural as he waited for the detective to return from the cake trolley. The house stereo was playing 'Frankie Teardrop' by Suicide, the pounding electric rhythm brutal and relentless.

He'd called the station and they'd told him about the attack on the detective. He'd called the hospital only to be informed that Van Hijn had checked himself out against medical advice. He'd finally reached the detective at his flat. Told him that he had to see him.

Van Hijn eased slowly into his chair. His movements were careful and precise as if he were moving through a space filled with invisible obstacles. Jon saw him wince when he sat down, a slight upturn of his lip, a glazing of the eyes.

'You okay?' he asked, unable to think of anything else to say.

'I will be once I get some cake,' Van Hijn replied.

Jon couldn't wait. The onrush of information was too much. He wanted to share his fears, hoping that they would seem pathetic, dope paranoia, that kind of thing. He told the detective about the testimony that Jake had left. The videos hidden in the CD cases. He watched as the detective took it all in, making the odd note. He told him about the Doctor, the man who followed him, perhaps the killer. Van Hijn nodded, not saying much, digesting the information. Jon thought he'd congratulate him but Van Hijn just looked up, tired and sick. 'You know I'm off the case?' he finally said.

Jon shook his head. He felt a sinking in his stomach. 'You're giving up?'

'No. But things have changed. It won't be as easy now.' He crushed his cigarette. 'I've been moved to a different case. Trouble at the zoo.'

'You're joking.' Jon felt his hopes drain away like the coffee in his cup. Without the detective there was only him and after outrunning the man that morning, Jon wasn't all that certain he could do it by himself. Or wanted to.

'No joke. A couple of the zoo attendants are running their own little side business. Opening up late at night. Apparently people pay good money to watch them beat the animals.'

Jon stared at him.

'Pay a little more and they give you a baseball bat and the keys to the monkey cage.' The detective coughed, stirred his coffee.

'What about the serial killer? The films? The case?' Jon said, leaning forward, trying to impose himself into the space that had opened up between them.

Van Hijn shrugged. He understood Jon's anger and enthusiasm, saw himself, younger, in Jon. But he could also see what it would lead to, the bitter disappointments and sleepless nights.

'I don't know that I can be any more use, Jon. There's others now, fresh to the case, perhaps they'll see something I didn't.'

Jon leaned back, grabbed his cup. The detective had changed. Something had gone out of him since their last meeting. 'I don't believe you're giving up.'

'I'm not giving up, Jon. I don't have a choice any more.'

'No?'

And Van Hijn didn't quite know how to answer that. Because there was always a choice. Was he running away from the past again? The past that existed only in his head but whose clutch was firmer than that of the present? He thought about the films. A certain seductive symmetry in that. He looked at Jon and felt envious of his vigour, his lack of apprehension, the way he'd followed this through despite all the warnings and obstacles. He was a different man from the shambling wreck who had entered his office a couple of weeks ago. Murder had made him a man, freed him from the restraints he'd imposed on himself. A strange irony indeed. 'Maybe you're right.' He motioned towards the waitress for another drink. 'Perhaps I've just forgotten how to live my life, in some way, perhaps that's it.'

Jon stared at him. Had the detective changed so much since their first meeting? 'How do you deal with it?' he said, a question that he'd been asking himself ever since his arrival in the city. He was curious to know what answers the Dutchman had formulated during his time as a policeman and he didn't want him to let go, not so easily.

'I don't really know. I ask myself this question over and over again and I come up with all sorts of answers, none ultimately satisfying, of course. I ask myself how I should react and when I weigh it up against how I do, I always find it lacking.'

The detective looked up from his cheesecake, his eyes locking on to Jon's. 'You know, you've got to stop every now and then and say to yourself, this is the best moment of my life up to now – it doesn't get any better than this. No, don't laugh, I'm serious ... you say it when you're listening to a song and the harmonies come in, in a way you didn't expect, suddenly flooding you with California

327

sunshine. Or when you bite into a piece of warm pastry, the heady smell filling your nose and then the crisp, crumbly texture and rich flavours that saturate your mouth . . . or when you find a book you've been searching ages for . . . you find it cheap in a discarded pile in the back of a secondhand bookshop – you have to say it to yourself, "It doesn't get any better than this," because if you don't say it at those moments, when are you going to say it? Those are the things that count.'

'Must be hard to continue.'

'Yes, it gets harder but it's also more of a reason to do it.' Van Hijn lit a cigarette, taking his time, drawing the smoke into his lungs. 'Make lists, Jon. Write down your favourite albums, your favourite books, the food you like eating most. Write it down so that when you need it, it's there.'

Jon looked at the detective and wondered whether he was right. Perhaps he was. Maybe you needed to make a balance book, the bad shit against the good. Tally it up. See where that takes you.

They had another round of drinks and Jon told him about the morning's pursuit. The unlabelled basement buzzer. He watched as the detective sat up, winced at the pain it caused him.

'I told you not to get involved.'

'Nothing happened to me. I can take care of myself.' Jon looked up. 'You know this place?'

Van Hijn nodded. 'It's a piercing parlour.'

'Somehow that doesn't come as a surprise.'

'I was coming back from there when I was attacked. Something doesn't make sense. They've arrested some kids, a gang, but it wasn't kids, Jon. The people who did this to me were wearing suits. That's the one thing I remember, black suits. That and the smell of the pavement.'

Jon looked away. Thought about what the detective had said: black suits. The shadow in black that had pursued him earlier. Was it possible they were one and the same?

Van Hijn rubbed his side. He tried smiling but he was in a lot of pain. He wondered whether he should tell Jon about *The Garden of Earthly Delights*, his own uncomfortable reading of the book, the sense of something not quite right underlying the text, the shifting of pronouns, the looseness of the tenses . . . Or tell him what he'd learned at AYN about the presence of SPAR in the city. But he could see that Jon had enough on his mind – his fingers were continually looking for something to do, his foot never still. No, better not to say anything, about AYN or about the fact that when he'd tried to trace them through property deeds and other records, he hadn't found a single mention of the organization. 'Your beard,' he said pointing to Jon, changing the subject. 'Makes you look more Jewish, you know.'

'I'm only learning what it is to be a Jew now. I never had much practice before.'

'You know what Isaiah Berlin once said?'

Jon shook his head.

'A Jew is a Jew like a table is a table.'

They both laughed. Jon leaned forward. 'You know, detective, I don't quite feel myself a proper Jew.'

'Why not?'

'It's because I wasn't in the Holocaust, my family weren't touched by it. I almost feel an impostor in my own race.'

'You think the Holocaust makes you a Jew?'

'No, but I feel, shit – I feel left out, if you really want to know. I sometimes wish that I had gone through it. I feel left out of something huge and defining.'

'You're fucking crazy. What do you think the Holocaust would have taught you if you'd been lucky enough to survive it? You think you would have learned anything if you'd gone straight to the gas chamber on your arrival?'

'Maybe it would have made me more of a Jew,' Jon said, knowing he was goading the detective now.

'What kind of Jew do you want to be, Jon? The kind that's had to witness all that atrocity, the one who's watched children and old women being humiliated in the streets and then killed? What kind of man is that? What kind of Jew? The one who has to steal from his own people to survive? Whose job it is to undress babies before the gas chamber? The one who has to eat human flesh and let SS officers fuck and torture him for fun? Jesus, Jon, is that the kind of man you want to be? Do you want to live the rest of your life embracing your hatred and need for revenge?'

'No, I didn't mean it like that,' Jon said, though he had. 'I was wrong,' he added.

Van Hijn took a sip of his coffee. Looked towards the slow moving boats inching down the canal. He knew he'd overreacted, understood how his own past coloured his words. What he wouldn't have given for his father to have been elsewhere. 'Don't be so consumed by your hatred that your life becomes empty without it, Jon. Find meaning in other things.'

Jon thought about Suze. The smell of her hands, the warmth of her breath on the back of his neck. But, fuck, it was the hardest thing to do – to let go. And didn't that imply they'd won?

As if reading his mind, Van Hijn said, 'You planning on staying for a while?'

Jon nodded. 'For a while. If you'll let me, that is.' They both laughed. 'There's something here. It feels so very different from London. I can enjoy small things, things I always took for granted – like you say, the smell of pastry, the sound of the cobbled streets. I love the way people mind their own business in this city, the sense of individual freedom.'

'Huh! That's just a mask. You think there's freedom here?' Van Hijn smiled, amused for the first time that day. 'It's just the same as anywhere else, only the laws are different. But the laws are still in place, still there. We can't let people run around doing exactly what they want.'

'Why not?'

'Why not? Because not all people want to mind their own business. Absolute freedom means letting people kill, torture, rape and get away with it. The Nazis had absolute freedom. So do most dictators. You come here and you think it's freedom but it's only the slightest shift in the rules, the foundations are still there. Unfortunately others make the same mistake as you when they arrive. But unlike you, they act on their desires and turn this city into the one that they originally mistook it for. And so you see how easily the imagined leaks into reality and becomes it.'

They had one last drink, the detective unable to resist another slice of the chilli and chive custard cheesecake that the café was famous for.

'It's fucking horrible!' Jon said, spitting his mouthful of the rancid substance into a serviette. 'How can you eat that?' Suddenly he felt the burn of the chilli shooting up his larynx, going nuclear in his mouth and behind that the sickly sweet, eggy aftertaste of the custard that had cemented on to his teeth.

'They also do them in whiskey and liquorice, apple and anchovy and marzipan and bacon flavour. The sweet and the savoury. I guess it's just not for you.'

Jon gulped down a full glass of water, ice and all. 'Ugh!'

Van Hijn laughed, clearly amused by the spectacle. 'So what are your plans?' he asked.

'I'm going to find out who's behind these films and from there, how the films led to Jake's murder. I think you were right. The films are fake, snuff. Somehow Jake colluded and they killed him for it.'

Van Hijn didn't say anything, not that he now knew the films were real or that he was certain Jake had been killed for them. It was funny how they'd changed sides, he and Jon, each believing the opposite of what they'd first thought. He could have told him what he'd seen in the preview but he knew he wouldn't. He didn't want Jon getting himself killed, better to let him follow a bad trail, better disappointment than death.

33

'I know someone who can show us the preview.'

'Preview? What are you talking . . .'

Her phone call had woken him from an uneasy slumber that was filled with the Doctor's face, his cackle and sneer, the whipflash of the city.

'Are you okay, Jon?' Suze asked.

'Waking up. Slowly.' He lit a cigarette, sat up on the bed. The first inhalation kicked his heart into gear. 'You mean the 49 reels?'

'Yes. If you don't mind seeing me again, that is.' She left it hanging. Jon took three more drags off his cigarette. He had to make a decision now.

'How?'

'A friend of mine owns a few porn shops. I was talking to him the other day, happened to mention the films and he said he knew where I could get to see the preview.'

'When?'

'Tonight. At seven.' She paused. He could hear her breathing. 'If you want.'

'Yes,' he said and put the phone down.

Friday night in Amsterdam and Jon couldn't believe the number of people swarming the streets as he wrestled his way through, heading for Suze's flat. Like the Vegas of Europe. Multitudes descended on the city every weekend in search of sex, drugs and a freedom that was not available back home. Groups of Eastern Europeans looking for sex, ravers pilled-up and bug-eyed, smugglers and students, businessmen and tramps, all congregated in the city every Friday night, shrinking the streets and alleys and shrouding the canals.

Jon felt uncomfortable as he passed through the smiling, expectant hordes. He kept walking, kept looking back. He was sure it was the same man that he'd eluded the day before. How the hell had he found him again? And who was he? The killer? Jon didn't want to think that. Had been trying to deny it all night, this morning too. A flight back to London suddenly seemed the sensible option. If he's the killer, why doesn't he just confront me, Jon thought. Better that than this endless unknowing fear.

'Hi.' She was wearing a beige suede halterneck, a long, flowing skirt and had managed to apply lipstick only to her top lip when she answered the door.

'You look nice,' Jon said, relieved to be out of the public gaze.

She stared at him and for a moment they were like strangers trapped together in a lift, looking for anything in common that could break the silence. 'Thanks, come in. I'll just be a minute.'

He sat down on the sofa as she went off to finish her make-up and began flicking idly through a film magazine that lay on the coffee-table. He couldn't concentrate. He looked at the mess on the table – spilled weed, empty wine glasses, a printout of Charlotte's diary, some photocopies of her work, CD covers – and thought how the table so mirrored her. He looked up and saw her in the other room, just movement. The Band was playing on the deck, horns wailing, voices overlapping, sepia drenched and filled with dread.

'Have a joint. There's some in my handbag,' she shouted through the open door.

He went through her bag. Took out the small sachet of grass, paper, a lighter. He also took out the canister that lay there. Mace. He felt safer just holding the small black tube, like a travel deodorant, its red button screaming Press Me. He looked back, she was still in the bedroom. He took the can over to the window, stretched his hand outside, pressed down. An explosion of fine mist spat out of the tube. Jon quickly closed the window before the noxious fumes could leak in. He smiled.

'It's great that women can buy these things legally here,' he said. 'In London they don't have any sort of protection.'

She came back into the room. 'Also means that the rapists have it,' she added. 'You want it?'

Jon nodded.

'Just don't go getting yourself killed.'

He smiled and placed the small canister in his jacket.

'It's a nightmare out there,' Jon said as he smoked the joint. Their speech was now filled with banalities. Afraid to say anything else.

'Tell me about it. Friday night and you can't even squeeze into your favourite coffee shop because of all the tourists.' She stood in front of him cleaning her glasses. She'd never looked more desirable and he felt a strong urge to take her then, lay her on the coffee-table and make love to her. Forget the past. Forget everything.

Instead he rolled another joint and thought about Jake. What had once seemed a simple murder, if there could be such a thing, had now taken on more angles and permutations than he would have thought possible. That such an event could have been the effect of all these lines drawing together. He knew the Doctor was the key. Dominic, somehow, the

335

link. The films, perhaps, the reason. But were they real? Tonight he would know. If they weren't, and were merely a fake, a historical genre snuff movie, then had Jake been roped in, on some pretence, and dispatched as soon as his role was over? That seemed the most likely answer. The detective had said as much. There were too many similarities between the death of Jake and that of the other victims. Coincidence seemed ludicrous.

But there was another option and though he'd been suppressing it, he couldn't deny its viability. Van Hijn himself had hinted at it. Perhaps Jake had made snuff films with the Doctor. It didn't seem like the Jake he knew but then neither did the corpse on the slab that day. Had Dominic found out about it? After Beatrice's death? And killed Jake when he came back from London?

And what about the Doctor? Where was he hiding? In some cellar or bolt-hole or an apartment furnished and paid for by the government? Jon's head began to spin. He lit the joint and took a deep swallow.

But if the films were real then everything was turned upside down. Did Jake find them in the museum, show them to someone, Dominic, the Doctor, someone else? Was he killed for them? After all they were worth a lot of money. But then how did Beatrice fit in? How did the other seven girls? Jon knew he couldn't discount them. The link between them and Jake was the only solid thing he had. That and the films he would get to see tonight.

He'd printed out photos of both Jake and the Doctor back in London. Freeze-framed the video and captured their fuzzy likeness. He had to find the Doctor. And Dominic knew where he was. He was certain of it. If only she would get in touch with Dominic. What else was she hiding? But no, he couldn't think like that. Seeing her made everything different and he wondered for whom, exactly, he'd come back.

'How's the thesis going?' he asked, trying to derail his thoughts.

She shrugged. 'It's not. Nothing's working. Nothing's right.'

'Are you sure this friend of yours can come up with the goods?'

She looked up, distant, and, he thought, so beautiful in that moment.

'I'm sure,' she replied. She knew how important it was for him. She thought of last night's phone call to Wouter. She'd hated doing it but she'd asked for the favour anyway. Had to endure his sarcasm and witticisms until he'd said, yes, he knew where such a thing could be watched. Then he'd asked her about Jon, prying little details. She'd put the phone down shaking. She'd thought Wouter hadn't cared that much about their split but it was obvious he had and she wasn't looking forward to the evening ahead.

'Where're we meeting your friend?'

'He owns a shop in the District, I said we'd meet him there.' She slipped on her glasses. Jon rose and, for a moment, they almost touched, almost fell back into the old patterns, but like poles of the same charge they turned from each other at the last minute.

'Jon, this is Wouter.' She introduced him to the tall Dutchman who sat behind a small table in the back of the porn shop.

'Glad to meet you, Jon.' He got up and shook Jon's hand vigorously, squeezing hard. 'Suze tells me you want to find out about the other Amsterdam.' He was grinning like a child. Suze could smell the burnt tangy coke in the air and could tell by his eyes that he'd been at it all day. She thought of taking Jon and walking away. But she knew he wouldn't leave.

Jon nodded, looking up at this mountain of a man, curious and a little scared. He heard a dog barking in the back room. The hum of elevators ascending.

'So, Wouter, where are you taking us?' Suze said, flicking ash off her cigarette for what seemed to Jon like the hundredth time that minute.

'Jon wanted to see the preview, that's where we're going. I have it all arranged.' Wouter looked at him. His eyes were close together and they seemed angled in a strange way as if he could see areas of the room that were obscured from normal sight.

'So, this is him then?' he said to Suze.

Jon looked at her but she didn't reply. He knew he'd missed something.

'Have a drag on this, you look nervous as hell,' Wouter said, handing Jon the joint.

He took a deep pull and suddenly his head spun out from his neck and his eyes screamed against their sockets. The world lit up. Suddenly, painfully there.

'Coke,' Suze whispered, taking his hand. 'Everyone here smokes it. Latest fashion, all very decadent. You'll appreciate it when we're out there in the swarm.'

Jon took three more monster drags before handing it back.

They walked past the Old Church and through groups of shaven-headed, middle-aged English men, drunk and bleary, staggering in each other's arms through the streets, shouting and abusing the window-girls they passed. It was a weekend and the binge tourists were out in force, walking in serpentine steps, puking in corners or sitting bug-eyed staring at a single cobblestone for three hours. They stumbled through the crowded streets of the District, between bar and sex shop, watching men choosing their girls for the night, the fathers who'd brought their sons to learn the facts of life, the lovers attempting to rekindle their sex lives and the latents trying to persuade themselves that a woman's body was still attractive.

The early mass of tourists had changed now, if not in number then in gender and type. Suze saw no other women except those behind glass and she felt sad at how the men who passed looked at her, even though there were far more beautiful girls on offer; but it seemed for some that was just too easy. She walked between Jon and Wouter sensing herself paraded here, wondering why she suddenly felt like that, having been in this area so many times before. She thought about what she was doing. Helping Jon with his search or still trying to stop him? More of the latter, she knew. She noticed how Wouter kept staring at him. It worried her. It wasn't all just surface, she wanted Jon to see that, to realize what lay beneath.

They stopped in a café and Wouter went into the back room with the manager, coming out a few minutes later.

'It's all set up,' Wouter said, checking his watch. 'In an hour, okay?'

'Who're we meeting?' Jon said, feeling better now that they were enclosed, away from the crowds.

'Mr Nagatha. He runs an establishment in the District. That's where it's showing.' Wouter shook a Marlboro out of his pack, flipped it into his mouth. 'There's something I want you to see first, Jon. Something I think you'll be interested in.'

He led them into the back room of the café. 'The manager's a friend of mine, keeps me updated about certain things.' Wouter stepped over to the desk and flicked the computer into life. He keyed in some lines of code and lit another of his foul-smelling joints. 'Nazi films isn't all there is. There's a lot of things that can be bought at auction these days.'

Suze and Jon looked at each other, blank and lost, as Wouter typed in the address and waited for the home page to download.

'We have to access it from this computer because of, how can I say? . . . security issues?'

The home page was basic, like a spare-time website, a white background with large type scrolling down. On the left frame was a series of hyperlinks:

Conrad   Billy

James   Russell

Francis   Benjamin

'What the hell is this?' Jon asked.

'Here.' Wouter clicked on the first hyperlink. The screen went blank.

As the photo slowly downloaded on to the screen, Jon felt a sickness rising inside him, a black nausea that swept his head and stomach. He took Suze's hand and held it, looking at the full-length picture of the naked boy and the group of stats beside him.

Age: 6
Country of origin: United States
Status: Untouched*
Acquisition date: January 1999
Training: No
Starting bid: $50,000 US
Reserve: Yes

Bid limit: None
Time remaining: 56 minutes

While we make every attempt to verify our information, we accept no liability towards false or misrepresented information.

Below that, a short description:

A rare and exciting opportunity to acquire such a fine specimen. As mentioned, he is untouched and has been kept off the market until this sale. He is good-natured and unproblematic and there is sure to be a lot of demand from bidders.

And:

Buyer arranges pick-up, shipping and all other attendant costs. Buyer must be a registered and cleared member. Bids from anyone lacking these credentials will not be accepted.

Jon looked back to the picture of Conrad, the thin boy's frame that hung dejected in front of the camera, his uncut hair and the sad twist of his mouth. He noticed that all the auctions were due to end in the next few hours and he wondered how many people around the world, at this very moment, were looking at the same page, clicking on the same links and reaching for their credit cards and secret passwords.

The electronic medium took away none of the horror, for he knew that behind the ones and zeros lay real boys in real rooms tied to real beds awaiting the rest of their lives.

'You see, you can get anything you want in this city,' Wouter said as he switched off the computer. 'You, my friend, know nothing.'

Suze noticed his voice was getting shriller and that he was

enjoying goading Jon. She sensed a maliciousness in Wouter she'd not felt before, a honing of his sarcasm and repressed rage. She wondered if this whole thing was a set-up. If Wouter had some plan, some way to get back at Jon, make him suffer. Perhaps this had been a terrible idea.

'You have the money, then Amsterdam has the goods.'

'Why here?' Jon asked, still thinking about the boy's mouth. Ghosts caught on film. Images of the dead. All around him now.

'Amsterdam is the new city of sin, every taste can be catered for here as long as you have the money.'

'You sound disapproving,' Suze said, her hand on Jon's knee. She felt she needed to take control of this situation, insert herself between these two men.

'No, not at all. It's good that all these things are on offer. You must know as well as I do that there's no point in pretending they don't exist or in outlawing them. They do exist, or rather the need and desire for them exists in certain people and you can't ever get rid of that. As they say, "Any crime that can be committed, is." But just because everything is on offer here, doesn't necessarily mean you need to have it.

'Everybody has to ask themselves how far will they go, and everybody needs to see what they are capable of. For me that is a basic requisite of freedom and if it means some bad shit will occur in the process then it's a small price to pay.'

Wouter took out another coke joint from his pocket and fired it up. He turned to an old tape deck and hit play. The opening notes of 'London Calling' came pounding out of the speakers, followed by Simonon's questioning bass line and finally Strummer's voice, ravaged and raving, a witness to the end.

Jon picked up his glass, saw that his fingers were resting on the breast of the woman moulded around it and downed the warm, stinging liquid. He didn't know what to say. His head was spinning faster than a waltzer. He couldn't get off this particular ride. Wouter made him uncomfortable and he wasn't sure why. He'd guessed there was something between him and Suze, something unrequited probably.

'Mr Nagatha, that's where he made his money.' Wouter passed Jon the joint. 'Take it,' he snapped when Jon feebly declined. 'Or so the rumour goes.'

Jon looked at Wouter. Was he the same shape and height as the man who'd been following him? It was near enough to make him shiver.

'He was a sex slaver?' Suze asked.

'Yes. Very careful about whom he picked. Only the finest specimens ended up on his private jet, bound for Africa. He had men roaming the capital cities of Europe, the holiday resorts of North Africa, finding and acquiring stock. A tourist goes into a shop in Tangiers to ask the price of a leather bag and never comes out again. Her husband waits patiently outside smoking cigarettes and when she doesn't appear he goes in and is told that they haven't seen any European women come into their shop today. The man will search the shop, tear the place apart, call the police, but all to no avail – by the time he's realized that she's even missing, she's already on her way to an airport. A cargo plane. A new life.'

'That still happens?' said Jon, shocked despite himself. The idea of just disappearing like that was terrifying. The world had so many holes into which a person could fall.

'Happens all the time.' Wouter laughed, looking at Suze. 'You hear about missing people and you know some of them are headed for the auction block. Nagatha quit a few years

343

back, sold his business and retired here, but countless other auctions still go on, every day. Remember, where there's demand there's product – the basic axiom of capitalism taken to one of its darker corners.' He lit a cigarette. 'You know, someone came into the shop a few weeks ago, had a range of home-made videos he wanted to sell me. I took him to the back room, and watched them. They were all crush videos. Footage of a woman stepping on rabbits and small puppies, breaking their spines slowly with her feet.'

'Did you buy them?' Suze asked, appalled.

'Hell, no. But someone else will.'

There was no sign above the door and only one bouncer to even suggest that anything was going on behind the black smoked windows of Mr Nagatha's. Wouter whispered something to the meat monkey, who checked on his walkie-talkie before allowing them in.

Jon had imagined chains, blood and the black wings of whips cracking in the smoky air. What he was not expecting to see was a smart restaurant full of people in suits eating and drinking amid the sharp Modernist lines of the decor. The only unusual thing, Jon noticed, as they were led to a table, was that all the diners were men.

'It's a fully functioning restaurant. Damn good food too. Took a few favours to get you two in. This, though, is just the waiting room,' Wouter added and poured them some wine. He kept staring at Jon and smiling in a way that made Suze feel uneasy.

Fifteen minutes later a waiter came up to their table and told Wouter that it was time. He led them through the restaurant, past the swinging doors and into the kitchen. Two men were clouded in a halo of steam and smoke as they fried something on the hob. A strange, bitter perfume filled the air. The waiter led them down some stairs and into a long room, dark and damp, where he left them.

Jon began to feel bad about all this. How well did Suze know this man? It was too late to ask her and now he was being led into the bowels of some mephitic establishment. He touched the can of mace in his pocket, wondering if it would be enough.

A door at the other end opened and an extremely small man, dark and wrinkled like a prune, made his way towards them.

'Thanks for seeing us, Mr Nagatha,' Wouter said, shaking the man's hand, encapsulating it.

'You brought some friends.' His accent was flat and without tone. He looked at Jon and Suze, his eyes like small black olives hidden in the folds of his face.

'Wouter said you could show us the preview footage,' Jon said, stepping forward, feeling both fear and excitement.

Nagatha laughed. 'Yes, that I can do.'

Jon's heart was pounding hard. Now he would see them. Now he would know if they were real. He reached into his pocket and pulled out the photos. He took the one of Jake and showed it to Nagatha. 'You know this man?'

The old man shrugged. 'No, never seen him before. Hasn't been here, anyway.'

Jon took the photo back, everything collapsing again. He thought perhaps Jake had left a trail through these establishments.

'Wait.' Nagatha put a hand on his. It felt cold and bony like the claw of a small bird. 'Let me see the other one.'

Jon handed Nagatha the photo of the Doctor.

'This one I know,' he said. 'Used to come here sometimes. Old German. Strange tastes. Had to take him off our list. Damaging the goods. Haven't seen him in a while.'

'How long?' Jon's mouth was so dry he almost couldn't speak. The room began to vibrate.

'A month or so. Lived up near Prinsengracht. One of my men used to deliver to him.'

'Deliver?'

'Oh, you know, videos, girls, whatever was asked for.'

'What happened to him?'

'As I said, we had to take him off the list. Made the girls do disgusting things with his dogs. Real fucked up. Treated them like shit. No respect for the merch. You see, I couldn't have that.'

'Dogs, did you say dogs?' Jon's head started rattling like a multi-ball frenzy in a pinball machine.

'Yes, why, you like that kind of thing? Perhaps I can find you some videos.' The human prune laughed.

'Did any of the girls disappear?'

Nagatha burst out laughing. 'Oh no. Anything like that had happened, I would have gone to see the old man myself, paid him a visit. You think I'm some kind of fucking fool?' He carried on laughing.

'Any chance you'd have the address somewhere?' Jon said, stepping forward, casting his shadow over Nagatha, who almost seemed to disappear.

Nagatha looked at him, thought it through for a minute. Jon saw the deep, etched lines in the man's face, the scars like small scarves wrapped around his neck. 'Normally I wouldn't, you understand. But this case is different. I don't owe the old fuck anything. In fact, he owes me. How about I tell you where he lives in exchange for a night with this pretty girl?' He smiled at Suze and put his hand on her breast. She pulled herself out of his reach. Nagatha laughed. 'Okay, I understand. Way it is these days. Money then. A thousand dollars.'

'You take credit cards?' Jon said.

'Most certainly.' Nagatha nodded, smiling. 'What shall I make it out for . . . services?'

Jon handed him his Visa. Nagatha took it and it disappeared neatly into his hand.

'Wouter, show them what they came here for. It'll take me a few minutes to get this information. I'll find you.'

Jon and Suze followed Wouter, who seemed to know where he was going.

'That was easy,' Suze said, still feeling the heat of the old man's clutch.

'And expensive,' Wouter added.

'Not really,' Jon replied. 'In fact, not at all.'

Wouter led them along a dark, narrow corridor and down some flights of stairs. 'In there.' He pointed to a door at the far end.

'Not many people here,' Jon said, wondering why the place was so quiet and empty.

'This is the special entrance. Come, follow me.'

He took them into a small, thin room. They were alone inside and Jon was beginning to wonder what was happening when Wouter pressed a button on the wall above him and the screen rolled back revealing the one-way mirror that looked out into the main viewing room of Mr Nagatha's.

It looked like a screening room. Widely spaced chairs dotted the floor. Men sat, stiff and still as concrete, their eyes glued to the screen.

'What's going on here?' Jon asked, trying to peer round to see what flickering images held these men in such captivity.

'Nagatha had the preview blown up, digitally enhanced and looped fifteen times. People are paying a lot of money to see this. This thing is all that people are talking about.' Wouter smiled, 'All the rage, you might say.'

Jon watched the men, upright, their hands hiding in the darkness of their crotches. Small, furtive movements. He wanted to leap through the glass, grab them, ask them what the fuck they thought they were doing. But more than that, he wanted to watch the film. To see what they were seeing.

'Come.' Wouter led them through the other door and down some more stairs. 'We have a special room reserved for this.'

They followed him through a labyrinth of tunnels, turning and skewing, almost like a ghost image of the city above being replicated below.

'What else goes on here?' Jon said, hearing strange sucking sounds coming through the walls.

'You don't want to know,' Wouter replied.

They sat in a small room and stared at the blank screen in front of them. Half the size of an average multiplex movie screen. Suze sat next to Jon and her hand slipped down to his, covering it. He didn't move it away. Wouter shifted in his seat, making sure he was comfortable, then pressed a small button on the side of the chair and waited for the film to load.

A man is strapped to a hospital bed, his limbs so emaciated that he seems to disappear as the camera swings around to reveal a short, bald-headed young doctor in glasses and a tall, stern-looking officer, impeccably suited and rigid, both watching the man on the bed. The young doctor takes off his glasses and cuts away the prisoner's trousers, revealing the shrivelled genitals. There is no sound, only the smooth movements of the doctor as he expertly removes the man's testicles and then sews up the incision. The stern-looking officer unzips his own trousers. Another inmate is brought in. A crack to the back of the head brings him down to his knees and in line.

348

A third officer walks quickly through the back of the frame. The prisoner on the table is writhing, screaming but there is no sound. Just a curious suspension of time. He is removed and a new inmate is placed upon the bed. The doctor smiles. Bends down. Wipes his implements on his smock. An SS man stands to the back of the frame, his face invisible now, cut off by the camera's limitations, only his hands visible, holding a stopwatch of some kind. As the doctor performs his task in the foreground the camera suddenly pans back to reveal the now not-so-stern-looking officer, smiling in the kind of way that a father would smile at his daughter's performance in a school play. When the doctor is finished, the officer walks up to him, shakes his hand, smiles once and then is gone.

They sat in silence and watched the operation as it looped and played again. The face of the Nazi doctor. The smiling officer. The jittery black-and-white pulse of the video, the slight break-up and buffering that meant thousands were watching the same footage when it was downloaded. It was only sixty seconds long but it seemed to last for ever. Each frame hanging in the space between moments like an unsure acrobat.

'Let's go, I've seen enough,' Suze whispered to Wouter, springing up from her seat.

'Yes. Fuck this, let's go now!' Jon added, not wanting to watch the film for the third time.

Wouter took them back into the viewing chamber where they saw a new set of men who were smiling and waiting in baited expectation and then back up through layers of staircases and hidden mezzanines until finally they walked through the restaurant where a waiter slipped a small piece of paper and the credit card into Jon's hand, past tables full of prosperous, good-looking men, drunk on the anticipation and excitement of pleasures to come.

*

That night they couldn't get close to each other. They sat on either end of her sofa and watched a late-night black-and-white film, not talking much, unable to say anything that wasn't shadowed by what they'd seen, disappearing into the folds of the film. Finally he fell into a restless sleep and she turned off the TV and moved herself closer to him, holding him tight so that he wouldn't go away.

34

It was still dark when he awoke and slipped quietly out of bed, trying not to disturb Suze's sweetly sleeping form. That restless beating of the blood pounded through his head and he knew he'd have to go out. That if his head was going to burst, it would be better that it burst in open space.

Outside the night had a strange luminescence, a feeling of immanence that Jon couldn't shake. He walked along the deserted streets and across the canals and thought about all the ugly things he'd seen that evening. Tried not to think about them but there they were, following him around as surely as the man had been following him earlier that night.

Now the streets were empty, the first time he'd seen them so devoid of the flash and friction of life, and he liked the way he could hear the slow ripples of canal water, the sound of rubbish twisting in the wind.

He passed by an all-night fried chicken restaurant and he stopped and looked through the window at the few people, sitting, staring dead-eyed into their food, hunched over with the kind of loneliness that drives you out in the middle of the night to such a place.

The night was filled with the emptiness of sleeping cities. For two or three hours, everything shuts down and collapses, even in Amsterdam. Jon walked through streets unrecognizable in their bareness, their lack of people, and it was as if he could feel the presence of that other Amsterdam, its dark, cluttered machinery pulling and cracking beneath his feet, humming behind the closed shop-fronts and cafés, alive in the swerve of canals and alleyways. It was as if for everything that occurred above there existed a shadowy twin living a life of its own, every now and then taking over the city and then retreating back to its domain, the mind, the underground, the dark recesses of a dream.

Tonight everything felt suffused with sadness, from an old man in the chicken joint to the policeman he saw walking alone across Dam Square.

He saw small groups of boys flicker across his vision, running silently from street to street, their purpose unknowable. A couple fighting on the steps of the town hall, screaming and hitting each other with a terrible fury. Stray dogs stumbling about, maimed and hobbling through the deserted streets looking for the remains of fast food. In a small alley off a square he came upon the broken wheels and seats of prams, many colours, all smashed and twisted by some unknown force. Ghostly garbage trucks slowly rolled across Damrak, fully mechanized, not a human being in sight.

Down by the first canal line he saw a small girl being punished by her father. The man ordered the little girl into a *pissoir* and made her stand there for five minutes while Jon watched, smoking a cigarette, cursing his cowardice. He followed the canals, finally sensing the order to them, the way the city rotates out from a circular centre and for the first time he could picture where he was in relation to his hotel, to Suze's place.

The streets slowly began to fill up with early-shift workers, women rushing to cleaning jobs, the whole menial underclass flushed out of sleep at half past five, like ghostly versions of what was to follow. He couldn't bear to see them. Couldn't bear to see the agony and disappointment in their eyes, the enormous tragedy of the dream in their immigrant shoulders. The years of anger and resentment that had carved them out into their present forms. The insurmountable obstacles of race and education, the great leveller – money – being all but unobtainable, except in the smallest increments. A dribble here and there, enough to make them come back to work the next day, enough to feed them sufficiently so that they can perform. Nothing much else but the constant erasure of dreams, the whittling down of hopes to something more realistic, more banal, and the eventual fracture of all promises. He thought about the men sitting in Mr Nagatha's waiting for their pleasures and he felt sick. He looked at the street-sweepers, beautiful African faces reduced to this, and the great sadness that he'd felt all night suddenly came crashing down on him.

Suze had heard him leave. When he was gone, she got out of bed, went to the window and watched his fading form recede into the dark streets beyond. She didn't know if he would come back.

She made herself a drink, aware that sleep was a luxury she would have to forgo tonight. There was no way she could relax, not with Jon being out of reach, perhaps for good. All she'd wanted was for him to realize the horror of it all, to show him how underneath all this pleasure lay only pain and suffering. Oh Jesus, she whispered, as it hit her how much she didn't want to lose him. She dropped her camomile tea, burning her foot. Please come back, she thought, please be gone only for some cigarettes.

She wiped up the mess, listening to *United Kingdom*, soaking up the sparse terror of Eitzel's songs, the feelings of dislocation and bitterness that permeated them like a disease.

She remembered what she'd told Dominic, about how much she cared for Jon, but this was different. Now that they had broken apart and come together again she understood how selfish she'd been, how her whole life had been unconsciously formed by her desires and the kind of men they attracted. No, this time it was different. This felt like someone had scooped out her insides. This was total and utter terror. The fear that he wouldn't come back. That she'd fucked it up again. That their coming together that night was only an arbitrary sharing of space and not a promise of things to come. What a surprise, she thought, me and my stupid games, screwing up again. Why did I have to be so open about it with Jon, why couldn't I have pretended to be normal, at least for the first few weeks? But she knew that would have been worse. There were enough secrets she'd kept from him. She let the cigarette's heat burn her fingers, thinking, this is the story of my fucking life, already written out to the last chapter.

Did I scare him away with my violence, the violence that I wanted done to me? She hoped he would come back so that she could ask him. She wanted to tell him that she was through with it if that was what would save their relationship. Some things were more important than fleeting pleasures. Some things had a chance to last. And perhaps she wouldn't miss it when she was with Jon. Isn't that how fairy-tales go? How they're supposed to go?

She turned up the volume on the CD. Eitzel was singing about a woman with a golden voice and how there was no heaven for him but the heaven of her hands. It was Suze's favourite song. She'd always thought it was one of the saddest songs ever sung, but she now saw it as the opposite. How could she have always thought that? If you can find heaven in someone's hands then that is, surely, more heaven than most people will ever know.

++++++++++++++++++

'I do not think you should go, Charlotte.' Madame Pecher looked at me with those full French eyes.

'But I must,' I replied.

'Why, Charlotte? Why?'

'Because there is a law and, since I'm Jewish, I thought it would be correct to present myself.'

I saw something cloud over in the landlady's face. Had she not known I was a Jew? She nodded, turned and went back into the kitchen, leaving me alone here in the untempered sun.

I have almost finished my paintings. I have run out of many materials but Madame Pecher has been kind enough to procure me things that I can no longer get for myself. The atmosphere down here has changed. Soldiers march up and down the promenade as if the sea too belonged to their German hearts. I no longer go out much. I have heard whispers, rumours of round-ups like the ones back home and though I do not believe that things could be that bad, still it is perhaps safer to stay at home. Someone told me about the exhibit that is touring the Côte. At present it resides in the main square, here. I am told that this exhibit of anti-Jew propaganda has made its tours of Europe. That it has been very successful. I remember the exhibit of degenerate art that made the rounds of Berlin before I left. I had to sneak in to see those great works. Beckmann. Ernst. Grosz. Hoch. I don't think an art exhibition has ever been that popular. Perhaps there is still hope.

*

The streets seem very different to me. Despite Pecher's warning, I do believe that I should go and register like the authorities said. I saw the posters and declaration that said all foreign Jews must be registered. Perhaps once I have done that they will leave me alone. So that I can finish the work. That is all that matters to me now.

There is a crowd at the station. Buses pull out constantly, smearing black exhaust tails in the air. German soldiers and French gendarmes are pointing, shouting, trying to herd the mass of people who've turned up. I wonder if Grandpapa is here or if he was allowed to register in Villefranche.

I wait in line. There is not much else to do. No one wants to talk. They are all wrapped up in themselves, looking down at the ground, as if perhaps we had got it wrong all along and that was where God resided, not in the infinite expanse of sky but in the very earth we tread.

The sun is hot. Midday. I have been standing for hours. Slowly the lines are being cleared. I thought this was just registration but I can see that the people in the line in front of me are all loaded on to buses. I wonder where they are being sent. Perhaps the registration centre is somewhere else. Two young men a few rows behind tried to turn back an hour ago. I didn't look but I heard the rifle's report and the sound of their bodies slumping to the ground. What is happening here?

It is almost evening. Thank God the sun is gone. They made us stand here all day. At one point a Nazi officer made a statement that all those who were having a problem with the sun, who wanted to sit down, get some rest, eat, recuperate – he said that's fine, you can go and join a special line and we will make sure you don't have to stand all day. I saw many old people, children, women move towards where the officer, this small dark hunchback called Brunner, who looked more of a Jew than I do, they all moved to where he pointed and were loaded into small trucks. I was tired. I wanted to sit down but there were others who needed it more than me.

Finally my turn comes and the officer looks startled when I speak German to him. He notes down my name in the file he is holding. His eyes refuse to meet mine. He points towards the nearest bus, already crammed with more people than it can hold. He shouts '*Schnell*!' and I have no choice but to follow his orders. I do not want to get on this bus. I want to go home and paint. There is no room on the bus for me. Where are they taking us? What will happen to Grandpapa?

They push me on to the bus. I want to tell them that there is no room. That I am happy to wait for the next one but they don't listen. A soldier presses his gun into my back and I know that I have made a terrible mistake.

'Where are we going?' a man shouts from inside the car.

The soldier laughs. 'East,' he says. 'Resettlement.'

I don't want to go East. What will become of my work, lying scattered on the floor of Madame Pecher's hotel?

I hear more shots. Bullets cracking the night. I can smell the fear of the hundred people that I am crammed against in this small bus. There is no room to move, very little to breathe. I hear the driver starting the engine. Berlin lies in the East. Is that what they mean? Or do they mean further East? And I remember the story that I heard back in Gurs and I start to choke, I can no longer breathe. Everything goes black.

*

357

The officer who noted my name down is moving towards the bus. It is fully dark now. He calls to me. Motions with his hand to come over. I look around but none of my fellow passengers have noticed. His signalling becomes more frantic. I manage to peel myself away and step down from the bus. I wait for the bullet to hit. The piece of wood to the back of the head.

The officer looks tired and angry. I walk up to him, watching his fingers twitching around his gun. He looks down at me. I realize that he is almost my age. That in another life we could have been lovers.

'Leave right away,' he commands me in German, pointing to the darkness-swallowed area to our left. 'Leave fast and don't come back; stay at home.' He is shouting but there is something else in his voice and before I can say anything he grabs my arm and pushes me towards the darkness.

I begin to walk. I don't understand what is happening but I walk and slowly the bus with its people squashed and twisted like characters from a Picasso fades into the darkness. The soldiers disappear. Suddenly everything is quiet and I keep walking, fast, though I know that if they want to find me, they will, and there is no speed that will outrun their hatred. But I keep walking through the darkness. I do not know this part of town. I do not know where I am heading. In the distance, I hear women crying, screaming, pleading. I see strange lights over the hill, in the town. I have no choice but to walk towards them. Behind me there is only death.

It is something quite unlike anything I have ever seen before in my life. Or heard. There are people screaming, crying, praying, singing – every human utterance you can imagine is here, a caterwaul of devotion, a desperate show of solidarity in a country that is no longer theirs.

The city flickers. Candles are placed in every hand and I too am given one, nod *merci* and join the crowd as I try to make my way across and towards the hotel in St Jean. The light is incredible. Twisting and turning on the wind it looks like something from one of Lang's films. The shadows continually change and quiver. The city seems unreal, like a projection of its true self. People walk by silent, awed, their hands carefully cupped against the candles they are holding lest the sea wind should snuff them out and leave the city to drown in its own darkness.

In the crowd I am nobody. I am everyone. No one looks at my face. No one wonders if I am a Jew. They are here to celebrate what has been lost. For an hour or two they don't care about anything else.

Last year the *Fête de Jeanne d'Arc* was a wildly celebratory affair. This year things are different. This year everyone wants something from that dead heroine.

I enter the main square and I can no longer move. People press against each other and I am reminded of the bus. Where was it headed? Where is it now, trudging silently through the black hills?

A great statue of Joan of Arc stands at the centre of the square. Someone is talking through a loudspeaker. I can make out most of the words. They talk about Joan. They call her the most complete symbol of our race. My skin prickles. I wonder whose race they are talking about. Suddenly all the women and children drop to their knees and begin wailing. I too fall. There is safety in it. I watch as they roll their heads and bow and praise this dead piece of stone they call Joan of Arc. I wonder how ironic she would have found this. The whole population is mesmerized. It is almost like a church, yet we all know, there is no longer any God.

*

I walked all the way back to the hotel. It took me all night but I knew that to stop would be death. I walked up to the office. Madame Pecher came out of her room, looked at me as if I were a ghost, then a huge smile broke across her face and she opened her arms and we stood there for ten or so minutes, crying in each other's embrace.

'Oh, Charlotte, I'm so glad you didn't go in the end,' she said and I didn't tell her any different.

I went up to my room. This small room that now seems like the last place on earth. All around me were the paintings. I knew that it was time to put them in order. To finish. I knew that time was running out. I have to complete it, no matter what the cost. What do I care about police or Grandpapa. I have to get back to –

There is no more time for images. There is no more time for digression. No more time for music. No time for love or memory. There is only time to write. There is only a small number of blank pages left. There is the sound of marching in the daytime. Rifle shots in the night. This room is getting smaller. The light is so bad that I cannot see what it is I am doing but I no longer have a choice.

I went back to the first page. The playbill. It was written by another woman in another time on another world. It will not do any more. I have no new paper to start over. I must write in the spaces that are left. The only colour I still have is red. Somehow that is fitting. I put it all together. It has weight. A certain dignity in its heft and volume. This is a year of my life. I will leave it at Ottilie's house. There, maybe, it will be safe. I have only one thing left to do. The dedication.

The author
St Jean, August 1941/42
or between heaven
and earth beyond
our era in the year
1 of the
New Salvation

+++++++++++++++++++

35

He dreamt of plane crashes when he finally got to bed that morning. The beautiful obliteration of the shattered fuselage. The rip and roar of metal, twisting in white-hot agony. The screams of the falling.

The phone woke him with its insistent fusillade of rings. 'Jon.'

It was her. He let the hotel's answering machine pick up the call.

'Are you there? Jon? . . . I hate these things. God . . . I was hoping that you'd come back last night . . . I'm at the seminar now but I'll be back home in an hour . . . call me, please.'

Jon waited for the beep, then got up. Checked the small piece of paper that Nagatha had handed him the night before. He looked back to the blinking red light, so insistent and desperate. Some things would have to wait.

The rain was constant as a heartbeat. It soaked through his clothes as he waited for the detective at the corner of Dam Square.

He'd had to get out of his room. The walls were closing in on him again. So he'd called Van Hijn, explained about the Doctor's address, said 'Meet me there.' The detective had demurred, but Jon had told him that he was going anyway, accompanied or not, knowing that Van Hijn would then not have a choice, or rather wouldn't allow himself the choice.

He watched the rain hit the streets like a shower of artillery, saw how people took up certain shapes to insulate themselves from it, unnatural angular modifications that they believed would protect them. Everyone running, hurried, pissed off and wet. Jon knew the feeling from London and how the rain closed everybody off in their own shell.

'Sorry, I'm late.' The detective smiled, his hair was wet and matted down and he looked as if he was drowning. 'Can't move too fast. Afraid I'll split if I make any sudden movements.'

'Good to see you're feeling better then. Hope I'm not keeping you away from your animals.' They shook hands, oddly formal in the rain.

Van Hijn smiled, spat out his cigarette. 'I'm sure they can live without me for a few hours.'

They were buzzed in by the landlord of the building. He inspected Van Hijn's badge as if he were an archaeologist staring at some new discovery, then nodded.

'He went away a lot. Haven't seen him for a couple of weeks but that's not so unusual.'

'Visitors?' Van Hijn asked, a puddle forming around his feet.

'Not many, no. Unless you count whores. A few of those.'

Jon showed him the photo of Jake. The landlord nodded again slowly. 'Yes, him I've seen several times. Don't know if he was visiting the Doctor though. People get buzzed in, I see them in the lobby but I don't know who they're visiting.'

'Thank you,' Van Hijn said, taking the master key.

They walked up the stairs, paint and carpet both peeling, Jon remembering Jake's description of the place, a chill sweeping through him, walking again in the old man's footsteps, trying to recover a ghost.

The Doctor's flat was clean and neat and empty. There was no sign that anyone had been there recently. No smell of food, rumpled sheets, temporary litter, none of the small accretions that coalesce around a life, the things you don't have time to deal with, that you leave for later. They walked slowly through the two rooms, silent, each alone in their thoughts and in what they expected from this.

In the main room, two faded, dust-soaked armchairs faced each other and it was easy for Jon to imagine the two old men sitting there, letting evenings ebb over a game of chess.

'Here,' Van Hijn called. Jon crossed the room and entered the bedroom.

The detective was holding up a small cine camera. Wires. A digital video camera. Jon felt his body shudder.

'No tapes,' Van Hijn said, throwing the devices back on to the floor. 'There's no fucking tapes anywhere. Someone got here before us.'

'You don't think he's coming back?' Jon asked.

Van Hijn shrugged. 'He probably knew that as soon as we found Jake this place would be compromised.'

'Fuck.' Jon expelled the word as if it had hooks.

Something snapped inside the detective's head. 'What did you think, Jon? That he'd be here waiting for you with a signed confession?' Van Hijn kicked a small box of leads across the room. He looked up, something softened in his face. 'Sorry. Guess I couldn't help expecting something too.' Van Hijn tried to smile but his face was grim.

Jon took the living room. He searched slowly through the accumulations of a life. Books in German and English, medical textbooks whose weight and gravity seemed to belong to another time. Small ceramic medieval coats-of-arms that littered the mantelpiece, the bookshelves, almost every flat surface. There were copies of old Dutch news-papers and he put them aside for the detective. A large folder containing drawings. There were so many clues here. Every object was a clue. Everything that wasn't here was a clue.

He got up, slowly stretching, thinking how this had been another colossal waste of time and expectation, when the window exploded.

The force of the blast and noise pushed him back and he landed on the edge of a table, a sharp piercing thrust in his spine, and then on the floor. Shards of glass scattered through the room as the carpet began burning.

'Get up!' The detective was pulling Jon's arm. He'd blacked out. The window was smashed. Black smoke was filling the room. The curtains roared with flames. A broken bottle trailing a rag lay in the middle of the carpet, flames licking the air around it.

Jon came to. His mouth dry and hot, tasting bitter, his arm and back screaming in pain, the detective's voice far away and muffled. All around him the light danced and crackled.

'Quick. The whole place is going up.' Van Hijn grabbed Jon's arm and draped it across his shoulder. He thought about his wounds. Would they split open? There was only one way to find out.

Jon began to feel his legs again slowly coming to life, taking his weight. The detective pushed him through the hall, the fire quickly gaining behind them. Jon got to the door first. Turned the handle. Nothing. Did it again. The same result.

Locked.

He began to scream.

Van Hijn pushed him out of the way. Pulled out his gun and blew the lock. The sound was terrible. Jon's eardrums felt as if they had been pierced. He was dizzy again and it took all his concentration to stay upright while the detective kicked at the door, once, twice, until finally it sheared away, spilling in light and oxygen.

Downstairs the landlord lay face-down on his table. He wasn't moving. Van Hijn lifted his head and it nearly came off. His throat cut ear to ear, the classic Colombian necktie. 'Shit, they certainly knew what they were doing,' the detective said breathlessly. Blood was pooling around the body and had already made its way to the edge of the table where it dribbled down on to the floor. A strange chemical smell in the air. Burning cocaine.

Jon watched as Van Hijn called the police and fire crews. He could feel it coming. A warm liquid onrush of fear and spent adrenalin. He leaned down and vomited on the hotel steps. He stood there shaking as he tried to light a cigarette to get the taste out of his mouth. Every time he blinked he could see the landlord's head and the slowly growing halo of blood surrounding it like some obscene replica of a Giotto saint. He spat out the cigarette, shaking still, knowing that there must have been something of value in the flat, something that had necessitated the destruction of everything to make it obscure.

36

He was behind him again. It was the same man he'd seen before. Jon began to walk faster, feeling the sweat prickly on his back, turning round every now and then to see his pursuer stop to light a cigarette or read a concert poster. He regretted now that he'd left the detective at the Doctor's building. Perhaps the man was just finishing the job. Jon fingered the canister that still lay in his pocket, a small but necessary comfort.

He began walking outwards, away from the clutch of the canals, from the dense squirm of people that made pursuit so easy. He got on a tram at Rokin and watched with relief as the man stood there, breathless at the station, getting smaller until he was gone.

Jon got off the tram when he thought he was far enough away. He walked past the stately buildings thinking about Suze, the brittle touches and smiles they'd exchanged the previous night. He continued to walk, under grey scudded clouds waiting to burst. He tried not to think about the places they'd visited. Tried not to think about the dead landlord or the fire in the flat. Thinking only made things worse.

He stopped to light a cigarette and recognized the street name. Coincidence or had his footsteps carried him here knowingly? It didn't matter. He walked up the street until he found her house.

He stood between the two stone lions, finished his cigarette and rang the bell.

'Mr Reed, how nice to see you,' she said as she opened the door, trying to disguise the smile that had appeared, spontaneous like a flower burst, on her face.

'Hello, Mrs De Roedel,' he said, explaining how he found himself on her street.

'No need for excuses. Come in, I'll make some tea. I also have some lovely pastries that were not meant to be eaten alone.'

He followed her down the empty hall.

Everything was gone.

The ornamental decorations, Empire plunder, paintings and adornments. All gone. The hall was bare. She led him to the front room and disappeared into the kitchen before he could say anything. He stared at the walls, previously splashed with painted ancestors, now vacant apart from the discoloration where the frames had hung, leaving only ghostly traces of what had been. Around the room were many white removal boxes. Taped and filled. There was something creepy about a room of this size being so empty.

'Lots of sugar, I remember,' she said as she slowly poured the tea into Jon's cup, making sure not to splash or spatter the liquid.

'Thank you.' Jon took the cup, cradled it in his hand, feeling the pleasing heat make its way through his bones. 'Looks like I just caught you in time,' he said.

Mrs De Roedel looked at him blankly for a second, then understood and smiled gently. 'Oh no, Mr Reed. I think I'll be here a long time yet.' She sat down, graceful as a china cat. 'I just thought it was time for a clean-up. Though it's not spring, I know. Time to redecorate, don't you think?'

Jon nodded, wondering how she could seem so resilient

when he knew her heart was smashed. 'What about all that stuff?' he said, pointing to the boxes, lined like tired soldiers across the perimeter of the room.

She shrugged, sipped her tea soundlessly. 'Most of it's going to the museum.' She put her cup down. It rattled and spilled on the table. 'Who else am I going to give it to?' Her hand went to cover her mouth. Jon looked down while the old lady made some choking sounds. 'It was her inheritance, all this. Stuff my family and my husband's had collected over the years. I guess we thought it was history. Maybe we were wrong. Maybe it's better in a museum. I'm beginning to think we shouldn't clutter up our life with things.' There was a silence in which the walls seemed to sag and then she looked up and asked him about Jake and he told her about the video that the old man had left him. How Jake had befriended a Holocaust survivor, a prisoner-doctor, and recorded his testimony. He mentioned his own reservations, the fact that the Doctor's testimony seemed to show only the worst. The arc of descent. He told her things he knew he couldn't tell Suze or the detective. Things he'd kept inside himself. How he was beginning to think that he'd been sucked, or maybe suckered, into this investigation. How Jake had laid certain clues that only he would find, and he told her that he didn't understand why the old man had done it, what he'd been trying to prove.

She nodded and refilled his cup, pushed the cake plate across to him. They sat and talked until the light dropped from the day.

'I have something for you,' she said as he was about to leave. 'I cleaned up Beatrice's room too. All her stuff. I couldn't stand being reminded any more, for all those clothes to have

369

no one to wear them, all those books with no one to read them. I found it behind her bookcase. I called the nice detective but they told me he was off the case. They didn't seem interested. I knew you would come back.'

She went into the main room. He heard every footstep as it diminished and then amplified. Every beat of his heart.

She took a small black object out of an envelope. He put his hand out. She placed it in his palm.

It was cold and plastic. His palm was drenched in sweat. He looked down.

It was a single reel of 8 mm film.

He got off the tram and entered the District, pulsing with the night swarm of pedestrians and shoppers. The film nestled in his inside jacket pocket, zipped up, constantly touched and prodded to make sure it was still there. He wondered if Suze had a projector. He thought that it would be a good way to get to see her. Neutral ground.

He wanted to call her right away. To see what was on the film. Holding it up to the light had just confirmed that it was indeed war footage, or at least bore a close resemblance to it. He would have to slip it through a projector, have it beamed on a screen to see why Beatrice had hidden this particular reel above all others.

The previous night had led him no closer to Jake, maybe only further away. The films were real and Jake couldn't be considered as a snuff extra. But now he felt something rising, a small sliver of hope that soon things would be answered, that one way or another, soon, he would know.

Then he saw the man again. Smiling this time. He was tired of being afraid, of always having to look over his shoulder. But he remembered the detective's words, the devices the killer had used, the pleasure he'd taken. His pursuer was too far away to make an identification, but looking at him, he felt something familiar about the man, a shudder of recognition. He turned, walked through the night, quickening his step, trying to keep control, not break into a full-out run, though a part of his brain was screaming to do just that. Through the tourists and crack dealers and the girls on their coffee breaks. He bounced like a pinball from canal to canal until he finally looked behind him and didn't see anyone following. He felt excited, proud for a moment that he'd finally eluded his pursuer. Felt the fear slip and ebb.

It was getting late and the streets were thinning out. The tourists had gone home and now only hardcore smokers and whorefuckers remained, their faces equally determined by their desires as they shuffled by him.

He walked past the Old Church, almost stumbling over a couple making love in its shadow until he found himself in front of the Skull & Roses tattoo parlour. He looked towards the basement. The buzzer glowed nicotine yellow. A piercing parlour, the detective had said. Jon moved nearer the steps. He could hear movement down in the basement and he saw the lights flickering and smelled the acrid tang of burnt coke. He thought of Wouter, the previous night, the burnt-down flat.

He looked to his left and right. There was no one around. He began descending the stairs, searching through his pockets, taking out the mace. He tested his fingers against the button. Stared at the door. He heard something creeping in the darkness to his left but could see only two bins, standing silent. A cat moved and he nearly maced it. He caught his breath. Laughed. Felt a sharp shred of nerve and fear pulse through him. He reached out his hand towards the buzzer, thinking, I have to do this, I have to see what's there, when someone grabbed his wrist.

37

Trains. Long, rust-caked and articulated like snakes. Trains rolling across the sleepy hills and empty towns. Trains, shuddering and packed, the tracks like black fingers uncoiling from Berlin and heading across the Eastern European plain.

He sat and watched the documentary footage, scratchy and pocked, as it narrated and speculated. Trains and time-tables. A skeleton infrastructure, stretched and spined across the back of Europe. Like the nerves that twisted around muscle and bone. A new network of capillaries, artery and vein, shunting new kinds of things away from the fatherland, cleansing as the heart beat faster and faster and the blood sped its way across the plain.

Quirk lit a cigarette, coughed, wiped the spit off his lower lip, dark and brown, speckled with blood, someday soon, he knew. He watched the programme change but there really was no change at all. Bormann stared at him. Bormann, whose skull became such a relic like the fingerbones of burnt saints. All the time now the TV was filled with images of that era. He'd spent thirty years forgetting, or kidding himself so. Living a small life, in small rooms, small cities, where the density of your surroundings always hugs you and will never let you fall. And then the programmes started. Every night. Every channel sometimes it seemed. Endless footage, run and rerun, black and white or, for novelty value, in colour. He saw the place he'd spent his childhood in. The barbed wire and dark forested blackness beyond. He didn't feel pain or loss or hate or any of those things. It was where he'd grown up. He hadn't known any different. It was nostalgic in the way every street corner is where you once played and joked and kissed girls. Though he'd never done that. Not much of any of that at all. And afterwards those things just didn't seem important any more.

Quirk stubbed the cigarette and flipped the channel. Another documentary. Another pit, out in the Russian forests, smiling officers, handshakes, yes, yes, yes. Were people so goddamn interested, he wondered. They must be. Otherwise why show all this. Education? Well, what the fuck could you learn from this? Death? Fear? A loss of belief? All that and more. Well, let them watch, they would never understand for to watch something is not to experience it however much it may set itself up as a facsimile thereof. Quirk had even heard of a 'theme' concentration camp down in the Bavarian hills. You paid your money and were given a pair of striped pyjamas that chafed and rubbed against your skin. Not much food. A night at most. See how it was, the adverts proclaimed. Understand. Feel. And so Germans, overfilled with guilt and shame paid for these humiliations, not understanding that choice was all. That in the morning they would give back their rough clothing, rub cream over their cracked and burnt skin, get back into their Volvos and stationwagons, talk to the kids, sigh deeply, shake their heads and then remember that tomorrow they're back at work.

He flipped again. Into cableland. The refuge of the documentarian, the fake historian, the ghouls and fiends who got a kick out of all this stuff. You could sit and watch torture and death non-stop if you wanted to. Modern day and medieval. All inclusive, one package. The new pornography.

He checked his watch. Karl should have reported back by now. Probably fucked it all up. Ten years he feeds them information and then when the big one finally comes around they send him some insecure, drug-addled muscle. Christ. Quality had definitely dropped. It had been so hard to part with the address. So fucking hard. But he knew that this way he'd get another chance at the 49 reels. The Germans needed a place to work on the man, convince him of the films' rightful place . . . and then perhaps his chance would come. At least he'd get to see them again, those films, those days. He lit another cigarette, coughed, not so bad this time and tuned into some glasses-wearing geek explaining how the Holocaust could not have happened, absolutely, definitively, because if they really had gassed so many people then more molecules of the chemical would have embedded themselves in the surrounding ground. And since, this geek asserted, there were only trace elements of those, then obviously the Holocaust was a lie, a myth set up by the Zionists to perpetuate their victimhood and consolidate their position as *de facto* rulers of the world.

The doorbell buzzed. Quirk flipped the channel on to the outside cam, saw the German and his woman standing there, flipped back to the programme and buzzed them in.

'Shhh,' he said, gesturing for them to sit. He watched the geek display his facts and provenance.

'Fucking Jew,' Karl spat.

Quirk laughed.

'Don't see why you find it so funny, old man. Who do you think these deniers are? Friends of the Reich? No. Jews. Set out to discredit the Führer's most palpable achievement.'

Quirk watched the woman. She hadn't said anything. It was the first time he'd seen her. Surprised, yes – he hadn't expected a woman, but he supposed times were changing. She looked pissed off and he immediately felt that charge that always fizzled and flashed between people who shared a bed. Dieter must have been short, Quirk thought, to send this lumphead and his fucking girlfriend. There was a sound outside. Quirk looked towards the door. Locked. Just kids playing. He wondered why he was so jumpy.

'These fucking liars,' Karl said, watching the TV flicker, shovelling another mound on to his card. The woman looked at him sharply but he ignored her, continued. 'They defile the Führer's glory. Every day trying to deny all we achieved and doing it in our name. If the Holocaust didn't happen then why do these same people profess to admire Hitler so much – because he conquered several countries for a few years? Fuck, everyone's done that at one time or another – Napoleon didn't inspire groups or meetings or ideology.'

'I know this,' Quirk snapped, suddenly impatient, disgusted with it all. 'It's done?' he asked though he could smell the tang of ash and flame that clung to Karl's clothes like cigarette smoke.

Karl nodded. 'As you said, old man. All gone. The whole floor, just to make sure.' He stepped forward, took the remote and flicked the set off. Quirk started to get up but then realizing it would be easier this way, said nothing. He was glad that they had at least achieved this small task. Now there would be no connections, no betraying trails leading back to here.

'You want to tell us why we had to burn that place?'

Quirk thought about it. 'No.'

'Well, what about the films?' Karl was bored, pissed off – they'd almost been caught by the policeman, fucking Greta arguing again, them both so tired and almost didn't notice. But no matter, it was done. The place was ashes. The heat had felt good.

'You have to make sure he has the films, the originals, before you do anything.'

Karl nodded. What did the old man know? Fucking

patronizing him like Dieter and the rest back in Frankfurt. Had Dieter told the old man he was Czech? Fuck. He knew he had to get these films, get them and store them somewhere safe, somewhere even Greta wouldn't know – these were his bargaining chips into the new world and he was damn sure not going to let them go. He moved towards the instrument table to his right, picked up several needles, different shapes and sizes, running his finger smoothly against the tips. 'You giving me this address suggests that you have already ascertained that.' Karl took two of the needles and slipped them into the folds of his coat.

'This is where the website comes from. The computer, you see. So what, you kill him and then search his flat, find he put the films in a safety deposit somewhere? How's Dieter going to like that?'

The old man had a point. Yes. The films were the most important thing, couldn't get carried away now, not when they were so close.

After they'd left, Quirk switched the set off and locked the basement door. He hoped they wouldn't fuck up. They looked as though they were more than capable of it, but surely Dieter wouldn't have left something this important in an idiot's hands. Shit, he should stop worrying. He'd owed Dieter the favour. He'd given him some bad information last time. Not his fault. Believing rumours became one of the hazards of the job. But Dieter had made the debt clear and Quirk knew that SPAR didn't fuck about. But Jesus, having to deal with these fucking imbeciles they sent! They're going to screw it up, he knew. And he just as surely knew that he would have to get the films from them, that they couldn't be trusted and besides he wanted, no, he *needed* to see the films just once before they went to Germany, to a black safe somewhere in a wall. He had to see them. Absolutely. And who would have more right? Dieter didn't care who got the films to him as long as he got them.

Quirk unpadlocked the door of the annex. He crawled silently through the dark, not needing light, knowing the spaces well, avoiding the heavy objects, and found the little crawl-away hole behind the fake fireplace. He pulled the face away and there it was – warm and comfortable and so . . . He bent down into the hole until his body was submerged and he could feel the cold, rich smell of earth around him, like sweet fruit, and he felt his heart quiet and when he pulled the fireplace back into position and the darkness swallowed him, then he began to feel good, with the soft earth all around him and nowhere to fall.

'You trust him?' Greta sat across from Karl at a small pizzeria. She wanted to get him off the subject of Holocaust deniers. He'd spent the whole time walking back from that piercing parlour ranting and raving about these people.

Karl looked up. Okay, so they weren't arguing. Maybe twenty-four hours, maybe longer. It felt good – still, there was that tension between them, the tingle that couples get when they know the words they want to say will come cracking out like whips. 'No. But we need him,' he replied. 'For the time being.' He didn't want to tell her of his plans for the films, not yet. He knew she'd be far more impressed after the fact, when he held them and he knew that Dieter would be too, impressed at his daring, his initiative and lack of fear. Yes, things were starting to look up. He thought about the whores he'd fucked since arriving and wondered if Greta could see their traces on his face. He thought not. Otherwise there wouldn't have been this temporary truce. No. But all he could think about was the next one. And how to get rid of Greta for the moment. Send her on some fool errand. And then he caught himself. Shit. He knew he should concentrate on the job at hand, how to make sure that the man had the films . . . but he thought perhaps he might try a brunette today, hadn't tried any of those yet, yep, that sounded like a plan and there was nothing that Karl appreciated as much as a plan well made. 'Greta, dear,' he said, offering her his most genuine smile (for he was thinking of those other women). 'We need rope and tape.'

'I thought the piercer was providing that.' She smiled, wondered what made Karl look so happy.

'We can't trust the old man to. We have to do this ourselves, otherwise, well, Dieter won't take any excuses, you know that.'

She knew. She got up. She understood what they needed. Better than he did. She always planned this side of things. And hell, the sun was out. Maybe it would be nice to get away from each other this afternoon, maybe it would make the night so much sweeter.

'I'll see you back at the hotel.'

'Don't be too obvious,' he said, meaning when buying the rope, but realizing, too late, that actually he was saying it to himself, and he noticed that he was hard, ready and hell, superwilling. He smiled, got up, kissed her on the cheek. 'I love you.'

He saw her face relax and break into a genuine smile. He'd said the right words.

'Love you too.' She kissed him, turned and was gone.

38

Van Hijn had spent the night crouching in the bushes. Hiding the trails his breath made and making sure that his partner, only three months on the job, held the camera correctly and shot what they needed so that he could be off the case as soon as possible. It was their third night at the zoo and this time they'd struck gold. They'd taped over an hour of footage, enough to make arrests and secure convictions.

He got out of the shower, towelled hard, trying to get the last traces of the animal smell off him. He made an espresso and watched the sun smear itself over the horizon. His whole body ached. He took a couple of painkillers and finished off the cheesecake in the fridge. Checked his watch: 8 a.m. Time to go again.

He rang the now familiar bell at AYN and waited for the door to be sprung. He felt every step of the long climb in his bones, felt his stitches giving way, slowly rending apart, but he kept going. He caught his breath on the landing while the camera verified that he was still the same person who'd appeared below.

'Hello, detective,' Piet said as he stood on the other side of the door, a last precaution.

Van Hijn smiled, walked past him and straight to the main desk. Piet followed.

'I need to know who's selling the films,' he said.

'I'm sorry, detective, but as I told you on your last visit that is information we cannot . . .'

Van Hijn slammed his fist down on the table. Piet jumped.

'I need to know now. This is no longer just about the films. People's lives are in danger. At least one person has already been killed . . .' A pause. 'I have an offer to make.'

Piet sat down, visibly unnerved by the detective's burst of anger. 'What offer?' he said, almost meekly.

'Give me the address and name. When I recover the films, I'll give them to you.' He stared at Piet, waiting for an answer.

'You don't expect me to believe that, detective. With all respect, the films will undoubtedly be taken for evidence, catalogued and shelved, and just as undoubtedly in a few months' time perhaps, another auction will be posted.'

'There will be no evidence gathered this time,' Van Hijn said. 'You will have the films, you have my word on that.'

Piet stared at him for a moment, gauging the detective's sincerity. He'd had the address for a week now, routed back through the auction site until it was isolated to a single line, snaking through a single flat. He exhaled deeply to show his disapproval and turned to the computer, punching some keys that, in turn, printed out an address, a name.

'Here,' he said, giving it, still somewhat reluctantly, to the detective. 'Don't let those films get into circulation.'

Van Hijn took the paper, slipped it into his pocket. He understood what was meant, the chance he had to undo the shadow of his father's deeds.

When he was outside, clear of the sweep of the cameras, he took out the paper. Read the address. A stone's throw from where Jake was found, or should that be a body's throw, Van Hijn thought to himself as he read the name, an English name, Dominic Ripton, and he remembered what Jon had said, about a Dominic being the only person who could help him. He had to call Jon, warn him. He stepped into a phone-box, rang the number. The hotel landlord told him that Jon hadn't been back all day. Van Hijn slammed the receiver down, cursed.

Perhaps it was already too late.

39

'Don't go in there.'

Jon wrenched his wrist out of the other man's grip. He looked up and saw the face, so familiar now, the one who'd been following him these last few days, present in his dreams, soaking his sheets, ruining his nights. He grabbed the man's hand and shoved him back. Something in his head snapped, a massive spike driven through his brain. Jon flung himself at him and they went down together. Scrabbling in the semi-dark until Jon was on top, his knee in the man's crotch, his fist pounding at his face.

'Stop, please,' the man screamed. Jon continued. 'Jon! Stop it.'

The sound of his own name snapped him back. He looked down at the man whose face was now bloodied and bruised, his hair a mess. 'How do you know my name?' he shouted, realizing just how out of breath he was.

The man tried to sit up but Jon kept his hand firmly on his collarbone, pressing down.

'How?'

'Jake told me you'd come. He said to expect you.'

Jon let go. Unable to think. He watched as the man slowly sat up, wiped his jaw, ran his bloody hands through his hair and smiled. 'My name's Dominic.'

Jon moved aside. Picked up the useless canister of mace, put it back in his pocket. Took out his cigarettes. Offered one to Dominic.

'We'd better get out of here,' Dominic said, accepting the cigarette, letting Jon light it for him.

Jon shook his head. 'Tell me here.'

Dominic exhaled smoke. 'I'm surprised they haven't heard us already.'

'Who?'

'The people who are after the films.'

Jon looked towards the door of the piercing parlour. He felt his skin go cold. 'But I saw you go in there the other day, after you followed me.'

Dominic leaned towards him. 'I made a mistake. I tried to rectify it that day. It didn't work. That's why I need you now. I need you to come back to my place.'

'No way,' Jon said, knowing how easy it would be to step into another trap like the one at the Doctor's flat.

'I have something for you. It's at the flat. You want it, you'll have to come with me.' He began getting up slowly, rubbing his side, wiping the blood away from his face. Jon grabbed his arm and helped him. 'Something Jake left?' he asked.

Dominic nodded.

They walked to Dominic's flat. Through the rain and empty streets. The silent stars. Jon stayed a couple of paces behind Dominic, both to make sure that he wouldn't run and to avoid conversation. They didn't say a word as they stumbled past the gardens where Jake had been found and up towards Dominic's studio flat. Jon noticed how it over-looked the park. He remembered the man in the bushes that first night.

'Why take a photo of me?' he asked.

Dominic looked round. 'So that I could identify you. So that, if anything happened to me, the police would have a photo of you . . . somewhere to begin from.'

Jon shook his head and gulped at his drink. The answer didn't satisfy him and he suspected Dominic had simply done it to scare him.

'I'm being followed too,' Dominic said. 'There isn't that much time left.'

Jon had no idea what he was talking about and was, instead, keeping his eye on the psychotic-looking dog sitting in the corner of the room.

'Followed by who?' Jon asked as the dog eyeballed him.

'I told you, those who want the films.'

Jon leaned forward; the dog loped towards him. 'The films are here? You have them?'

Dominic shook his head. 'You don't think I'm that stupid, do you?' He disappeared into the small kitchen enclave.

Jon inched up to the dog and stroked it.

'Jake liked Bill. Took 'im walking a lot,' Dominic said when he returned. 'Take a seat.'

Jon sat on the small armchair, sinking deep down into its faded and tattered cushion. 'I still don't understand why you had to follow me or how you even found me.'

'Jake told me to.' Dominic waited while the information sunk in. He could see that Jon was having trouble with it.

'What are you talking about?'

'Jake came back from London. He told me all about you. Even said you'd be coming soon. I had no idea what he was planning to do but I knew that he wanted you here.'

Jon stared at his feet, the grainy floorboards below him. 'In Amsterdam?'

'Why do you think he left your phone number in the book? I guess you found the recordings he made.'

Jon nodded, still unable to say anything.

'You want to know why, of course you do. But don't look at me. I didn't want you or anyone else involved. It was

Jake's decision and he never fully explained it to me. I think he thought you'd find it "educational" – at least that's as much as he told me.'

'And it wasn't because of Suze?' Jon finally said.

'What do you mean?' Dominic shifted in his seat again.

'You know exactly what I mean.'

Dominic tried to light a cigarette, burnt his fingers on the match. 'Okay, what the fuck do you want me to say? But that was not why I followed you. Not at first. But then I had to know. Things were changing between us. Progressing. I knew she'd see me in a different light once she found out about the films . . . and then you come along and fuck it all up. Jesus, I wanted to kill you. You stole her from me.'

'I didn't steal anyone. She wasn't an object to be stolen.' Jon wondered what Dominic thought their relationship was like, all roses and romance probably.

'She would have been mine,' Dominic said, slumping back in the armchair, the fight draining out of him.

'If that was true, then she'd be with you now. It's not my fault.'

Dominic put his hand through his hair again. The thin blond locks looked like a hay bale torn apart by terrible winds. 'I know. But I had to blame someone.'

Jon accepted this. 'And now?' he asked.

'I told you I made a mistake. I need your help.'

'And why should I give it to you?'

'Because it's for Jake, not for me.'

Jon edged forward, tried to keep his voice under control. 'Who killed him, Dominic? Was it you?'

Dominic laughed. 'You still haven't guessed, have you?'

'Then tell me.'

'I can do better than that. I can show you.' He looked up at Jon. 'What do you know about the 49 reels?'

Heart beating fast: 'Only what's on the site, what I've been told, but I know they had something to do with Jake's death.'

'With Jake's death?' Dominic paused, contemplating what Jon had said. 'I suppose they did in a way. You know I hadn't thought of that but I suppose you're right, Jon.' He exhaled the cigarette smoke and watched it dissipate above him.

Dominic got up, went to the kitchen and came back with two mugs of coffee. How perfectly English, Jon thought, mugs of coffee. It was the first time he'd seen that in Amsterdam and it was strangely comforting. He looked at all the computers and black plastic devices, projectors and editing boxes that filled the walls of the room and at Bill who'd curled up beside his feet. He was restless, wanting to know, sensing that things had come to a certain point of unravelling. 'What mistake did you make?'

Dominic sipped his coffee, burning his tongue. 'Jake realized too late that Quirk had betrayed him. He'd trusted the piercer, thought he would help us with the work, his background, all that. But you can never tell, can you? I went there the other day because I wanted to nail that sonofabitch Quirk.'

'What happened?'

'I told him I knew all about him. He jumped me. Old fuck's quicker than he seems.' Dominic pulled up his shirt. There was a large purple-black bruise spreading over his left kidney. 'That's what happened. I've been pissing blood for the last two days. I fucked up. Happy?'

'How did you get out of there?'

'The buzzer went. He was distracted. I kicked him in the balls and ran. What else could I do?'

Jon thought about what the detective had told him. 'What was Jake's connection with Quirk?'

'Quirk was a survivor. Another one. A kid in the camp,

387

been in and out of institutions most of his life. The Doctor introduced them. Of course Jake found it useful that this man was a piercer. I think he used him for that. But Quirk promised us. He pretended to be part of the cause. His background . . . we thought . . .'

'What do you need me to do?' Jon interrupted.

'I've hidden the reels.' Dominic leaned forward, bridging the gap between them. 'I knew that someone would eventually trace them back here. I always knew that. It was never a concern. No, time was, that was all. I had to get them converted into MPEGs.'

'Where are they?' Jon asked, feeling himself being drawn in again, like a sea stone caught in the drift of a whirlpool.

'I hid them in the museum, the JHM.' Dominic laughed. 'Kind of fitting, don't you think? In the basement. Room 435. Where they keep all their film archives. The auction finishes tomorrow. I didn't need the originals once I'd digitally encoded them. It was too much of a risk keeping them here.'

'You're going to sell to the highest bidder come Sunday?'

'No chance.' Dominic splashed the mug down on the table.

'No?'

'That was never the plan.'

'The plan?' Jon was getting frustrated with his half-replies, with the sense that Dominic still wasn't telling him everything, still playing games.

'Jake's plan. He had the films. Kaplan gave them to him as a special present. A farewell gift, you might call it. Jake needed someone who knew how to transfer them on to a computer, how to post it on the net, so we worked together.'

'This was all Jake's idea?' Jon said, a light starting to glint through the darkness.

'He thought these films needed disseminating. He became obsessed with it. He was right.'

Jon shifted in his seat. 'What happens Sunday midnight?'

'The complete footage goes out on a live video feed to anyone who wants to see it.'

'My God, why?'

'Why? Christ, Jon. Jake said you weren't much of a Jew. Don't you see that these films are unique? That they need exposure? People need to see this. They stand outside of everything we've seen about the Holocaust. Nothing like this has ever been unearthed before. Don't you see the possibilities?'

Jon wasn't sure which possibilities Dominic was talking about but he nodded anyway, sure that the strange York-shireman would explain himself.

'These are pure images compared to what we've already watched. It'll reawaken the Holocaust, redeem it from the banality and comedy it's become. The auction is just a medium through which to open up interest, electronic fore-play in an age where the brevity of 8 mm is a symbol of a gone world.' Dominic laughed to himself, then stared right back at him.

Jon wondered if all the men around Suze were like this. He remembered Wouter's preachy epistle on freedom and sin. Now this. Did she attract this kind of man or was it just coincidence?

Dominic continued: 'There's something to them beyond mere images, Jon, there's a palpable sense of history there, a sense of something lost in the last fifty years, frozen in time and revived again in this new century to redeem what has been corrupted in the interim.' Dominic stopped to take a breath. 'Don't you see how badly we need this?'

'Who's we?'

'Everyone! This is our only chance at redemption. Our salvation. And with the net we have the possibility of disseminating it to untold receivers. To put it into the mythstream, into the living body of knowledge.'

'Don't you care how some people might use this footage?' Jon said, thinking back to the night at Nagatha's. Thinking how much more interest there would be in the full, uncensored object. 'Is that what you want to do, remind everyone of what beasts we are? Is that the fucking point?'

'No! Jake wanted the opposite. He thought these films were strong enough to repel those thoughts.'

It made sense. A brutal, disgusting kind of sense. All those visits by Jake to the museum. The recordings of Jake's and the Doctor's testimonies. There was a certain logic, deluded perhaps, to Jake's actions. 'And you, why are you doing this?'

Dominic looked away. 'Jake was a friend of mine,' he said.

'Is that all? You're as obsessed by it as he was.'

'And you're not? Anyway, what, only Jews are allowed to be obsessed by it? It belongs to everyone. This is where it begins. It was the start of the new millennium right there and then.'

'What are you talking about?'

'Auschwitz was the last nail in God's coffin. The last belief blown away by the crematorium fires. The last hope sublimated down into soap. After the Holocaust we had to come to terms with all our worst fears. That there was only us, only this life.'

'What about Nietzsche and Marx? They said that way before.'

'There's always been people who've said it. We always had a hunch it was true. The Holocaust was just the last strand. It was like the veil of reality was lifted and instead of it being all illusion, we saw that it was all terror. It's the hinge on which the twentieth century flaps. You think it's a coincidence that Sartre wrote of existence being the only remaining thing? Or Brando in his leather jacket, saying "What d'ya got?" The beat generation? Rock and roll? The emergence of the counter-culture? Work it out for yourself.'

Jon listened to everything Dominic said, making as little facial movement as possible, thinking, he's making sense but he's lost all sense of proportion. Dominic's tirade didn't stop, he looked like a victim of road rage, his muscles tight, his mouth exhaling words and smoke with the fury of a Gatling gun. 'Christ, Jon. You picked Jake up off the streets, you thought you were saving him, saving his soul, but you were wrong, so wrong. It was you whose soul needed saving. Jake told me that when he came back.'

Jon didn't know what to say. All this time, he'd never even considered it. Dominic seemed further away from him, the room almost boundless. 'Why did Jake come back to Amsterdam?' he asked, trying to deflect the previous comment.

'He read about Beatrice. He didn't need to see her face or hear her name. He knew it was her. Knew that the Doctor had tried to get the film from her.'

'What was her role?'

Dominic looked at him, spat out some loose tobacco from his gums. 'Jake asked her to help him film his testament. Then the Doctor's.'

'He must have known he was putting her in danger.'

Dominic smiled sadly. 'You didn't know Beatrice. Danger would have been like a red rag to her. Besides, Jake believed we're all responsible for our own actions. She knew what she was doing.'

'I have the single 8 mm reel he gave her,' Jon said.

For the first time, Dominic looked genuinely surprised. '*The* reel?'

Jon smiled.

'Jake gave it to her to hide. How the hell did you get it?'

'Never mind that. Why's it so important?'

'You haven't seen it then? Watch it, Jon. Suze can get hold of a projector. Watch it, remember what Jake left for you in London. Compare faces. You'll see what I mean.'

'What are you talking about?'

'It's something you'll have to see for yourself. Only then will you accept it. Jake was the same. He kept looking for this one thing and then he found it but it was not what he thought it was, in fact it was the very opposite and it broke his fucking life. Far worse than anything else, worse than what his father had left him in that will. When he saw it, he left Amsterdam. His life cracked like an egg under a truck wheel.'

Dominic got up, walked over to his CD case and came back with a clear plastic pouch in his hand. 'This is for you. Jake made this when he came back to Amsterdam. After London. He wanted you to have it. He knew you'd come.'

Jon's heart cranked up three gears. He'd suspected there might be a third CD all along but not that Jake would have made it *after* London. 'What's on it?'

'Watch it and see. Give you an excuse to visit Suze. Not that you need that,' he added sourly.

Jon let that ride. 'I still don't understand why you had to go through the pretence of running the auction.'

'It wasn't a pretence. The auction is real.' Dominic smiled, almost cackled, Jon thought. 'Except they don't get what they paid for. People who bid for these kind of things, the last thing they want to see is their rare item out in the public domain. Where it should be. I want to rub their noses in it. They've spent all week getting fired up about owning such a unique item. I wish I could see even one of their faces when the live feed goes out.'

Jon smiled, finally seeing it, starting to sense that the answers were indeed out there, eminently graspable. 'And the Doctor?' he asked. 'Where is he? I need to find him.'

Dominic laughed. He shook out a cigarette and lit it. 'Watch the video, Jon, watch and you'll understand.'

Jon slipped the disc into his pocket, along with the single 8 mm reel, stroked Bill. He knew he'd got what he could out of Dominic, what Dominic wanted him to know.

They shook hands and Jon walked back through the early hours to his hotel, watching the first smears of light creep in from the east, his head so filled with all this new information that he feared it might explode. He thought of calling Van Hijn and telling him where the 49 reels were, the auction, but he knew he wouldn't and why. Because of Jake. Jake had obviously trusted Dominic and Jon knew that he would wait another day, let this thing reach its end, before informing the detective. Jake deserved that at least. He felt the hard presence and poke of the disc in his pocket, the third instalment in Jake's story. It would mean he'd have to go round to Suze's in the morning, and the thought of that made him smile for the first time in hours, perhaps even days.

40

The next morning he sat in the hotel room, now more familiar than his own flat, and stared at the single reel of film, the final CD.

He reached for the phone. No hesitation.

Dialled Suze's number.

'Jon. How are you?' She sounded excited to hear him. He took it as a good sign.

'I'm fine, I guess. Suze, I really need to use your computer.' He ground his foot down into the floor. It was not what he'd meant to say. His abruptness surprised him, he'd once been the opposite, so shy and reluctant to come to the point.

'So that's why you called me?' She tried to make it a joke but realized from his tone that it hadn't worked.

'No, not just that. I saw your friend Dominic last night. He gave me the last of the CDs.'

She knew this was not the time to talk about personal things. Not now. 'Jake's CD?'

'Yes, and . . .' His words hovered in the space between them. He took a deep breath, felt his hands clench in his pocket, heard the hum of distance in the wires. 'And I miss you, Suze. Shit, I know that sounds . . .'

She cut in, 'Don't say anything.' There was a pause in which neither of them spoke.

Then: 'Suze, have you got an 8 mm projector?'

'So, you just want me for my machines?'

He laughed. 'Of course, what else did you think? No, I have a reel of film that Jake gave to Beatrice to hide. Not one of the 49. This is different. I think it's why she was killed, why Jake was killed.'

'Over one reel of film?'

'Over what's on it.'

She lit a cigarette. 'I can borrow a projector from the museum. Meet me at the flat in an hour.'

He heard her exhale smoke through the wires, saw her lips pressing up against the plastic of the phone. 'I'll see you then.'

Dominic had woken up with a bad hangover and a feeling of having done something wrong. He looked around for Bill, saw the dog standing by his water dish, just watching it, and decided it was time to get out of bed. He brushed his teeth, tearing away at the fast food and sugar skin he'd left on them the night before and went through all the possible variations of tonight's auction closing.

The thought made him smile for the first time that morning and he suddenly felt as if a whole mountain of shit was gradually lifting from his back. He fed Bill, somewhat concerned by the dog's unenthusiastic eating and put on the Birthday Party's *Junkyard*, enjoying the noise and dissonance of the music as it filled and splintered the room. He smoked two cigarettes and drank three glasses of gin with the overwhelming feeling of anticipated relief that hits you when you know the scariest rollercoaster ride of your life is almost over.

'It's good to see you,' she said and put her arms around his neck, moving her body closer to his, feeling the warm rub of his skin. She felt him move back at first, tense and coiled like a barbed-wire fence, then easing, letting his body drape into hers. They both stood back. Looked at each other, each unwilling to say anything that might break the moment. He put the bag down on her table.

'You want some breakfast?' she said, opening the curtains on a rare slice of sunshine. 'I've got bagels and croissants.'

'No, I'm fine.'

'Tell me about Dominic.' They sat on her sofa, one at either end, facing each other, the hum of a Richard Buckner CD pulsing in the background.

'He's been following me for days. I thought it was Wouter but it was Dominic all along.'

She moved towards him. 'Why? He's a bit creepy but . . .'

'This.' He pointed to the bag that lay innocently on the table. 'It all has to do with this. Jake's murder. The serial killer. Everything.'

'The Nazi snuff films?'

He shook his head. 'He's hidden them. No, this is Jake's last video.'

She sat there unable to say anything else. Dominic, behind the films? It made sense, made more sense than she wanted to admit. His preoccupation these past few weeks, his connections and evangelical fervour. 'He was doing it for the Council,' she said.

Jon shook his head. 'No, he was doing it for Jake. For himself too.'

'What's he going to do with them?'

'Post them on the web for everyone to see.'

'Christ!' she said, lighting a cigarette, moving towards him.

'You disagree?' He thought she'd be thrilled, that it would be the apex of all that the Council believed in. He stared at her crumpled form and realized how wrong he'd been. 'I thought that's what the Council's theories were all about?'

'I thought that too, until I realized that we were wrong or

perhaps just too simplistic, too idealistic. There have to be other ways of disseminating this information. The bottom line is how do you live? Can you live with all that hate filling up inside you? Can you do something positive with it or does it just infect you and make you into the very thing you despise?'

Dominic spent the day hiding in the shade of corner tables in small coffee shops around the District. He knew that staying at home was not an option. Even if nothing happened, the anticipation of it doing so would have driven him crazy. Today of all days he wanted to remain sane.

He sat in an early show of a Belgian porn film. A couple on a holiday island fall in love with the local donkey. The man who owns the donkey and who, by day, rents him out to small children for short rides, agrees to let the couple have the animal, nights, for a larger fee than he charges the kids. Dominic watched as the couple made love to the donkey without ever touching each other. He got bored after twenty minutes, the couple were still discovering the joys of their newfound friend at night and the kids were still riding him by day though a few of the children had complained that Pablo, their favourite beach burro, was acting a little weird these last few days. Moody, they said, and Dominic heard the man in the seat behind him grunt feverishly, reaching an orgasm. Dominic noticed how the man had come as soon as the screen was filled up with children's faces and he felt suddenly disgusted, smelling the sour stench of spunk all around him, its sticky purchase under his feet.

He left the cinema and started walking through the District, trying to keep his face hidden, his movements banal, *El Hombre Invisible* like Bill Burroughs, and he fortified himself with the steely image of the gaunt writer wandering through the streets of Tangiers, a ghost flitting through the city.

At the corner of Zeedijk, he saw an amazing sight come towards him. At first he thought she was a whore but no whores were that good-looking, not even in Amsterdam, and anyway he could see that she was holding a map in her left hand. He stood there stunned as she came up to him and in a slight, lilting German accent asked him the way to the Old Church. 'It's my first day in Amsterdam and I don't understand this system at all.'

'It's a bitch to master,' Dominic replied, trying not to look at her breasts.

'Is it far?' Her eyes were like pools of cool water on a blistering summer day.

'No, about two minutes, just take the left . . .'

'Please, could you show me the way?' She tilted her head towards him, put her hand on his arm. 'I'm scared of being lost again and this place frightens me. What if they think I'm one of those women and start touching me? They already look at me like that here.'

'No problem, I was walking that way myself.' Terribly English and terribly proud of himself, Dominic took her hand, surprised that she let it stay in his and walked with her the long route to the Old Church, enthralled by the way she spoke and the way she looked.

'Please, if you could, I know you've been very kind already but I need to go to this place. I was told it was by the Old Church.' She took a piece of paper from her cleavage. Dominic saw the paper come up and a breast nearly follow it, revealing a tease of darker skin before she adjusted herself.

Dominic watched as she tried to read the paper. A whiff of harsh chemicals flooded his nose and then, from behind, a sudden shadow. He barely had time to feel the metal making contact with the back of his head before the darkness swallowed him whole.

41

Van Hijn arrived at Dominic's flat, realizing immediately that he was too late. The door hung open. Light spilled on to the hallway carpet. He stepped inside, his gun at the ready this time, but no one was there. Only the mess that was left when the place had been searched. A quiet, contained fury evident in the scatter of objects. He walked around the small flat quickly, trying to ascertain what remained. Though the flat had been turned over there was no apparent sign of struggle. Nothing to suggest that Dominic had been in when they'd arrived.

He tried booting up the computer but it was busted, the hard drive lying in fragments at his feet. Then he heard whimpering.

It was coming from the closet. He drew his gun. Reached out and opened the door.

The dog lay wrapped in barbed wire at the bottom of the closet. He was shivering and crying, small sobs coming from his throat, blood pooling about him.

'Jesus Christ.' Van Hijn put the gun back in his pocket, dropping to his knees and reaching out to the dog. He could see one glassy eye turn up towards him and he wondered if the dog would go crazy, unleash all its pain on him. But it just moaned. The detective noticed a long, thin needle lying next to the animal, spotted with blood. It looked like the one he'd seen at Quirk's. He flashed on Quirk's smile, the folds of the old man's face, his buried accent, the secret room. Jon's pursuer disappearing into the basement. He'd been meaning to pay the old piercer another visit. Looking around the wrecked flat he realized it was all he had left.

Van Hijn grabbed one of the strands of wire and slowly began unravelling it from the animal's body. If the dog was in the way they could have just killed him, he thought; this was for pleasure, an added bonus. He spent the next few minutes carefully unwrapping the animal, who seemed to understand that the detective meant him no harm. The dog whimpered and screamed every time the wire caught on his flesh or took off a piece of fur. But he never lashed out.

Van Hijn realized he was crying. He wiped his eyes on his sleeve and took off the last bit of wire. He went to the kitchen, found a bowl, filled it with water and brought it to the dog. He looked on as the dog slowly lifted its head, in considerable pain, and began lapping up the liquid. With that done, his chest heavy and choked, Van Hijn locked the door behind him and headed for Quirk's piercing parlour.

Dominic watched as Karl argued with Quirk, hoping it would prolong the time before he started to work on him. He knew it was coming though and wondered how he would stand up to it. He hoped he would be the person he believed himself to be.

It had all led to this.

He shouldn't have been surprised. It had started as something right. Something necessary. He had done what was needed. He'd done everything so that the films would go online. So that people would see once and for all. Sitting there, strapped to the piercing chair, watching Karl, the girl and Quirk, he made a promise to himself: not to tell them where the reels were even if it meant his death. He thought there was not much chance of him leaving this room either way and strangely, he felt alive then. He heard every word they spoke and noticed every part of the room, the small table with the piercing instruments, the broken chair in the corner and the black bag that was next to him on the floor. I will not say a thing to them. I will not feel any pain, he repeated to himself as he saw the piercer come towards him.

'One last time. Where are the films?'

Dominic shook his head. The German turned towards him. 'I suggest you tell him,' he said. 'Quirk here has perfected the art of piercing *through* the nerve, I don't think it's something you'll appreciate.' He laughed.

Dominic looked at him blankly. Quirk smiled. 'Okay, I prefer it this way too,' he said and reached for his equipment.

He put the first needle into Dominic's left thigh. It went in cleanly, smoothly, like a breath of cold air on the skin. Dominic looked down at the piercer's bald head and his withered hands manipulating the needle, finding the right place, then pushing it in.

There was a moment when he didn't feel anything, when everything stopped, the room, the people, all stopped dead as if they'd been freeze-framed. And then it hit him. Like a punch, a kick to the balls, like nothing he'd ever experienced before, and he squirmed and cried out and puked and pissed himself as his whole body flared up in pain. He saw Bill running through a field of brilliant green in migraine sunshine and then he passed out.

Karl took out a small bottle of smelling salts.

'Much quicker, you see,' Quirk said, looking at Karl, quietly proud of himself.

'The films?' he whispered. Dominic struggled but managed to shake his head and even peel back his lips for something approximating a smile. He could still see Bill running and he knew that as long as the dog ran, he would be okay.

Quirk grinned. He liked the tough ones, the ones that took more to get them to break. Worthy vessels for his undoubted talent. He took another needle, wider, curved; showed it to Dominic. He rolled up Dominic's sleeve, pressed his cold fingers on the skin, feeling for the right point. When he had it, he took the needle and slid it past the membrane and into the nerve. Dominic screamed and lost consciousness again.

When Dominic came out of the blackness he saw Quirk holding another needle in his hand, long and thin like a shark's tooth, smiling, ready to strike. Bill was gone. The field and the flowers were all gone. Only the pain existed. A sweet, exquisite toothache pain that pulsed through his arm and leg, throbbing in his veins. 'No!' he screamed. 'No, I'll tell you where they are. No more! Please!'

Karl took a cigarette from his pack, lit it and placed it gently in Dominic's mouth, gesturing for Quirk to move away. 'Where?' he asked Dominic, his tone solicitous and smooth as a salesman closing a sweet deal.

'They're in the museum. The JHM. Room 435,' he said, trying to catch his breath. It seemed so hard to breathe suddenly and his stomach felt extremely hot.

Karl smiled. He looked at Quirk. 'Finish up with him. I believe the man came here to get some piercings. Do it.'

+ + + + + + + + + + + + + + + + +

LATE SEPTEMBER, 1943. VILLEFRANCHE/DRANCY/
POLAND

They will come for us.

Everyone else is gone from town and no one smiles any more. The nights are filled with screams and the groaning of their trucks taking more people away. I am here with my new husband. Alex. It still feels strange to say that, but there it is. We are hiding out in Ottilie's villa. I do not know of anywhere else to go. The soldiers are everywhere.

We got married in the late summer heat. We stood on the steps of the hall and we kissed and I never imagined it would be like this. I always thought that it would be me and Alfred and music would be playing, the stars twinkling, the very earth would heave and groan and the wild sky would break apart. But instead it is filled-out forms, lazy handshakes, wry smiles and this baby that is now five months inside of me.

It is autumn and the sky is closing in. The last week of August brought storms terrifying and unstoppable, wrenching the water out of its nest, waves breaking against the small sea-front hotels. Rain like I have never seen it. Not Berlin rain but something else, denser, so that you almost choke to death in its spray.

Someone gave us up.

I heard the truck approach, saw the men step out, their black uniforms slick with rain, and I screamed.

Alex told me to hide but I couldn't leave him. We stood up together when the men entered our room. Two young German men. In another life they could have been my sui-

404

tors. In this life, they were smiling. The officer took out a whip and began beating Alex with it. I screamed again but only heard them laughing. My dear Alex fell to the floor and began to shake.

They told us to pack our things but there was nothing left to take. All I still had were those awful things I had drawn in Gurs. I do not know why but I took them, folded them and placed them inside my shirt. They broke Alex's ankle with a stick and dragged him by the hair out to the truck.

We arrived at the hotel. Alex could barely climb out of the truck. I tried to help him but the officer began to beat me until I couldn't hold on any longer. They marched us into the Excelsior. SS stood like dustbins every few yards. A short, dark, hook-nosed man stood on the balcony smiling. They took me to a room that I was to share with other women. Alex was taken elsewhere. The women looked at me as I made my way to the empty space in the corner. I fell on to the floor and revelled in its cold, hard kiss.

Someone told me that today is 24 September. They said, remember this day. I do not know why. Today I was reunited with Alex. They lined us up with about thirty others. Brunner screamed and shouted. He picked an old rabbi out of the line, started beating him, ripping his clothes off. I looked away just before I heard the shot.

We marched up the main street towards the railway station. The French stood on the pavements and watched us. Some cheered. Others, I could see, were trying to hold back their tears. I managed to grab Alex, help him stand, and no one saw us, our hands clasped, as we marched towards the train.

*

The camp here at Drancy is much larger than the one at Gurs. But there is a different feeling here. Everyone feels that this is the worst, that once we are moved, things can only get better. Yesterday, Brunner handed out postcards that had been sent from other resettled Jews. The cards were postmarked Oswiecim, and on the back they told of better times. Of a place where they are left alone. Where there is food and education for the children. They spoke of better places. We each held on to the cards for as long as we could, loath to pass them on, as if in their surfaces we too could find such comfort.

We know that we are going to Poland. They took our money on entering the camp and gave us receipts, vouchers in zlotys which we would be able to cash once we arrived. Everyone felt much better, knowing how the Germans liked to keep things in meticulous order, everyone thinking we are going to a place with shops, where things can be bought and we all held on to those little slips as if our lives depended on them.

I think it is October. I do not know any more. Today we are leaving. They called our names this morning and we stood for six hours out in the cold, still naked from sleep, until the roll-call had been repeated to Brunner's satisfaction. They loaded us on to a bus. I lost track of Alex. The local kids threw stones at the bus as we were marched in.

Alex is gone. Maybe he is on another bus. Maybe he managed to get away. I hope so. Or I hope that I will see him on the train. Or in Poland. Where we can live as a couple, have this child, forget these awful days.

I cannot believe that they expect us to ride in these trains. The compartment in front of me is filled. People are squirming and crying and the stink is terrible. I stand in line. I have seen many shot today. I will not do anything out of line. I want to see my Alex in Poland. I will do as they tell me.

The compartment is filled. I hear the SS shouting out 'Close transport 60', and suddenly all the light disappears. I do not know how many of us are in the car. There is a steady undercurrent of tears. Nearly everyone is standing. My face is almost pressed against the door. I was the last one in. Some of the old people have managed to sit between other people's legs. I cannot see further than that. No one is screaming. Not yet. But I can feel it in their throats and in mine. This rising scream that threatens to unleash at any minute.

There is shouting from outside. I cannot make out what they are saying. Suddenly the door is opened and I nearly fall out. Someone grabs me from behind and stops me. Air drifts into the car and a few people sigh, thinking maybe it was all a trick and now we were being let off. But I could hear the soldiers shouting. They were talking in my language.

'We're full. The list has been completed. You know we can't add people who are not represented on the list. He will have to go on the next transport tomorrow.'

'No. It is imperative he goes now.'

'What's so special about this Jew?'

'He is English. An English Jew, can you believe that? You see, the quicker we dispatch him the better.'

'Okay, but you will have to report this to the Obersturm-führer. He does not like it when the numbers are wrong.'

I hear the crack of wood on bone and then they shove him into the car. He is face-to-face with me. Blood is running down his head and if it wasn't so cramped in here he would collapse.

The doors shut.

Darkness again. The train begins to move. People sway and fall into each other. I hold the man in front of me. I can hear the deep twists of his breath.

'Do you speak English?' he says.

I nod and then realize he can't see me. 'Yes, some I speak,' I say, hoping that is right, trying to remember what I can. I think he smiles but I am not sure, perhaps it is only the moonlight leaking in through a crack in the door.

'Hello,' he says and his breath is warm against my cheek. 'My name is Jon Reed and I don't know what I'm doing here.'

'I am Charlotte,' I say. 'And I don't know what I'm doing here either.'

He presses against me and puts his hand on my stomach. I can feel my child kicking inside and I know that he feels it too. We stand like that, stomachs pressed against each other, in this terrible heat.

'I can feel it,' he says.

'Yes.'

+ + + + + + + + + + + + + + + + + +

42

Van Hijn stood outside the piercing parlour and shook the rain out of his hair. The light was on inside. No sounds, no movement that he could discern. He tried the door. Locked. He pulled out his gun and blew the lock, shielding himself against the exploded fragments of wood and metal that spat back at him. He looked behind him; the street was empty. He shouldered the door and spilled into the room.

Dominic was laid out on the piercing chair, his head drooping. Van Hijn had to look away, then forced himself to look back.

A pool of blood had converged around the bottom of the chair. Dominic was naked and it looked as if he'd been pierced with fragments of a skyscraper. Or been caught in a hurricane of shrapnel, white-hot and hissing. Bits of metal protruded from his side, from where his liver was, curling in strange shapes as they reentered his body lower down, one in his thigh, the other through his genitals. His tongue hung loose from his mouth and had been bisected by a sharp metal rod that quivered with a faint blue electrical charge.

The detective checked his pulse, but it was just routine. He looked away from the dead body, noticed the other door. The gleaming padlock. He held his hand up to his face and shot it off.

The light was so bright that it took him a couple of seconds to focus on the shape of the piercer slipping across the room.

He fired one shot. Quirk went down. Van Hijn heard the

satisfying collision of metal and bone and watched as the piercer's ankle bloomed a sudden red.

He moved towards the man. Applied pressure to his broken ankle. The piercer screamed.

'Where are the films?' Van Hijn shouted.

Quirk grimaced. Shook his head.

More pressure. The soft giving of flesh and cartilage. Quirk shook his head.

Van Hijn handcuffed the old man to the radiator. He called for back-up. Stood, caught his breath. Then explored the room. It was tiled white. A strange, rotting smell sat heavily in the detective's nostrils. Once another piercing room perhaps, before that a hiding place for Jews during the war. In the centre of the room stood the Judas Cradle, solid and monumental like a remnant of some forgotten empire or a work of groundbreaking modernist art. In the corners, other devices lay silent and occluded. Tongues of metal and steel, leather and wood, spikes and clamps and shackles. He walked across the floor, trying to breathe through his mouth, saw the clogged drain, leaned down, felt his fingers slide through the mulch, hair and skin and blood. He wiped his hand on his trousers and looked up at the empty tripod, the overhanging halogens.

He was drawn to the screen in the corner, like something you'd find in a radiology unit. Gun-metal grey. He looked behind and saw the video camera mounted on a tripod. His heart boomed through his chest. But there was no tape inside. Nothing at all. He felt the floor sliding away from him as he stared through the camera's eye at the centre of the room, the Judas Cradle looming perfectly positioned and focused in his field.

Van Hijn ran back into the room. Quirk was lying on the floor, quietly moaning, holding his ankle.

'Where did they go?' Van Hijn shouted.

'Go to hell,' the piercer replied. His voice sounded as if he was gargling stones.

Van Hijn walked up to him. Put his foot above the bullet wound. 'I'm not going to ask again.'

Quirk said nothing this time. Van Hijn applied pressure. The piercer started coughing, convulsing, then passed out.

'Motherfucker!'

He was too late. Too fucking late.

Dominic must have told them where the films were.

He could hear the sirens of the approaching ambulance and police crew. He didn't feel like talking to them, explaining what he was doing here. He left the basement and disappeared back into the rain. He stood behind the Old Church and called Jon.

43

She carefully threaded the film through the projector's teeth. Her hands were shaking and it took three attempts before it slipped smoothly into the machine's clasp.

'They mind you borrowing that?' Jon asked, surprised at her resourcefulness.

'They don't know.' She flicked her cigarette, missed the ashtray and hit the floor. 'Long as I have it back before the museum opens, no one will be the wiser. There.' She fed the last bit through, her fingers slipping over the old, brittle celluloid, careful not to crack it, to erase this most precious of objects. 'The reel from Beatrice's room or Jake's video?' She looked at him, wondering how he could act so calmly at a moment like this when every bone in her body felt as if it was shaking.

'Beatrice's reel,' Jon replied, lighting what seemed to be his fortieth cigarette that day.

The insect whirr and creak of the machine filled the room like an old man's breath as the far wall flickered and jumped until an image rested upon it. Jon moved closer to Suze, taking her hand, his breath shallow and irregular.

'What if there's nothing on it?' she said, voicing his worst fears.

He didn't answer. The film had started.

A courtyard. Was that barbed wire in the distance? Hard to tell. A line of SS officers standing in the sun, smiling and congratulating each other, a mood of conviviality settled about their faces. Perhaps it is a Sunday afternoon. It has that relaxed country feel. Another officer steps out of a black car and starts going along the line, handing out medals, commendations, handshakes and smiles. Each recipient smiles back in close-up . . .

'Jesus! Fuck!'

Suze was the first to see it. She got up, turned the switch and the film rewound on the spool.

'What?' Jon asked, almost off his seat.

'Wait,' she said and switched the gears back into forward.

They watched in silence as his face came into the centre of the frame. Dressed impeccably in his SS uniform, all those straight angular lines, to-die-for collars, shiny leather boots, the small death's-heads on the jacket and yes, those eyes, those same eyes.

'Pause it,' Jon said.

'I can't. This isn't video.'

'It's him, isn't it?' He watched the Doctor move forward, shake hands with the officer, accept his commendation.

'That son of a bitch!' Suze screamed. She got up, hit a switch on the machine, the film slowed down, stopped, disappeared.

'What the fuck is Kaplan doing in Nazi uniform?' Jon said.

Suze turned to him. 'There is no Kaplan. There never was. He *was* the Nazi doctor, not the prisoner. He was Dr Werner and not his so-called assistant, Kaplan.'

'It can't be,' he said, thinking of those long evenings the two old men had sat opposite each other, Jake's attachment, the whole damn thing. 'No.'

'Jake must have found the film in the JHM. Must have recognized Kaplan. You were right, the Doctor killed him because of this. Because he'd discovered his true identity.'

Jon sat there, everything upside down. The world was

suddenly silent except for the faint hum of the machine, the ebb and flow of their breath.

Kaplan was a Nazi doctor. All along. Had Jake known? He couldn't have. Unless that was the point. But no, he wouldn't have filmed him if he'd known. Jake must have stumbled upon it, recognized the Doctor, confronted him.

'We have to see Jake's video.' He got up, took the final CD out of his pocket, walked over to her computer and loaded it in the tray.

'Oh, Jon,' she said. She thought of the Doctor sitting in on group meetings, his friendship with Dominic and Beatrice and she wanted to scream.

She moved towards Jon, pulling up a chair beside the computer. 'Are you sure you want to watch this?' she asked.

He replied by pressing Return. The machine sputtered and groaned as it whirled the silver disc around, read its secrets and then, in a flourish that alchemists would have envied, transformed those simple numbers into a face, the life of a man, his voice and only remaining presence in the world. Even more wondrous than turning lead into gold, Jon thought, as the old man, his old man, the tramp, Jake or Jakob – whoever he was – lived and spoke again.

'Jon. It seems very different now that I know to whom I am addressing this.' Jake looked older, his face as if it had been folded many times, his voice heavy with smoke. 'It was better, I think, when I spoke to the camera. There was something about that, the purity of it, that seemed to fit what I had . . .'

The phone made them both jump.

They looked at each other and laughed, releasing some of the tension that had built up. Jon paused the disc, the old man for ever frozen, a mass of pixels flickering on as Suze picked up the phone.

'Van Hijn,' she said, passing it to Jon.

The detective didn't waste time on greetings. 'Dominic's dead,' he said.

Jon took a deep breath.

'He must have told them where the 49 reels are. It's too fucking late. We've lost them.'

'No, it isn't,' Jon said, breathless, heart pounding hard. 'I know where he hid them. Meet me at the JHM. Fifteen minutes. The films are there.'

44

The rain was terrible. But they got lucky. For the first time since they had left Frankfurt, things went smoothly and they arrived at the museum's doors just as the old man was locking up.

Karl emerged from the rain and grabbed Moshe from behind, his arm slipping quietly to the old man's neck. Greta followed the two men back into the museum, taking Moshe's keys and locking the door behind them. Outside the rain continued pounding the pavements. Inside, quiet had descended.

'What do you want?' Moshe asked, though he already knew.

Karl stared at him, smiling. 'Don't worry yourself, old man. We'll be through faster than you think. No harm will come to you.'

Moshe had heard similar things before. He looked down at the floor and noticed that the cleaner had missed a spot. Mud lay caked on the tiles.

'Room 435?' Karl said, pointing his gun at the old man.

'Find it yourself,' Moshe said. In German.

Karl smiled. Took his gun, twisted it round and let the handle slam into Moshe's jaw sending the old man spilling on to the dirty floor. 'I won't ask so politely again.'

Moshe pushed himself up. Wiped the blood from his chin. 'That way.' He pointed into the darkness of the main hall.

'No, you're coming with us,' Karl said, lifting the old man

416

up, surprised at how little he weighed, like a small girl. 'Make sure he keeps up,' he told Greta.

They were about to enter the main hall when they heard the front door opening.

'I thought you locked it,' he said.

'I did,' Greta replied.

45

'You've got keys, right?'

Suze nodded. 'What did the detective say?'

He looked at her, knowing that there was no way round it, that he had to tell her. 'Dominic's dead. Van Hijn thinks he told the killers where the films were.'

She put her hand to her mouth, but the scream she thought would come, did not. Instead this blind, choking vacuum filled her lungs. The floor seemed to float. The room to shake. Jon moved to steady her but she turned away, not wanting him to see her like this. She looked out of the window and tried not to cry. She closed her eyes tight but that didn't help. She thought of the last time she'd seen Dominic and how awful it all was, but that still didn't make things better. She'd never have guessed that his death would move her so. She felt it instantly, as if the world had suddenly sprung a leak, and out of this gap came her tears, only a pale imitation of the rain outside, but endless, or so it seemed to her.

She let him come and wrap his arms around her. She felt him fold into her gaps, the places where her body gave way, and put a hand to her face.

'I'm sorry, Suze.' He held her for as long as he could but he knew that the detective would be waiting.

'I don't mind going by myself,' he said eventually.

She shook her head, turned but, still caught in his embrace, said, 'No. I can't stay here. I'm the only one who knows the layout of the place, you need me.'

418

And he wanted to tell her that, yes, that was true, but a sudden gust caught the limb of a nearby tree and sent it crashing down into the roof of the car below, making them both jump, scaring them out of the moment.

46

Van Hijn watched as the police cars circled the parlour. Through the rain, the red and blue lights took on an almost hallucinatory feel, flicking and strobing, cutting through the dense mist of the night. He saw Beeuwers walk towards the entrance, slow, sinewy and muscular like a creature which had skipped a couple of evolutionary stages. At least the captain would make sure that nothing got fucked up, Van Hijn thought. The captain would know when he saw the little room that the killer had finally been found, or one of them at least. Van Hijn's phone call would have been recorded, no way for Beeuwers to take the credit for himself. But all these lights and cars? He was just an old man with a bullet in his ankle, harmless now. But people wanted spectacle. They wanted flash and glam. The bright halogen lights of cameras and insect buzz of television. He could see the various news crews approaching. The captain would have tipped them off. Good publicity for him, good copy for them. Nice how that worked.

The night illuminated and cordoned, Van Hijn turned and walked away, hidden in the rain, his hair smeared over his scalp, his clothes no longer resembling anything but misshapen rags. He headed east towards the museum, towards the real end of this thing, not the flash splatter headlines that he'd left behind him but something that he knew could be found only in the darkness of the past.

He got there first. The museum doors were closed, the

place locked up for the night. He walked around the perimeter, noticing how the new modern buildings had been so effortlessly joined to the older synagogues, a marvel of architecture, something you could perhaps truly appreciate only on such a wet night with things still ahead.

He hid behind some bushes. His favourite pastime lately it seemed. Waited until he saw the two of them approaching the main entrance.

They hadn't talked much on the way. They'd decided to forsake the tram for the privacy of the storm, the caterwaul that would drown out anything but the loudest screams. Jon watched her walking two steps ahead of him, and wondered what Dominic had really meant to her. He quickly dismissed the thought. That was her life, the parts of it that existed without him, and he had no right to probe there. He could never understand her true feelings, it was hard enough to get a grip on his own.

He thought of Jake, the waste of his life, the pain and fear that had grown up with him like errant siblings, always there when he turned off the light. The slow spiralling descent that he'd let himself tumble into. How had he felt watching that reel of film, seeing his friend, his new friend, in that uniform? Was there any way back from that?

Jon watched the canals roil and rumble, water swishing over the sides of the boats as the rain pounded them. As he walked, he saw the Doctor's face on most of the men passing through the District, each smiling at him, all melting into other faces when he looked too closely. He wondered if it changed anything, the Doctor being a Nazi and not a Jew. It was a clever disguise, one that no one would question. But it had occurred to Jake, somewhere along the line, and though he'd denied it, he'd still gone on looking for the evidence. And found it. That was why the Doctor had killed him. The 49 reels were only a distraction. It was the single reel that had led to Jake's death. Beatrice's too. Killed, tortured terribly as the detective had said and yet she hadn't told the old man where the film was. And where did the others fit in, Jon wondered, seven girls all gone? Were they just fodder for the Doctor's dreams?

'The place is locked. No one here.' The detective smiled at the couple as he emerged from the bushes.

'Suze has the keys,' Jon said.

Van Hijn nodded, his expression oblique as alabaster, a cigarette slowly burning between his fingers. 'Are you sure the 49 reels are in there?'

Jon nodded. 'That's what Dominic said. Did you find the Doctor?'

'No. I found something else though.' Van Hijn wiped the rain from his eyes. 'The room where they killed the girls. At Quirk's piercing parlour.'

'The alarms are off.' The rain was so loud that she had to shout to get their attention. She was standing by the door, looking at the still camera above her, its dead eye recording nothing. 'I think they're in there already. Moshe never forgets the alarm. Not once in all the time I've been here.'

Jon looked at the detective. Van Hijn pulled out his gun, held it at his side. 'I'll go in first. You two follow me.'

Suze gave him the key. The detective took a deep breath, steadied the shaking of his hand and unlocked the door. His stomach winced and wailed.

'The light's on your left,' Suze said.

Van Hijn crawled slowly through the dark until he reached the switch. Behind him he heard Suze lock the door, the storm muffled behind the thick glass. He pressed the button and the light snapped on.

Suze screamed.

47

They were holding Moshe underneath the huge, dangling Torah at the centre of the room. The woman had her hands around his neck while the man was pointing a gun in his left eye. Blood ran down from Moshe's thin, white hair and settled on his grey lips.

Van Hijn aimed his gun at Karl, keeping his eye on the woman to his side. 'Put the gun down,' he said. 'Put it down, now. There's nowhere to go from here. The police are on their way. Put it down and no one gets hurt.'

The man laughed. 'Why should no one get hurt?' he said, in English this time. 'Where's the fun in that?' He poked the barrel of the gun further into Moshe's eye. 'Drop your gun, detective.'

Van Hijn stared at the man holding the gun, watching the twitch on his face, his dilated pupils. He looked towards Jon and Suze. They were staring at Moshe.

It was up to him.

If he gave up his gun, he knew that there was no way out for any of them. These maniacs would surely think nothing of shooting them here. And Moshe was so old, over a hundred at least, had to be, Van Hijn rationalized, lucky to have another year in him. He knew that he could kill both of them before they could turn their guns towards him or Jon and Suze. He knew that this was the right thing to do in the circumstances. That it was the logical thing. That whatever life the old man had left was nothing compared to the rest of them. He looked back at Jon and Suze; their expressions hadn't changed. He cocked the gun. Saw Karl move his head, attuned to the sound, cocking his now too.

'Last fucking time,' he shouted at the detective.

Van Hijn considered it once more. Then threw the gun down on the floor. Kicked it over towards the man.

'Good decision.' Karl said, signalling to Greta to pick it up. He lowered his own and grabbed Moshe's shoulder, threw him down on the floor.

'Should have died sixty years ago with the rest of them,' he added, taking the gun from Greta, inspecting it. Suddenly his arm flicked open like a whip. The gun pointed at Van Hijn. The room exploded with the noise of the shot. Jon watched the detective go down. Falling to the floor screaming.

Karl stood motionless in a cloud of smoke. He pointed the gun at Suze and Jon. 'Don't move towards him.'

They stood there, dead still, afraid to move a muscle, to even breathe.

Jon saw Van Hijn on the floor, his hand around the hole the bullet had made. The detective had been sick and was breathing heavily and unevenly. He clutched his stomach, and Jon could see that he was biting his lip. Small droplets of blood leaking from his mouth.

'Greta, check his pockets for a phone. You two.' He pointed the gun at them. 'Come with me.'

Jon stepped forward and in front of Suze, a last stupid measure of defence. The sight of the gun made him quickly back away.

'You work here, don't you?' Karl took out a pack of cigarettes and offered Suze one.

Suze shook her head, saw the pack smeared red with Dominic's fingerprints.

'I've seen you here.'

She nodded, not knowing what else to say. Looking at Jon, hoping he wouldn't do anything stupid.

'Room 435. Take us there.'

Suze nodded. Pointed towards the older part of the synagogue.

'No, you first,' Karl said, then turned to Greta. 'You stay behind. Keep an eye on the policeman. I don't think he should be any more trouble but keep an eye on him anyway.'

'You want me to finish it?' she asked.

Karl smiled. 'No. Let him suffer a while. I have other plans for him.'

Greta stared at Karl, nodded stiffly. 'No problem,' she replied.

Suze led the way, Jon shuffling behind her, gun at his back, Karl breathing heavily at the rear. She unlocked the door that led to the basement, the storehouse, the place of dead ends, forgotten and unclassified history. She appreciated the irony of Dominic hiding the films down here, where they mingled easily with all the other artefacts. She'd never spent much time in room 435. It was where Jake had buried himself for days, sitting in that small, air-conditioned room, picking films and spools randomly from the mess, all the time, she now knew, searching for the Doctor's face.

They arrived at the dark wooden door, the small plaque that told them this was the right room. She could hear Karl breathing in sharp, staccato gasps, excitement flowing through his blood. She wished he'd have a heart attack and die right there. Wished this was all . . .

The pistol hit her in the jaw and sent her flying against the wall. It felt as though a car had crashed into her face. The wall bounced her back and she saw Jon reaching out for her, then the gun pointing at him. She fell hard on the floor, swirling in blackness and nausea that drowned her.

'She kept her end of the deal, what the fuck are you doing?' Jon screamed. Staring into the barrel of the gun, the cold and cracked smile of the man behind it.

'Exactly. Who needs her now?' Karl said, extracting a joint from his upper pocket, keeping the gun steady. Jon watched as he lit it, heard the frantic sputter and spark as it caught and smelled the heavy, acrid fumes. He saw Karl's eyes like pinwheels expand and shine. Sweat started pouring down his forehead as he took another drag. 'Open the fucking door,' he snarled.

Jon turned the handle. The door wasn't locked. Inside, it was dark and smelled of damp chemicals, mouldy films, old books, history discarded and boxed up. The walls were lined with filing cabinets, deep, high and black. Next to them were piles of brown boxes, taped up and wedged wherever space allowed. Karl pushed past him and into the room.

This was his chance. He could escape now. But he couldn't save Suze. She was lying on the floor, unconscious. He could save himself but not both of them.

'Finally,' Karl said, then turned and pointed the gun at Jon, motioning him to enter the room. Too late now. Too late to do anything but obey.

He watched as Karl ripped open the first box he came across. Saw a look of horror and frustration spread across the German's face. Then rushing to the next box, ripping open the cardboard, shouting in German, then in English, shouting fuck, Christ, damn and a hundred other imprecations at God, ripping open more boxes, pulling out reels and reels of film with his hands, loose and messed up, looking like black octopuses in his grasp. He threw them against the ground. Took a long drag off the joint that made it sizzle wickedly in the quiet of the room.

'Where the fuck are the films?' He turned to Jon, his

complexion the colour of an elastic band stretched so tightly that it becomes transparent for a brief moment before snapping. 'Tell me where they are.'

Jon looked at him. 'In here,' he said, then added, 'somewhere.'

'Fucking Christ!' Karl sputtered and pulled out another handful of films. 'Start going through them.' He was screaming now. 'We're not leaving until we find the right ones.'

'But there's thousands here.'

He pressed the gun into Jon's face. Jon could taste the oily metal and smell the gunpowder. He nodded, turned and opened another of the crates. He looked inside. Maybe a couple of hundred reels, quite a bit of loose film, some video cassettes – and that was only one crate. There were another forty or fifty in the room and he couldn't help but smile at Dominic's guile. Hiding the films here, where they would merge with all the others, a Herculean task to find them, necessitating going through everything, hours and hours of work, days and months, a whole lifetime if he'd scattered the films in different boxes.

He watched as Karl frenziedly undid reels and held them up to the light, trying to spot what was on them, then throwing them back down in disgust. He knew that this would be the only chance he had. That this was it and if he fucked up, he'd get shot, killed. Dead.

But he didn't have too many hopes either way. The man would not find what he was looking for. Even if he did, he'd kill them all. There was no doubt about it and that made Jon's decision easier. No, no more time for discussion, Jon told himself, no more time for fear.

'Here!' he shouted. 'I found them. They're here!'

He had his face buried in one of the boxes at the far corner of the room. He heard Karl make his way towards him. He draped himself over the crate, so that the other man couldn't see where his hands were.

He felt in his jacket, yes there it was – so glad he'd forgotten to empty his pockets that morning. He heard the man nearing, smelled the heavy cocaine funk of his breath.

'They're here. All of them,' he said as Karl approached, turning quickly when he estimated the man was almost right behind him and let loose with the mace, pressing down so hard on the nozzle that his thumb would be bruised for days to come.

At first there was nothing, just Karl's quickly comprehending face as he tried to step back, the joint dangling stupidly from his lips. Then it all exploded. A fine white mist that sent Jon reeling backwards. Karl's face disappeared in the fog. Jon could feel the spray claw into his eyes and choke his chest but he continued spraying, hearing the man scream. Orange flames began dancing around the joint, covering Karl's face with a kinetic Catherine wheel spark and flash as he reeled backwards, holding his throat, the gun clattering to the floor, heaving, wet sobs wrenching his chest.

Jon felt as though knives had been pushed slowly down his throat, he felt like being sick, felt suffocated. His eyes were being scratched from the inside by rats. He leapt forward, landing on the writhing German, picked up the gun and began to hit him with it. He breathed in the smoke and fury. His eyes almost blinded. He smashed the gun into the man's jaw, heard it crack. Smashed it down again, hitting the floor, sending pain reverberating through his hand. He threw the gun down and used his fists. He was still punching, puke dribbling down his mouth, his eyes red and streaming, when Suze came into the room, picked up the gun and pulled him off.

'Enough!' she shouted, horrified by his stare, his wild eyes.

429

His smile. 'No more,' she screamed and this time Jon heard. 'It's over.'

He got up, began to cough and puke, fell on the floor, sat there watching Karl's still body as Suze smiled, the gun in her hand, by her side. 'Over. All over,' she said and there wasn't anything he could add to that.

Epilogue

'Not tonight, Jon.'

'We've got plenty of time,' he said, booting up the computer.

'It's New Year's Eve,' she replied. She didn't really mind. In fact, was as eager to watch Jake's last CDR as Jon.

He turned from the humming machine. 'Exactly,' he said and walked over towards the kitchen. 'Kind of fitting, don't you think?'

He took the bottle of Maker's Mark and a couple of glasses off the worktop. 'Once we've seen the film, we can start to leave it behind.' He poured two large shots, wondering if such things could ever be left behind. He understood that he was not the same person he'd been before Amsterdam though if Suze or anyone else were to ask him to detail these changes, he wouldn't be able to. Yet there was something different in the ordinary things, in just waking up, or sitting, waiting for the sun to expire – something that he wanted to hold on to. 'I just thought it would be good to do it this way,' he added and handed her the drink.

Outside, the noise of the crowds was deafening. It had taken Jon ten minutes to get to Suze's from his new flat, a journey which usually took only two. He'd spent the day with Mrs De Roedel, walking with her through the elegant, silent halls of the Rijksmuseum, his anticipation slowly growing, the evening looming, bursting with possibility.

Strange to think it had all happened over a month ago. That awful night in the belly of the museum.

Suze had stayed overnight in the hospital, a minor concussion, nothing more. A sexy scar like a wobbly eclipse the only memory of that night. The detective had been in a wheelchair for a while, his name appearing in all the tabloids, revered as the saviour of Amsterdam. Deliverer of the city from the notorious serial killer that had been stalking its streets for so long. Beeuwers had found the handcuffed Quirk and the secret room. The flash of cameras had captured the chamber in all its gory delight. Close-ups of the devices were splashed across the Sunday supplements; 'Inside the world of the dead', 'A look inside your local charnel house', features proclaimed. They found the video camera mounted behind the wall, the halogen lights and the forensic smears of nail and skin and hair.

If he could have had it his way, Beeuwers would not have mentioned Van Hijn's involvement at all but, as it was, they needed the detective to tie up the links for them, which he did in a way that he thought they would both understand and accept as the way it really was. Which it wasn't. But, nevertheless, residents of the city felt they could walk along the canals and alleys in the safe knowledge that the dreaded beast of their nightmares had finally been caged.

No one mentioned the Doctor, still missing, or the dark beginnings of the case in what was now another century. Quirk was charged with the murders of the eight women. He was found in his prison bunk, still on remand, with his genitals cut and inserted into his mouth. His eyes had been removed. No one had put him in protective custody. Karl and Greta were charged with various crimes, among which the shooting of a police officer made sure that neither would leave the country for a good many years. And that was it. There was no need to upset the public. Useless speculation and unresolved anxieties were washed away like the winter leaves.

Van Hijn's face was splashed across newspapers and TV reports for the next couple of weeks and some closed-door negotiations were held whose outcome was the reinstatement of the detective to his full former position, a rising media star that the department now could not afford to lose.

Jon himself couldn't remember anything but waking up in the hospital in a room full of cops. His lungs were fucked. He wheezed and sputtered and thought that someone had set small fires in his throat. He explained to the policemen what had happened. He coughed and spat as they took notes.

They'd never got back to watching Jake's last CD. He'd left it at Suze's and, for a few days after the incident at the museum, they hadn't talked about it. Both secretly dreading watching this final piece of the puzzle.

They'd kept putting it off in the days after, always finding something else to do, getting to know each other again, walking the soaking streets, reading each morning the newspaper write-ups and, of course, Dominic's funeral.

Poor Dominic, Suze thought. They'd buried him a week after the incident in a small churchyard outside Amsterdam. Apparently his parents had been informed but had declined to come. It had been a sad affair, rain-lashed and tortuous, Bill whining constantly, Jon morose. It had seemed to her then that things could only get worse and she scolded herself for the pessimism she'd let herself slip into so easily. Shit, there was enough of that already.

That was why she'd bought the tickets. She was waiting till the stroke of midnight to tell him. Corny, she knew, but she enjoyed the arbitrary symbolism of the event just as much as he did. Things were definitely looking up, she thought, there was a chance there somewhere, a chance for something good, something new and uninherited.

She could sense that things were different between the two

of them. That, while he still fell into silences and sometimes drifted beyond her reach, he found her distant too and that these things were normal and shouldn't be seen as portents of doom.

That was why she'd bought the tickets to Phoenix. She hadn't told him, knowing how he would raise objections, find reasons not to go, but she knew, deep in her heart, that it was the right thing to do. They were leaving the day after tomorrow, just enough time to recover from the New Year but not enough to see the looming months ahead.

She wanted to show him the desert, to show him the mini-mart where it all began twenty years before. She wanted to climb high on the mesas with him, away from this city, from the noise and light of civilization to somewhere gentler; the dark, brooding hills that had framed her youth, the endless salt flats and dust devils of her dreams, that wild and eerie country that was like no other on earth.

She wanted to go back home.

He returned from the toilet and looked through the mess on her desk. 'Are you sure you put the weed here?' he asked.

'Yes,' she replied.

He ploughed through her papers and cuttings, looking for the joint they'd rolled earlier. He picked up one of the pieces of paper, looked at it. 'This your thesis? I thought you'd quit working on it?'

'I have,' she said. 'That's something new.'

He looked at the piece of paper, began reading:

+ + + + + + + + + + + + + + + + + +

SPRING, 1940. VILLEFRANCHE

Grandmother threw herself out of the window today.

The sun was brilliant like all the days before and the sea

quiet, like it knew what the hours would hold. We knew it was coming. Grandpapa had joked about it often enough. I had seen it in her eyes, in the way her breath slowly escaped her mouth as if loath to do so, in the distant echoes of her speech, her faded skin, the weight of the collapsing world.

+ + + + + + + + + + + + + + + + + +

'I didn't know Charlotte wrote a diary?'

Suze shook her head. 'She didn't. I did.'

'Why?' Jon looked down. He had taken it for genuine. The tone of voice, the feel, everything about it. But Charlotte had produced a visual diary, not a written one. 'Is this part of your thesis?'

'No. That's over. Boxed up and forgotten. It wasn't going anywhere. I couldn't get at the truth in the thesis. Its parameters were too strict. I could only do that through fiction. Through this diary. I understood that there would be more truth in this lie than in the list of dates and places, the ideological discussions, all that. So, I began to write her diary, the one she never had time to start.' For now, she didn't want to say anything more.

'Will you let me read it?'

'In the New Year.'

He slumped back down into the sofa, drink in hand, the dog curled up at his feet. Suze bent down to stroke Bill. The dog would have been put down, she guessed, after Dominic's death, but Jon had said he would take him. She'd been scared at first that Jon would go back to London after all that had happened, but his acquisition of the dog seemed to her a positive move towards staying in the city.

Jon took a deep breath of air. Let it sit in his lungs until he was almost gagging, then exhaled, as Jake's face appeared once again.

'Jon. It seems very different now that I know to whom I am addressing this.'

Jake spoke slowly, his voice coming through Suze's small speakers, looking recognizably like the version of Jake that Jon had known. More bedraggled than in the earlier footage, his tone slower, more contemplative.

Jon and Suze settled back. There was an unease in the air, palpable in their sudden silence and hushed anticipation. It would almost be better not to watch it, Jon thought, to keep Jake as he was, but he knew that was not an option open to him. That today was to be the day, a symbolic date perhaps but a necessary one.

Jake continued, a slow rhythmic cadence more subdued than the staccato delivery of the earlier footage.

'If you are watching this, Jon, then I belatedly thank you for your hospitality, for your flat and for so much more. You see, I was in really bad shape when you met me in London. I had been there three weeks, my old city, what for most of my life I had believed to be my birthplace and it seemed different, darker and I, the alien, shifting through its streets. I had to return though. Had to get away from Amsterdam. From the Doctor.

'We'd been having our regular chess evenings and chats all through the summer. He seemed pleased to have someone to tell his stories to and me, you know, I'm a good listener.

'And then I saw the film. And you can understand what a shock it was and yet, somewhere deep inside I'd suspected it all along, even hoped it was true. You see, it was somehow more acceptable to me

438

for him to have been a Nazi and said all those things than if he was a Jew. And it was amazing how easily he slipped on that costume, how with only the slightest of shifts he became a Jew. So, I went back, played chess, kept this secret to myself, my power over him, or so I thought.

'I often wondered if my family had followed the point of his finger. I felt that the only thing left connecting me to them was the Doctor. I don't entirely expect you to understand that, I don't entirely understand it myself, but I feel it to be true none the less. My father, my fake father, always said, "Follow your gut, boy, your head will only cheat and deceive you, follow your gut and you won't go too far wrong." Of course he died of stomach cancer so perhaps it wasn't such good advice but I've never been able to really shrug it off either.

'I think the old bastard knew. I think he guessed that I had discovered his secret. I noticed that he treated me differently, that he was no longer so couched and gnomic, small slivers of pride leaking out of his smiles. So I confronted him. I told him about the reel of film I had found at the JHM. He laughed when I said that, laughed and clapped his hands. "You are the first person to have discovered me, Jakob, I truly respect that," he said. I wanted to hit him. Kill him. Right then and there. And that's when he told me about the 49 reels.

'He had filmed them all himself and they'd been meant as a record of their achievements at Auschwitz. He knew that the films were a great liability, an invitation to a hanging, but he kept them even after Eichmann had given the order to destroy all evidence pertaining to the Final Solution. He said he always knew that there would come a day when the films would be appreciated for what they were. I never asked him what that was, it didn't bother me by then. I knew what I had to do.

'I said, "Why don't we watch them?" He told me his projector was broken but that he had something better if that's what interested me. I just nodded, eager to see what he would come up with. He put a tape into the video, and as soon as I saw the girl tied to that horrible device, I knew.

'She was screaming, crying, pleading. Her scream reverberated through my head long after the tape had been switched off. I recognized the room. Quirk's long bony fingers adjusting the ratchet. And her scream slashing through red hair and eyes. When I go to sleep her scream is the last thing I hear before sleep divests me.

'The Doctor was smiling as we watched the video. Proud and bashful as a teenage boy who's just had his first fuck.

'I looked back at the girl on the screen and I recognized her from the papers, the fourth victim, Elena something, and I knew then what I should have guessed all along. My head was bursting. I could feel my heart sticky with hate. I walked out on him, that evening, without saying a word.

'Perhaps you think I should have gone to the police, but it was far too late for that. For him and for me. I knew that our paths had crossed for a reason and I now began to intuit what that was.

'I look at the Doctor and I try to understand how someone from a well-to-do family in a cultured, civilized country could have done what he did, and my father's words keep coming back to me.

'I hate the way Kaplan wraps himself in language as if that explains everything. I hate his little justifications, his *bons mots* and ancient quotations, and I hate their subversion of language, the way they labelled the gas chambers "disinfecting showers", the Jews as the rotten appendix, the lie in the sign above the gates of Auschwitz. It should have been "Death liberates all" – the only axiom valid in such a place.

'I think of the writers I loved as a child, I think of Goethe and Schiller, the excitement of Spengler and Nietzsche, the drama of Wagner, the intense intelligence and liberating philosophies of Heidegger and Hegel, and I wonder, was that a prelude, did that make it all possible? Is it even possible that art can create such a hole in the nation's soul, an ever widening hole that can be filled only with the machine-gun rattle and fury of the speech at the Nuremberg Rally, the funny little man with the moustache, whose last will and testament, written minutes before doing his final duty to his mistress, his dog and himself, ended with a proclamation for the German people to keep fighting the disease of International Jewry?

'I began to detest our little meetings and yet I still went, even after I'd seen the video of the girl and knew that, among his collection, the previous seven would be present, entombed in those plastic graves. I can't explain that to you, perhaps it was just that he made me more aware of myself, I don't know. After a night with the Doctor I often found myself, the next day, spending prolonged periods in the basement of the museum watching through the endless hours of survivor testimony. I clicked the tapes into place and watched them tell their story. I would sit all day among their faces, listening to their tales and remembering that no matter how horrible those stories were, these people were the lucky ones. These people could come and sit before a video camera and speak. These people could find what tatters remained of their families, and the videos began to stand for something else, for the millions missing, the black hole in Mitteleuropa that will never be filled.

'Every day I said to myself that this would be the last time I would see the Doctor but every night I went over to his small flat and played chess and listened to him talk.

'He made me a Jew. And for that I both admired and hated him. When I'd read my father's last testament, when I'd found out about my family, when I'd gone through the briefcase full of faded documents and yellow stars – I had known I was Jewish. The evidence was clear to see but I did not feel it until I felt like killing the old man. Our identities are formed from oppositions that are there despite ourselves, despite our trembling efforts to escape them. I hated him for that, for being the one to make me see, and when I finally let myself accept this fact – I had been in denial for weeks – I immediately went and bought a ticket to London, knowing that I had to get away from him.

'London seemed mean and ugly. I walked through streets I'd known all my life and they felt different. I tried to escape the Doctor, but, even in London, the sound of his finely clipped accent kept swirling through my brain. At that point, I had no idea of my future. No desire to go back to my old life, that just seemed like a child's game to me now, one that you discover many years later in the attic and wonder what the hell made it so fascinating all those years ago. Amsterdam was out of the question. Amsterdam was a city of ghosts for me.

'I had made the journey to Westerbork one day in the summer. Caught the train from Amsterdam and arrived there in the early afternoon. The sun was shining on the fields and windmills spun picturesquely in the background. There were few visitors and I walked through the small museum and over the fields where once the Jews of Amsterdam had been housed, waiting to be squeezed on to cattlecars for the great migration east. I stood on the ground where my whole family had been. It was just a piece of countryside now, an empty green field, innocent and ignorant of itself, and I began crying, standing there alone, my tears splashing hot on the soft grass below. The knowledge that they had all once been here, all once been alive, shaking on this very ground, was too much, too much for me to bear.

'I went back to Amsterdam and on the train I picked up an old copy of an English newspaper that someone had left folded on the seat opposite me. I saw the photo on the front. The trains carrying another race of people to their deaths. The lines of misery stretched out waiting to board. Dogs and soldiers and guns. And the Kosovans looked just like the Jews had fifty years ago, full of fear and resignation, boarding the trains with that goodbye look in their eyes. And then I began reading. And my heart choked with anger. So-called liberals, the intelligentsia, the people I always thought of as my

442

people, were decrying the American intervention. They preferred rape camps and genocide to anything American. The Kosovans didn't give a shit about ideology, they just wanted to sleep at night without the knock that drags you into a hell of black cells, they just wanted their missing back. We were living in a world that had been turned upside down. This was the shape of the future, the New Nationalism born out of impotent unheated flats and age-old hatred, a Socialist Nationalism, equal parts Marx and Hitler. Politics, like everything else, at the end of the century, had become merely fashion.

'Once in London I thought I would never go back to Amsterdam. Until I read about her on the news page, dead, unidentified but I knew exactly who she was and where she'd ended up. And though it was her choice, it was I who had run, who had left her to these dogs. I stared at the screen for a few minutes and I knew that I had to go back. That I hadn't managed to escape anything. That there is no escaping. No place to hide from yourself. I read and reread the small fifty-word piece on Beatrice's death and I knew what I had to do.

'The night I arrived back in the city, I called the Doctor. He told me to come round, that he could do with a game of chess, he hadn't been feeling too well. I walked through the rain and climbed the stairs to his apartment. After all those weeks of sleeping rough my body was not what it had been and I strained and struggled that last floor, catching my breath before I knocked on his door.

'His flat smelled of sickness, that clotted, heavy smell that seems to reside in your nostrils for days afterwards. He was lying in bed and looked older than I had ever seen him. His face was white and his eyes, milky and uncertain. I was almost disappointed, I had wanted him strong.

'We played a little chess though I could see his heart wasn't really in it. He apologized. Told me he'd be back to normal in a few days. It was just a cold but he was an old man and his body weak.

'I looked at him lying there in bed, pathetic and grizzled, and I saw

443

Beatrice's face as she stared terrified at his video camera. I heard her scream and I thought about the other girls the police knew about. Their screams. And the ones they didn't, the ones who slipped the net. That would for ever go unremembered and unmourned. I leaned over the Doctor and he saw the look on my face and I think he knew then.

'I put my hands around his throat and began to squeeze. I looked at him and he stared back at me. Our eyeballs locked. I squeezed tighter, feeling the loose skin of his neck fold under my hands and, when he grabbed my wrists, I steadied myself for the impending struggle but he didn't try to prise my hands off. He held them tightly, pressing them down on to his neck until they relaxed completely and I looked into his eyes and saw nothing. I took the films, the videos, some drugs from his medicine cabinet, and locked the door behind me, locked it shut on everything.

'That happened twelve hours ago and I can still smell his death on my hands. It is slowly creeping up my arms and heading for my chest. I can feel it like little breaths of air sliding up my arm. It's almost sensual but it also freezes my blood.

'I burnt the videos. There were eight of them. All neatly labelled and filed. Beatrice's smile – still nervous, still there. So I set them on fire. Made them sublimate into smoke. If they got into the wrong hands . . . there was too much at stake. Those women had been abused enough, and while justice was perhaps not done, a certain closure was at least effected. I can only hope he never made copies.

'I left his body where it was. I ran all the way to Dominic's flat. I told him what had happened. How the Doctor had told me it was filmed at Quirk's piercing parlour. An old friend from the war. A real Jew, he said, a survivor. I'd been shocked. The Doctor had introduced me to Quirk a few weeks earlier. He'd bumped into him ten years previously. Quirk recognized him but instead of blabbing and going to the police, the piercer had collapsed at the Doctor's feet, weeping with gratitude. He'd been a small child in Auschwitz and the Doctor was the closest thing to a father he'd known. They gradually found they had certain things in common, certain lusts, and their friendship grew from there. I could see that it was as much of a surprise to Dominic as it had been to me. I gave him the films. He assured me that he would clean up the mess. We talked about disposal and we both agreed that the Doctor would find peace at the bottom of a canal, among the mud and ooze and broken glass. He left an hour ago. I will not be here when he gets back.

'These are my last words. These are the final things I have left.

'I lost. I fucked up. I blew it. I let the Doctor get inside me. I let him corrupt me. I thought he was making me a Jew but he made me a Nazi. He passed on his inheritance of hate and anger to me. I was his son, and he, my only real father. And so this is my inheritance to you, Jon. Don't make the same mistakes I made. Pull your head out of the fucking sand . . .

'And now I can see what the real tragedy of the Holocaust was. Not the millions dead and the conveyor-belt executions, not the bars of soap or the rotting bodies in pits. Not the dead, but the living, those who would come afterwards to sit in classrooms and watch jerky black-and-white newsreels trying to comprehend, so full of anger, hate and despair that they could never really live again, never open themselves up to another person or laugh at a stupid thing. The millions of men and women for ever folded into themselves, used up and useless. And I'm not talking about Jews. I'm talking about anyone who ever heard the word Holocaust, whose mind was immediately beset with those flash-frame images of barbed wire and jutting bone. You see, it wasn't us who were the swelling, infected appendix, but them. And when it burst, it sent bits of their disease all across the world. Escaped Nazis taught South African police how to kill blacks. They trained the South American military dictatorships of the 1970s, taught them how to extract information. They ended up in Damascus and Tripoli, explaining how bombs can be made, terror spread, the fight continued. But they also affected us on much

445

deeper levels, they infected our consciousness, set it on a different track, launching us into a new kind of century. Their garden of earthly delights came crashing down, exploding and fracturing, sending its fragments across the oceans and over the mountains, a new kind of rain, a new kind of world.'

Jon and Suze watched as Jake took the syringe off the table next to him. Jon leapt forward as if to shout, 'No, don't do it' – then, realizing his stupidity, leaned back into the sofa. Watched transfixed as the old man held the needle to his skin.

'I am going out for a short walk now. Find myself a park, somewhere to lay myself down. I need to sleep in the air.

'Let there be no mistake about this, no speculation of murder or accident. That would be a betrayal. My body is not mine any more. It rides a carriage made of bones through a dark and terrible place and my riding companion is the Doctor – now I finally give it over.'

The image cut to blue and then back to the start-up screen.

'Christ!' Jon said as he got up and looked at the monitor, shaking uncontrollably, his knees buckling and swerving, steadying himself, hand placed on the table.

'Come here,' Suze called out to him but he didn't make any move towards her, just kept shaking his head.

'I can't fucking believe it.'

'At least it was his choice.'

'That's what makes it even more terrible. That and the fact that he wanted me to fall into this. The way he planned it so meticulously.'

'Wanted you?' She tried to get closer to him but it was as if a force of electromagnetic energy surrounded him, making the air between them unstable.

Jon looked up at her. 'My phone number in the book – that stupid code that he knew only I'd get. The CD's. From the start he planned this all out.'

She wanted to tell him that if it hadn't been for Jake, they would never have met, but it was such a trite thing to say, especially at a moment like this. It was what she felt but she could not say it. 'Why, Jon?'

'I don't know. He wanted me to wake up. He thought I was asleep. He wanted me to realize where I came from but all I realize is that it doesn't matter. That it's only surface now. Those times are gone.'

'He was really fucked up.'

'Yes,' he replied, only fully acknowledging it now. 'Yes, he was.'

Jon stared out of the window at the dense layers of rain that peppered the street outside and remembered the days when he'd sunk deep into the arms of suicide, the dark days of the failure of the magazine and of his hopes and dreams, and he remembered the beautiful temptation of it, its promise and allure. He cursed himself for having thought like that and most of all he cursed himself because he knew that, like Jake, it had taken murder and genocide to make him see.

'Jon,' she cried out, startling him. 'Oh my God! There's something else on the CD.'

He turned around and looked at her. 'What are you talking about?'

But the answer was obvious in her face. He moved towards her so that he could see.

They stood there in silence. Unable to quite believe it: a simple zipped contents file on screen, divided into 49 segments.

She moved the mouse until it highlighted the first segment. Pressed Play.

They sat there, both knowing what was on this last hour of the CD, staring transfixed at the black-and-white images that poured from the screen, the swift and jerky movements of a lost time, another world. Outside, it went strangely quiet, as if the earth's very atmosphere had sagged. The film began, the first reel unfolded. They heard the countdown from the street below as all around them rose the voices of happiness and jubilation. A rising scream that came from everywhere and everything.

This is how it begins.

Postscript

This is how it began. In a small room off Westbourne Grove. It was September 1999 and my twenty-ninth birthday had come and gone. Earlier that year I'd quit my job at the BBC to concentrate on writing. I had a vague idea of what I wanted to write about and a part-time job as a music critic allowed me to spend most of my time on the novel. I thought it would be easy. I thought it would be quick.

September was cold that year. My then partner was on a six-week trip to Japan. I was alone in the flat. I woke up every morning and stared at the blank screen. I went through my notes. I read books. I knew where the novel would be set. I didn't know anything else.

That summer I'd been to Amsterdam for the first time since I was seventeen. I saw a different city now, a palimpsest of history and libertarianism populated by the ghosts of the receding century. I saw red and blue lights swirling against the cobblestones and canals. We were in the red-light district after all, but this was a very different kind of light. A crowd had gathered at the head of one of the narrow, window-studded alleys the city is so famous for. Two police cars and an ambulance blocked the other end. The red and blue lights strobed and sprayed against the glass. A body was stretchered out of one of the rooms, a white sheet covering its face.

Looking back on it now, this was where it began. The image stayed in my mind, nagged, shouted, and insisted I create a context for it.

Once I knew the novel would be set in Amsterdam, everything else followed. Landscape is both history and plot. I knew the book would have to deal with the city's notorious libertarianism and issues of freedom. I knew the shadow of the Second World War would hang over every page. I couldn't imagine writing a book about this city which didn't address these things.

And then there was the tramp.

He stood outside the cashpoint, opposite the high windows of my small room. He was there every day, regardless of the weather. He never asked for money or held up a sign or paper cup. He looked distinguished, out of place; his bearing, the way he held himself, his long white hair and beard. He always carried a pile of books with him. He was always barefoot.

I would look out the window that autumn and see him standing there. I was stuck in a room with the blinking cursor, the empty screen. I looked out the window a lot those days. And I began to invent his life. I made up stories, speculated, guessed and conjectured, but I never asked him. We would exchange a few brief words in the morning when I left my room for coffee, but that was it.

I thought about letting him stay in the flat but I didn't think about it for long. I was living in a tiny space with my girlfriend and all our accumulated possessions, mountain ranges of books and music. We had been together for seven years, but lately something in our hearts had started to drift. We didn't realise it at the time, but we'd begun to cancel each other out. The flat was composed of areas, demarcated and rarely kept to.

I had a million other rationalisations for not inviting the man in and letting him stay. So instead I did what writers do

– I posited that essential what if? question and the answer was *The Devil's Playground*.

It was not an easy book to write in all the ways that books aren't easy to write. I had only written one novel before, *The Great American Desert*, a story about an English couple who go to LA for their honeymoon. They rent a car at the airport and immediately get lost. They are carjacked and the woman is shot dead. The man, in a state of shock, drives. He has no idea where or why. He ends up in the south-western desert, befriends a contract killer, and together they go searching for a legendary astronaut turned mystic televangelist. It taught me how not to write a book. Every sentence you write teaches you what is wrong with it.

I stared endlessly at the blank page. I knew what I wanted to write about, the landscape and themes I wanted to pursue, but it took me a long time to find the right medium for them. And, even after I'd finished the book, I still didn't realise that what I'd written was a crime novel.

Ian Rankin says he was an accidental crime writer and that's a phrase I like a lot. My literary heroes were William Burroughs, Thomas Pynchon, Cormac McCarthy. But they were also James Crumley, Jim Thompson and James Ellroy. I loved the dense figurative language and ideas of the former group and I dug the adrenaline-pumping plots and reconfigured histories of the latter.

But this is all hindsight. When I started writing *The Devil's Playground*, I wasn't thinking of genre, I was only wondering what would be the best way to tell this story. That's the beauty and heartbreak of your first published novel. As a writer you'll never write anything like that again. The first novel exists in a place of uncertainty, before you have an audience, before readership expectations, before you realise your own limitations. You try and cram everything you know between their pages. They are the sum product of all the years leading up to them, while every novel that follows is structured by time and the constant swerve against diminishing returns.

So I began, as I always do, without a plan. I knew what I wanted to talk about but not how. I knew the novel would have at least eight POV characters and I started telling their stories. The months passed, my partner came back, the old man disappeared from the street, as if he'd served his purpose. The characters in the draft told their stories. The stories began to revolve around similar themes: violence – its justifications and representations. This was the central gravitational field that pulled all the disparate ends together. But without a plot this meant nothing. As draft followed draft, the story began to creep in, and a detective made his presence felt.

I can't remember how many drafts I wrote for *The Devil's Playground* but it's in the ballpark of twenty. I still do ten drafts when I'm writing a novel nowadays. Each draft layers a different part of the story into the text, each draft weeds out clichés and gets you closer to the right word, the perfect shocking twist. The draft went through many changes. I still have two hundred pages of extra material that I cut for reasons of pace. The title changed too. It started as *Holocaust Studies*, then turned into *Inheritance*, then became *Rain Dogs*, which finally mutated into *The Devil's Playground*.

The process towards publication was not an easy one. It very rarely is. I had approximately forty rejection letters from agents. I worked on the manuscript with two agents before I found the right one. I almost threw her letter away. It looked like a form rejection, but I opened it. She liked the book and sent it out to editors. If it wasn't for Lesley Thorne, I would probably have abandoned the novel. I remember a Friday afternoon, sitting at home, watching Fellini's *8½* when the phone rang. She told me Penguin had made an offer on the book. I looked at the mute monochrome face of Marcello Mastroianni and tried to remember how to breathe.

The novel came out and got better reviews than I could ever have hoped for. It was shortlisted for the CWA John Creasey Dagger.

I thought this was it. I thought my career and life were on the right track. But this was only the beginning. There were many more endings first and it was five years before my next novel, *The Black Monastery*, was published. I was living in a different flat by then, with a different woman, and contracted to a different publisher.

Sometimes you have to go through the wrong door to get to the right room. Faber felt like the right room. My editor, Angus Cargill, understood what I was trying to do and knew how to make it better. He always liked this novel. It's because of his tireless advocacy that it's now in your hands.

I haven't re-read it. I've never re-read any of my books once they've gone into print. It's like watching scratchy home movies, that curious split between acute embarrassment at your own youth and a nostalgia for the fire and flare of those days. I hope the novel stands up. I hope readers of my later books will find something to like here. It's not the easiest book to read, but the subject matter meant I couldn't take any shortcuts. It's also the book where all the music crammed into my head was finally put to use. I inserted songs wherever I could. People complained the songs were obscure but nowadays you can easily look them up online. In my subsequent books there are very few music references. If I've done something in one book, I don't like to repeat. But, in the chapter I wrote today, Jack Carrigan bought his first CD in a long time and was about to put it on. The themes explored in *The Devil's Playground* ricochet through all my subsequent novels and I have no doubt they will continue to do so across the ones to come.

Stav Sherez,
November 2013

ff

The Black Monastery

Welcome to Paradise . . .

People used to come to the Greek island of Palassos for the
historic ruins. Now they come to take drugs
and party all night.

The horrific ritual murder of a teenage boy in the grounds of
the old monastery has haunting similarities to the
cult murders of two boys in the 1970s – a painful
episode in the island's history which the inhabitants
have tried hard to forget.

When a second body is discovered local police chief, Nikos,
and British tourists Kitty and Jason, are thrown
together in a desperate bid to unravel the mystery which
has held the town in its grip for thirty years.

'Truly exceptional . . . Viscerally suspenseful,
thoughtful and exciting.' Lee Child

'For an atmospheric thriller, look no further . . . dynamite fiction.'
Independent

Available in paperback and ebook now

Also by Stav Sherez

ff

A Dark Redemption

THE FIRST CARRIGAN AND MILLER NOVEL

Shortlisted for the Theakston's Old Peculier
Crime Novel of the Year 2013

Some people will go to any lengths to keep a secret . . .

A Dark Redemption introduces DI Jack Carrigan and DS
Geneva Miller as they investigate the brutal murder of a
young Ugandan student. Plunged into an underworld of
illegal immigrant communities, they discover that the
murdered girl's studies at a London college may have
threatened to reveal things that some people will go to
any lengths to keep secret . . .

'Masterful.' *Daily Mirror* ****

'Fast-paced and slick.' *Guardian*

'Sherez is superb at evoking the unfamiliar world of immigrant communities . . . Although there is nothing more conventional than an
unconventional cop, Sherez has beaten the odds and created an
original detective in Carrigan.' *Daily Telegraph*

Available in paperback and ebook now